A Dance in Time

By the same author

Lovers' Hollow

A Dance in Time

ORNA ROSS

PENGUIN
IRELAND

PENGUIN IRELAND

Published by the Penguin Group
Penguin Ireland, 25 St Stephen's Green, Dublin 2, Ireland
(a division of Penguin Books Ltd)
Penguin Books Ltd, 80 Strand, London WC2R ORL, England
Penguin Group (USA) Inc., 375 Hudson Street, New York, New York 10014, USA
Penguin Group (Australia), 250 Camberwell Road, Camberwell, Victoria 3124, Australia
(a division of Pearson Australia Group Pty Ltd)
Penguin Group (Canada), 90 Eglinton Avenue East, Suite 700, Toronto, Ontario, Canada M4P 2Y3
(a division of Pearson Penguin Canada Inc.)
Penguin Books India Pvt Ltd, 11 Community Centre, Panchsheel Park, New Delhi – 110 017, India
Penguin Group (NZ), 67 Apollo Drive, Rosedale, North Shore 0632, New Zealand
(a division of Pearson New Zealand Ltd)
Penguin Books (South Africa) (Pty) Ltd, 24 Sturdee Avenue, Rosebank, Johannesburg 2196, South Africa

Penguin Books Ltd, Registered Offices: 80 Strand, London WC2R ORL, England

www.penguin.com

First published 2008
1

Set in 13.5/16 pt Postscript Monotype Garamond
Typeset by Rowland Phototypesetting Ltd, Bury St Edmunds, Suffolk
Printed in Great Britain by Clays Ltd, St Ives plc

A CIP catalogue record for this book is available from the British Library

ISBN 978–1–844–88053–9

www.greenpenguin.co.uk

For Ida and Ornagh
my mother, my daughter

The words are purposes.
The words are maps.

Adrienne Rich,
'Diving into the Wreck'

The infant daughter also desires its mother but it is
unthinkable, either in myth, in fantasy or in fact, that this
desire can be consummated.

Edna O'Brien

First Words
Star
2008

Christmas Eve, 1982. My mother opened the front door of Doolough Lodge, saw me standing on the step and rubbed her eyes. Fury surged in me, sudden and complete, and the good intentions I had nursed all the way across the Atlantic Ocean were instantly swept away.

It wasn't surprise that had Mom acting like a character in a bad movie. No, this was her clumsy effort to hide the reflex that always kicked in whenever she saw me: the slide of her eyeballs away from the sight, then the conscious tugging of them back.

She did her damnedest to hide it, but whenever my mother looked at me it was my fat that hit her first.

That hardly made her unique, but you expect more from your mother than from the rest of the world, right? She just couldn't help it. My excess flesh was her shame too. Public evidence of her failure to win Greatest Mother of All Time Award.

'Hello to you too, Mom,' I said.

'Darling, I'm so . . . Come in, come in.' She ushered me into the hall and pulled me towards her.

'Wait,' I said. '*He's* definitely not here?'

'No, no. I told you.'

'And not coming back?'

'No.'

'Okay, I'll come in' – she reached for my backpack, but I held it – 'provided you promise there'll be no tears and no sorries. I haven't come for a grand reconciliation.'

'Oh.'

'To be honest, I didn't even know if I'd make it all the way here. I kept thinking I'd turn back.'

'But you didn't.'

'No. But that doesn't mean – Everything I said the day you left Santa Paola . . . every word of that still stands.'

'Okay, darling. I understand. But can I just say that –'

'No, don't "just say" anything. Let's agree to not discuss it.'

'I understand,' she said again, but I could see she'd be off first chance she got. She wouldn't be able to help herself.

I shouldn't have come.

She stood aside to let me in and led me down the hallway, towards the kitchen. It was strange to be in my grandfather's house again. I remembered its old-house smell, but now there was an extra layer, the tang of disinfectant.

'How is Granddad?' I asked.

'He's low today. It's great you've come.'

Last time we were here, her father had run us out of the place, yet she spoke as if I was an ordinary granddaughter paying a loving sick call. Dear Mom, she did so love to play happy families.

In the kitchen she put on the kettle and sat down opposite me. Before it was boiling, she had begun again. 'Star, I am sorry, so deeply, deeply sorry about what happened. I never –'

'You're unbelievable, Mom. What did I just say out in the hall?'

'But if we don't –'

I held up my hand. 'If you're going to insist on talking about this, then I'm out of here. And I won't be back.'

'All right, all right . . . Calm down.'

She got herself busy with cups and tea bags, while I took off my coat and searched in the pocket for cigarettes. As I shook one from the box, I heard myself sigh, so long and deep it sounded like the last breath I'd ever take.

She turned. 'Darling, how are you? Can I ask you that? Are you okay?'

2

'No.' My hands were shaking too hard to light up. 'No, Mom, I am not "okay". I'm livid.'

'Oh, Star.'

'I want to bulldoze houses and cut down trees. I want to set fire to all the fields and dump poison into all the rivers. I want to hurt everybody, *everybody* in the whole wide world and see if *that* makes me feel any better.'

'Honey, please . . .'

'Don't worry, it seems I won't do it. I'll just go on, apparently, the way I always have. But inside I'm seething.'

She looked at me, stricken.

'Seeing as you asked.'

It wasn't always like that between me and my mother. I remember being a little girl and her singing to me. *Twinkle twinkle little Star, how I love you, all that you are.* How her strawberry-blonde hair would fall forward as she bent over me, shimmers of starlight in it too. How I thought that song was mine and hers alone, and was amazed when I went to school and heard it in other mouths, with different words. I do remember that.

My mother had a story she loved to tell about W. B. Yeats, her favourite poet. Apparently, when informed that he had mispronounced Benito Mussolini's name, he supposedly said: 'I am told the name is not Missolonghi but Mussolini – but, does it . . . really . . . matter?'

Mom thought that was the coolest line. To me, it sounds affected – like the floppy bow tie and black clothes he used to wear in his youth so that people would know he was A POET – but what Mom loved best about old W. B. was his disdain for fact. 'Only a breath separates fiction from non-fiction,' she said to me the last time we talked about this book. 'That half-breath is the backwind to my story.' (To which I could only cry: 'Ugh! Pretensho!' – what my girlfriend Veno and I regularly used to shout at her when we were teenagers.)

Me, I like facts. To me, turning real lives into fiction seems suspect. Mixing imagined and historical events, mingling invented thoughts with those gleaned from real-life letters or diaries, making dialogue out of published poetry and prose . . . I find it, as one of her 'characters', Ezra Pound, might say – very, very bughouse.

Yet I am here.

Last week I sat beside my husband at an over-polished mahogany table listening to over-polished lingo from my mother's solicitor. We walked out of that office considerably richer than when we went in, but with me also hefting a 600-page manuscript and a self-serving letter. Dealt the ultimate deadline by breast cancer, my mother had decided to ask me to see her only unpublished manuscript through to completion. To tie together its loose ends and find it a publisher.

What I have found so far on these pages is shocking to me. I'm only on page 124 and already I've had numerous parts that made me jump up and shout at the page, 'That's NOT how it was.' Part of me would like to hurl the thing in the fire, but curiosity and dying-request guilt will, I know, propel me to the end.

Good trick, Mom. You win again.

Okay, then, I'll do it.

But I'm going to have my say too.

My better half thinks this is wrong of me. He says I shouldn't have written that scene at the beginning from my point of view, or this foreword, or the footnotes either. This is my mother's book, he says, not mine. I am merely the editor. My job is to ensure that what *she* wanted to say is said – truly and clearly and unambiguously.

Fair enough. Nobody knows better than me how it feels to have what is yours taken over. So I'll let go many of my mother's asides about my body, my mind and my motives, even when I know her to be wrong, wrong, wrong. But some things do have to be said.

Actually, I believe Mom expected me to 'write back'. She all but said so on that last day in Laragh churchyard.

'It's your story too,' she said.

She sat so erect on the bench that day as we talked, her legs angled to one side. Old and ill and frail but somehow still lovely, her hair highlighted to a crisp ash-blonde, all trace of strawberry gone. She wore it long, too long, some would say, for her age. Usually pinned into a coil at her crown but at that moment folded over one shoulder, falling in a curtain over the place where her breast used to be.

Then she added: 'And Iseult's, of course.'

Ah, yes, the other Iseult. She always had to be brought in. That's the bit I can't understand.

Or stand.

Once I asked her whether she ever resented the number of hours she spent on the Gonnes and their cronies. 'No,' she replied, 'they were my most significant hours.' (Ugh! Pretensho!) But why? Why were they so important? What was there in the life of Iseult Gonne that she couldn't let lie?

When I think about her fumbling around the chasm between one piece of evidence and another, trying to touch a dead woman – trying to touch that particular dead woman – I get mad as hell.

But who am I mad at?

Maybe you can tell.

My mother was a writer and a thinker and just about the last person anyone would expect to commit murder. And not just murder, *patricide*. Yet – strange thing – when she said she hadn't done it, few people believed her. This, her book, tries to explain why.

Only you can say whether it succeeds, whether it throws light on those events that almost destroyed us, and whether, between us, she and I manage to give you the truth, the whole truth and nothing but . . .

Or indeed whether, in the words of the great W.B. (all bow down, now), any of it . . . *really* . . . *matters*.

Maya 'Star' Creahy
2008

A Hollow, Pearly Heart

. . . I will my heavy story tell
Till my own words, re-echoing, shall send
Their sadness through a hollow, pearly heart;
And my own tale again for me shall sing,
And my own whispering words be comforting,
And lo! my ancient burden may depart.

W. B. Yeats, 'The Sad Shepherd'

I

I'll begin with my father's journals, tumbling from their secret compartment at the back of the bureau, landing on the floor with an unforgiving thump. A large, thick notebook, with red hard covers, born to be a shop ledger. Inside, four hundred pages of his familiar handwriting, marching through pink vertical lines as if they were not there. And five smaller diaries, with black soft covers, full of shorter notes.

My pulse, already pounding, skidded at the sight of that writing. I knew I had found what I was looking for, even though I hadn't realized, until that moment, that what I was engaged in was a search. A memory of him sitting at this bureau to write rose in my mind. The bent back hunched over, the thick fingers clasped around a skinny pen.

Traces of him were all over these pages. Not just his words but creases and dog ears. Some kind of oil all over page 287. An ink spill on the cover of one of the smaller ones. Even those pages that seemed clean would have been brushed by his hand trailing across. His DNA could be reconstructed from these.

I turned back to page one, hand to my chest. *6 August 1914.* A new beginning for all of France and millions across Europe. On the inside cover he had stuck his conscription card and his medical records. I touched them and they came away, the glue dry and dead.

Yes, that's where I'll begin.

I could start a little earlier, with the moment when I first spied the hammer sitting under the corner table in the kitchen. Left there since I nailed a sprig of holly over the kitchen door – my poor attempt at Christmas decoration – it had caught my eye when its two fingers, usually used for prising out nails, seemed to twitch. To beckon me across.

Something clicked closed in my head when I saw this hammer. I picked it up, tapped its flat head against my palm, felt the weight of what I was about to do. Pulling my mind shut – no more thoughts allowed – I let it swing, hard and fast, into the TV screen. *Smash.* Shards of glass went spiking through the air. *Smash* again. The glass cabinet this time. I regretted that Star and I had cleared the glasses and ornaments from the shelves a few hours earlier; I would have loved to unleash myself on them.

Thump. I brought the hammer down on the little side table, but it made only a dent. I found myself throwing it aside, then running through the kitchen and out the back door. It was dry outside and not cold, not for December. The automatic security light came on, spotlighting the weeds that cracked through the gravel. My hands slipped as I jerked the bolt on the shed open, grazing my knuckles. I sucked on the pain, my tongue moving across bone and blood. I felt like a hurricane, like a snowstorm, like a wild and raging ocean, a wild throb of hurry keeping thought at bay.

In the corner of the shed, I found what I was looking for: the sledgehammer. Its heavy head pulled me down as I ran back inside, where I went entirely amok. I smashed the coffee table and the sideboard. I smashed the fiddly occasional table that always wobbled, making us fearful for the lamp. I smashed the lamp. I turned my back on the piano – that I couldn't destroy – and when I came to the bureau, I also hesitated. My father's most precious piece of furniture: bought in Paris and transported back to Ireland, the only physical relic of the time he spent there. All through my childhood I had watched him sitting at this desk to write, or do what he called 'the books', the accounts that measured his income against his expenses, the largest of which was me.

Smash. The hammer put a deep V into its top and the back

folded apart. As it did, a torrent of paper tumbled out. Money. Hundreds of notes: old pound notes and fivers and tenners and twenties. One of my father's secret stashes. He had them all over the house: in a biscuit tin under the floorboards in his bedroom, inside an old plant-food container on a high shelf in the back pantry and doubtless in lots of other places that I knew nothing about.

It was the other bounty, though, that made me pounce: the notebooks. I picked them up with both hands. What would it do to me to read them? The thought set my heart fluttering around its cage of ribs, as if he were still alive to catch me. I sat down in the middle of the devastation and opened the largest one, hand to my chest as I started to read.

It was quite a while later – I have no idea how long – when the doorbell rang. Since Dr Keane's questioning at the funeral two days before, I had been half expecting a call from the police; yet, when I heard the bell, my thoughts flew unbidden to Zach. Could he have come back to me?

No, of course not.

The bell rang again.

No.

I had made my choice, and we both knew what it meant.

I pushed myself up from the floor and picked my way through the wood and glass and debris, the large notebook in front of my chest like a shield. I moved slowly, with reluctance, because anyone but Zach was an unwelcome intrusion.* On my way, the bell rang a third time, and when I finally opened the door, I saw from the faces of the two policemen standing there that I hadn't done myself any favours with the delay.

'Detective Inspector Patrick O'Neill,' said the one who wasn't wearing a uniform, flipping a badge under my face. 'And this is Garda Shane Cogley.'

I tried to steer them towards the kitchen, but the Inspector

* Including me?

11

– with what detective instinct? – headed straight for the parlour. The three of us stood in the open door and took in the destruction, the fivers and tenners all over the floor.

The Inspector turned his world-weary, mind-made-up eyes on to me. 'What . . . ?' he asked, pausing for emphasis. 'What . . . in good God's name has happened here?'

Without further preliminaries, he said he was investigating the murder of Martin Mulcahy – his full name, as if he was someone unknown to me – and that he wanted me to go down to the station to help with their enquiries.

'You're not serious?' I said, knowing from TV what that meant.

'Just a few routine questions.'

Garda Cogley snapped his notebook shut and put it back in his pocket.

'Do you need to inform anyone?' the Inspector asked, as he turned to lead us out.

I shook my head, dazed. 'There's nobody to inform.'

'Your daughter . . . ?'

'She's not here.'

'When will she be back?'

'I'm not sure.'

'We need to know, Mrs Creahy.'

'Mulcahy.'

'Mrs *Mulcahy*.' His look told me this was not the time to ask for Ms. 'We need to know her whereabouts. She'll have to be interviewed.'

'She's gone travelling around Ireland. Sightseeing. She only left a couple of hours ago.'

'You didn't go with her.'

'No, I had to stay to look after my father's affairs.'

'Yeah,' he said, pointing an ironical eyebrow at the devastation. 'Right. Come on, let's go.'

2

I could start earlier in the tale, with my father's funeral.* Star
and I, chief mourners, daughter and granddaughter of the
deceased, in our places in the top pew, the back of our black
coats to the rest. The questions I knew the congregation were
asking pinging into my back all through the prayers and the
readings and the hymns: That must be the daughter, is it? When
did she get here? Where was the boyfriend gone? It couldn't be
true what some people were saying, could it?

The event was organized as my father had decreed. Remains
to Stafford's Funeral Parlour in town. No wake. No viewing.
High Mass in Doolough at 10 a.m. Six priests. 'Ave Maria'. 'Be
Not Afraid'. 'How Great Thou Art'. Throughout it all, Star and
I played our parts, standing and sitting as required, heads bowed,
faces blank, but I felt like somebody had punched a hole in me.
Where I should have had a core, I had only space.

Sitting in our front pew, I hadn't realized how many people
were piling into the church behind us until the end, when we
turned to follow the coffin down the aisle and out. All the seats
were full, and crowds were bunched around the doors, upward
of 400 eyes nailing us. In rural Ireland, anyone considered a
local will have a good turnout for their funeral, especially someone central to the community, like a Garda sergeant – even if
he was long retired and not especially popular.

Out we trudged, into the churchyard cemetery for a rosary at
the graveside and afterwards, continuing under orders, we went

---

* So, right from the get-go, we find Mom telling us she's going to do one thing
(begin her story at the point of finding the journals) while doing something else
(taking us further back).

for a soup-and-sandwich lunch to the local pub, Maguire's. It was there, once people had settled in over their spoons, that Dr Keane – who had had his eyes on me ever since coming into the pub – leant across the table where I was sitting with Star and Pauline and Mikey and asked if he might have a word.

'Of course,' I said, pushing my untouched food aside.

Dr Keane was Jimmy to my father, his oldest friend. Despite their different rankings in Doolough's finely tuned social scale, they were bonded by their active history in the Irish Civil War, when they had both fought to uphold the Treaty with Britain that others thought a sordid compromise.

'We'll step outside, if you don't mind,' he said to me, causing a look to fly around the table, the kind of look that made me glad I would be leaving Doolough soon. I put down my napkin and followed him through the crowd. It was cold out, a point he remarked on, pulling his scarf tight around his ancient, scrawny throat and offering me a cigarette. When I shook my head, he lit one for himself and started to talk about the funeral and praise my father and recount some of his memories of their boyhood. Eventually, when he couldn't put off any longer what he had to say, he threw his cigarette to the ground, squashed it with the toe of his boot and said, 'The autopsy found something wasn't right.'

At first, I didn't let in what he was saying. 'If everything was all right,' I said, 'I guess he wouldn't be dead.'

'This isn't a joke, dear.' He looked at me over his glasses, making me feel ten years old. 'The cause of death was an overdose of morphine.'

'What?'

'Yes.'

'But that's –'

'It's beyond doubt. The pathologist said she never saw so much morphine in a body.'

'The pump, maybe. Maybe the pump was faulty?'

'It's been checked. The pump was fine.'

'What about the pills?'

'We don't know about that.' He folded his arms across his chest, let a silence grow. 'We were hoping you might be able to help.'

'How? Help how?'

'Like I say, we don't know. All we know is what the toxicology reports say. An unholy amount, apparently.'

Toxicology reports? Pathologist? Autopsy? With my father's medical history?

'Doctor, does it matter? You and Pauline know what it was like for my father at the end. Pain, babyfood, sleepless nights . . . An animal would have been put out of its misery long before.'

'If I were you, m'girl, I wouldn't be going around saying things like that.'

'If he hadn't died that day, he would have died another day soon.'

'Aren't you wondering who did it?'

'Did what?'

'I'm telling you that somebody killed your father by giving him an overdose of morphine. And all you have to say to me is that whoever did it, did right.'

The nausea I had been feeling all day rose up my wind pipe. 'It's not that. I just can't believe that *anybody* did it. Who could have? Who would have?'

'Who indeed?'

'Maybe . . . Could he have done it himself?'

'I spoke to him a week before he went. He said nothing that sounded suicidal to me.' He tightened his scarf again. 'I wanted you to be told first, that's only fair.'

I thought of the looks exchanged around the table as I got up to leave and knew that, in fact, I wasn't the first. Already, he or the pathologist or somebody else had been talking. Maybe that's why there had been so many at the funeral? They hadn't come to pay their respects to the little-liked sergeant at all but to take a look at the daughter who was being rumoured to have seen him out.

I could begin further back again, with Christmas Day, 1982, the day my father died. The day Star arrived from California. The day Zach left.

Or further back again, when Zach came to rescue me from my father's onslaughts. Or when I decided to return to Doolough to nurse that ungrateful man. Or why not the day I met Zach? The day Star was born? The day I left Ireland with Brendan? The day my father brought me to see Iseult Gonne? The day I was born myself?

Beginnings are for beginners. When you get to my age, you know that you can go back for ever and never get to the start. As I look back now over the long tale, the moment that seems most significant is bending to the floor to pick up my father's journals.

Later, when Inspector O'Neill brought me off to the barracks, all I could think about was these notebooks. Strange? Maybe, but I was fired by more than daughterly curiosity. By this time I had spent more than five years writing about Iseult Gonne, trying to unlock the meaning of her life.

The first fruit of those efforts had been a BA dissertation, 'Suffer As Your Mother Suffered: The Life of Iseult Gonne', but, before I even climbed the podium to accept the parchment, I knew that what spoke loudest to me about Iseult's life was not citable. Where we touched was not in the record but in the gaps and oversights, in the silences where whispers rise.

Not knowing what to do about this, I went back to my sources and citations, and pushed and pummelled the evidence, trying to make it yield. But it wasn't working. Iseult's life remained an enigma, closed to me in some way that I couldn't unpick. Now with the journals, and letters and photographs that I had found here in the house, I felt I was being given a new set of keys.

My father had always boasted of knowing Iseult and her mother, Maud Gonne, in France. Maud was quite the celebrity in her day, a patriot and propagandist who had dubbed herself 'Ireland's Joan of Arc'. Having known her was one of the ways in which my father impressed upon others that he was no ordinary Garda sergeant.

Iseult was all over that big notebook of his – the short read I'd had time for had shown me that – so, as I listened to the Inspector's questions, what I was longing to do was read more. In there was the something I'd been seeking. I knew it. It was what Zach would have called an Intuition – a word, like Prayer, that he always capitalized. ('A Prayer is you talking to the Source; an Intuition is the Source talking to you.')

Looking back, I can see that I was not quite sane in those days after my father died. For twenty years I had carried him around in my head. In coming back to Ireland to nurse him, the picture I held – a broad, red-faced bully – was reduced as age and illness shrank him to little more than skin shrouding bone. Now both versions of him were gone. The strong arms that used to reach so readily for the strap: gone. The sour smell of his sickroom breath: gone. The size fourteen feet that had to have shoes and boots specially made: gone. The shrivelled genitals and wispy, grey fuzz that surrounded them: gone.

The young version and the old, the fearful and the pitiful, all gone, gone, gone. I knew it, but something about it was unknowable.

So when the Inspector told me he was arresting me and said that line I had heard in TV police dramas, about my not having to say anything but knowing that what I did say might be used in evidence against me, a part of me was unable to take it seriously. What I said, according to the *Wicklow Gazette,* which took a personal interest in my trial, was 'You must be joking', but already another, deeper part of me was whispering something that didn't want to be heard.

Establishing values other than (*better* than) my father's;

stripping away his influence: these were the aims that had guided my life since I ran away from Doolough. I had travelled far in my effort to escape him, more than 6,000 miles, but even at that distance he held me. My body might be in Santa Paola, California, but my deepest thoughts never strayed too far from Doolough, County Wicklow; regurgitating what had been, what should have been, what might have been, each twist and turn only tightening the ties.

And when I was needed, I came back to Doolough to tend him and to see if I could find the closure that my Californian friends recommended. He was no easy patient, but I prevailed and thought often of the time to come, when I would be alive and he would be dead.

It wasn't much, but I had thought it would be enough. It would be over. I would have peace at last.

Wrong, Izzy. Wrong, yet again.

3

'Take your head out of that book,' my father says, coming into the kitchen. 'We're taking a ramble.'

Eleven-year-old me looks up, half hearing. 'What?'

'A ramble.' His word for paying people a visit. He often brought me along when going to see someone, as a sort of armour. 'Now.'

I put *Jane Eyre* aside and get up from the window seat.

'Will ye be back for tea?' Mammy asks, from the sink.

'Of course, woman. It's only half past three.'

Mammy puts on her sorry-for-asking face and goes back to her work. I put my book in my bag. Sometimes on his visits he gets talking so hard he forgets he's brought me and I get to read.

Outside the car is waiting, his blue Ford Anglia. In Doolough at that time, only the publican, the doctor and the priest had a car, and in other villages the sergeant went around on a bicycle. Most of my father's journeys were also made on two wheels, but he loved owning this car and he loved an excuse to take it out – a drive to Dublin, or to the beach, or on a ramble.

'It's a lady in mourning that we're going to see,' he tells me as we climb in. 'She's just lost someone she used to call her aunt but in fact was her mother. So she's in need of a visit and that's that.' My father's conversation often ran like this, with him answering arguments you never made.

'Who is she?' I ask, as I'm supposed to.

'Her name is Iseult Stuart. Though some still call her Gonne.'

Daughter of the more famous Maud, whose funeral he had gone to in Dublin the week before. He had come home from it in a state of unnatural excitement that was hard to read,

19

that had him taking whiskey from the cupboard he called the medicine chest. All through the week he kept reading us bits about her from the newspapers, as if she were a relation.

'I think we learnt about her in school,' I venture, unsure how he'll take it.

'What did you learn?'

'That W. B. Yeats was in love with her. That he was always asking her to marry him.'

'Oh, that was the mother. But wasn't half of Dublin always proposing to the both of them? And half of London, and Paris too?'

He turns right at the end of the lane, and right again at the village on to the Glendalough road.

'I thought you'd like to meet her,' he says, 'because it was from her I got your name.'

'But you said it was from the story.' A legend about Iseult of Ireland, a princess loved by an aged king and a young knight.

'None of your backchat now,' he snaps. 'Who do you think *she* was named for?'

I pull myself over to the window side of the seat, knowing better than to deny or defend anything. It's May out there, my favourite month, and the trees are bursting with leaf, but in here, as always in the car, my father feels too close. His six-foot-two frame spills out of the small seat and his knuckles bulge round the steering wheel. He begins to tap out a tune on it.

We settle into not talking.

It was Miss McNamara, our English teacher, who introduced me to Iseult, through the writer she called Ireland's greatest poet: William Butler Yeats. 'He wishes for the Cloths of Heaven', she taught us first, a poem in which he portrays him-self as a sort of cosmic Sir Walter Ralegh, laying down the heavens under Maud Gonne's feet. She read in the slow, mannered style that she called Yeatsian, which made the entire class crack up, trying not to laugh.

Miss McNamara didn't notice. On the final line, 'Tread softly because you tread on my dreams', she bowed her head. She had moved herself to tears. My friend Pauline, sitting in the desk beside me, gave me a nudge and I rolled my eyes, afraid to admit that I too was affected.

Next day, Pauline brought in a picture of Maud Gonne that her mother had at home, a picture taken around the time Yeats had written, 'I never thought to see in a living woman so great beauty.' It was a beauty lost on the girls of the Convent of Our Blessed Lady in 1953, a time when the favoured female look was blonde and busty. The almost-masculine, handsome-rather-than-pretty ideal of the Edwardians couldn't have been less fashionable. Looking at Pauline's photo, the girls of 2A picked Maud's image apart: her face was too broad, her chin too strong, her jaw too set, her forehead too high . . .

'Maybe she didn't photograph well,' I suggested. 'Maybe you had to be in her presence to get a sense of her.'

'"In her presence",' jeered Pauline. 'Oooh!'

'You know what I mean. Sometimes it's like that. She was six foot tall. And her auburn hair went down past her waist.'

I didn't say what I was really thinking: that we might sneer but would any amongst us ever inspire such wonderful words? All through this time I was wafting around school and home in a befuddle of Yeatsianisms: burning youths with beating hearts and glimmering girls with pearl-pale hands. Apple blossom hair, bound and wound about the stars and moon and piteous sun . . .

So imagine my chagrin when, a couple of days into our work on Yeats, Miss McNamara casually mentioned that in his middle years the poet had moved his romantic attentions from Maud Gonne to her daughter. I was so offended I only half registered my surprise that the daughter bore my name, the name that was so unusual and difficult to pronounce for everybody, except my father. Her daughter? Her *daughter*!

'No,' I cried out into the classroom. 'He couldn't have.'

Whereupon everybody laughed.

Blink-blink, blink-blink: my father has pressed the indicator and turned off the road into a rain-rutted lane not unlike our own but with rhododendrons on both sides just coming into bloom, massive pink heads nodding at us all the way up. A house comes into view. Grey, immense and brooding, with a castellated roof.

'Here we are,' my father says. 'Laragh Castle.'

The lane runs straight to the hall door, but he parks away from it, over by the hedge. Then he sits, nothing moving except his two thumbs, which are ferociously circling around each other.

'Daddy?'

'All right, all right,' he says, as if it is me who has dragged him here, and he gets out so fast he nearly trips.

Near the hall door is a pyramid of empty dog and cat food cans, giving off a meaty smell. We ring the bell. As we stand, waiting, on the doormat, something rubs against my ankle. *Miaow!* A cat has appeared from nowhere to wind herself around me.

The door opens.

'Sergeant?' Surprise flickers across the face of the old lady standing there, then she sees the cat. 'Sophie, *what* are you doing? Where are your manners?'

She has an accent, a French roll to her *r*. *Whairr arre yourr mannairrs?* When young, she was beautiful, with the sort of beauty that made people stop in the street and gasp, but she is not beautiful now. Her ankles are thick and ropy. She reminds me of a picture I saw in a book in school, a photograph of a famous old Indian in his feather headdress, eyes saturated with sorrow.

'Would you', she says, looking at me, 'be terribly kind and pick her up for me?'

I bend and sweep the warm squirm into my arms. A furry eel.

'Thank you so much,' she says, smiling, as I hand her over.

'I'm afraid if *I* bent down that far, I should never get back up.'

With the cat held against her, she turns to my father. 'Do come in, Sergeant.' *Searrrrgean'*.

In the hallway, we have an awkward moment while she waits for me to be introduced. When nothing is forthcoming, she holds out her hand to me. 'I'm Iseult Stuart.' Her married name.

'I'm Iseult too,' I say. 'Iseult Mulcahy.'

'How wonderful. I so rarely hear the name in Ireland. Do you like it?'

'Most people call me Izzy.'

She nods. 'Probably wise. Our poor namesake is far too tragic for modern times.'

My father cuts in. 'I just came to pay my respects.'

Again, a splinter of surprise. 'That's very kind.'

The clock ticks. 'Shall we go to the garden?' she says, as another pause grows too long. 'It's such a beautiful day.'

She leads us through to the back of the house, through rooms that are dark and full, every surface, including the floor, covered. Books, pictures, cups and plates, gramophone records, knitting wool, newspapers, photographs in frames and out, lie in mounds that have taken years to construct and haven't moved in months. A shovel and pick lie against one wall, a child's scooter against another. On the couch are two empty pudding bowls upended, pens and pencils, more books, ornaments, old shoes, over-flowing ashtrays and, on top, a glass half full of an unknown liquid set thick. All preserved in dust. If Mammy was here, she'd be having an anxiety attack.

'Excuse the mess,' she says, dismissing it with a lofty wave of her hand as she shepherds us past. 'I normally bring visitors to the drawing room in front. But it's such a lovely afternoon.'

After the chaos indoors, the garden comes as a lovely surprise, like a cool drink on a dusty day. All the colours are woven together into an order that feels exactly right, that feels magical, like places I've only read about before. A secret garden, a wonderland. I feel that we three – my father's green trousers,

23

her blue cardigan, my red tights – are part of it, this rhythm of colour that seems to glory in itself. Somewhere near by, a stream rushes, and the smell of pines from the mountains tangs the breeze.

'This garden is a beautiful job,' my father says.

'It gives me great pleasure.'

She directs us to the bench against the south-facing wall, full in the sun. As soon as she sits, the cat appears again and jumps into her lap. We sit too, my father in the middle, the three of us looking at the garden as if it is a cinema screen. I take out my book, hoping they might talk more freely if they think I'm not listening.

'What are you reading?' she asks. 'Ah, *Jane Eyre*. Dear Jane, so passionately moral. We should all be more like her. You are fond of reading?'

I nod.

'It will be a great consolation to you,' she says. 'All through life.'

'Would you like a cigarette?' says my father, dragging her back again. She takes one, and the light he offers, inhaling the smoke deep into her lungs and letting it out in a long line.

My father, by contrast, jabs at his with short, sharp puffs.

They begin to talk about her mother, Maud, while I pretend to read. 'It is hard to understand why somebody who spent her whole life giving', she says, 'had to suffer so in the end.'

'She was a great woman, entirely.'

'She found it disgusting and despairing that her suffering, instead of spiritualizing her, only made her more selfish and materialistic. As it is also my experience with this rotten heart illness, I could only wretchedly agree.'

'I agree myself.'

'You are ill too?'

'No, healthy as an old hog, thank God. I meant it's what I've seen.'

None of his usual sarcasm here, or any of the cynicism he

brings on other visits, to old men with tattered faces and wrinkled caps.

'I'm glad to say it was all redeemed by her death, which was one of those really beautiful things one reads of in holy books and doesn't quite believe in. The day before she died, after she got the last sacraments, she had some kind of mystical experience and looked radiantly happy and young.' She is animated now. As her voice warms up, her hands move in time with her words. 'Almost the last words she spoke were: "I feel now an ineffable joy." Then she went to sleep breathing lightly, like a child.'

My father is appalled at this talk of death, even more so when she says, 'I think I shall soon be joining her.'

'Nonsense. You're only . . . what? . . . Sixty?'

'Fifty-eight. But I have already lived much longer than I thought possible with such pain and decrepitude. Unless things take a miraculous turn, this coming winter may well see the end of it. I'm not saying this to make myself pathetic. I'm actually quite jealous of Moura now, thinking of her in what she used to call the predestined dancing place.'

'I'm sure it can be arranged. Do you still have that old gun inside?'

She breaks into a laugh that seems to be conspiratorial but also aimed at herself. A lovely laugh that is surprisingly young, that seems to lift her up out of her old body, and the disorder and clutter of her house, that makes her head lean towards us and her eyes open out.

He is delighted. 'What are you laughing at? Didn't you just say that's what you want?'

The laugh collapses into a cough. 'What I want? It has so seldom been in my power to get it for myself that I confess I hardly know any more.'

He sighs. 'It's hard to see all right, why we have to suffer the way we do.'

'No generation ever saw more of it than ours.'

'That war.'

She nods. 'And the last one too, Sergeant. That awful bomb.'

'Nothing left to us now but the prospect of us blowing the entire world open.'

'What disenchanted times we live in. The Easterns believe that all suffering is self-created. Whether we know it or not.'

'I think I've seen a bit too much to believe that.'

'Their understanding is not ours, but I know what you mean. Those wars.'

'That bomb.'

'Earthquakes.'

'Famine.'

'Heart disease,' she laughs. 'No, Sergeant, do not speak. No more or we *shall* end up going inside for the gun. I insist on closing with my execrable heart.'

He concedes. My *father* concedes.

I sneak a look. He is sitting back, arms folded, happy as I have ever seen him. 'You'd wonder what it's all for, all right, so much suffering.'

'It's so we won't mind going,' I say, the words popping from my mouth. Or so I remember it.

They both turn to me. She is beaming, he less taken. '"So we won't mind going,"' she repeats thoughtfully. 'Oh, my dear, you are so right. It's so we can let go of this world. What a delightful, intelligent girl you have there, Sergeant. What a *special* girl.'

I bathed in that blessing for the rest of our visit. Sometimes I think I bathe in it still.

In the car on the way home, his good humour makes me brave. 'What were you saying to the lady about the gun, Daddy?'

He takes his eyes off the road to look at me. 'I can't be telling you that.'

'Please.'

'It's state business.'

'I'm eleven, Daddy.'

'Don't I know? I can hardly credit it. When I was your age, I was working weekends and holidays, putting together a few bob. I tell you, you youngsters don't know you have it made . . .'

This is an old refrain, but his mood doesn't lean far in that direction this afternoon. He wants to talk about her as much as I want to hear. 'You're not to go blabbing it about at school, now.'

'I won't. Of course I won't.'

'All right so. It was ten years ago, during the Emergency, the country was awash with German spies. One evening we got a call at the station to say one had parachuted into Meath and made his way down this far. We were to go up and do a search at Laragh.'

'For a spy?'

'They were harbouring him there. It wasn't her, of course. He was sent across by the husband and –'

'Her husband was still alive then?'

'He's alive yet, the blackguard.'

I am surprised. She hadn't seemed married. 'So where was he today?'

'He doesn't live at home. Mr Stuart backed the wrong horse in the war. Went off to Germany and declared his love of Hitler and so is not welcome back in Ireland.'

Hitler? She is married to someone who loved *Hitler*? My idea of her splinters around that information.

'Anyhow, he prefers to go careering around Europe with other women instead.'

Hitler? I think of her admiring Jane Eyre. *So passionately moral.*

'On the night in question we were given orders to search the house for the German spy. As I went round, I opened a drawer in the sideboard in the parlour and found a gun. I quickly closed it again and said nothing.'

'Why?'

'I felt I owed her that much.'

He's evading now, but the burn of my curiosity makes me risk asking again. 'But why?'

'She treated me fine once, when she could easily have done otherwise.'

'So you saved her.'

'I did my best for her, but she and her mother had bought clothes for yer man, including an overcoat. When he was captured, they traced the clothes back to her Switzers account and gave her a fright with a month in Mountjoy and a trial by the Special Criminal Court. But I had the satisfaction of knowing I had no act nor part in it.'

I don't understand. I don't understand any of it. He looks at my puzzled face. 'Oh, it's too hard to explain. Maybe when you're older.'

That is it, he's said as much as he feels like saying. He starts humming to make sure I know it, and after a while his good mood breaks into a whistle. 'Don't Fence Me In'.

When we get back to the house, on our way out of the car he says, 'Don't go telling your mother where we were, all right? It would only upset her.'

When, many years later and many miles away, I first started to find my way back to Iseult Gonne, it was through her mother. In those early research days I found Maud more beguiling. Maud, the radical Irish revolutionary, the celebrated beauty, the unattainable muse, always dashing and bedazzling and *doing* . . .

Iseult's attractions were more subtle. I had to spend years squinting beyond the sparkling characters around her, straining to hear her voice through their clamour. And, of them all, none was brighter or more voluble than the alluring and alarming Maud.

The real surprise was that writing about them led me into writing about myself and the cauldron of emotion sizzling between poor misunderstood me and my poor misguided father and daughter. For years I resisted writing like this: the autobiographical, the confessional, the first-person narrative so beloved of Freudianism and feminism. The insistent I. I-I-I-I. It still feels self-indulgent, but nothing else will do, that's what I've come to know.

That's what I was coming to realize in the days after my father's death and what was confirmed, beyond doubt, on finding his journals. The small books told me things like he cut back the ditch at the bottom of the garden on Friday 16 July 1924; that rain prevented him from finishing the job the next day; that he wrote poetry, sporadically and badly; that he never forgot the war. He kept them diligently, a new one for every year, though only five (1924, 1925, 1937, 1951, 1960) survived.

The entries in the large book are much longer. It was started in France, during the war, and he added to it all his life, in spurts. One break between entries, from 1926 to 1937, is almost eleven years long. Anyone else would have started a new notebook but not my waste-not, want-not father.

Miss Gonne, he calls Iseult in earlier entries, Mrs Stuart later on.

And, on reading what he had to say, I realized I had been having so much trouble with my book about Iseult because I was telling part of the tale. That the truth about her could only be told by also writing about me.*

Initially, that realization dismayed me. I knew it would certainly have dismayed Iseult, who would have detested being hauled into biographical fiction – one of the most despised corners of literature, awash with the blood of beheaded queens and the tears of the used and abused. A generic outpost far removed from her beloved poetry and philosophy.

I resisted, but in the end I had no choice. This was the only literary home that had room for us both, the only method that allowed me to reach into the secret spaces we shared.

So here I am, stepping out from behind the footnotes and

* And me, apparently!

citations into the breaches. Putting it all together, all that I've learnt from my reading and from my own living. Laying us down on the page together, the Gonnes and my own people, side by side. Martin 'The Mule' Mulcahy and Lucien Millevoye. Brendan and Francis, Zack and Ezra, Star and Dolores. And Willie Yeats, of course, the poet who touched us all.

Oh, and me. Don't forget me, the teller caught in the tale.

All of us squirming and breathing, laughing and dancing, suffering and dying. A story. Not only that, but a true story.

Or as true as I can make it.

4

After Dr Keane delivered his bombshell, I had to go back into the pub and stay to the very end, my mind clanging with his insinuations. Star sat opposite me at our table, chewing on her pudgy fingers and disdaining to join in the talk. I switched out too, let the conversation churn around me and waited, waited, for them all to finish their food and their drinks and take themselves off. It was hours before they cleared, but eventually only the stragglers, freeloaders and alcoholics were left, and Pauline, more attuned to the niceties of Doolough behaviour than me, said it would be okay to go.

'I will never set foot in that place again,' I said to Star as we walked out together. 'Never, never, never.'

'Ah, now,' said Pauline, coming out behind us, putting an arm around us each, 'I thought it all went off grand.'

Mikey, her husband, was waiting outside to drive us home. We sat into the back, and I was grateful for everybody's silence. I was drained from taking condolences and from watching people straining to find nice things to say. We drove through Doolough, past the school and the smattering of houses known as the heart of the village (as if Doolough had a heart), and out on to the Avoca road. Past the high walls of Doolough House. Past the police barracks. As the car drew towards the house, I said: 'You can drop us here, Mikey, at the end of the lane. We'd be glad of the fresh air.'

'Are you sure?' asked Pauline. 'Do you not want me to come up?'

'Not at all, Pauline,' I said. 'You've done so much already.'

Pauline twisted her head round to Star. 'It's great you're here now, love. Your poor mam has been a slave to your grandad's illness these past months.'

'Ah, now . . .' I said.

How easily I had slipped back into these Irish phrases that you don't get anywhere else.

She patted my hand. 'You let Star look after *you* now.' She got out of her front seat and folded it forward, so we could climb out. We waited side by side, trying not to see Star's struggle to extract herself from the small car. Why are fat people's exertions so painful to watch?

'I'll be round tomorrow at one o'clock,' she said, 'with a bit of dinner.'

'Thank you so much for everything, Pauline.'

'You're sure you're all right?'

'Positive.'

Star was out.

'Ring me now if you need anything,' Pauline said, sitting back in. 'Middle of the night or whenever. I won't mind.'

'You're too good, Pauline.' I closed the door on her. 'Thanks, Mikey.'

'Thank you,' said Star, her only contribution since we'd left the pub.

We waved and they were gone, the chuggy sound of their engine carrying across the fields as we walked up the lane back to the house where I was raised – or reared, as they like to say in Ireland, as if you were one of the cows or sheep of the fields. The short day was coming to a close; the late-December light was as pale as water and fading fast. Through the naked stalks of the trees we could see my father's house: tall, white, Georgian, protected by a circle of faithful ash trees, with two chimneys either end of the roof in which jackdaws nested and cawed.

Is it an Irish or an American saying, that when it comes to money or possessions 'you can't take it with you'? If you could take anything to the place beyond, this house would be it for my father. There had always been a question mark over how he, a Garda sergeant, had accumulated the money to buy it.*

I matched my pace to Star's slower, more tentative steps – the heavier Star becomes, somehow, the less solid she feels – and we walked up the lane in gathering darkness, two feet by two crunching along the gravel as we drew close. Eight front windows – six above and a large one either side of the front door – stared us down. It was ours now, this house, unless my father had another surprise waiting for us in his will.

Since she'd arrived on Christmas Eve, Star and I had had no time alone. My father died the next day, and since then it had been nothing but people coming and going and funeral arrangements and things to do. Now I wanted her to myself for a while. Our old way of being together had evacuated, and we needed time if we were to replace it with something new. I wanted to show her Doolough and all the beauty spots of County Wicklow, especially Laragh, where Iseult had lived, and Glendalough, where she was buried.

Yet I didn't know how to ask or how to tell her any of this. Imagine that: lost for words with your own daughter. When she was a child, if somebody had told me this would happen, I would have laughed. The breach of adolescence, the generation gap, is no secret, but it's like other women telling you about their birth pains: you only dimly perceive what you are being told until your own experience smacks you into knowing.

And Star and I had complicating factors, if ever a mother and daughter had. Her refusal to discuss that made other talk impossible.

I let her in through the back porch, followed in behind. Beneath those dyed and gelled spikes, just below her hairline,

---

* Mom said to me once that it was rumoured to be IRA money. My grandfather had returned to Ireland from France in 1918 and, like many Irish ex-WWI soldiers, found that the War of Independence unleashed the nationalist within. But I don't know what she meant by IRA money, or if it was even true.

was a birthmark about a square inch in size, the shape – if you closed your eyes and tilted your sight a certain way – of a five-cornered star. I used to kiss that mark after every feed.

I did my best, Star, I screamed internally at the spine that was so hunched against me as I followed it into the house. *I did my best.* Even as I was thinking it, I despised the thought. The anthem of the failed mother.

Forget all that. Instead find words that might reach through that anger of hers and persuade her to stay. If we were to salvage anything worth taking into a shared future, I *had* to get her to stay.

In the kitchen I put on the kettle and had an idea. I'd show Star some of the family photographs and letters that I had found in the bureau in the sitting room. Draw her in, then ask her to stay on, for a few days at least. I fetched them from the bureau drawers and laid them out on the table in front of her while I made tea. The first one that caught her was one of Daddy and me at the beach. Me, aged seven or eight, in a hoop-striped swimming costume with a frilly skirt piece, standing in front of a sandcastle. My father, already old, sitting upright on a plaid rug behind me, his shirt buttons undone showing grey hair across his chest. Both of us squinting into the sun.

'You were so cute,' Star said, her voice as wistful as if she were looking at her own memory, not mine. 'Who took this?'

'Your granny, I guess.' I'd spent so long trying to forget that all my memories felt unreliable. 'We used to go to the beach on summer Sundays when she was alive.'

Star was handing me another photograph, but this one was an illustration, cut from a book. 'Who's this?'

I knew the picture; I had seen it in more than one publication. Iseult, *circa* 1918. Aged twenty-two, not much older than Star was now. Posed in faux-peasant style, her hair a long curtain down her back, shoulders covered in a rough shawl. I suspected Maud's hand in the arrangement: her daughter, the Irish colleen.

Except it didn't work. Iseult's expression was too intellectual, her beauty too ethereal. 'That's Iseult Gonne.'

'Iseult Gonne? That writer woman you used to study?'

'Exactly.'

'But what's she doing among Granddad's photos?'

'Your granddad had a bit of a thing for her.'

'He did?'

'Yes. You know he named me for her.'

'Did I? Did he date her or something? Before he met Grandma?'

I laughed. 'God, no. My father was a Garda sergeant; Iseult was Ascendancy.'

'Huh?'

'The old ruling class. And foreign. And cultured. They would have been poles apart.'

Star's forehead creased, producing those lines I always felt like smoothing out with my thumb. 'But you've just said –'

'Iseult was . . .' I searched for the right word. '. . . a kind of obsession to your grandfather.'

'Ah ha! So you *did* have something in common with him.'

I turned my back on that comment and reached up to the high shelf over the fridge. 'Here,' I said, slipping a letter out of a bunch held together with a blue elastic and opening it. 'Read this, here.'

She tried. '*You'll be interested to hear, Mammy, that we visited* – is it? – *visited the house of* . . . *of Major John MacBride and Maud Gonne the other evening. I'd never seen nothing* – is that right? – *nothing so fine in my* . . . eh . . .' She was stumbling over the crooked handwriting, the strange spellings, the back-to-front Irish idioms. She looked up at me. 'What *is* this?'

'It's a letter home, from my father. From when he lived in Paris.'

I took it from her and, more familiar with his writing, I read it for us both: '*You'll be interested to hear, Mammy, that we visited the house of Major John MacBride and Maud Gonne the other evening. I'd never seen nothing so fine in my life as that house. And you'll not believe what else. I caught a look at the young wan she keeps there, ten year old or so. So I'm sorry to have to tell you, Mammy, that all they say about her is true indeed. Seems like she's a different person in Paris from what we get in Ireland . . . Though knowing you, you'll probably still refuse to believe it.'*

I paused, looked up to see how Star was taking it. Her expression was unreadable. 'The "young wan" is Iseult.'

'I guessed.'

'He hadn't had much of an education at that stage,' I explained. 'He left school at fourteen to go to France.'

'How spooky is that? You writing away about her all those years in the States and now finding this letter.'

Spooky was the wrong word. Zach would say synchronous. For Zach there was no such thing as coincidence. It was all an unfolding of The Source's plan, all happening as it ought to happen in a great interconnected arrangement. Corny? Oh, yes, but it was Zach's gift to make you believe and open those realms for you.

Zach would have understood my need of Iseult at this time. He would have talked to me and bestowed his calm, quiet attention on me, so that after a while my words would have come to seem too loud, then too one-dimensional, then super-fluous altogether. That's what I needed now, but instead I had Star, perplexity oozing from a too-fat, over-furrowed face. 'I don't get it, Mom.'

'What?'

'Any of it. You and Granddad. You and this . . . Iseult Gonne person. Your attention on all that now, at a time like this.'

How could I explain? I looked down at the artefacts of Iseult that my father had saved for decades. 'She had that sort of effect on people. She was superbly herself but selfless too. Beautiful but retiring. Excitable but shy. Discriminating but kind. Arthur Symons called her a Virgin Vagabond, and I remember the first time I met her . . .' I trailed away. She wasn't listening.

'Mom, you know I'm leaving tomorrow?'

'Star, please. At this time, wou–'

'I'm sorry. I know you'd like to lay on the guilt, but you also know that would be unfair.'

'I'd just like you to stay for a couple of days, now you're here.'

'Oh, yes, now I'm here.'

'What does that mean?'

'What if I hadn't decided to come, Mom? How long would I have had to wait before *you'd* have got in touch?'

I stood up, began to tidy up the table. Here it came, the attack.

'Not a word, nothing, for *months*. *I* had to fly 6,000 miles. *I* had to hire a car in a strange city and drive into rural Ireland, asking my way of strangers in the dark, not knowing who'd be here when I arrived. And if I hadn't . . . ?'

She reached across and took my wrist. 'No, don't get up. I get why you ran off, just about, though did you really *have* to leave for Ireland, quite so quickly? Well, maybe. But what I *don't* accept, Mom, what I will *never* accept, is the great silence that came after.'

I looked down at her, at the shuddering of her jowls in her anger. For a moment I was tempted to do what she was doing: to let myself think of nothing but me-me-me. What would I say to her? *Cut me a break, Star. Don't ask any more of me than you ask of yourself. Move on. Let me and Zach be.*

But I didn't, of course. Star was American; I, for all the years in Santa Paola, was still of Ireland, where – in my day, at least – the national motto was Whatever You Say, Say Nothing.

And I was the mother, trained into biting my tongue. Daughterly anger we might survive but maternal self-pity, I knew, would kill us off. 'It's all so complicated,' I ventured.

'Complicated? To pick up a telephone?'

37

'I didn't think you wanted to hear from me. You said –'

'We both said a lot of things that day.'

In fact, I had said very little. It was she who had ranted and raved before stomping out of the house but this didn't seem like the time to say so.

'Couldn't you have written me a letter? A note of your telephone number here? After what you did . . .'

What about all the years before my unintended mistake, Star, day after day after day of mothering and giving? Did that not count for anything? Should that not be weighed against my sin?

Oh, Star, my daughter dear, go easy on me. Go easy or you might come to regret it.

5

Iseult Gonne's story begins on a hot summer afternoon in Royat, a spa town in the mountainous centre of France, where her mother and her father are just about to meet.

Twenty-year-old Maud Gonne is sitting under a tree in the town square, in a white shimmering dress, fanning away white shimmering heat. Sitting between her great-aunt and her sister, she surveys the town and in her head announces to herself that she is bored. Bored, *bored*, BORED.

Royat, in the Auvergne, has long been the favourite health resort of her great-aunt Mary, the Comtesse de Sisseraine, and it is the old lady's pleasure to stroll her two beautiful nieces – Maud and her sister Kathleen – along the gravelled paths, so that young men in straw boaters and gold-braided caps might admire them. This afternoon, though, is too hot for walking, and so they sit in the shady square, beneath a tree, listening to military music from the bandstand.

Maud's boredom is the restless kind: she is gripped by a feeling of premonition so strong she can barely sit still. 'Something is going to happen,' she whispers to her sister from behind her fan, but Kathleen says it is only static from the coming thunderstorm.

Tedium, Maud has come to realize over the past months, is not just the preserve of her deceased father's military set in Dublin. Society everywhere, it seemed, trades in the same surface trivia, the same insincere talk, the same lack of purpose. She felt it when she moved to the London milieu of her English aunts after Tommy died, and even here, in glamorous France, with her favourite aunt, the social timetable of balls and crushes, dinners and soirées, parades and casinos, has become a round of duties. Duties in which she takes no more delight than Tommy would have taken in a military review.

A couple of unknown men are approaching, are being welcomed and introduced. From the moment the exceedingly tall Frenchman bends over her hand, pronouncing himself *enchanté*, Maud knows this – he – is what she has been expecting. As he straightens and smiles, she sees that he is older, by a decade or perhaps even more, and saturninely handsome. Tall – one of the exceptional men who soars above her own six feet. Thin face. Straight nose. Small ears. Thinning hair (a pity, but one cannot have *everything*).

It is his mouth that is most intriguing: something about it, barely visible under his handlebar moustache, fills her with fear, fear of a most delicious kind. His eyes protrude slightly from his lively face, but she perceives concealed shadows. Behind his ostentatious display of admiration lies a little melancholy, the same subdued sadness she used to sense in Tommy. It ignites in her a feeling she hasn't felt since her father died: a desire to win this man's admiration, not for her beauty but for herself.

Such men deserve to be gratified.

The talk is all of the impending storm, of how it would be too hot to play at the casino that night. Aunt Mary elucidates her great fear of thunderstorms, a fear she considers femininely becoming, and the other ladies and Kathleen murmur their concurrences for the same reason. Maud, still fighting her alarming inclination to dance about, forces herself to sit, twirling her parasol and her smile. The imposed stillness intensifies her strong, strange sense of *déjà vu*. 'Monsieur,' she says, 'I do believe we have met before?'

'*Mais non*, mademoiselle. *C'est impossible.*' He smiles a meaningful smile. 'If I had met you, I should not forget.'

'I am sure we have met somewhere, sometime,' she repeats. 'But it is too hot to think.'

A few heavy drops of rain fall, and Aunt Mary rises. The men accompany them back to their hotel, and, as they reach it, the storm breaks in great flashes of lightning and crashing thunder, releasing rain in torrents. Aunt Mary leads them all upstairs to the salon, where she orders the blinds and curtains to be drawn and the gas lights lit, to keep out sight of the storm. Then she summons Figlio (the young Englishman she refers to as her secretary, though everybody knows his real function) to play the piano. It will distract them from the thunder, she says, which is now so close that each clap shakes the building.

Figlio begins to play. While the attention is on his performance, Maud – without looking at her Frenchman – slips through the thick curtains, out on to the roofed terrace. The rosebushes in the garden below are being dashed to pieces by the driving rain, the petals sending up an intoxicatingly sweet aroma. She would love to go down into the garden amid the havoc of the flowers, but, restrained by thoughts of her new dress and hat, contents herself with leaning forward from the terrace, stretching her bare arms into the rain.

His voice from behind, though half expected, makes her jump. 'Mademoiselle, your aunt has sent me to look for you, to tell you to come in.'

'I cannot. How can one leave a storm like this?'

'You are not afraid?'

'Oh, no, one must never be afraid of anything. Not even death.'

This was Tommy's doctrine. He said those very words to her when she was only four years old, too young to understand, but, because he said them on the day her mother died, and because his voice was so strange and faraway as he spoke, she has never forgotten.

The Frenchman comes to stand beside her. 'Death? What a strange thought in one so young.'

'I have always been careless of death. I believe that is why I have survived so long.'

'My dear girl, you are all of – what? – eighteen?'

'Twenty, monsieur.'

'You need hardly fear death just yet.'

She does not tell him of the lung disease that has been her trouble since childhood and, later, she will learn that he suffers from the same affliction. 'Oh, I don't think of death at all,' she says. 'That is what I'm saying. I think only of life, of how life might best be lived.'

'That is easily answered. Life is best lived in love.'

'A pretty answer, monsieur, but I am afraid love leads to marriage. And that is not how *my* life would best be lived.'

He chuckles. 'I thought all beautiful young ladies wished to marry.'

'In December I shall be twenty-one, free at last from the bondage of my elders. Why should I then choose to go into the bondage of a husband?'

'And what do your parents make of this unorthodox doctrine?'

'Both are dead, Monsieur Millevoye. Hence the freedom that will shortly come my way.'

'Oh . . . My condolences, mademoiselle.'

She waves her hand. 'Thank you. My mother died many years ago and my father last November. The latter bereavement has left me, I will confess, a trifle raw. But also, soon, truly independent.'

'You have my sympathy, none the less. The death of a parent is always a grievous loss.'

She bows her head. 'We were very close, Tommy and I. People who did not know us often mistook us for husband and wife.'

Lucien raises his fine eyebrows.

'Oh, you see, he looked very young for his age, and I was an exceptionally tall child, five foot ten at the age of fourteen. At that age, I persuaded Nurse to lengthen my skirts and let me put up my hair so I could accompany him.'

'And this he permitted?'

'Welcomed.'

'An unconventional father.'

'He did try sometimes to be conventional, but it did not become him.' A memory breaks a smile in her. 'Once after a visit to Rome he became disturbed by the arrival of numerous letters to me with an Italian postmark, and he thought he should confiscate and read them. So I told my correspondent to write to me with milk on the edges of fashionable papers that Tommy would unsuspectingly hand over. This he did. When I received one of these despatches, I sat Tommy down and showed him what we had done.'

'Did that not rather ruin your fun?'

'Tommy was far more interesting to me than the writer of these letters and his education far more important than the attentions of a beau. So I sat him by the fire and held the paper close to the flame and showed him the love letter gradually emerging in brown letters. "This, Tommy, is what you have just handed over," I said. "Don't you realize how absurd this inspection of correspondence is? In four years, I shall be of age and able to marry this young man, and you won't be able to prevent me. If he goes on writing like this, I shall certainly *not* want to marry him, so please, stop making him interesting by opening his letters."'

Lucien burst out laughing.

'That's just how he used to laugh. You remind me of him . . . a little.'

He made a small bow. 'I am immensely flattered, mademoiselle.'

The lift of his lips twists something inside her. She turns, moves away from him, to the far edge of the terrace. The rain is easing, falling in spatters now, and the air feels clean, purified by the downpour.

'You miss him,' says his voice from where he stood. She had thought he would follow her across.

43

'The night before he died,' she says, speaking into the garden, 'I dreamt of watching a funeral procession go down Dublin quays. Military bands were playing the Dead March, and the small shops along the quays had their shutters closed in mourning. At the port, the coffin was lifted from a gun carriage and hoisted on to the boat.' She turns to face him. 'And that was precisely how it happened at his funeral, every detail just as I dreamt it. Do you think that strange, monsieur?'

'You have the gift of second sight.'

'Sometimes I believe so.'

'You have, I feel sure, numerous gifts.'

Now he approaches, drawing in close. She can see the reflection of the terrace gas lamps in his eyes, streaks of orange amid the green.

'*Where* have we met before?' she whispers. 'I *have* met you, try to remember.'

Being a Frenchman, being Lucien, he takes this as an invitation and kisses the top of her dripping wet arm. His lips are hot, and his moustache prickles her bare skin. She shivers.

'I'm afraid you misunderstand me, monsieur. We speak a different language.' She turns away. 'Let us go in; Aunt Mary will be anxious.'

Of course that was not the end of it. If it was, how disappointed she would have been. Or if he had accepted the other gentle rebuffs she dealt him over the following days. He was an expert at the game of love and she no match, partly because less experienced but mainly because she could not bother to hold back the tide of her emotions when what she most wanted was to let them flow.

After that first time, they met every day: at the springs, at the promenades, in the evening at the casino. He wooed her partly with his eloquent words but mostly by his demonstration of a different way to live. Far from being an empty socialite, he was just the sort of person she wanted to be in the world. The grandson of a famous poet, he was knowledgeable in all the fine arts, skilled in the use of sword and pistol, deeply concerned for animals and for his people.

His hero was General Boulanger, the soldier who had turned the French army into a force capable of winning back the French territories of Alsace-Lorraine, stolen from them by the Prussians. Boulanger, he told her, was their great hope of unseating the cowardly, double-dealing scoundrels of the government, of installing a manly administration, one that would instigate the necessary war to regain the lost provinces.

As he lay with Maud in a cornfield or woodland by day, or walked with her under the high dome of a starry Auvergne sky, he would whisper to her of Boulangist schemes or hum in her ear the ditty that all France was singing that summer – '*Il vient de délivrer/Le Lorraine et l'Alsace!*' – to make her smile. For back then everyone, not just Lucien, was mad for *le brave général*. One could wash with Boulanger soap, suck Boulanger sweets, eat food off Boulanger plates . . .

When Lucien gave Maud compliments or flattery, it stirred little in her beyond mindless repartee, but when he demonstrated his disdain for the government of the Third Republic, his fire lit a matching glow. As he stomped around the room ranting against governmental iniquities – 'The empty parliamentary debates! The endless, futile crises! The despicable corruption!' – she squirmed with admiration.

When she told him she thought to become an actress, he was scornful but not for the conventional reasons of her London relatives. 'You don't understand your own power,' he said. 'An *actrice*, even one as great as Bernhardt, only portrays the life of another. Where is the glory in that? Why not devote yourself to a more noble aim? Free Ireland from Britain, just as Joan of Arc freed France.'

At first this sounded preposterous, until he said to her that anybody could do anything to which they truly devoted mind and heart. This again reminded her of Tommy, of how he always said that *anything* was possible, if you willed it enough.

Lucien offered her an alliance: he would help her in her work to free Ireland if she would help him in his work to regain Alsace-Lorraine.

'The Germans and the English are but one and the same,' he said. 'To hit one is to hit the other.'

This was the day she told him that he did, after all, speak her language. They rode deep into the Clermont-Ferrand country-side and found a secluded place to be together. He brought a rug, some bread and cheese and a pitcher of red wine, and orchestrated the afternoon, from the moment that he flicked out the blue rug across the grass to when he bent over her reclining body, blocking out the sun.

She gave herself to him – that is how she always thought of it, even when she came to write her memoirs fifty years later – gave herself there, in the open air, under the gaze of the Puy-de-Dôme and the other looming mountains of the Auvergne, gave herself gladly, knowing that Kathleen and all her friends would think her wrong.

(Doubly wrong as he was married.)

Other young women might be happy to wallow in cowardice and call it morality but not Maud Gonne. She loved; ergo, she would give her love. To her, a vacillation or a quibbling would have been the true dishonour. In her, action followed emotion as freely as Dagda, her Great Dane, jumped into pursuit at the sight of a rabbit.

Stop and think? Weigh and measure? Might as well ask Dagda to consider the sense of the chase. So she thought she never would regret the decision she took that summer in Royat, the decision she took and took again, whenever he wanted her. What else could she have done, being who she was?

6

Star and I sat in her hire car, driving to Glendalough. She had seen little on her way down from the airport on Christmas Eve, but today was a day for sightseeing. One of those days that the Irish winter occasionally throws up, just when you despair that the ceiling of grey has turned solid. A day that seemed to have wandered backwards out of springtime, with a clear-blue sky and golden light. A gift of a day.

I breathed deeply, trying to inhale some of its tranquillity. We were climbing, the little engine whining as we negotiated the bends. More accustomed to an automatic, Star kept crunching the gear stick. As we topped the crest, a bog-plain opened out, miles of tufted peat and raw earth on all sides. 'What do you think of the scenery?' I asked.

'Sure, it's pretty.'

It was the wrong word for the ruggedness of this part of Wicklow, but nothing was going to dampen my mood. We were together, my daughter and I. We were taking a day trip. I hadn't told her where we were going, just instructed her to take the Military Road, but our destination was Laragh, the village where Iseult lived, and nearby Glendalough, where she was buried.

'What time do you think we'll be back?' Star asked.

'I'm not sure. I thought we'd make a day of it, have a spot of lunch?'

'I have to leave in the afternoon.'

'Oh.'

'Mom, don't give me "oh". You know. I told you.'

'But not where you're planning on going.'

'I've booked some time in a monastery. Mount Melleray Abbey.'

'What?'

'It's in County Waterford,' she said.

'I know where it is. It's well known.' An enclosed order of Cistercians on the bare, windblown slopes of the Knockmealdown Mountains. 'A Catholic monastery, Star? Are you sure?'

'I better tell you. In March, I'm going to be confirmed.'

It was so long since I'd heard the word used in this context that for a minute I failed to recognize it. 'Confirmed?' I repeated, puzzled. Then I realized. 'Confirmed as a Roman Catholic?'

'Yes. I've been going to Mass and taking classes.'

'Since when?'

'Since . . . oh, a long time.'

Star was baptized for the same reason her father and I got married: because in the 1970s nuns and priests and Christian Brothers provided a better education than the public schools. (These were the days before 'paedophile priests' or 'child sexual abuse' entered the lexicon.) We wanted the best for our darling, so, capitalizing on our Irish Catholic backgrounds, we married and had Star baptized Maya Bernadette, the name she took through school and college and out into the world, though to us she was always Star.

And, though she got plenty of Jesus, Mary and holy Saint Joseph at school, at home we counterbalanced it with our secular view of life. In her teens, she had moved away from the Church as she did from all aspects of her childhood, and became angry and rebellious – but also a thinker, intelligent and introspective. How could somebody like that sign up for the self-serving, conservative and duplicitous RC Church? Her father would have cried to think of it, and I couldn't help but feel it was just another way to get at us.

At me.

'I'm always surprised when young people sign up for organized religion,' I said.

'I'm not asking your permission, Mom. I'm just telling you.'

'I didn't mean . . .' I let my explanation trail away. It wasn't important, not beside our other differences. I would also ignore this insistence that she had to leave today. She had said that yesterday too, but I had managed to get her to stay on.

'You'll be interested in where we are going, then,' I said. 'Glendalough was once the Christian capital of Ireland.'

We began our descent into the sheer-sided, forest-covered valley (*Gleann*) cupping two elongated lakes (*Dá Lough*). For 900 years, from the 500s, a monastic city had thrived here, and now, after centuries of near-terminal decline, it thrives again as a tourist spot. As Star and I emerged from the car park by the lake, the mountains seemed to have reared up around us. The distant humming rush of Poulanass waterfall underlined the silence that overlaid all like a haze. It settled on me, and I felt my muscles unclench.

Star was finally impressed. 'Wow! This place is something.'

We set off. Star was no walker. Because of her size she was propelled not by her legs but by her belly, her steps somehow delicate as well as full of effort, as if the force of gravity was precarious for her. I knew each pace she took brought her discomfort and that, in a few moments, her forehead would be lined with a sheen of sweat.*

Yet it was good for her to walk, surely? Not to give in to her disinclination? I fell into slow step beside her.

Groups and couples passed us in their coloured rainwear, their faces ruddy with fresh air, nodding and smiling. I took her up the back way, through the ruins, the remains of cloisters and chapels left over from the monastic heyday. 'That round tower is something,' she said, as we stood at the base of it, looking up. 'What was it for?'

'A beacon for pilgrims. A bell tower. A refuge when the Vikings came to plunder.'

---

* This feels like fatism to me, even though I am no longer fat. Does it need to be said? What does it add, Mom?

'Hard to imagine plundering Vikings now. It's so peaceful. What a place to be buried, eh?'

I pushed open the gate into the graveyard. 'It's typical of Iseult to be somewhere so lovely, though she actually didn't want to be buried at all. She had a big interest in Eastern philosophy and had requested a cremation.'

'So why didn't she get it?'

'I don't think it was allowed in 1950s Ireland.' The Ireland of my childhood, a bigoted theocracy, steeped in stringent thou-shalt-nots. Browbeaten by the Church my daughter now wanted to join.

'There it is.' I pointed at the grave behind the gate. A tall, narrow headstone curved at the crown. Cut into it at the top was an arched opening, like a church window, within which nestled a plump stone bird. Echoes of Saint Kevin, patron saint of Glendalough. A standing stone, tamed and Christianized.

ISEULT STUART. BORN 1894. DIED 1954.

The plot was covered in cobblestones with a fern at the centre and a rosebush at the foot. On the wall, holly and ivy flourished and, alongside, leaves of primrose plants, promises of spring. Shoots of some kind of spring bulb were visible too: snowdrops or daffodils. It had been a mild winter.

It felt strange, looking at Iseult's grave with Star, thinking of what remained of her skeleton beneath us, under the earth. Did Star now believe that another part of her, an all-knowing part, knew we were here? Zach did, though his understanding differed from the Christian belief of life after death. And me? I didn't know what I believed any more. He had tossed me up and now I was falling back to earth without his arms to catch me.

'I think I remember reading somewhere that she didn't want a headstone either,' I told Star. 'That silver birch there by the wall: that's her style. Her son planted it for her.'

The roots of the birch tree cracked through the stone wall.

'What happened to him?'

'He's an artist. He still lives near by.'

'Maybe we should visit him, ask him what he remembers.'

We. She said 'We'. I'd drawn her in despite herself. 'Maybe we should.'

'I bet he'd be flattered.'

'I don't know. I wrote and asked if I could interview him about her, but he didn't reply.' I bent and plucked a weed from between the stones. 'I think it was he who designed the gravestone, or maybe his first wife.'

'It is lovely.'

'Sure, I'm not saying it isn't. But I hate that she never got what she wanted. What she wanted was so simple. A home, a wild piece of earth, love, peace ... But she had this horrible depression that used to settle on her and rob her of will and energy. She –'

Star's face made me break off. 'The way you talk about her, it's so weird. Like she's someone you know.'

'I do know her. I know her better than I know some of my friends.'

'I just don't get it.'

I tried to explain, told her about my hazy, dazy view of love when I was a teenager, about Miss McNamara and Yeats, but I could hardly explain how my romanticism had led me into marriage with her father and the mistakes that arose from that. 'Iseult was like a talisman of truth to me,' I said. 'I was such a sucker for romance.'

It sounded weak even as I was saying it.

Star shrugged. 'I think you're just plain old-fashioned star-struck, Mom.'

Her voice was teasing, light. Glendalough was working its magic. Whether Star got it or not, Iseult was bringing us together.

'Would you like to see where she lived? It's a bit of a walk away. About twenty minutes.'

51

A wave of scarlet flooded her round face. 'No,' I hurried on, 'actually, thinking about it, it's a bit longer than that. Let's take the car.'

It took minutes to drive there. 'Laragh,' Star said, as we approached the road sign. 'Laragh?'

'Yes. Drive on through the village and turn –'

'Laragh? Isn't that where Dad came from?'

I had forgotten she knew that. I had half forgotten I knew it myself. 'Yes, it is.'

'Oh my God, Mom, you are unbelievable!' She jerked the car to a stop, making the car behind us hoot.

'Star!'

'Don't you think, Mom' – she was speaking slowly, as if I were a child . . . or an idiot – 'I might be more interested in seeing the house where my *father* grew up than the house of this Iseult Gonne person?'

'Gosh, honey, I don't think I even know where your dad's home place is. Once before I tried to find it, from his description, but I couldn't be sure –'

'But not even to *say*.'

'I half forgot. I'm sorry.' (Sorry, sorry, sorry, sorry . . .)

She interlaced her fingers on the steering wheel, rested her forehead on them. Then: 'Were you never in it, you know, before you left Ireland?'

'No. No, we left very soon after we met.'

'Did he *never* go back?'

'No, I don't believe he did.'

'Why? I've never been able to understand that. What had they done to him?'

'He never told me. He flatly refused to talk about it.'

'You should have made him. Maybe if he had talked about it . . .'

This was a new riff on her old refrain, of her father's failings being all my fault.

'All right, then,' I said. 'Let's see if we can find his house too.'

52

I directed her to turn at the bridge, near the old mill, and we drove up to the house that I believed might have belonged to Brendan's family, parked the car a little way beyond, walked back. A bungalow, low and squat without a single attractive feature except the shrubbery. 'The garden's pretty, isn't it?' I said. 'Even at this time of year. Somebody in there has green fingers.'

'I think we should go in,' Star said.

'Absolutely not.'

'I think we should.'

'I would never have brought you here if –'

'Come on. Why not?'

'I'm not even sure that it's the right house. If it is, they could well be dead by now. And, if not, what on earth do you think we can go in there and say? "Oh, hi! I was married to your son, the one who left when he was eighteen and never contacted you again. This is your granddaughter. Nice to meet you."'

'But, Mom, they don't know whether he's alive or dead. Whatever happened, that's just not right.'

'Agreed. But going in there and putting the heart crossways in a mother or father who must be in their seventies by now is not going to make it better.'

'But –'

'It's too late, Star.'

'No. Don't say that. You always say it's never too late.'

'If you want to do this, you'll have to do it another day. On your *own*.'

'Or on my own, now.'

'Okay. Give me the keys and I'll wait for you in the car.'

She rummaged in her bag, handed them across. I turned and began to walk back down the hill. I hadn't got far when she called out to me. 'Stop. Wait.'

I turned.

'Maybe you're right,' she puffed, as she caught up.

'You could write to them first. That might be an approach.'

'I probably won't even do that. As usual I'm in a funk.'

'You just want to know more about him.' I took her arm. She let me, and I gave it a squeeze. 'It's natural.'

'Why didn't you tell me more when I was growing up? Why did you keep it all from me?'

'Star, I know you're really angry with me for that. It was a mistake, I've admitted that to you. I've told you how sorry I am. And I am. Really, really, really sorry. I did what I thought was best.'

'It wasn't.'

'I know. You've said.'

Over and over: the same thing. Was she never going to let it go? These reproaches were the flip side to the excessive love she used to lavish on me when she was little: 'I love you, Mommy,' holding my head in place with her two little hands, so I couldn't look away from her.* Twice in my life I had wronged her. The first time in relation to her father, and I knew that, in her mind, our recent travails were connected with that – a connection she would never explain and I could never fathom.

I realized I was going to have to say something, take hold of the subject we were both avoiding. 'This isn't just about Brendan, is it?'

'Mom, don't. I'm warning you, just don't.'

'I gave him up for you, Star. I loved my Zach just as much as you loved your Shando, but I gave him up for you. What more do you want?'

There it was, out in the open.

She snatched back her arm. 'Okay, that's it. This sham of a day is now officially over.'

---

* I'm not going to comment again on my mother's fatism, or on the passive-aggression that lines every second word she writes about me. But I really have to ask: how can a child's love be 'excessive'?

'I know it's hard to talk about it, honey. But I *really* think we should.'

'Dr Aintree told me this would happen. That you would annihilate me again.'

Dr Aintree: her therapist, a good doctor. And a nice woman. 'Annihilate you?'

'We are driving home now, Mom, and then I am going to pack and leave as planned.'

'*Annihilate?* You cannot be serious. Annihilate?'

'I can't do this. I refuse. I'll give you a lift back to Doolough if you want. But only if you come *now*. And only if you don't open your big mouth around one more word.'

7

'Think of it,' says Maud Gonne. 'A human entity is about to be brought into existence upon the earthly plane.'

Lucien rolls his eyes, for these two are no longer in the first flush of love, or even the second. It is more than a decade since they first lay together on that picnic rug in Royat. Tonight they are in a carriage, twisting and turning through the outer roads of Paris, speeding towards Samois-sur-Seine. Dear Samois, Maud's favourite village in all of France, where she has been so happy (and so *un*happy). Samois: the fitting place for this ritual to be enacted.

She places her hand on Lucien's wrist. 'Don't you wonder where Georges is now, before the deed is done?'

'I do not.'

'I imagine his soul as a ghostly vapour, hovering somewhere in space out of time, waiting for us.'

Again, that cynical upward flick of his eyes. Oh, it *is* a naive image, she knows that, but she holds to it only as a symbol of a deeper truth.

Is it not wondrous that this child towards whom they hurtle exists as yet only as thought and feeling, swirls of sensation in their bodies? In her: a clamminess of the hands, a churning of the stomach, a tightness of the neck and shoulders. And in Lucien, if nothing else, an anticipatory stirring in the groin. She knows she can count on that, and tonight, for once, his priapic constancy is welcome – though his failure to show equal interest in other aspects of their ritual is . . .

No.

Banish such thoughts.

It is not propitious to fret. In a short while, all succeeding, she and he shall come together within the crypt at Samois cemetery where Georges, her beloved little Georginet, lies embalmed. At stroke of midnight, egg and seed will unite, sparking his dear little baby soul, once again, into being. Two Irish friends who are great seers have sworn it so.

But if success is to be theirs, if her timing is not to be set awry, then the coachman needs to *hurry*. Midnight is – she checks again the Victorian pocket-watch that once belonged to her father, Tommy – a mere forty-five minutes away. Snapping the timepiece shut, she sits back in her seat, twists her thoughts again to Higher Things. How far does the act of reincarnation change the alchemy of flesh and blood and spirit? Will the essence of new Georges be a replica of the old, having the same soul as before? Or, being of new flesh, possessed of a different inner nature? So many of her questions have no answers, and on such matters Yeats and Russell, her Irish mages, were unclear.

The coach takes a sudden swerve, almost throwing her on top of Lucien. As she lifts her eyes to his, she sees that he is smiling at her. A small stretch of the lips under his moustache, but most certainly a smile. A coil of triumph turns within her. Without Georges, she has had nothing to hold him, nothing of hers to set against his first, legal family, but once they again have a son, the issue of his stock and hers – fighting stock, not the milk-and-water blood of Madame Millevoye – he will truly be hers again.

Truly.

She lifts the curtain, tries to peer through the blackness to check where they are. Trees flash past, dark denizens of the great forest of Fontainebleau, telling her nothing.

Samois – about four miles from the town of Fontainebleau – is one of those somnolent villages that line the Seine outside Paris, of the type immortalized by the painter Sisley. Ochre-coloured stone houses with green-shuttered windows squatting smug between river and forest.

Thirty minutes before, the village day ended with the return to home of the last customers to leave Lepotier's *taverne*. By now, Monsieur Lepotier has emptied his till, sorted and hidden his francs and centimes, tidied the stools, the kegs, the bottles of absinthe and cognac, and climbed the back stairs to the chamber he shares with his wife. He finds her turned towards the wall, eyes resolutely closed. *Ça fait mal, ma cherie?* he asks her in his head, as he unlaces his boots. *Pas de tout,* he answers, lying into the creaking bed and thrusting a purposeful hand under her nightgown.

Other acts of sexual intercourse are already under way in Samois. The dry, weekly conjugation of Monsieur and Madame Dupont; the latest instalment in the affair between Monsieur Castor and his pretty, plump sister-in-law, Jeannette; the first coupling of the sixteen-year-old Michel Patton, the son of a local merchant family, and Jean Raspile, a young butcher, who have sneaked out of their bedroom windows to meet in a dark clump of the forest . . . We will avert our eyes from the furtive deposit a certain Monsieur Doneille is making into the taut, tight body of his eight-year-old niece (Why do men do such things? Because they must? Because they can?) and peep instead at the impressive sexual acrobatics of the recently married Bernards. Young Monsieur Pierre is, at this very moment, running his tongue along Madame Bernard's inner ankle bone to the accompaniment of her rising breath, and they will still be enjoying each other long after Iseult's mother and father have finished their experiment.

The other five hundred or so villagers have chosen the lull of sleep over the dance of sex. It has been dark since five o'clock, with the sun not due to surface again for another eight hours, and cold. Cold with winter damp, the sort of cold that seeps through to the bones. What else to do on such a night, but sleep, sleep . . .

But here comes the carriage, hooves and harness jangling open the night-quiet. Closer it comes, all the way along the winding road until it reaches the cemetery, where it halts with a jerk. The horse whinnies, then quiets, so that, for half a moment, all folds back into silence. Within the carriage, this half-moment communicates itself to Maud, and it feels to her as if the world is waiting, holding its breath at what is to come.

She resists the notion. Where is the wonder in what is about to happen? What is more everyday on this earth than the creation of life? Yet it's undeniable, this sense of significance: she feels it in the night sky with its hammering of stars above, in the broken road beneath the wheels of the carriage, in the breathing of the trees and in the sly bulk of the gravestones waiting in the cemetery, frosted sentries of the dark.

Enough! No more of this imaginative indulgence. She pushes the carriage door and steps out, one hand to the mantle that covers her distinctive auburn coiffure. They are travelling in-cognito, and one never knows who is about, even here, even at this hour.

Lucien steps down behind her, his arms full of candles wrapped in a blanket. '*À bientôt, Roger,*' he calls up to the driver, who has his instructions to return for them in an hour, at 12.30. Roger lifts his tall hat in assent, his face impassive. '*Cimetière de Samois,*' Maud can imagine him saying to his friends later, at his tavern. '*Les petites folies de la petite noblesse.*' With a flick of his reins, he leaves them, and they stand watching the carriage disappear round the bend, listening to its rumble and clatter fade across the fields.

One hour to change all. She shivers and takes Lucien's arm, steers him towards the cemetery gates left unlocked by a bribe to the sexton. Oh but it is cold out here in open countryside. Together they walk a slow, curiously formal walk, side by side, step for step, as if she were a bride and he her father escorting her up the aisle. Wearing their evening clothes and each of a height, they make a handsome couple yet, even if there is nobody but the tombstones to see them.

At the furthest side of the cemetery, Lucien lays down his bundle before the finest mausoleum. He tries the key but the lock on the vault is troublesome; after wrestling with it for a time, he begins to throw petulant looks back over his shoulder. *Tut*, clicks his tongue. And again: *tut*. Maud closes her eyes to shut him out. He wishes – she can hear his thoughts clearly, as if he spoke them aloud – to blame her. Why, he would like to ask, has she allocated to *him* the task of opening up when the difficult lock is so much more familiar to *her*.

Oh, Lucien, Lucien . . .

She will *not* permit him to disturb her equilibrium. It is hardly her fault that he has visited his son's tomb so rarely that he doesn't know the knack of unclicking that bolt, really quite simple when you are used to it. And has she not agreed with him the timetable of this evening, the exact distribution of tasks and duties? Agreed it over and again during the past days, so often that he told her to desist, that he needed no more directives or instructions? So what is this huffing and tutting for now, this giving of himself over to pique?

She inhales deeply, wrapping herself inside what is to come, so his vexation cannot infect her and the work they have to do. The key clicks, as she knew it would, and the door opens with what seems like a sigh, puffing stale, malodorous air into their faces. Maud gasps: that dead stench, so much more concentrated by night, holds all their early grief in it. It slides in under the rivets in her mind, freeing incarcerated memories, allowing them to pierce her again: her old laments about a death-bird pecking at the window, her fear of the Grey Lady of her dreams, who showed herself to be a child-killer . . .

She wills them from her mind, as she has so often before. With her will, she can do anything. *Anything.* Isn't she here tonight to prove this once again?

She extends her hand to Lucien, a mute request for him to hand over what he carries so she can take it down into the crypt.

60

'I do not think you can manage alone,' he says aloud. 'It is so dark down there.'

He has spoken. *Spoken!*

She wants to slap him to silence but restricts herself to placing her index finger on his lips. *Be quiet*, this finger insists. *You know what is agreed.*

He pulls back. For one moment she thinks he might turn and march off, past the watching gravestones, out the cemetery gate, into the night. She sees him consider it, knowing the reluctance she has had to overcome to get him here tonight, for his parliamentary enemies would like nothing more than to have such a *scandale* to spread . . . His eyes lock with hers in one of their mute struggles. Always so vexatious with each other now: it exhausts her. Such a waste of energy – and tonight it cannot be permitted, it will corrupt the mood.

She pulls herself up to her full height so she can transfer to him her thoughts. *We seek a reunion of the spirits. Our task is sacred. Let us banish petty human aggravations. Let us lay ourselves open to the spark of fire of the soul. Let us cast ourselves down in humble surrender so that we may become instruments of rebirth.*

He drops her gaze, in what feels almost like a bow, and her heart shudders: he has made her a pledge, a most grave and solemn promise. With the act that is to come, all will be reprieved.

She takes the candles and blankets from him, enters the crypt. Some might fear to go into a vaulted tomb by night but not she. It is only Georges down there, nothing to fear. Only her darling little Georginet. She closes her eyes: in this darkness, sight will not serve her, she must rely on other senses. Hugging her armload, she takes a step forward, the flat of one foot engaging the whole of the ground, then the other. She is glad she wore her flattest boots.

It is colder in the crypt, and damp. She lays down her bundle, feels among the candles for the tallest, fattest pair, the two she would place on either side of the coffin. The touch of cold candle wax recalls her son's embalmed limbs: the same unbending texture. Tonight the warmth of flame will soften the wax.

The rasp of a match never sounded so loud, or the glare of its flame so bright. One wick, then another, and the little crypt is suddenly filled with light. She stretches out her arms to place one hand either side of the tombstone and bends until her forehead touches stone.

O, great spirits, purify and strengthen us and seal our lips for the work. Titans of light, higher souls: make of us your instrument.

She recalls the swollen face that was Georges and not Georges, his tiny starfish hands laid one upon another and now always to be thus. That she can bear, but she must push away the recollection of those fingers live, reaching up to touch her face, the wonder in his eyes at the brush of her skin. Go! Be gone! *Spear of Lugh, pierce the night. Let the essence of God, the spark of fire of the soul, flow down into the cauldron of regeneration and rebirth.*

She takes up the smaller candles and places them in as wide a circle as the walls permit, wide enough for two tall people to lie within. In the centre of the tombstone she lays the two blankets – folded lengthways into two strips – at right angles to each other in the form of a cross. Then she briskly lights the rest of the candles, all forty-eight of them, before kneeling for a final, quick invocation.

She has to hurry now; it is almost time.

Tonight they make amends.

Tonight atonement and retribution will be theirs.

She stands and, trying not to shiver, begins to peel off her clothes.

Above, sheltering in the small space between the door and the top of the stairs, Lucien smokes and waits, the base of his cigarette flattened between two frozen fingers. He can hear her moving about below, see the faint glow coming on at the end of the stairs. He knows she is lighting the candles: forty-eight small ones, two thick, large ones: fifty in all. Already the chill of night is seeping through to his bones. *Sacré bleu,* why the devil did he agree to this madness?

He blames her crazed Irish friends for this. It is they who are responsible for all her follies. Poets are always mad, but the Celtic types are the worst. He had said as much to her last week.

'But, Lucien, it was you, not Yeats or Russell, who gave me the idea,' she replied, and reminded him of the time he tried to persuade her, she who wanted to conceive an Irish patriot hero, to make love before the altar of Jeanne d'Arc in Paris Cathedral. He remembered then: how he had bribed the sacristan, but it all came to naught. And now, years later, this eerie travesty of his intention. On her terms. She really was the very devil of a woman.

The way she looked him in the eye before she went below, her finger pressed to his lips, attempting to subdue him. Hah! Once such behaviour would have delighted him, the challenge of breaking her, of turning hauteur to need. Once he treasured that arrogant head of hers but now he knows it for a sham. All her fire is surface, as is the beauty that once consumed him. Beneath, she is the same as the rest.

Women are at their best when barely known: time always turns the outer charms transparent. One comes to see the snarl of complications beneath, the chaos that lies at the heart of all females. It is true what he said to Déroulède last evening: a mistress held too long becomes another wife.

Slap – slap – slap: from the foot of the steps come three loud handclaps, his cue to go down. He drops his cigarette, sparks falling through the dark, and crushes it underfoot. She pretends to mastery and he to submission, but they both know the truth: it is pity that has hauled him here tonight.

Yet what power these women wield in their weakness.

In the crypt, all is light, giving an illusion of warmth. Two candles, tall pillars of light, stand sentry over the tomb. The smell in here brings it all back, fells him all over again. Perhaps Maud is right, perhaps *this* is the great sorrow that changed everything?

Perhaps.

There she is, surrounded by the wide ring of candles, naked to the skin. Lying on the tombstone like Christ on his crucifix, arms outstretched across two blankets she has folded for the purpose. Around her neck she wears her father's timepiece while candlelight gleams on the pale mound of her belly, along the skin of her thighs, across the rise of her breasts and her erect nipples, standing to attention. Is it just the cold – or has this bizarre ritual injected the sex act with the excitement it no longer holds for her?

Impossible to know as she keeps her eyes closed, her face impassive. Her father's fob watch is open, reading nine minutes to midnight. What if he were to leave her here, naked and unfulfilled? Is that not what she has done to him so often, with her fastidious aversion? And not just since Georges's death, though that is what she likes to pretend. What if he were to leave her, to know for herself that humiliation? Bah! Why does he torment himself with this nonsense? He knows he will do as he has pledged.

All he has to do is squint his eyes a little so he can forget what festers between them. Limit his attention to her fine physique. She is, after all, the most beautiful woman in the world, and not just according to that idiot journalist Stead. So centre on those two peaked breasts, those long thighs, the shadow of promise between them. Why think of saying no, what man would? See, already it is working.

Already, he feels the stirring he needs. He shrugs off his overcoat, lets it lie where it falls at the end of the steps. Removes his jacket and waistcoat, his trousers and shirt, his under-garments and his stockings, until he is as naked as she. The chill air on his bare skin feels almost solid. The cement floor under-foot is not dry. Just damp, he hopes, and not the secretions of some animal. Stepping into the circle of candles, he kneels on the edge of the blanket in front of Maud. No response. He bends to kiss her lips, lying along the length of her. Her skin is ice, she is like a corpse, her lips rigid under his. Her body holds its crucified position. Is she to be unmoving throughout, a passive receptacle? In her little lectures about who was to do what, she never covered that detail.

He reaches for her hands, splaying his arms out along hers, but she holds them in two tight fists. The devil! He will make her open at least her hands to him. With his fingers he prises hers apart. Something is clutched in her grasp, something woollen. He holds it to the candle: a knitted bootee, one in each hand. Georges's bootees.

Her lips are moving but making no sound. He moves to close her murmurs with his mouth. Forget the bootees, forget the coffin . . . the lace robe . . . the small, solid, half-pouting baby mouth . . . Forget, forget . . . He feels for her breasts, squeezes the mounds of flesh, thinks to take one in his own mouth. Yes, yes, a surge of strength swells in his veins. He is in command, a man again.

Maud is glad she has kept her eyes fastened. He is quite, quite lost to her now, sunk into his own coarseness, almost hurting her. No matter – she had anticipated as much. Tonight is about more than male pleasure. Tonight he is for her what she has so often been to him, a means to an end.

This is what he has done to her, to them.

She turns her head and, without making it obvious, checks Tommy's watch. Almost time. She opens her legs, guides Lucien into place. As he breaks her, she cries out, a small surprised shriek. Not her cry of old, but he, with his thickening breath, shows no sign of knowing that. Another glance at the time – one minute to go – and she touches him on the buttocks, their signal, and he increases his rhythm, plunging in and in again. She feels his moment approach, the moment he wants to last for ever, the moment that heralds its own demise. She arches her hips to meet it, once . . . twice . . . thrice . . .

May the spirits rise to meet us. May perpetual light shine upon us. May the great Mother move to bring forth life. Life out of death, life out of death eternally . . .

As he climaxes (at – yes! – *exactly* midnight), as his seed shudders through her, she is flooded with gratitude. Tears, which since the death of Georges are always too ready to overrun, rise, but she squeezes them back. No tears, no tears: they have succeeded.

After a time, Lucien lifts his head from her breast and tries to shift, but she grips his shoulders, pins him with her eyes. 'This', she says, 'is our greatest act together.'

His eyes swivel from hers, unwilling to follow her thought. Exasperating man. Then, almost to their own surprise, they are drawn back. He stares at her and, wonder of this wondrous night, through this staring intensity, she feels him submit. It is as if he seeks to gaze into her soul, his expression is so intense, so *solid*. He has need of her still.

'We have succeeded,' she tells him, with great, definite tenderness.

'How can you know this?'

'We have succeeded.'

Life out of death. Light from the darkness. Unto us a child is born.

In truth, Lucien barely hears or sees her. He is gazing not at her but at the reflection of the flames dancing in her eyes. Past the steaming fervour of Maud's certainty, into the mystery of light.

8

So Iseult begins, as we all began, in the channel of a woman.*
One infinitesimal spark of time during which Maud Gonne's
egg accepts one of Lucien Millevoye's sperm and – *voila!* –
where a moment before there were two entities, now there is
one. A single cell. A microscopic bud of potential.

The cell pauses, as if overcome by what has just happened
or perhaps to gather itself for what is ahead. Then it launches
itself upon a precarious passage down the oviduct, towards the
womb. Intent on implantation, it subdivides itself as it travels:
from one cell to two, two to four, four to sixteen, sixteen to
256, 256 to 65,536, 65,536 to . . . Thus begins the gradual firming
of potential that will take months to complete.

The entity that will eventually be Iseult is only halfway
towards the womb before Maud is telling her dear friend Ghénia
that she knows, just *knows*, her endeavours have been successful:
she is *enceinte*.

'My dear, how can you be so sure?'

'One just knows.' Maud smiles her most theatrical smile.
They are talking to each other through a looking glass, trying
on bonnets in the millinery department of Printemps. 'Tell me,
what do you think of this one?'

'I preferred the green.'

---

* Point of fact: this is my mother's conception of Iseult's conception. When
Iseult was a four-year-old secret, MG confessed her existence to WBY and told
him a version of this reincarnation-in-the-crypt story. WB put it in his memoirs,
and the story hardened through telling after uncontested telling. Truth is, Iseult
Gonne may have been sired in a comfortable bed, between clean sheets, with a
good fire warming the grate – perhaps not even by Lucien Millevoye at all. Only
Maud could know for sure; we all rest on her words.

'Yes. Simple lines are always best, are they not?'

'And that colour is so becoming to your hair.'

Maud is glad of a little frivolity today. The knowledge of her condition has come trailing fronds of memory: recollections of little Georges's weight in her arm, the smoothness of his baby cheek beneath her fingerpads, his smell, cleaner than lilac, softer than powder ... Memories that, before this pregnancy, were unbearable can now, she finds, be borne – though not at all times and never for long.

This pleases her. To cower from her thoughts was not something Maud Gonne ever wanted to do, but, during that broken, incoherent autumn of 1891, each memory was a scalpel slicing her wound wider. For a long time, too long a time, survival called for denial.

'I think to give the good news to Lucien on Christmas Day,' she says.

Ghénia frowns. 'You are sure he will be pleased?'

'Of course. Think of the trouble we took. There is nothing he wants more. Nothing.'

In the mirror, Ghénia opens her mouth as if to speak, then closes it again.

'Yes,' Maud repeats. 'What day could be more fitting to make the announcement that another significant son is about to be born?' She ties the two long ribbons of her bonnet into a bow under her chin and turns her head this way and that in the mirror, taking care not to see her friend's frown at this blasphemy. 'Yes, Christmas Day it shall be.'

On Christmas Day, 1955, I was thirteen years old. It was a mellow day, I remember, part of an unseasonable warm spell that had taken us all by surprise on the day before Christmas Eve. Walking back from Mass, everybody was talking about it – old timers saying they'd never seen a Christmas like it, Mrs Fox fretting because her entire household had colds and a good frost was needed to kill off the germs, the rest of us delighted with the reprieve from porridge-coloured skies.

After we went back to the house from Mass and Mammy had the turkey prepared and placed in the oven, my father looked up from his newspaper and said, 'Are you two going for that walk?'

Which made me look up from my book. What walk?

'Yes, good idea,' Mammy said in a strange voice, as if she were on stage. 'Would you like to go for a walk by the lake, Izzy?'

My mother might walk to the village shop for messages, or to Mass, but in all my life I'd never known her to take a walk for its own sake. 'It's such a lovely day,' she said.

'Put that book away and go on with your mother.'

I did as I was bid, telling myself that it *was* Christmas, hyacinths and holly time. Family time. Was that it? I knew it wasn't. I knew what was really happening was that Mammy was going to tell me she was sick.

Really sick.

Dying.

I already knew, but they thought I didn't.

I got my coat and out we went. The white mist of sunny winter mornings was still down, here and there, in wisps, and I felt we were two ghosts walking down through the orchard, past the beech trees and the old yew, down to the pathway. The lake looked like a sheet of black glass in the yellow morning: still and silent, seeing and knowing all, from the reeds that were part of it to the heights of Doolough Mountain so far above and beyond. It held all in its depths and reflected all back.

'Let's go sit on the bench,' Mammy said.

My father had put this crude construction together by wheel-barrowing two long gateposts down the pathway and setting them in place on the eastern shore, to hold his food and his fishing gear. We walked round to there and sat. I waited. She didn't speak. After a time, I picked up a pebble and threw it as far as I could into the water. When she found her words, they weren't what I'd expected. 'Izzy?'

'Yes.'

'You know you're adopted?'

Adopted. The word plunged into my depths, like the stone I'd just plunked into the lake. It gave form to a truth I had always known. *This* was why I never fully felt part of this family, *this* was why my father was so horrible, *this* was why I always seemed to look through outsider's eyes.

As the awareness sank into me, I felt another feeling rise. Joy. My mother might be dying (I wasn't sure), but, if she was, I had another mother somewhere. My father might be a tyrant (no doubt there), but never mind, I had another father somewhere.

He jumped into my mind fully formed, this other father, a cross between God (but with a shorter beard) and Santa Claus (but not so fat). A kindly mouth, a gentle twinkle in his eye.

'Yes,' I said. 'I've always known.'

'Did he tell you?'

'No. I just knew.'

She looked wounded.

'I don't mean –'

'Oh, no, I know that.'

I wanted to ask her about my real mother and father but was afraid to hurt her, so I started to say, 'Would you have told me this if . . . if . . .' but I wasn't able to finish that sentence either.

'If I wasn't going to be leaving you?'

I nod. So there it is. Another unspoken, said.

'I would of course. We'd have had to tell you sometime. I always said that to Martin.'

Now fear chased away the strange joy. This was my mother, my protector, not some stranger I'd never met. He, not some stranger I'd never met, was my father. And she was going to die and I was going to be left alone with him.

Whenever I did something wrong, my mother was always

70

summoned to my father's side, to play her part in my punishment. It was his way of blaming her, of punishing her too. The routine was set each time. First, I was made to take down the cane, which was held in the recess of the mantelpiece, attached by two thin hooks in the corner. Ever present but not obviously visible – except to those who knew it was there.

I'd hand it to him and then he would stand, gently slapping the palm of his other hand with it. When he gave a small sharp nod, we fell to our knees in the correct order: first me, then Mammy, then – more slowly – him. Next came a prayer, made out of whatever was in his head. 'Dear God and His Mother in Heaven, let this child know that to steal cake from those who are given the charge of rearing her and caring for her in this world is a true sin . . . Make her realize that defiance is the root of all suffering . . . Jesus, Mary and Holy Saint Joseph, give her strength to do her daily tasks without being disobedient to her parents or teachers . . .'

Eventually 'Amen' would be reached, followed by a period of silence, while he waited for God to inform him how many blows he was to deliver unto my bare bottom. That was the worst part of it, that kneeling and waiting. I always imagined myself leaping up and running out the door, but the unknown of that must have been more frightening to me than the certain pain and humiliation to come. Up he would rise, with a heavy air of reluctance, and summon us to my bedroom. A prod of his finger was my silent order to lean forward over the bed, then he would raise my skirt and pull down my knickers and go to work. Mammy's job was to count each lash aloud: 'One, two, three . . .' If at any point I cried out, he would go back to the beginning and start again.

Afterwards, I had to apologize to both of them for whatever it was I had done and then lead the three of us through five decades of the Rosary. The Sorrowful Mysteries, naturally. Any break in my voice, any sign of hurt or emotion he interpreted as a lack of due humility. I would have to start over, or – once

– go back to lean over the bed again for another caning. Only when five decades were completed in calm capitulation were we allowed off our knees.

Yes, he did all that and more. He was hard on me, and on her. Now there wasn't going to be any her. But when?

'Did the doctor say how long, Mammy?' I asked, looking down at my skirt. New, bought for Christmas. Only half an hour ago that had felt important.

She shifted on the makeshift bench, wiped invisible crumbs off her coat and said, 'Four months, maybe six,' then immediately recoiled on to the other subject. 'When your father is hard on you, it's not that he doesn't love you, you know that, don't you?'

This was an even bigger shock than talking about death. 'Love' was not a word used in our house.

'I remember when he brought you here first, he took you out in the pram for a jaunt. Only he got such a hard time about being soft from the other men at Mass that he never did it again.'

Pushing me in a pram? I couldn't imagine that. But until she suggested it, I had never thought, not through all the punishments, to doubt his love. He was my father. Brutish and bossy and sometimes sinister but my father. Except now it turned out that he wasn't.

'If we'd stayed in Dublin near his family, I always think it would have been easier for us. A couple of his sisters were very good to me.'

'Why didn't you?'

'He fell out with them all, the sisters, the brothers, the mother . . . And he had a dream to live in the country, in a place just like this. It sounded impossible to me, but he made it happen. There was a time I thought that man could make anything happen.'

She told me everything then. After they married, they were a long time without children, and he was growing bitter and ashamed. In those days, everyone wanted a big family, and he, who had shut out his own people, wanted it more than most. And he was frustrated. It was the first thing he'd ever truly wanted that didn't come good for him. He most dearly wanted a son, someone to whom he could gift the house and the money and the land he was amassing, but a daughter would do. Any child.

'He grew obsessed. I think it was partly a distraction from how he hated being here, in Doolough, with the war going on in Europe. He was awful restless for the duration of that. Thought the whole world had excitement, except those stuck here in this backwater.'

He sent her to hospital for tests, in Dublin so nobody would know, and the results showed she was barren. (That was the word she used.) He was so angry, with the doctors who couldn't fix her, with God above, but most of all with her. That was when he bought the car. He started driving up to Dublin and going with other women, younger women, then coming back to tell her all about it. He was trying to humiliate her, as he felt she'd humiliated him.

Then one of the girls, an eighteen-year-old, got pregnant (he was fifty-two at the time). When she gave up the baby for adoption, he said he wanted to take it home.

'To humiliate you more?'

'If that was in it, Izzy, it was only the smallest part. Truly. By then he'd been to the orphanage to see you and he wanted you for yourself.'

'Really?'

'Honest to God. He knew it would go hard for him, here in the village. Everyone was against the idea. The priest. Dr Keane. My sister, the nun. All wanted him to leave well enough alone, but he kept quoting those Gonnes at us, how they always did what they felt to be the right thing and never let public opinion interfere. He kept saying it was all wrong that his child should be wasting away in an orphanage.' She pulled the collar of her

73

coat up around her throat, gazed away from me, out at the lake. 'He did it in spite of us all, yes, me too, Izzy. That's what I wanted to say to you today. How wrong I was in that and how sorry I am for it.'

'It's okay, Mammy.'

'It was the only time I ever stood up to him – and I was wrong in it. I thought this the worst thing he could do to me, but it turned out to be the best. The very best thing that happened in my whole life. Do you understand what I'm saying?'

'I do, Mammy.'

'Do you? You're such a good girl.'

The lake water made small, slow lapping sounds.

'The thing is, Izzy, you can't let on you know any of this.'

'That I'm adopted?'

'No, he knows I'm telling you that today. He thinks it will make it easier . . . when the time comes . . . that I'm not your real mother.'

'You *are* my real mother, Mammy. Of course you are.'

'Ah, thank you, pet.' She opened her arms to me and I shunted closer on the bench, our feelings spilling into a long, awkward hug.

'You're such a good girl, always,' she said.

She was patting and stroking my hair. I wanted to stay on the bench with her always and never move again. Getting up and going back to the house, to my father, felt impossible. I couldn't carry the weight of all she had told me. 'What is it, again, that I'm not supposed to know?'

'That you're his.'

'I'm to pretend he's my adopted father, not my real one?' This set off a brain loop that made me giddy.

Something in my tone made her concerned. 'You're so young, Izzy, to have all this put upon you. But you can't . . . God, Izzy, you can't let him know that you know.'

'It's a bit of a –'

'No, listen to me.' She took hold of my sleeve. 'If he thought

74

you knew what he did in those times . . . Going to Dublin, and all. He'd never forgive you for it.'

She was frightening me, but she was right. I could hear the direct-line conversation he'd have with God on the matter ('This ungrateful girl, this cheeky hussy with her opinions on her elders and betters . . .') and my body flinched to think of the punishment it would bring on. 'I'll be careful, Mammy. I will. I promise.'

Later, much later, during consciousness-raising sessions in California, when I listened to testimony from women who were furious with their mothers for failing to protect them from fathers or uncles or brothers, I knew that wasn't how I felt. I always understood my mother's fear was my own.

'I had to tell you. Now or never, don't you see?'

I did.

'Tell me I did right,' she said, plucking my sleeve. 'Please tell me I wasn't wrong.'

'Of course you did right. I'm glad to know.'

'Thank God. Oh, thank God.'

She took my hand. I wanted to ask about the girl who had to give her baby away, of what had happened to her, my other mother, but I couldn't. Instead I stared at the reeds and grasses and trees reflected in the winter water. The lake had nothing to say to me, not that day. It was calm, so calm that the images did not ripple, not even once, on the stillness of its surface.

9

Sixty-two years earlier in Paris, the morning of 25 December dawns late and grey. At 8.30 Maud Gonne's eyelids snap open to a noise, a windy burst of heavy rain rattling upon the glass as if it wants to be let in.

The noise has jerked her out of a demented dream: that Grey Lady she dreamt of before was there, appearing to her in some sensational way that she cannot now recapture. And she was running down a dark ravine . . . Or was it a tunnel? At any rate, she was fleeing, being pursued . . .

Only a dream. Look around. Everything is in place, all as it should be. The little dressing table under the window and darling Dagda still asleep in his basket beside her, his great breath purring like an engine. She pulls herself up on to her pillows and lights the candle on her bedside locker. Queasiness is already stirring inside her, like a hatch of flies swarming into life. If she gets up, she knows she will be vomiting within minutes.

Fortunately it is Christmas morning and Lucien is not due until late afternoon. She can lie here quite still, for as long as it takes this wretched nausea to pass. Smoothing the skin of her forehead now with her fingers, she attempts to subdue physical discomfort by focusing her mind on the deeper place that lies within. This morning she will think only thoughts that are beautiful.

Dagda stirs in his basket, lifts his head.

'Good morning, my darling,' Maud says into his eyes, eyes still cloudy with dog dreams. She will give him a minute to rouse, then let him out for his morning trot. How quiet the apartment is without Josephine. Normally she would be rattling

76

the fireplaces by now, but she has gone to Brittany, to spend *nativité* with her family.

So here Maud is, in her aloneness, nausea sucking her energy. Or is it her dreams that sap her? Ever since the night in Georges's mausoleum, her dream-life has been spectacular: the Grey Lady and other evil doers and doings, fleeing and being pursued, falling into rushing rivers and waterfalls, and all sorts of wild beasts … Often she wakes in the night, trembling, wondering if she can stay true to her resolution to renounce chloroform.

Dagda lifts himself up on to his legs, nudges her arm with his nose. She takes his lovely head in her hands, ruffles his neck. 'Yes, my darling boy. I will let you out now. Just give me a moment.' Holding her nausea in check, she slides slowly from the high bed and goes in search of her wrap. In the hallway Dagda's big tail almost sends her little statue of Cuchulain flying off the table. Poor darling, he has grown too big for this place. Soon she will find a bigger apartment, big enough for a baby and nursemaid. She opens her front door and out he bounds, with delight, to splash through morning puddles.

'Be careful,' she calls after his departing back. She envies his joyous energy, his clear sense of purpose.

Back in bed, the embrace of pillows and bed linen gives her a momentary comfort but her mind is full of disquiet, and the wretched nausea threatens her still. Perhaps a little reading, something elevating, something that might still her thoughts, take them to another plane. Willie Yeats's *Countess Kathleen and Various Legends and Lyrics*, perhaps. It is not on the bedside cabinet, so she leans out to look under the bed. Yes, there it is, halfway under.

She will reach under and fish it out, read 'The Two Trees'. He wrote this for her, and she is flattered by his vision of her soul. The language is so lovely, it must be heavenly to be able to express one's thoughts like that.

She leans out, trying to reach under the bed, and is hanging upside down when her stomach lurches. Instead of the book, she has to reach quickly for the bowl she has taken to keeping under there, beside the chamber pot. She gets it to her mouth just in time. Vomit spurts into it, stinging through her throat. Almost immediately she heaves again. And again, a third time, with less violence. A small respite before a fourth, almost dry retch.

That is the end of it for now: heart thudding, she leans back into the pillows, the bowl on her chest. Already, she feels better. It is over for another day. She lies on her side, her knees curved into her chest, her heart thumping too, too hard. With the palm of her hand, she traces the flat of her abdomen: no distention yet.

Behind the curling folds of her abdominal organs, inside the wall of her womb, lies Iseult, who's been on quite a journey – gathering size like a rolling snowball as cells frenetically divide, patterns and combinations accumulate and shift, and she grows ever more stable and fixed. Zygote to blastocyte, blastocyte to embryo . . . Her feet are already becoming webbed, anticipating her toes, and she is forming eyelids that, for now, she holds wide open. Once she's survived twelve full weeks of these transformations and mutations, she will merit the term 'foetus', and her most significant pre-birth changes will be complete. All she will need to do then is strengthen until she is what they call viable, able to survive alone without her mother's breath and bloodstream.

All this cellular activity is what is stealing Maud's energy. It's not Iseult's fault, of course not, it is just the human way, but we must surely pity her mother, lying there, able for nothing more than watching grey Parisian light stream through her bedroom window? She pities herself, thinking it anomalous that this, the most tiresome stage of pregnancy, wins her no sympathy or encouragement. That will come later, when she will feel wonderful but be forced into confinement – but in these, her most wretched weeks, she will have nothing but the solace that morning sickness is supposed to be a sign of a healthy child.

She cannot rise, she feels too weak, though the bells have begun to chime. Christmas bells: first the royal chimes from the palace and then the boom of the great bell of Notre-Dame. Perhaps she should have gone to Mass? She could go yet. Though she is officially a member of the Church of England, she has little empathy for that narrow denomination. Roman Catholicism, the religion of the Irish and the French, has rituals that are ancient and beautiful, and in L'église de la Madeleine this morning, the theatre of High Mass would provide an elevating spectacle.

But it is too late now to rush up and hither. And the weather is wretched. Rising from the bed feels beyond her.

At least she has ensured that Lucien spends some of this day with her. Last year he devoted all of Christmas to his family and she had energy to make only a feeble protest. This year, having her annunciation to make gave her strength to insist on his obligation to *her*.

Insistence and resistance: oh, how they are changed! On their first Christmas together, only four years ago, they didn't rise until four in the afternoon, driven from bed only by the need to eat. She was heavily pregnant with Georges then, and all their talk was of divorce, of how his absurd matrimonial tie to a woman so unsympathetic to his needs and ideals *must* be broken. Of how the coming baby, their darling patriot boy, *must* bear his father's name. Of the formidable alliance they would make when they were truly, properly together.

The year after that, Christmas 1890, they spent at lovely Saint-Raphaël, with pale winter sunshine glinting off the Mediterranean and Georges between them, one of his soft hands in each of theirs, training his chubby, tottering legs to stand. If she could have those days back, she wouldn't waste them on frustration with Madame Millevoye's stubbornness and Lucien's unwillingness to force the divorce. She knows how such vexations would pale in the horror that was to come.

Their *annus horribilis* . . .

But no, no! One must meet defeat with action! Thus thinks Iseult's mother, as she presses her hands against her abdomen, massaging its flatness, as if Iseult can be kneaded into being from without.

It is as well that the bells do not induce Maud to rise and hurry across the city to L'église de la Madeleine. For, in the very moments that she is being distracted from her memories of her *engagements* with him, her lover is mounting the marble steps into the church with his wife and their son, Henri. As the brass bell clangs above their heads like a thunderclap, Lucien flinches and the young Henri laughs.

'*Regarde*, Maman. See how Papa jumps.'

Madame Millevoye smiles down at her boy, made happy, Lucien thinks, by seeing him look foolish. Lucien is suffering greatly this morning but nobody cares. Though he is dutifully here, attending Mass *en famille*, no thanks or praise are his. He arrived at the house this morning bearing gifts, to be told in a matter-of-fact voice to leave them under the tree, that they would be opened after Mass. When he divulged details of his aching head – a pounding pain that was not, he knew for sure, just the consequence of staying up too late the night before at Déroulède's, drinking inferior wine, but a more pressing, disquieting ache – his wife only shrugged. It would serve her right if it were something serious, a brain haemorrhage like that which took their acquaintance Pontin last year.

The small family proceeds together up the cathedral steps. The frown on the face of both Henri and Lucien is identical, placed there by different thoughts but giving the boy the look of the man, so that they are unmistakably father and son. They move up the aisle and into a pew on the right side. Madame

Millevoye kneels, her face in her hands, and the boy copies her, but Lucien sits, two hands on his silver-handled umbrella.

At ten o'clock precisely the choir – forty-two pre-adolescent boys resplendent in white surplices – begins the joyful descant of 'Adeste Fidelis', heralding an entourage of clergymen on to the altar. When the choir finishes the hymn, the priest leaves a silence, then intones the Latin of the Mass in a fine masculine timbre that flows down the aisles and up into the height of the rafters.

The words stretch towards heaven, but Lucien Millevoye is in hell – one of his own making but none the less hellish for that. Though he knows Latin almost as well as he knows French, though this priest is a master, though every effort has been made by the architects of this cathedral to entice him out of his daily troubles into the worship of God – lights and stained glass and paintings and statuary and arches ceiled with carved wood pointing soaring shafts – not one holy word pierces his soul. He is present in body only, his mind is away, trapped in a sealed world where he besieges himself with swirling thought.

The nub of it is that he allowed himself, last summer, to be duped. For months he has revisited the sorry sequence of events, trying to see how he might have behaved differently, but he cannot. Thus he knows that he must be guiltless. At the root of his downfall was an entourage of Jewish financiers, who tried to corrupt the public men of France. One good man after another went down, some for the most innocent of dealings, yet somehow, through it all, Prime Minister Clemenceau, *l'homme sinistre*, survived. Though proved to have taken money from the Jew Cornelius Herz, still he strode through the Chambre, reckless, aggressive, triumphant . . . What a travesty!

So, naturally, when papers emerged proving what had long been suspected, that he was in the pay of the English, *naturally* Lucien had given them attention. Thus was he deceived, ushered into making false accusations, in a scheme worthy of the Venetian Republic.

Why did nobody believe this? Five years ago, he had hopes of being Finance (or even Prime) Minister in a Boulangist government; now he had not even a seat. *How* had this come to be? (*Sacré bleu*, how his head hurts. And he has a thirst that would not be slaked by an ocean of water.) *What* has happened to France when Jewish financiers – those cosmopolitan wayfarers without any nationality who will take any employment, straight or crooked, so long as it pays – are allowed to rule, while a man who has the imagination to dream and the courage to try to make his dream come true, a man who wants nothing but to be *un grand Français,* can come to naught?

. . . *Tandeum est.* The Mass is over. The massive organ pounds the opening strains of the closing hymn. Lucien escorts his family out before the hymn is over, for he cannot wait a single moment longer: he must have relief.

Outside, while he scoops mouthfuls of fresh air into his lungs, Madame gives Henri a new yo-yo, one of his many Christmas presents. Lucien waits, two hands to his silver-handled umbrella, anxious to be gone. Once the crowd emerges, he will be forced to exchange pleasantries with some ass, and now he really must have water, or fall down in a heap like a swooning damsel. At last they are off, Lucien setting the pace, striding out, swinging his umbrella. Henri, unfurling his new toy, falls behind.

'Be careful,' Madame Millevoye calls back over her shoulder. 'Watch your step, darling.'

Rapt with concentration, he doesn't hear her.

'Slow down a little, Lucien. There is something I wish to discuss with you.'

Words to sink a man's heart. 'Yes, my dear.'

'It is about Henri's schooling. He is getting too old for Monsieur Rambaud.'

'Is he? He is only . . . What age is he now?'

'Seven. Eight in June. It is time for us to be thinking about sending him away to school.'

'Is that really necessary? At this time?' The woman persists in acting as if he had not lost his seat at all, and with it an annual income.

'Really, Lucien, I think if I can make the sacrifice to let dear Henri go, though I shall miss him every moment . . .' Her lower lip is trembling. 'We must do what is best for Henri.'

There is no need for histrionics. If he had his choice, he would send him to L'école Clamais, with Henri de Rochefort's son. A boy emerged from Clamais groomed for power and influence. But the fees were ninety francs a year. 'This is not perhaps the place for this conversation,' he says.

'Very well. We shall discuss it at home.'

'Home?' says Lucien, his voice vague, as if he never heard the word before. But it is just that his attention has been snatched by the sighting of a girl. She is 300 yards away, advancing towards them up the long, straight hill of the quiet street, but even from this distance he likes the swing of her hips. Her dress is an unusual combination of green and red, some newfangled feminine fashion that he has not seen before. He slows, so he can observe her advance. As she draws closer, he sees he is mistaken: her clothes are not fashionable at all but a poor attempt at respectability, an attempt doomed by her bosom (too high, too prominent, too much *décolletage*) and her walk . . . This girl is no lady.

From behind his wife's back, he raises his eyebrows at the temptress, and she holds his look a moment before draping her eyelashes down into a simper. The snip! She then turns down a side lane, towards Rue Caulaincourt, proof – if any more were needed – that she is what he thinks she is. If he were to follow her down that lane, he knows what he would find in the warren of small streets behind . . . He stops walking. Is that not the very distraction that he needs this morning? Why, yes, indeed.

83

The very thing to lift this infernal headache, and clear his body of the miasma instilled by last night's intemperance, precisely what he needs to take his mind from his worries.

For, damn it all, it *is* Christmas. Is he truly expected to spend the morning in his marital home, a house that now chokes him with its cloying, female atmosphere, all trace of him dispatched? In that house, he cannot breathe. And in the afternoon, to attend at Maud's, where he will no doubt have to face demands of a different kind? This baby obsession of hers (she *must* have a baby, he *owes* her a baby), which may even – dear Lord above, pray he is mistaken – be a prelude to her starting once again on her divorce obsession. She has promised that she has no such thoughts, that she understands how impossible it is for him, a member of Parliament – well, an ex-member of Parliament but still a man of some influence – to divorce. In France, all affairs of the heart are permitted, so long as they are discreet, but discretion is not one of Maud Gonne's virtues.

How the devil has he got himself into such a predicament? While the rest of the world is enjoying itself, eating and drinking and making merry, he is expected to divide Christmas Day between two harridans.

'I am sorry, my dear. I find I cannot attend today after all.'

'What? But we are almost home.'

'I know. I am sorry. This wretched headache. I find I am not well enough to eat. That I need to return to bed.' (That part, at least, is not a lie.)

'You can lie down at home.'

'I wouldn't dream of inconveniencing you so.'

She whips him one of her coldest stares. 'Lucien, please. Not today –'

'I shall probably return. Later. If I find I have recovered.'

She gestures back towards the boy, who has fallen a way behind. 'For Henri, Lucien, *please*. He has been so anticipating this day with you.'

He has already turned. 'You can give him my present; you know where it is.'

Henri lifts his head from his yo-yo. 'Papa?'

'I shall be back presently, Henri. Be a good boy for your mother.'

I don't want to follow Iseult's father as he walks away from his family down where straight boulevards quickly narrow to crooked streets, then lanes; where the even line of buildings breaks into a crazed jumble of roofs; where windows are cracked and black and brickwork is open to passers-by. I don't want to feel his thirst growing as he walks down the twisted streets and, with it, his other need. I don't want to hear his negotiations with Madame la Brothel Keeper, who has a voice like a consumptive pirate, or his indignation at the price – two francs for wine and three for the girl – or her excuses about it being Christmas morning and her false expressions of apology, as if it were somebody else imposing the extortion.

I don't want to watch him shrug a reluctant agreement, though wine is the last thing he wants, simply because he would rather be damned for all eternity than thought parsimonious by one such as her and because he is driven on by something he refuses to examine and so cannot understand. I don't want to see his expression as he turns down the offer to have any . . . ahem . . . special requests fulfilled for a small extra charge.

I refuse to follow him into that over-warm room. I can't bear the sight of it, to tell you the truth, with its candle-blackened ceiling, its long red curtains puddling into dinge at the floor, its toxic smell of stale wax and smoke and semen. And that girl who will be turned and twisted and prised to order. (Her story – for what it is worth – is a common one. Sent to Paris by her relatives to find work when her parents died; met at the Gare du Nord by Madame; brought to this house and kept here with the help of opium, to which she is now addicted; gives herself away, time after time, with no idea of how much she earns for others.) Brothels' scornful exploitation of male need are never comfortable places for women who bestow sexual favours for free, or for a different, more complicated price.

And I fear I am being a little unfair to Lucien. When Iseult is old enough to discern his character, she will nickname her father *Le Loup*, 'The Wolf', but there was more to him than that. This, after all, is the man who won Maud Gonne – a woman who received marriage proposals from dukes and marquises, from poets and artists, from distinguished soldiers and politicians in many countries. So many men, yet it was Lucien she chose.

It thrilled her – would, she believed, thrill any woman – to see him standing up in Parliament, bending his great height over his papers, then throwing his head back to declaim his opinion on the issue of the day. His height and carriage; his sophisticated humour; his finely trimmed moustache; his gentleness with a cat or a rabbit or a bird; the tenderness that combined with principle to make him a committed vegetarian and anti-vivisectionist; his powers of oratory; his noble patriotism; the passion of his thought; the turn of his head. For all these qualities, and others, Maud Gonne loved this man.

He's been having a difficult time and is feeling the strain. Under strain, do we not all break at our weakest point? For Lucien, that is sex. So let's leave him to his prostitute and return to a different *quartier* of Paris, where ceilings are high and ornaments are intricately wrought, where the order and ease at which Maud Gonne excels might make us believe that what is fine in human nature is what dominates.

How is Maud now? After we left, she did let her head fill with thoughts of Lucien and of how he is still, to her, so frustratingly dear. She did ruminate further on the twists their lives had taken since they first met, did fall back to sleep where she suffered more preposterous dreams. Did, in short, all that she had promised herself she would not do. And now, somehow, it is late afternoon, and it will be a rush to get everything done by the time he arrives.

She rises, stiff from lying too long, and goes to the drawing room, where she sets a match to the fire Josephine laid before leaving. She plumps some already plumped cushions, draws the drapes and lights some candles. Though it is not yet dark, they give the atmosphere she seeks. In the kitchen, Josephine has left food prepared in the larder. Partridge to start, then some pressed beef and ham; a chicken, some potato salad, a mix of melon and nectarine, a fruit slice. She conveys it, plate by plate, to the dining room and lays it out on the large table. Later, she may heat the meats by slicing them and placing them in a bain-marie, if that is what Lucien wants. Now, though, she must bathe and dress, the most time-consuming task of the day.

She is in her bedroom, standing before her mirror in her 'health' corset and stockings, thinking how *corsetière* Madame Gaches-Sarraute should truly be anointed the patron saint of women for having produced this wonderful garment that keeps the waist small but still allows for breathing and movement, when her doorbell rings. Three sharp peals. Once – twice – thrice: his signature ring. He is early.

She grabs her petticoat, steps into it, then throws her dress on over her head. A tea-gown, soft films of rose chiffon with lace trimming on a bodice that clings tight to bosom and belly – she may as well wear it while she still can – and thirty-two slow buttons. Her fingers move, dexterous and fast, but not fast enough. His key turns in the lock below. The door opens, allowing in the sounds of the street. 'Maud?' he calls up the stairs.

A glance in the mirror. Up with the chin, adopt the walk and the look that they all seem to like so much, the attitude that Willie Yeats likens to the goddess Pallas Athene, a poise of elegance and femininity, of hauteur and mystery.

'Maud?' he calls again.

'Yes, Lucien. I am here.'

She sweeps out of her bedroom and down the stairs to greet him, a procession of one.

While Maud is sashaying down her stairs towards Lucien, across the English Channel the poet whose work so sings her praises is stomping up his, fleeing his exasperating family. Speechifying father, damaged mother, clinging sisters and soon-to-be-married brother, he repudiates them all. All.

In the year that is coming, he tells himself as he reaches his room and slams fast its door behind him, he *must* leave this house. He must find an independent flat in London, no matter that he cannot afford it.

W. B. Yeats's* London is no longer the city depicted by Dickens, where rich and poor, healthy and afflicted, comingled public and private lives on thronged and narrow streets. It is 1893, and London's streets have crept like a rampant ivy across the fields, devouring grass and trees and hedges, coiling around farms and villages and towns. Its hub, especially on the East side, now teems with the thin and dirty poor, while the middle classes have taken themselves off to the more salubrious outer edges.

Among the rows of grey, one cluster of houses, near the Hammersmith line, stands out. Built in the warm red stone that is now commonly called London brick but was, in those grey times, very much more uncommon, Bedford Park's flash of colour offers the Victorian sensibility the same pleasure as the glimpse of an Irish peasant's scarlet petticoat. Uncommon too is the way details on these houses vary, thus avoiding the regimental look of other middle-class suburbs. The inhabitants of these houses, indeed, never refer to their neighbourhood as

* My mother's favourite poet. As a child, I thought of him as Double-You-Be.

a suburb at all. Bedford Park is a 'colony', or a 'quarter', or sometimes a 'village' – anything that resists the spirit of the age. For Bedford Park is not inhabited by bowler-hatted Mr Pooters, swinging their brollies towards the 8.15, but, in the main, by artists, writers and academics.

This young man who flings himself, like a teenage girl, upon his bed in the back bedroom of No. 3 Blenheim Road is son and brother to artists, but his vocation is words. Already, at not yet thirty, he is making a name for himself as a poet of Ireland. A mystic whose childhood days in County Sligo inspired his celebrations of the mythic and spiritual attractions of mountain and cloud, lake and moon, wind and stars.

Now he lies, face into his pillow, impaling himself upon his emotions. He loves! He loves! But five yearning years of hopelessness have reached a crescendo. He is coming to believe he must set it aside, this love that keeps him in unctuous celibacy. Most of his friends have mistresses or, at need, go home with a harlot; yet he has never, since childhood, kissed a woman's lips. Only last evening at Hammersmith Station he saw a woman of the town walking up and down the near-empty platform, and thought to offer himself to her. This is how he thinks of it, a strange verb for a man to use in this context. In the event, he made no offer, held back by the old thought: No. I love the most beautiful woman in the world.

But the most beautiful woman in the world has abandoned him. Once he believed they would be together, he the poet–priest of a new age, she the human incarnation of female divinity, but now she neglects their occult interests and freezes him with business letters. Is it that vague desire of hers for some impossible life, some unvarying excitement, like the heroine of his play *The Land of Heart's Desire*? The vague idealisms and impossible hopes that blow in upon us to the ruin of near and substantial ambitions?

Or has she given up on him?

A few nights ago, when dropping into sleep, he saw an image

of a thimble, followed by a shapeless white mass that puzzled him. The next day, on passing a tobacconist's, he saw it was a lump of meerschaum, not yet made into a pipe, and he understood: she was complete; he was not.

That vile old nurse of hers told him that he would never see her again, that she was lover to another in France, indeed perhaps two others who were to fight a duel for her. He might be inclined to believe this had he not heard around Dublin another of her slanders: that Miss Gonne's illness of last summer arose from an illegal operation and that *he* was the father.

Miss Gonne. Maud. Miss Maud Gonne. She is the cause of all his despair, including the trouble downstairs that saw him race from the Christmas table, food untouched. It began harmless enough, with Papa starting a Christmas speech on the state of the family, of how Jack was soon to marry and become a substantial man, with a cheerful kind-hearted wife and an open-handed welcome for his friends. This stubborn cheerfulness wilted Willie's spirits. They all know Jack's fiancée is tying up her money so that her father-in-law won't be able to get his hands on any of it.

Papa then turned his glass on him. 'And Willie will be famous and shed a bright light on us all, with sometimes a little money and sometimes not.'

He drank and sat, signifying the end of the toast, whereupon Lolly's face began to redden. When his other sister, Lily, reached over to pat her hand, a gesture that only doubled Lolly's fury, Papa noticed and hastily stood back up. 'And Lolly will have a prosperous school and give away as prizes her eminent brother's volumes of poetry.'

This, naturally, only enraged her the more. At that moment, Maria arrived in and plunked the plate of potatoes on the table. When he reached for one with his fork, his belligerent sister turned her wrath upon him: 'You might wait for grace before meals, Willie. You might wait until Mama is settled.'

He had looked at the potato sitting on the end of his fork,

like a head on a spike, and said, 'I think to go to Paris,' taking himself by surprise.

'What?' Lolly had replied. 'You think to *what?*'

Her objection was financial, and she launched herself into a great oration about how *she* would like to go to Paris, but there would never be money out of her wages by the time the household expenses were met. That there would never be enough time either, or permission from any of them to just take herself off, wash day or some other female task would prevent it, etc., etc. He hardly knew what she said, he was so appalled to see in her again the same detestable excitability from which he suffers himself (she has Mars in square with Saturn, while he has Moon in opposition to Mars). He determines again to exclude this irritability from his writing and speech, to escape it through adoption of a gracious style. Is not one's art made out of the struggle in one's soul? Is not beauty a victory over oneself?

Papa tried to rescue him, asking about his intentions during the trip, and whether he was taking any letters of introduction.

'From York Powell to see Mallarmé, actually, and from Symons to Verlaine.'

Which impressed Papa and surely must highlight to the misguided Lolly the difference between the needs of a poet and those of a kindergarten teacher. But no. Since taking up that Froebel training, the wretched girl has become even more strident. What poor delusiveness is all this 'higher education of women'? Men have set up a great mill, called examinations, to destroy the imagination. Why should women go through it? Circumstance does not drive *them*. They come out with no repose, no peacefulness, and their minds no longer quiet gardens full of secluded paths, but loud as chaffering market places.

'This trip of yours,' she said. 'It has nothing to do with a certain Miss Maud Gonne, I suppose.'

The eyes of Lily, his other – kinder – sister, closed, and Papa interjected again. 'Now, now, Lolly.'

'Like a little lapdog,' she spat, her face burnt ugly red. 'You should be ashamed.'

Willie decided to be solicitous: 'Are you tired, Lolly?'

'Tired?'

'Combined housekeeping and kindergarten anxieties too much for you, perhaps?'

Such elaborate courtesies always incense her. A while ago, when she complained of household tasks, he got up one morning to make her tea before she left for school, and the memory of her annoyance amused him for a week. Today his little gibe raised her rant some degrees higher, while her face grew as red as a fishmonger's, but he drew no pleasure from his small victory. She appalled him.

He found himself pushing away from the table, saying, 'I am no longer hungry.'

His father told him to sit back down, and Lily said in her most plaintive voice, 'Please, Willie, it is Christmas,' but he ran from the room as if pursued.

Despite what Lolly thinks – what they all think, except maybe Papa – it is not just for Maud Gonne that he makes this trip to the French capital, though, yes, while there he would endeavour to progress the work on their Celtic mysteries, through which art's secret symbolical relation to the religious mysteries might be reborn.

In Paris, unlike in London, the pride of the mage is easily coupled with the pride of the artist and in February, the French capital will see a performance of Villiers de l'Isle-Adam's *Axël*. Five hours of elevated drama where all the characters are symbols and all the events allegories. He needs to see this play, as a model and validation of his own dramatic work. Only in France would a drama five hours long be tolerated.

Thinking of the Rosicrucian wisdom that inspired *Axël*'s creator restores his equilibrium a little. Perhaps he would never marry but like those esoteric lovers, he would love his chosen woman unto death. Thinking about her, her high, almost arrogant carriage, he finds his hand journeying under his leg, towards the forbidden regions. He corrects himself, tucks them into two fists under his chest.

It is a torture to him, this enforced celibacy, for he is not naturally chaste. This continual struggle wears his nerves but he knows of old that giving in to the impulse is worse. In that direction lies ruin, the loathing of self. He turns determinedly, with a great sigh, to lie on his back.

A knock comes to the door, jerking him bolt upright on the bed. It is Maria, the less appealing of their two servants, bearing a tray.

'Miss Lily said you'd better prefer to eat here, sir.'

His impulse is to spurn it, but he knows solicitous Lily would return with it herself. He waves Maria towards the table, and she thumps down the tray, thumps across the room and thumps the door closed behind her. This tray of food presents him with a quandary. He has made of poverty a virtue. No matter how rich he becomes in future – and though he is indigent still at almost thirty he knows that one day his writing will make him rich – he also knows he will always walk to his work, and eat little meat, and wear old clothes, for asceticism has become one of his ideals.

So what of this food, here, now? Should he, after his protest, eat it or leave it?

He gets off his bed, lifts the lid. Ham that arrived anonymously on their doorstep two evenings ago from some tactful friend. Without such kindnesses, and the income earned by himself and, especially, the girls, whose work has at least the virtue of regularity, this household would have fallen apart. Willie never knows whether he considers his father admirable in this, or negligent. The leg of a goose, sent from Sligo. Potatoes and buttered swede. Beside it, brandy pudding and a slice of cake.

He pulls up a chair and begins to eat, mindlessly ingesting mouthful after mouthful, without pause, taking no drink. Think-

94

ing. He shall ask Miss Gonne to accompany him to *Axël* and explain to her its importance. 'The greatest work you can do for Ireland is to raise our literature,' she has so often urged. 'Others can give speeches and attend meetings. You have higher work to do. For the honour of our country, the world must recognize you as one of the Great Poets of the century.'

Was this not dew shining through a love decayed by slander-ous tongues? Yes, yes, he thinks through his swede and potatoes, he shall go to her in Paris.

As Maud descends her stairs, she finds Lucien hanging his cape and putting his umbrella in the stand. In her last home he was as her husband, coming and going as he pleased, but after their quarrel in 1891, she gave up those rooms. In this temporary abode, which she took when they reunited, he has always been a curious mixture of *habitant* and guest.

He hands Maud a box of chocolates, and she gives him thanks most charming, though in truth she thinks little of such a thoughtless present. Then she leads him into the draw-ing room, where he stands now, before the fire, as is his way, rubbing his hands together.

'A drink?' she asks. Maud drinks little alcohol herself, but she keeps a good cabinet.

'I shouldn't. I had too much last night, with Déroulède.'

She waits.

'Perhaps a small glass of claret.'

'How is our friend?' she asks, as she locates the decanter.

'Tolerable. As good as a man can be who has lost everything.'

'Hardly *everything*, Lucien. He still has those who love him and he still has work to be done.' Her look as she hands him the crystal glass is pointed. 'Just because he is no longer in Parliament does not mean there is no work to be done.'

She leads the way to the dining room, and, as they enter, a gust of rain bursts against the large window. 'What a damnable day,' he says, his face scored with displeasure.

95

'We are well out of it.'

She won't ask him about heating the food, she decides, not in this mood. They shall have it as it is. She resolves to be tender: he is always unsettled by time with Madame. *She* must be charming, soothing, in contrast.

'So,' she says, lifting her glass. 'To a new year and a better one.'

'It could hardly be worse than the last.'

'Oh, come, *mon cher*. You do not need to take on so. You must fight back, so that in the next election, you regain what you have lost.'

'Don't you ever tire, Maud, of the fight?'

'Certainly. And when I am tired, I rest. Thus I gather my strength for the next battle.'

'I am forty-three. Too old for battles.'

'Pouf! That is what you said after Boulanger's suicide. That you were finished.'

'And maybe I should have finished then. Then the forgeries débâcle would not have happened.'

Still he smarts. It is understandable. For her too recollection of his humiliation can make her quail. She was in London, staying in the Clarendon, when she first heard, from a headline on the newspaper being read opposite her. DEPUTY MILLE-VOYE'S 'REVELATIONS', it squealed. Those hateful, ominous quotation marks.

She had sent the boy for a copy of *The Times* and read it with a faltering heart, her breakfast pushed aside: *Monsieur Millevoye stood before the deputies, lifting one by one the sheets and reading from them passages that were supposed to be incriminating of Monsieur Clemenceau, but which were in fact quite devoid of serious interest. Hearing them greeted only by jeers or ironical laughter, he began to see the ridiculousness of his plight . . .*

She had wanted, there and then, to dash across the English Channel, to give him comfort. Months on, the unforgiving words remained with her: *Monsieur Millevoye then pretended that*

there were some sentences that discretion forbade him to read but the
Chamber saw through this. Each time he paused, they urged him with
cries of 'Go on, go on.' When he conceded to read the passages, they greeted
them with long bursts of hilarity . . .

Paul Déroulède was forced from the chamber that day and, when the papers were proved to be forgeries, Lucien had to follow.

'I have a suggestion for you,' she says now. 'Something that will help reverse old misfortunes.'

He groans and ducks his head down into his shoulders.

'It is a fine suggestion. Don't you want to hear?'

'Why can you not just let me be?'

'Because, in reality, you do not want to be so let. Shall I tell you?'

'Can I stop you?'

'Jules Jaluzot is looking for an editor for his newspaper *La Patrie.*'

His eyebrows go up. Aha! She has at least surprised him. Jaluzot, director of the department store Printemps, is one of the richest men in Paris, and in Paris every man who climbs to political or financial eminence hedges himself with a newspaper, which, like a parapet, serves both to prevent him from falling and to shield him from the stones that may be flung up from below.

'And what makes you think he would accept me?'

Jaluzot and she have already discussed the possibility, but she doesn't want to reveal this. 'Ah! So you *are* interested.'

He shrugs.

'Of course he would want you – a writer of your calibre.'

He makes a face.

'You know it is true, Lucien. Nobody uses words like you. How was it that Englishman described your writing: "sinewy"?'

'"Sinewy and mellifluous".'

'And he was right. He was right. You can make words dance like champagne.'

'But *La Patrie*. Who reads it?'

'It is not worth reading now. But you are the very person who could make that little-read paper an instrument with which to rebuild our work.'

He takes a long draught of wine. She refills his glass, enjoying how the cut glass makes the liquid shine like rubies in the glow of the fire. 'It would take time, yes, but with it you could regain your old influence a hundredfold.'

'I don't know, Maud. Sometimes I think the Boulangistes and all we stand for have had our time. That we are a hangover from another, more noble age.'

'Lucien.' She pauses for effect, places her hand on her abdomen. 'Our son will want a father whom he can admire.'

His eyes widen.

'Yes!' She can feel the smile splitting her face in half. 'Our undertaking at Samois was successful.'

'You are sure?'

'Quite, quite certain.'

He shakes his head slowly. Ruminatively.

'And the stars were auspicious,' she says. 'I have checked.'

He drains his glass, picks up the decanter and pours himself another.

'When he is born, I shall get Willie Yeats to do a proper horoscope.'

He swallows again, the sound loud. To fill the gap he is leaving so wide, she says: 'Did I ever tell you that I myself was born on a full moon at the exact moment of the winter solstice?'

'Yes. You know you did.'

'And what it means? According to Willie Yeats, Mercury and Neptune both stopping their march across the sky like that is a moment associated with the birth of gods.'

'Yes, Maud. You have told me. Many times.'

'But wouldn't it be wonderful if such a sign were to be given to us at *this* birth.'

He shrugs.

'You do not seem happy.'

'Happy? I am, I suppose, a trifle overwhelmed.'

'Yes, that is natural. But it is wonderful, is it not? Truly, Lucien, I believe that today represents –'

'When is the date? The summer?'

'Early August, I am told.'

He nods, slowly and definitely, then seems to give himself a shake. 'I am sorry, *cherie*. Of course you are right. Of course this is good news.' He picks up the decanter and his glass and – thrillingly! – comes across to sit beside her.

'Do you mean our child?' she asks. 'Or the newspaper job?'

'Both.'

'Oh, Lucien, truly?'

'Yes. Yes. Both.'

'Darling, I am so pleased.'

'Have you told anybody else?'

'Only Ghénia.'

He grimaces. He and her feminist friend have unending disputations.

'You should wait a while, I believe, before telling anybody else,' he says, his voice holding a gentleness that recalls bygone times. He takes one of her hands in his. 'Remember what happened with Madame Millevoye.'

'Lucien!' What a thing to say. Does he not know how it hurts her to hear him so casually mention that woman and her miscarriages, evidence that . . . ? No, begone. Centre instead on the concerned timbres of his talk – she has not felt such concern from him in many a day. Recline back into this beautiful consideration, as Lulu the cat lies back into a warm shaft of sunshine. Yes, that is better. He places a hand on her knee. When she does not rebuff it, he places the other on the dip of her waist and leans across to place his lips on hers.

'*Chérie*,' he says, pulling back from the kiss to look in her eyes. 'You must take greater care of yourself.'

Something flutters, deep in her. She has created this new

tenderness so like the old. He kisses her again. A small flick of his tongue she allows. A little more, still permitted. He lets a sigh and she is surprised, as always, by the speed and intensity of his rising need. She does not halt the tentative brushing of her breasts through her clothing, the sliding of his other hand behind her back, his first fumblings with her neck buttons . . . But by the time he has got through a quarter of them, her flickering ardour has dissolved, insubstantial as ether. Her hip hurts. He is leaning too heavily, pushing a corner of her pelvis against a hard bar underpinning the upholstery. She shifts. Better.

She lets him proceed. Why? Not because he intimidates her – she is not one of his *chanteuses* – but to stop him now would be to break the unspoken code they have evolved between them: that if she is not willing, she should turn aside or otherwise deflect his advances before or just after the mouth-on-mouth kiss. Now he drops soft kisses to her lips and eyes, while he negotiates the detestable buttons and offers attentions that he thinks pleasing to her. This will, she determines, be the final time until after their son is born. From now on, her condition will excuse her. He begins to draw patterns on the surface of her body.

It is when she feels his hand fumbling with the front of his trousers that she knows she can't go on. 'Lucien . . .'

'*Mmmmmm . . .*'

'I'm sorry. I –'

'*Chérie*, you are so beautiful. *Quelle belle.*'

Faithless, false and meaningless words. She puts her hands to his shoulders. 'Truly, Lucien, I cannot. I feel a pain . . .'

He opens his eyes, perplexed, stops his hand so it wavers above her body.

'I am sorry, I do not feel well . . . My condition.'

'Oh, your *condition*. Pardon me.' He snaps away from her, turns to fix his breeches.

His back is a surly hump. Of course he is angry, he has a

perfect right to be angry. She must bring all her tact to bear now; if she does not soothe him, he might leave, and this she could not bear, not today. Not Christmas Day, the day of their joyous announcement.

'Thank you, Lucien. I am –'

'*Thank you.*' His voice is bitterly sarcastic. '*Thank* you? Oh, you are welcome, Maud.'

'Please. Do not be vexed.'

'Vexed. Pah! Your vocabulary is poorly chosen, my dear.'

'Lucien, let us not fall out over this small thing when we have so many momentous things to be glad of today.'

'It is true, what Déroulède said.'

'Déroulède?'

'Every man who sees Maud Gonne wants her, but the sensible man soon sees that she is as cold as the ocean bed.'

'Lucien, please –'

'You are frigid, mademosielle.'

Oh, frigid. What is that? A man's word for what is not his to have. 'It was not always thus, Lucien.'

'I should have followed my friend's advice, beaten my retreat long ago.'

Why is he goading her, drawing her into saying what should not be said again? Today of all days.

'Cold, cold, cold . . .'

Enough. 'If I *am* cold, you well know why.'

'. . . as the ocean bed.'

'It is not *I* who betrayed our love, Lucien. It was you who did that when you asked me to sleep with De Rochefort to further your career.'

Within weeks of that awful event in 1891, horrifying punishments were visited on their lives. Boulanger, Lucien and France's great hope, committing suicide on the grave of his mistress. Parnell too, the uncrowned king of Ireland and her great hero, dying of a heart attack in the arms of *his* mistress. Indication enough. But it was the striking down of their darling

Georges by meningitis that made it undeniable: these horrors were Lucien's punishment for his faithlessness.

And hers, for being unable to hold him.

He has jumped to his feet. 'Ah, *non*,' he says. '*Non*. Not this again.'

She stands too, tries to get him to look at her, to get beyond the hurt. 'This pregnancy we have been given: it is a sign of forgiveness, Lucien. Don't you see? We have been given another chance. We must protect it.'

'By not making love?'

'Now that our love has resulted in a child, we should be content.'

'Pah! One could as easily say, now that our love has resulted in a child, we should love more often.'

She shakes her head.

'Fine,' he says. 'So be it. We shall never be lovers again.'

She takes his hand in both of hers; his fingers are bony. 'Lucien, that is *not* what I want. It is what the gods demand. And not for ever, just for now. We shall know when it is right again.'

'Oh, yes. When *you* deem it right.' He slips his hands from her grasp. 'We should never have got back together.'

'*Lucien!*'

'Why reunite, if nothing is forgiven? I have apologized to you, Maud, over and again for what happened with De Rochefort. Explained my misunderstanding –'

'Don't use that word for it, *ever*. I have told you.'

'Laid myself prostrate before you, but there is no forgiveness.'

'It is not my forgiveness that counts, Lucien, but that of the gods. Otherwise we are doomed. See what is happening to us right here.' So long as he refuses to acknowledge his sins, she is forced to be a moral nature for two.

'Pah! We never have to worry about the gods' forgiveness for Maud Gonne's errors.'

He turns away, towards the door. 'I bid you goodnight, mademoiselle.'

'Lucien, don't go. We can –'

But he has already marched from the room with such purpose that to follow would be pure humiliation.

So she sits back down amid the remains of their day, the half-empty decanter, the candles and chocolates, listening to him retrieving his cape and slamming the door behind him. Oh, why didn't she just let him have his way? It wouldn't have taken long; by now, they would be sitting happily together, talking.

She pictures it again, the image she clasped to herself for weeks: the pair of them reclining in togetherness on the *chaise*, she in the crook of his arm, exchanging gentle whispers about their darling baby-to-be. She making the suggestion that they should name him for his dead brother, who himself was named for the *brave général* Boulanger. And explaining to Lucien how this baby is both the acknowledgement of all that went before but also, crucially, an *entrée* to a new life together.

That, still, is true. And is it not *he*, the coming child, who is the point of significance? Yes . . . yes. What does another quarrel signify? She and Lucien have quarrelled before over similar rejections. He forgave then and would forgive again. He has to, does he not, now that she carries his child? A child who will grow to be the saviour of France or Ireland – or perhaps even both? A patriot son to redeem all their losses.

11

Dear Izzy

Your dinner is on the table. Put some boiling water from the kettle into the pot on the stove and put the plate on top. Simmer the water for about fifteen minutes. Don't take the foil off. I'll be back before you're home from school tomorrow. Be a good girl.

Bye bye,
Mammy

PS   Don't burn yourself.

On the kitchen table, my place was set: glass for milk, side plate, knife and fork either side of a cork place mat, dinner plate wrapped in tinfoil with a smaller foil pack on top. I ran through the days of the week in my mind. Wednesday. So beneath the foil was bacon and cabbage. And in the small pack, my dessert: two chocolate biscuits. I left my schoolbag on the floor where it fell, opened the biscuits and began to eat (before my dinner – such badness!).

For the first time in my life, I had let myself into our house. Mammy had gone to Dublin, to the hospital. 'I have to go,' she had insisted the night before, as if I were trying to stop her. 'I'll be back as soon as I can.'

The biscuits were doing little for my physical hunger, though they were satisfying another sort of longing. I put my feet up on the table to better enjoy them, and looked about me. The kitchen looked different without Mammy in it, doing her chores. Her foostering, Daddy called it. Emptier and quieter. I felt nervous and for a time I didn't know why. My gut, fluttering as if it had been colonized by a battalion of butterflies, was ahead of my conscious thought.

It wasn't until I had the biscuits demolished and the crumbs wiped from my mouth that I allowed the idea: with all of them out of the house I could have a bath.

Doolough in those days had not progressed to showers, and baths were permitted only on Saturdays, or on once-in-a-lifetime occasions like First Communion or Confirmation, and then only in three or four inches of water, just enough to do the job. In our house, having a bath necessitated turning on the immersion heater, which was controlled by a big red switch in our hot press that neither Mammy nor I was allowed to touch. Daddy kept the bath plug in a hiding place in his bedroom.

In my room I had a bottle of green bubble bath given to me last Christmas. I could, if I hurried, heat enough water to cover myself entirely. This was, I had discovered since going to secondary school, the proper way, the way that most people, people who did not have to live with my father, took a bath. I filled my head with an image that allowed room for no other: me reclining under hot water, covered in bubbles, like one of the models in Mammy's magazines.

I crossed the room, opened the door of the hot press and flipped the red switch to 'On', blood leaping at the sound of its click.

Emboldened by my own daring, I then had a look in all the cupboards I was usually forbidden to open. I found the rest of the packet of chocolate biscuits. For the first few, pleasure outweighed guilt, but then it was the other way round. Yet, even after the worry rose so high that I was no longer enjoying them, I kept stuffing them in, knowing they would be missed. What was I at?

Then came my dinner, or as much of it as I could manage after the choco-fest. After washing and tidying up (I hadn't gone entirely berserk), I put my hand to the immersion heater. Hot. Hot half the way down. Face flushed, I took two towels and went upstairs in search of the bath plug, a search that would require a forage into forbidden territory: my parents' bedroom.

There was no visible sign of my father in that room, except for his hairbrush and a smell, a smell that is still in the house to this day, even after his death. Fear was thick in me as I went around to his side of the bed, and with good reason. He might well decide to drop over from the barracks as he sometimes did during the day. Especially today, he might do that, as I was home alone. If caught, I would bring upon myself unimaginable punishment, yet on I pressed, compelled by something stronger than fear.

His bedroom locker was one place kept free of my mother's housekeeping. In it, bundles of papers and letters were jumbled with two pairs of reading glasses, a screwdriver, some golf tees and a golf ball, a whiskey glass full of copper coins and other debris. Under a stack of *Ireland's Own* and *Reader's Digest* magazines I found it: the bath plug. And beneath it: a brown envelope torn in one corner. I peeled back the tear a little. What impulse led me to open the envelope, heart banging against its cage? It was as if I knew before I knew.

Listeners never hear good of themselves, they say, and those who pry are punished by what they find. My father's magazine was full of pictures of half-naked women. It would be considered innocent now, the sort of images that have become everyday to us, delivered to our breakfast tables in daily newspapers and to our sitting rooms by TV. A dark-haired girl in a leather hat brandishing a cocktail glass, her sweater pulled up. Another reclining naked on a fur coat, fabric carefully arranged to cover her pubis. Another lying in the bath, soaping herself, leg bent to block a view of anything too blatant. Anatomically innocent, but in its intent the same as all porn, and it was the intent that held thirteen-year-old me riveted with shock.

I was at an age when I was just becoming aware of breasts. My own were budding, and I had started surreptitiously eyeing the bulges beneath the blouses and jumpers of the females around me: teachers in school, sixth-year girls, neighbours at Mass. I had never seen anyone else's naked before, and now here was a profusion of them in every variety. And the look on these girls' faces. Saucy, as one of the captions said. Yes, they were girls but girls of a different species. They had allowed somebody to photograph them like that because they liked it: so said the little paragraphs beside each picture. 'Hi. I'm Sophie, and I've always wanted to be a nude model.'

Something I was just coming to know about women and men was writ large in this magazine, in my 65-year-old father's keeping it in a brown envelope in his bedside locker. I wanted to put it back, pretend I'd never seen it, but I also wanted to see more of it. I wanted to know everything it had to tell me.

I proceeded into the bathroom and turned on the taps. Water gushed forth, steam rising. I opened the magazine out on the shelf, at Miss September, the centrefold, a kneeling beauty who was using the top half of her bikini to cover where the bottom should be. I put a bottle of shampoo to hold open one edge, a cake of soap the other. Then I remembered the bubble bath and went back to my bedroom to find it.

As I searched through the shoe box at the back of my wardrobe where I kept all my precious things, a noise outside in the corridor made me jump. It sounded like a footstep. My heart started to flutter and flap like a bird caught in a room. I turned my ear up urgently to listen. Nothing. Nothing, you silly. Nothing, except the old house creaking. Finding the bubble bath, I hurried back to the gushing taps. I nudged the half-open bathroom door and a chasm dropped beneath me. It hadn't been nothing. No. It was my father.

My father, bent over the bath, turning off the taps.

When he felt the door move, he swung round. He was dressed for rain, in his policeman's cycling cape and pull-ups. The strap of his hat dug into his jawline. On the shelf beside him, level with his head: Miss September, her chin thrown back, her protuberant breasts on offer, nipples pushing out of the picture.

Our eyes connected for an infinitesimal moment across the silence that had replaced the gush of water.

Then I turned and ran.

12

In March, Maud makes her last public appearance, and life hangs heavy without her fund-raising dinners, her meetings with politicians and journalists and other men of influence. She detests confinement: the word and the concept. Ghénia agrees, and they spend much time considering the wrong that women are expected to hide themselves away at this time, as if they have done something wrong. This Maud refuses to do – even though in her case pregnancy has layers of shame. She travels to London for her sister Kathleen's wedding, causing consternation among her English aunts.

Iseult lies within, oblivious to these disputations. By now she is able to jerk her body, bend her lengthening limbs, hic an occasional hiccough. She has a chin, a large forehead, a button nose. The tiny bones inside her ears have hardened, so she can hear the rumbling of Maud's digestive system, the beats of her heart, the underwater echo of her voice. Her vaginal plate is now intact, confirming her sex. She has tastebuds that can distinguish bitter from sweet. And a brain that is growing so fast it has to wrinkle up like a walnut to fit inside her skull. The cells she needs for conscious thought are forming, the beginnings of the ability to remember, and thus to learn.

July passes. The city slips into torpor. In shop windows in every *quartier*, little paper cards announce that this or that *patron* is away until a date in late August or the beginning of September. The air grows heavy along the streets and boulevards, so that to poor Maud breathing feels like eating.

This is the first year since she came to live in France that she has spent a summer in the city. How she longs for the cool of Clermont-Ferrand, or Cap Saint-Vincent, or even the little house in Samois where she and Lucien were once so happy, where grass and trees cool the temperatures, and the air is free to blow. Perhaps once the baby is born, an escape might be possible. For now, time has slowed to the watching of one fat second slumping down on to another.

In London too the weather is uncommonly hot. On the morning of 6 August 1894 – the most significant day in Iseult's life – Willie Yeats sits to his desk to write a letter to a new woman friend, Mrs Olivia Shakespear, an authoress of what Willie thinks of as 'little' novels. With this letter, he launches himself upon the affair that is to lose him his unwanted virginity. When he visited Maud in February, he had found her cool and distant. In the months since his return from Paris he has been telling himself that if he cannot get the woman he loves, it would be a comfort, even but for a little while, to devote himself to another.

So today he writes to Olivia, thinking of her beauty, the kind of beauty that holds within it the nobility of defeated things. She has a love sorrow of her own: married to an incompatible and much older man, who has not paid her court since the day they wed. Of course his letter addresses none of this. His subject is her writing. He tells her how he admires the tremulous delicacy and fragile beauty of her prose and makes a suggestion. Should she perhaps reconstruct her villain to be one of those 'vigerous' (Willie was always a poor speller) fair-haired men who are very positive and what is called manly in external activities and energies.*

Having proffered this suggestion, he takes another sheet of paper and begins to doodle. Three letters repeated over and over in a multitude of angles and sizes: WBY, WBY, WBY . . . The letters have the air he is seeking. Begone, the detestable appellation of his boyhood – Willie – the name so cavalierly

* The type, in other words, who is the opposite of him.

bandied about by his family. A boy's name. With a blotting rag, he wipes the nib and stares at the page as if it were one of his finest creations, quite forgetting his letter until a banging door downstairs makes him jump out of his reverie. He finishes rather hastily, expressing the hope that he might meet her when she returns from her holiday with her husband in Brittany.

This they will do over the coming autumn and winter. Months of meetings will pass without Willie making any sexual move, until eventually Olivia will be forced, on a day trip to Kew Gardens, to take the initiative and give him, in the railway carriage, what he calls in his memoirs 'the passionate kiss of love'. Even after this, more effort will be required to get him over what he calls her pagan past (possible prior lovers), and, when she finally beds him, he will be impotent at first, from nervous excitement.

All this lies ahead. This warm August morning he does not even know that he is playing suitor. After he signs his name, his mind turns to Paris, to she whom he considers to be 'the greatest of her tribe', to why she no longer shows concern for their mutual interests.

The reason why is today making Maud exceedingly uncomfortable. A stroll along the Seine had seemed like a good idea after lunch, but now strange sensations have begun to unfold inside her. Might this be it? In the hallway she lifts her arms to hang the wrap without which no respectable woman can walk around Paris, no matter how high the heat, and feels something shift in her lower abdomen, as if a band of muscle is opening out. 'Like London Bridge,' she said afterwards to Ghénia. This is followed by a faint muscular contraction. Yes, it has started.

Iseult feels it too, this momentary pressure that is over before it begins. For some hours she has been squirming with an inchoate sensation of discomfort, brought on by a flush of hormones designed to push her from her womb home. The contraction tightens the feeling. And here comes another, a little stronger than the last . . . She wishes they would stop, that she could be left where she is, but, even as she clings, a contrary impulse is also rising. The contractions intensify, until the balance between wanting to remain tips towards having to move. When the time comes, she'll be ready.

Maud calls Josephine, sends her to alert the doctor and nurse. Georges took twenty-six hours to appear from first contraction: the doctor is likely to come, take a look, then go away again to dine as he did last time. Still, she would like him to arrive now and check that all is well.

13

On the drive back to Doolough from Glendalough, Star turned on the radio so we wouldn't have to talk. At the house I said to her, 'Will you help me clear away your granddad's things before you go?' If I could get her to darkness, she might stay another night.

She didn't want to help, but she could hardly say no, so we set to it, working through the house with boxes and black plastic sacks, separately and in silence, like burglars.

It is surprising the amount of detritus that even the least accumulative life can gather, but my father was a hoarder. He hadn't smoked for years before he died but he'd kept all his old pipes in a shoe box. Of footwear, old and new, I counted seventy-eight pairs: wellington boots, walking boots, best shoes and second best and long, long past their best. Wardrobes and cupboards stuffed with clothes and knick-knacks. Ornaments and pictures, brass plates and candlesticks, holy water fonts and ancient bedside lamps.

As the shelves and drawers emptied and the bags and boxes filled, I saw how objects separated from their owners become pure junk. Without him, the blue woollen hat he wore when fishing was repellent: greasy and redundant. Star and I worked for over two hours, clearing everywhere except my bedroom and the parlour. 'They've already been sorted,' I lied. It would be too awkward to allow her into those two rooms that Zach and I had made our own.

She took a carriage clock as a memento, along with the photograph of me with my father, and another of my parents sitting on a cliff side. You could read their futures in that photograph. My father dapper in a three-piece suit and trilby, a cigarette smouldering between his fingers. My mother thin, too thin, with her eyes raised to the camera from beneath the brim of her hat. Hers was the last generation to esteem hats; she kept a selection, immaculate in hat boxes, atop her wardrobe. My father's arm is taut around her shoulders, she shrinks from the camera's attention, and you can see, even in two-dimensional black and white, that he is driving their day.

I brought out the last of the bags and when I came back into the kitchen, I was shocked to find Star beside the stove, crying.

'Darling?' I put my arms around her shoulders, and she let me, just about, her spine stiff as a tree. Then she shrugged herself away, dabbed each eye dry with the back of her wrist.

'Oh, Mom . . .'

'It's okay, Star. I understand. You have to go.' I knew what I had to do was keep talking, fill the space between us with meaningless sound, hums and burbles and fuzzy static that would get us through. 'And thanks for helping with the clearing. I needed to get as much of Granddad out of here as I could.'

I imagined myself stripping further back, taking up the carpets and polishing up the wooden floors. I fed myself that vision in my head, and I liked it. Painting every wall white. Turning this place into a new canvas. Maybe that was what I would do, when she was gone.

'It's too cold to go down to the gate,' I said, afraid I'd break if I had to watch her go, the backpack in her heartbreaking, chubby grip. 'I'll wave you away from upstairs.'

I left her then, so she could get on with it, and went up to the spare bedroom. This was my favourite room in the house, a corner room with a window on three sides. I went to the one that overlooked the drive and the lane. It was only four thirty, but the day was already faded so that I could barely make her out below, head bent to the rain, one hand holding her coat together. She threw her bag on to the back seat and waved up to me once, unseeing. Then she folded herself in behind the steering wheel.

114

The car lights came on, front and back, and the red vehicle slipped down the laneway. Moran's dog, who hung around every part of the neighbourhood, appeared out of somewhere to go running after the back wheels, until it sped up and he relinquished the chase. I watched on. It turned the corner of our lane, out on to the road and I followed its lights with my eyes until I could see it no more.

I was reeling with absence: first Zach's, then my father's, now Star's. Thoughts threatened to explode my head. So I went back down, into the kitchen, and turned on the TV. It was then that I spied the hammer sitting under the corner table, its two fingers beckoning. I picked it up, tapped the flat of its head against my palm and you know what happened next.

Within a short time I was being escorted from the devastated room into a police car, stopping only to collect the notebooks. Inspector O'Neill and Garda Cogley were quiet for our short drive to the barracks, and I was thinking about the times I walked the distance between these two buildings in my childhood, sent up with a tinfoil-covered dinner plate or 'a message' for my father.

When they brought me into the lock-up room at the back, I remembered him showing me – small, wide-eyed, knee-socked me – this place where the bad men were kept. Thirty years on it looked the same. A shelf-like bed, a chair, a naked bulb swinging from the ceiling above. Garda Cogley had to put a hand to my back to nudge me in.

He later told the *Wicklow Gazette* that he was surprised to find me, when he came by later to check, 'calmly writing, oblivious to all'.

'Is it letters you're writing?' he asked me, and I told him no, that I was writing a story.

'A crime story?'

I laughed a broken laugh and said, 'Maybe you could say that.'

That I had laughed, the newspaper said, was surprising to

Garda Cogley. Shocked, it said he was. Disbelief, it said he felt, that all through the time I was waiting for my bail to be organized, I kept calmly, assiduously filling pages with words. It was a queer way of going on, he thought, for a woman in my position.

Tears would have suited Garda Cogley better. Fear. Lying awake all night, contemplating the horror of my position. But in those first hours in prison, writing felt like survival, the only way I could manage what was happening, a way to cut through the confusions and make some sense of it all.

Before my time with Iseult and with Zach, I would have thought that inferring sense from the random events of life was self-delusion, a childish inability to understand or accept one's own unimportance. It was they who made me feel that there *were* connections that would lead to understanding – perhaps even to release – if I could only uncover their meaning.

As I sat in Doolough Barracks with the Inspector firing questions at me – Had I liked my father? Had I loved him? Where had my boyfriend gone? Where was my daughter? Did I want to get back to my own life in California? – it was Iseult I held in my mind.

His questions revealed that a number of people had been alone with my father that Christmas Eve afternoon. Zach to say goodbye before leaving, disregarding, as always, my father's bony silence to pay him his due respect. Pauline, on a check-up visit. And Star. The first thing Star had done on arrival was to go into his room to see him. All three had had the opportunity to feed him morphine, and I didn't have to think too hard to give each a motive. One was more likely than the other two, but the idea of any of them actually doing it was unthinkable.

As unthinkable as the idea that it was me.

I could tell, though, from the tenor of the questions and the way they spat from the Inspector's thin mouth – What had my father eaten that last night? What had he had to drink? How had he looked? How had he slept? What had he said? – that he did not agree. I answered him as carefully as I could, aware all the time of the tape machine recording in the corner. I watched spittle spray from his mouth as his symphony of questions reached its crescendo – What about the morphine dosages? What about the pump? What about the pills? – and I gave my answers, while holding fast in my head words that Iseult once wrote about suffering: 'Doubtless there's a meaning in it, but it's one that one can only see from a distance, safe in the heart of well-being.'

14

The room is dark and full of sound, great gusts of breath. Summer night is falling as the birth moment approaches. The emergent darkness is lined with the sound of Maud's breathing and crying, crying and breathing. Her revolutionary activity, her fine physique and physiognomy, her political passion, her strong will: none is of use to her here. Here she is nothing but mother: source, vessel and channel.

The candle flame burns straight and tall in the muggy heat. The nurse mops her brow. Josephine runs hither and thither with jugs of water and cloths and glasses of iced lemonade. The doctor murmurs consolation. 'Not long now. Not long.' Maud withstands the pain, disdaining to cry out, but as the labour comes to crisis she begins to emit the unmistakable, universal female sounds. Her whimpers turn to cries, then shouts. All her breaths are gasps. Then comes a long scream as her skin is stretched wider than skin can stretch, and Iseult's head pushes through, tearing her open.

Through her scream comes Iseult's cry, small and faint. A fragile sound, yet everyone in the room turns towards it.

'*Elle est parfait*,' says the nurse.

'*Elle?*' Maud gasps, as if a girl were some mysterious creature of whom she has only just heard.

The nurse holds up the baby, and Maud gasps again at the reality that is Iseult – no longer a notion inside her but a solid squirm of fleshy limbs, a squawk of throat and lungs. A baby in the world. A girl.

They stare at each other, Iseult's infant eyes still glazed with the blood and fluids, Maud's eyes riveted upon her genitals. Then her mouth widens into a dazzling smile, and the attendants around the bed let out a breath. Maud holds up her arms and careful hands pass the baby.

She pulls her in close and sniffs her skin. She had no female name chosen but in the rush of emotion a name comes to her, a name that carries in it all the sorrows and mysteries of womanhood. A gift from her beloved Wagner. She whispers it now in the child's ear: Iseult.

She thinks of her man, so unfaithful and unreliable, and of how a boy would have settled him better, but the thought is swept away in a flood of hormones and love. Maud is good at loving and now again has someone worthy of her devotion. She folds the miniature body close to hers, feels the little chest rising and falling in quick baby breaths. Her insides clench. Pray God this one will be stronger than her brother.

She drops a kiss on to her red and wrinkled forehead, inhales her scent, the scent of her own insides, a smell of blood and secrets.

'You and me, then,' she whispers into the tiny, curly conch of an ear.

She turns to find Josephine, who is rinsing a cloth in the corner. 'Josephine, the letter on the bureau. Open it, please, and bring me my pen.' Josephine does as she is asked, and Maud removes the sheet of paper from its envelope. It has no salutation or signature, in case it should fall into the wrong hands. Just four stark words: 'Your son is born.' She scratches out 'son', replaces it with 'child'. And adds two more truncated sentences: 'A daughter. Iseult Germaine Lucille.' Then she holds it up to dry, waving it in the air.

Nestled in the crook of Maud's other arm, Iseult has no idea what her mother is saying, or even that somebody is speaking. Her eardrums will take time to tune up to the full range of sounds in this new, noisy world. She barely feels the touch of her mother's lips and only a few photons of light from the candle pierce her retina. This protection from full sensory onslaught will last some weeks but a familiarity in the voice does reach her and gives her ease. She lets her eyelids droop and drops into her first sleep in this new world.

Congratulations, Iseult. You are born.

The Phantom, Beauty

... ever pacing on the verge of things,
The phantom, Beauty, in a mist of tears;
While we alone have round us woven woods,
And feel the softness of each other's hand ...

W. B. Yeats, 'Anashuya and Vijaya'

Christmas Eve, 1982
Izzy

Early on Christmas Eve morning, hours before Zach left or Star arrived, my father asked me to kill him.

I'd spent some of that night in a chair at the end of his bed. At one point he woke and started to panic, then, remembering, reached up to push the button that released liquid morphine into his veins. Through half-closed lashes I saw him settle back, his breathing hoarse and loud, a sound like the sea pressing through a blowhole.

'Better,' he said, as the pain relief kicked in. 'That's better.'

His hand went up to press the machine again, but I knew nothing would issue from it so soon. Maybe he believed it had, because he dropped off immediately into a more settled sleep and didn't wake until breakfast time, when I brought him a bowl of mashed banana and yoghurt. His eyes clicked open and he said, in a surprisingly clear voice, 'I need a pill.'

'What about the pump?'

'No, a pill.'

I took the container, a new one, nearly full, from its place on the window and shook a single pill into his hand. He took the glass of water and gulped to swallow, his whole throat working over it. He coughed, then drank again.

'I need more.'

Thinking he meant water, I reached for the jug.

'More pills, I mean.'

I looked at the phial in my hand. 'You can't, you know that.'

He turned his eyes on me. 'Help me. I've had enough of living like this.'

His eyes held on to mine, as only ever once before.

'Please. You'll know what to do.'

'Let the one you've just had take effect. You'll feel better then.'

'There's no better for me.' He put his fingers on my wrist, his grip surprisingly tight and strong. 'Please.'

But the pill was already beginning its work or maybe it was the effort of making the request, of taking my arm, of saying such words. His eyelids began to droop.

'You're a clever girl, always were,' he whispered. 'You'll know what to do.'

His eyes closed on the first compliment he ever gave me.

15

On the night Star was born, I stood at the window of an adobe that her father and I shared with five others at that time, watching the sun radiating purple beams through patches of silver-clouded New Mexico sky. Outside, the earth was palest yellow, the colour of a lion's hair, flat and treeless, naked except for a smattering of sage. Across the plain, Taos Mountain seemed on alert, as if it knew what was happening to me, and in the sky a strange cloud formation filtered the rays, iridescent and full of significance, like direct messages from Above.

Down at the end of the room, circled around our big, communal dining table was ... everybody: our housemates Madeira, Zane, Emma and Jade and Quicksilver, together with Buff and Jalope, who had moved in two days ago and would stay as long as they were needed. We had laid in plenty of food, and they each took turns to cook, except for me. 'Mama Lightning' was excused from all duties except rest.

In the other corner was the child's paddling pool in which I would give birth. Jade, who had been a midwife in her other life and studied underwater birthing in France, was going to help deliver the baby. Zane had borrowed a car, in case anything went wrong. But nothing would, I knew it as sure as I knew that Taos Mountain would not fall down.

For thirty minutes I had been pacing around the long walls of our living room, stopping each time at the big window that faced west, timing my way round so that I'd have my contractions there. Snakeskin – as Brendan called himself now – looked up from his card game each time I passed, to show me he cared. 'You okay, Mama?' he'd ask, and I'd nod, wanting to keep the baby to myself as long as I could.

I was expanded to twice, to ten, to a million times my normal size by pregnancy. I'm not talking about my enlarged belly but inside. I was a fruit, ripe with knowledge. I had become the one the others came to with their problems. Me, Lightning! They called me 'Mama' as a joke but I was changed, we all knew it.

My cramps clutched me again. I struggled to the window, this time making only a pretence at looking out. Thunder clattered in the clouds, and a shriek of lightning tore across the sky. A jackrabbit ran through the sage. In the distance, across the plain, rain started to fall, slant and stretched, the kind the Pueblos call Long Walking Man. We were still bathed in sunlight.

'Sunlight,' I said, turning to the others when my breath returned to me. 'The baby will be called Sunlight.' With a piece of my name in him or her.

Another pain came, too quickly, bending me over. When I looked up again, night was surging across the sky from the east, and Jade was beside me. 'It's started, hasn't it?'

I turned to find Brendan. He was at the table, talking. I waited until he lifted his head so I could connect with his eyes. Only then did I answer her: 'Yes, it's started.'

He got up, smiling that smile of his, hips meandering across the room to me. What a smile that man had. That was all it took for me to feel as if he had just covered us both, me and the baby-to-be, in wild roses.

Yes, yes, I know. Lightning and long rain and wild roses. I know – but back then we didn't care. We were beatniks and proud of it. We lived in a commune and let ourselves say what the wage-slaves feared to think. Our men wore goatees and berets and played bongos, while our women danced in black leotards. We were open, wide open. To peace and sunlight, to sex and drugs and complicated love, to any kind of living that wasn't the kind we deemed a living death.

It was all a long way from Ireland, and it was this edgy, complicated man who had spirited me away. I had known he would the moment I saw him, long before he was Snakeskin, when he was just plain Brendan Creahy of Laragh.

We met in Molina Dancehall, one of those Irish arenas of pleasure thrown up on the side of a road in the middle of nowhere, summoning every young person for miles. Boys on one side, girls on the other, bottles of soda pop – we called them 'minerals' – clenched in our fists, the sweet fizzy liquid sucked through straws. At sixteen I was one of the youngest there. I had sneaked out the window of my cramped bedroom. Looking back, I can't believe my daring.

'If my father catches me, he'll kill me,' I'd said to Pauline, my friend from school.

She took it as a figure of speech, but I was working on a logical extrapolation. Given that being five minutes late home from school could bring on a beating that might last twenty minutes, sneaking out a window to a dance could well be putting my life in danger. I could feel the blows and the form they would take if I were caught. Yet still I went.

Something bigger than our small selves kicks up in adolescence, or in a certain type of adolescent, and, as with all revolution, the firmer the grip, the fiercer the resistance. I cringe to recall the ferocity I brought to those teenage romances of mine. At sixteen I had already experienced a series of them, each blazing through me with its own particular and ridiculous fervour. I'd like to deny half of it, pretend I was never like that, but for me at that time each new male was a potential Him, a funnel for the thoughts and feelings I was not allowed to indulge for their own sake. Later, I would see the same energy seize Star and her friends. Passion's passion for itself.

So there I was, risking I knew not what for the dubious pleasures of Molina Dancehall, my teenage-girl radar scanning the room. Brendan must have felt my burning eyes on him, because he turned, cigarette still in his mouth, to face me, and his eyes, half closed to the rising smoke, popped open. I instantly regretted my clothes, a sleeveless dress covered in big red roses and cinched at the waist with a red belt – it felt far too Sandra Dee to attract a boy like him – but no, it was okay. He was crushing his cigarette underfoot and walking across, the prospect switching on his smile.

Skinny and crevice-skinned even when young, Brendan wasn't the best-looking guy in the world, or even in Molina Dancehall, but, oh, that smile of his. His teeth were white and perfectly aligned, unusual in the Ireland of the time, but it was more than that. The smile changed him, chased all the edgy moodiness out of his face and latched on to you, made you feel like you were what drove the bad times away.

He spun me out on to the dancefloor and pulled me into his arms. Within an hour he was telling me how he hated Wicklow and the whole godforsaken dump of a country we lived in, and I was telling him things about my home life that I had never told Pauline or anyone else. Next day I met him at the end of our lane, where he was waiting on his Honda with two helmets.

He had a motorbike and a leather jacket and a guitar. He taught me how to drink Guinness. He took me on a picnic and fed me food from his hand. He brought me to the cinema and spent the two hours watching me instead of the movie and afterwards told me how he had loved seeing the lights and colours on my face.

I loved how he was astonishing himself with the telling. All the telling. There was nothing we did not tell each other. Or so it seemed at the time. So when – just three months after we danced our first dance – he asked me to go with him, to climb on to the back of his motorbike with all I owned and get out of soggy, miserable Ireland once and for all, I went. He was a poet, he said, a writer of songs. And at that time I was wild for poetry. Really wild, swooning over it in my single bed. It never occurred to me to want to *be* a poet, but secretly I longed to be married to one.

I went because I wanted him and because of the miracle of his wanting me.

I went because I wanted something other than cooking my father's dinner and hanging our clothes and going behind his back for any enjoyment I had and studying for my Leaving Certificate at his kitchen table while he dealt out his complaints about me. *Tea: one shilling and six. Butter: two shillings. Eggs: one and eight. Sausages* ... The cost of feeding me, read out from his parchment-covered notebook.

Brendan – soon to be known as Snakeskin – was my breakout clause, doing for me what I couldn't do for myself.

At my request, the birthing pool was brought over to the window. He and I got naked, except for a tank top over my breasts, and got into the pool. The others formed a 'circle of love' around us, with Zane playing his guitar and the rest singing along, beating hand drums or pots, or rapping spoons. Every so often one of the girls would get up to boil a kettle of water and carefully tip it into the pool to keep us warm.

What Jade had promised me came to pass: I had birth pains but in the water they were bearable: more than bearable – effective, essential. Outside the day faded into darkness, and the stars came out to shine.

'I've changed my mind,' I said to Brendan between two sets of contractions. 'Let's call her Starlight.'

It had been more than a year and a half since we left Doolough, with nothing to our names but his bike and twelve pounds, eight shillings and ninepence. First came a short stint in London, but we quickly gave up on England, where it was so hard to be Irish. We sold the bike and flew to New York. A Brooklyn winter was followed by our best time, when we bought a VW van, painted it up and kitted it out with bed and camper stove and followed the sun down the East Coast, picking up bits of work as we went. Cape Cod. The Carolinas. Sarasota.

Across to New Orleans. Then back to the coast and northwards again, as it grew too hot for our Irish skins. Brendan drew pictures and strummed songs, including some of his own, on his guitar. I wrote poems in a brown, leather-bound notebook he bought me.

Just when we were wondering where we'd go next, we saw a TV programme about the Beats that reported groups of what the TV commentator called beatniks gathering in San Francisco. Our eyes met across the screen. We gave ourselves new names, started to grow our hair and took off. It was a wet afternoon full of plump rain turning to snow when we arrived in Taos, with an introduction to a friend of a friend. We drove up a long dirt road lined with olive trees, as instructed, to be told that the friend was long gone, but that we were welcome anyway, to stop the night.

Almost a year on we were still here.

Sounds were rising in me, unrecognizable as me but unmistakable. Universal, female sounds. My breaths became gasps, my whimpers turned to wailing. Soon all I could hear was my own pulse, my own breathing, my own crying. I became nothing but mother-body: source, vessel, channel, bringer, giver. The rest of me had faded, become a small sharp observer whose observations were puny here.

Jade mopped my brow, Brendan held my hand, Emma brought me drinks of water and glasses of iced tea.

'Not long now. Not long.'

My skin stretched wider than skin can stretch, and I screamed with the searing heat of the rip. The head was through. Then a slither through the soreness and then a cry. Smaller than my cries, faint and fragile. So faint, so fragile, yet everyone in the room turned towards it.

'A girl,' Jade said, with her serene smile.

She placed her on my belly. The baby's eyes were glazed, but she looked at me and I looked at her, both of us astonished. What the look held wasn't of my world but of hers, the world she had more recently left. Brendan was observing us, proud but lost. The outsider, for once, and not liking it.

The cord was cut by somebody, I don't know who, and I pulled her in closer. The rapid rise and fall of her body breath made my insides clench.

'Look,' Jade said. 'She has a birthmark.'

We looked. On the back of her neck, just below a fringe of dark hair lining the base of her skull, was a wine-coloured smudge, about the size of a bean but five-sided. Almost like a star.

Madeira took up her guitar and started to play, a song of Joni Mitchell's, a favourite with us all.*

'You are golden,' I whispered in the baby's ear. 'Stardust.'

---

* Must have been a different song. I was born in 1960, but Joni Mitchell didn't cut her first record until 1968.

16

'AU REVOIR, Mr Lynch.'

'Goodbye, Mr Synge, thank you so much for coming.'

'Mr MacKenna.' Maud inclines her head with grace. 'Until we meet again.'

Observe, Willie thinks to himself as he watches her pass from one of her guests to the next with smiling sympathy, see how the subtle artifice of her beauty leaves each of them feeling elevated by association. Look how Lynch is not happy to leave until he has taken her hand and palpated it, as if it were the handle of a village pump.

He himself is no longer affected by such attentions paid, or indeed denied, to her. In the almost three years that have passed since his last trip to Paris, he has detached himself. Won by the kindness and patience of Mrs Olivia Shakespear, he has had many days of happiness, days that have inoculated him against the old lure. This time he is in Paris not to make love to Maud Gonne but to further their shared mystical endeavours.

'Goodbye . . . goodbye.'

Some more lifting of hats and buttoning of coats and tying of scarves against the winter air and then they are all gone, all except Miss Delaney, now officially the secretary of L'Association Irlandaise, who is still in the dining room, stooped over the big red book she is writing in, greatly conscious of her responsibilities.

Maud Gonne's mood is high and exalted. 'I do believe that went just about as well as we could have hoped.'

All her suggestions were taken up. Gatherings and monster meetings are to be held throughout the coming year in Ireland,

and she will ensure a French presence at each. Funds are to be raised to erect monuments, and she will write notices for the press. They need a sympathetic publication here in France, so she intends to fund and edit one. *L'Irlande libre.*

Her skin is flushed by the plans, and her hair has come a little loose. He turns away from this excitement. It will take all his power to calm her for the real work of their day. A conflagration of the soul of a man and woman leading to a spiritual rebirth: that is what they seek. It is, she has always insisted, the reason they have been brought together, and they are on the point of attaining a revelation. They both feel it trembling just beyond the veil.

His interest in her now is purely in her seership. He cannot influence her outer actions, but he can dominate her inner being and in so doing guide her clairvoyance to produce forms that arise from both minds – though mainly seen by one. He pats the pocket of his jacket, feels the reassuring swell within, the drug that will help them slip into the altered consciousness they need.

The summer before last, while staying in Ireland, he found what she and he had so long been seeking: a site for their Castle of Heroes. A tiny, uninhabited island in the centre of Lough Key, in the county of Roscommon, with a ruined castle at its centre. The roof is sound, the windows intact and there is even a stone platform for meditation. With a little money, it could easily be made habitable.

The work they have been engaged upon since is coming to fruition. That is why he is here in Paris, instead of in his rooms in London with Olivia. (Dear Olivia.)

Miss Delaney is packing books into her bag in her self-conscious way, hoping to be invited to stay. Willie hopes she will not ask him about her writing. Some months ago Maud Gonne gave him stories of hers to read and if possible to place, but he has not tried: he cannot be associated with writing of such deficiency.

She turns his way. 'How do find Paris, Mr Yeats?' she asks in her strong brogue. 'Do you like it?'

Like? What a word for the city where one can spend an entire day with Moreau's chimeras and demon lovers, where Loïe Fuller nightly tantalizes the theatre with her veils, where in cafés and salons everywhere one meets young men of letters who talk naturally of magic . . .

'Mr Yeats thinks he might move here,' says Maud Gonne. 'He thinks only Paris is able for the advanced theatre.'

'Wouldn't we all be delighted?' Miss Delaney says. 'Honoured indeed.'

He bows a small acknowledgement of the compliment. 'Nothing is settled.'

'I agree with you, Barry. He should move. It is not good for an Irish poet to live always in London.'

He wishes she would not talk so to this vulgar woman. At the same time he regrets he cannot offer her simple kindness, as Maud Gonne does so naturally. Why does the struggle to come at truth take away one's pity, and the struggle to overcome one's own passions restore it again?

In this moment, he shrinks from Maud Gonne – as the lover so often does shrink, without understanding why, from the strain of relating to the woman who is always in his thoughts.

But no, he forgets. No longer. Dear Olivia.

Miss Delaney's bag is packed yet still she lingers. When no invitation is proffered, Maud Gonne sees her out. On her return, she says: 'You had no luck placing Delaney's writings?'

How can he tell her that he did not even try, a decision that at the time seemed like the only one possible. Now, in her generous presence, he wonders how he could have failed to do this small thing.

'Oh, I know she is not artistic,' Maud Gonne says, tucking her skirt underneath to sit, a gesture he experiences as both earthy and ethereal. 'But I thought the sensational weirdness of some of them might suit a certain class of not very cultivated people. And it would be doing such a charity to the poor girl.'

'Perhaps it might be kinder not to encourage.'

'I do not think it is our job to *dis*courage, Mr Yeats. Who knows what may come if she is resolute? Why would the gods give Delaney the impulse to write if the world has no use for what she has to say?'

Her monkey peeps at him around the corner of her chair, then scurries behind the pouffe. 'Come here, my little Chappie.' She takes a pistachio nut from the bowl before her on the table and cracks the shell. The monkey snatches it and runs off, with a mistrustful greed that makes them both laugh. Monkeys are degenerate men, Willie thinks, not man's ancestors.

'So,' she says, shrugging off Miss Barry Delaney, her tones reverting to her earlier, mocking lilts. 'Tell me – this news I hear of you from Dublin. Is it true?'

'What news?'

'Taken up, I am told, by the London papers.'

'You speak in riddles.'

'Come now, Mr Yeats. Do not play coy with me.'

'I assure you, I know not –'

'Is it true that you have lately married a widow?'

'Married! If such a thing were true, don't you think you might have heard it first from me?'

She smiles. 'I did think that we were sufficiently friends for you to have told me. But then, on reflection, I thought: perhaps not. Marriage, after all, is only a little detail in life. I said to myself: if he did marry, it would make no difference to his character or life or to our work together. So I began to think it quite possible that you had married and not thought it important enough to report.'

Such bantering on such a topic. Surely this is a mask? She speaks as if he had never proposed that she should share the little kingdom he would make.

'You well know whom I would choose to marry.'

'Come, Mr Yeats, I was only –'

'Oh, Miss Gonne, why do you not give up this tragic declamatory struggle and come sit with me in the kingdom I am making and be its queen?'

'Are you not tired of asking me that question? How often have I said that you and the world would not thank me for marrying you? You make such beautiful poetry out of what you call your love and your unhappiness. Marriage would be a dull affair in comparison.'

He shakes his head vehemently. 'If not for me, do it for Ireland. You have more to offer our country as symbol than as organizer or propagandist.' He leans forward to persuade. 'Ours is the voice of the renaissance that is coming, Miss Gonne. The renaissance of the soul against the intellect.'

'Mr Yeats, please . . .'

She squirms in her seat, but at least he has broken through the teasing mask. She is his again, the only woman who knows all the subtlety of his thought.

'Oh, we will make no more than a beginning, I know that,' he says. 'But centuries after we die, cities will be overthrown because of an anthem we once hummed, or a fabric full of meaning that we hung upon a wall. For that, you will accept me.'

'If you begin to make love to me again, Mr Yeats, I will not be able to see you and that will distress me very much.'

'For that, you will accept a penniless suitor. And for that I will relinquish pure devotion to my magic and to my poetry in order to further your political causes. That is the price we will pay for our happiness.'

'I do not want you to give me such a place in your life.'

'We shall be martyrs together. For pleasure seekers who pay no price are immoral. True lovers are united by their payment to Iseult and Brünnhilde and all the saints of love.'

'Are you listening to me, Mr Yeats? If you find that an absolutely platonic friendship – which is all I can or ever will be able to give – unsettles you and spoils your work, then you must have the strength and courage at once to give up meeting me.'

'Every desire, every joy, has its martyrdom. By that it is uplifted above the world and becomes part of revelation. Miss Gonne, I will do whatever you like, work for any cause you see fit, live as you tell me to live. I should die to serve you and think it happiness.'

She stands. 'Mr Yeats, I am only a commonplace woman,' she says, as though she repeated words she knew by heart. 'And you are, I think, a man of genius. Yet some day I know you will understand what I am telling you. This martyrdom of which you speak is the *very opposite* to that which you are called to make. It is not your work that you are called on to sacrifice, it is me.'

Can it be so? The monkey makes little melancholy cries at the hearthrug. Oh, that clear unwavering voice of hers that bids him what to do, that firm air of decision: is not that part of the gentle mastery that is so much her charm?

When he does not answer her, she says in a gentler voice: 'What is best for your genius, that is what must always be your first consideration. For the honour of our country, the world must recognize you as one of the great poets of the coming century. Your genius belongs to Ireland and you have no right to allow anything to injure it. Not even our friendship.'

If he could but prove himself to her by putting his hand in the fire until it burnt, would not that make her understand that devotion such as his was not to be wasted? The flames flicker and lick at the chimney, and he thinks to do it but does not, held back not by the fear of pain but the fear of being thought mad.

Is he mad?

'Do you understand me, Mr Yeats?'

Yes, he understands. Like Lancelot, he must love his queen to the last. 'If you do not love me now,' he says, 'you will come

137

to love me in time. A love as great as mine must have some meaning.'

To his dismay, she laughs.

'Oh, come,' she says, and crosses towards the cupboard with purpose. 'Let us put talk of love aside. Let us begin the work.'

Outside, Paris is winding down from the enjoyment of its gayest holiday, *le jour de l'an*, the first day of the year. Since morning, the toyshops, the flower-shops and the four rival princes of the bon-bon trade – Siraudin, Boissier, Guerre and Jullien – have been open for business, but now, as daylight begins to dim, their bustle has slowed. Darkness seeps from the unlit corners of streets and alleyways, and along the arc of the Seine the breath of dusk rises, ruffling the blackening waters.

In *le jardin zoologique*, the animals are being fed their evening meal, giving pause to visitors who were in the act of leaving. Near the western exit, on the path in front of the aviary, a little girl is bent over the lawn. She knows nothing of feeding time. Whatever she sees among the blades of grass has all her attention.

'Iseult, please,' her father says again, from twenty paces ahead, but she does not lift her head.

He knows that even if she did, her eyes would wear that dark expression he finds so unnerving. Do all children of this age look so cognizant? He does not remember it, with Henri. Certainly not all two-and-a-half-year-olds are so *stubborn*. The lengthiest days of provocative debate at the Chambre have not tried him as has this one day with his daughter.

When Maud dropped the girl over to him – a crisis provoked by some visitors from Ireland and Ghénia de Sainte-Croix suddenly becoming unavailable – he had thought he should quite enjoy the experience of a day with her. He has been very busy of late and had not seen her for some weeks. And at first, yes, it was a pleasure, walking with her small hand in his past the wine shops and the cab stands and tobacco bureaux, accepting cheery good wishes: '*Je vous le souhait bon et heureux.*' A child brings out the best in people, and she is an exceptionally beautiful child.

In the chocolatier's, as he lifted her up into his arms so she could point to her choice of bon-bon, the fat feel of her legs against his hands and the excited beauty of her face and the sweet smell in the shop and her arms around his neck – all welled in him, taking him by surprise. So much so that when the shopkeeper said, '*Ah, monsieur, quelle belle,*' with the sincerest admiration, he had to dip his head to hide his face in her hair. (With every passing year, it seems he grows more sentimental.)

Marrons glacés, she chose, and when she asked that Tassie too might have some – Tassie being that ridiculous rag doll she insisted on carrying everywhere – he shared the shopkeeper's smiles and indulged her without wincing at the price (seven francs to the pound!). He set her gently to the floor, and, when he handed her the two glazed-paper cornets and she looked up at him through her silky lashes with a gaze of unadulterated adoration, her arms full of her beloved Tassie and the bon-bons, he felt himself well rewarded.

All most gratifying.

But then began the trouble. She wanted to eat them there, instead of at the zoo, and when he declined his permission for this, what a tantrum! 'Tassie want bon-bons *now*!'

He had to secrete the cornets into the inner pocket of his jacket, which very much ruined the line. She would not be calmed, and before they had gone a hundred paces her tantrum was attracting such attention from passers-by, and he so feared a sticky mess on his best grey wool, that he ended by giving them to her after all.

It was the first of many such noes throughout the day. Did Henri ever behave in this tiresome fashion? Lucien thinks not: Madame Millevoye would not have permitted it. Maud is too lax, that is the problem, and the result is that Iseult is a perfect little savage, giving in to every impulse.

Now, he takes out his watch to check the time. Almost 4.15. It seems as if he has been for ever on this path, trying to leave this wretched place. He cannot stand this dawdling, it makes his legs ache, but she will not let him carry her.

He walks back towards her. 'Iseult, we must hurry. The gates will be closed and we shall be locked in. All night.'

'Oh, yes!' She claps her hands. 'That is good, Papon.'

'No, it is not, my dear. The night would be dark and cold, and the big bear would come out and eat us.'

The darkness glows in her eyes. 'Bear in cage.'

'Not at night. At night all the animals come out. And if they find a little girl still left in here, they will eat her up. Now come on.'

Once again he turns and walks, but this time with only a half-hope that she will follow. Sure enough, when he looks back, she is bent, rapt, over the grass. She calls him. 'Look, Papon.'

'We have no time.'

'Papon, look.'

'Truly Iseult, I must insist –'

'Papon! Looooooooook.'

'Oh, for goodness' sake, what? What is it?'

He returns to her and looks at what lies beyond the little pointing finger. He can see only a bug. Black. Hard-shelled. *Un cafard*, a cockroach.

'Leave that, Iseult. It's not nice.'

'Iseult look Papon.'

What she means is that she has made him look. This afternoon he has become more accustomed to her lingo. 'All right. Very nice. Now let us *please* go.'

'No.'

No again. Must everything today be 'No!' and 'Look!' and 'Don't want to!' in that bossy tone so reminiscent of her mother's? The cockroach is suddenly forgotten and an ordinary leaf on an ordinary bush has all her attention as she shows it to her rag of a doll, stroking its surface. All the monkeys, lions and giraffes put together are no more to her than this leaf she is caressing.

Lucien walks slowly on, hoping she will follow, past the aviary and up towards the caged tiger. In front of the rust-wired cage, he stops to lament magnificence confined. Even in the gathering gloom, the glory of the beast's striped limbs is manifest. This zoo in the *Jardin des Plantes* – the world's first to be opened to the public rather than kept as the private plaything of an aristocrat – was intended to be a zoological Louvre, stocked with creatures seized from Europe and beyond by the Revolutionary armies, its exhibits displayed in cages scattered among Rousseauesque parkland designed to imitate what Parisians call *le nature*. In actuality, it is a disgrace, cramped and unclean. The terrarium smells like an open sewer, and far too many of the cages are too small. He counts the tiger's paces: one-two-three-four-five-six . . . Only seven paces before it has to turn to walk in the opposite direction. One more than the polar bear he observed earlier.

Lucien is one of a group of reformers who has put pressure on the zoo's committee to make improvements. It is one of the reasons he thought to bring Iseult here today, to check on progress. True liberty is, of course, impossible to grant to the animals, but some of the buildings and parts of the park have been modified to give to visitors an impression of freedom. It is too little and for the wrong reasons – the managers are moved less by reforming instincts than by the falling levels of visitors to their facility.

He looks back. His daughter has not moved one step, still focused on the grass, dark hair falling forward. 'Come along, my dear.' How can she remain so unmoved by the sights around her? He had thought she would love it here, but he might as well have brought her to the local park. Is it that she is too young? Or too like her mother, who, though she claims to be such an animal lover, responded to his campaign by saying that many a Dublin tenement family – not to mention the denizens of the prisons and workhouses and lunatic asylums – would be happy to be confined in quarters as roomy as the tiger pen at *le jardin zoologique*.

'Come, Iseult. Come now.'

Iseult doesn't want to walk. She is tired, though she doesn't yet know herself well enough to identify the sticky fatigue that has stopped her in her tracks. In her short and inward-pointing life, no experience has happened regularly enough or lasted long enough to be held and named. Fatigue, hunger, pain, pleasure are sensations that rise in her like winds through the grass. So it is not she who cries, it is sadness; not she who stamps her foot and refuses to budge, but frustration. The sticky drag of feeling won't let her walk. Her head is marshmallow, and all the animal names Papon gave her knock about inside it, making it hurt. If she had a tower of bricks in front of her now, she would kick them right over, though she doesn't know why.

She holds up Tassie to show her a bush that looks like the one outside the grove of wonder in Passy Park. Tassie looks at the leaf, and Iseult takes it in her fingers to show her how it feels. 'Furry,' she whispers into her ear. The feel reminds her of Lulu, the cat. As she whispers, Tassie jerks, then flies up into the air, like an arrow from a bow.

'Tassie!'

'Stop that noise, silly girl. Look, dolly is leaving. Come along. Follow dolly.'

'Tas-siiiie!' Iseult screams, then screams again louder, and Tassie's face returns, looming large and close against Iseult's own, her stitch smile glad to be back. Iseult reaches for her but again she jerks away.

'Dolly wants you to follow her, Iseult.'

'No! Papon! Tass-ie!'

'Come and get her, here she is ... Phew! I do believe the thing smells. Come ... Here she is. She wants you.'

Iseult cannot run after her. Gluey tiredness has her sealed in place. She starts to scream. 'No-ooooo!' The noise she makes frightens her, and she howls louder.

'Stop it at once, you naughty girl. Your dolly is here. You are to come to her.'

'No!' Iseult screams again. 'Me-eeee want Tassi-eeeeeee!'

'Stop. Here is your stupid doll. Stop it at once!'

Tassie is back. Iseult clutches her tight. Poor Tassie is crying too.

Papon's face comes down to hers. 'Iseult, please. You must come. For Papon.'

Tassie says no. Tassie says Papon is bad.

'Iseult, I am warning you now. I shall have to smack you. I do not want to smack you.'

He grabs her hand, begins to drag her along.

Tassie starts to scream, and Iseult copies her. 'Aaaaaeeeeeek!'

'Stop it, you wicked child.'

Her hand is being grasped, turned over. A smack lands, sharp and stinging. Pain and shock stops her scream. Another smack, harder. Her breath constricts. Then a third.

Iseult has never been smacked before. She finds her breath and begins to sob.

'A ... mour,' she sobs, cradling her injured hand in her armpit.

'Enough,' hisses Lucien. The release of physical punishment has only added shame to the cocktail of feelings that assails him.

'Amour ... Iseult ... want ... Am ... our.' She starts to raise her voice again. 'AMOUR! AHHH- MOUR!'

The girl is impossible. Maud has asked him to keep her for the entire evening, until Ghénia returns to collect her, but how can he?

'Come now, Iseult. No more nonsense.'

She crouches, her face puckered like a pug dog's, theatrical

143

sobs shaking her body. Very well, then: he picks her up. 'We shall see, my little *anarchiste*, who is the person in charge here.'

She begins to kick. 'AHHH- MOUR!'

He tightens his grasp.

'Papon, NO! My LEG! You hurt LEG.'

'Why do you scream so, Iseult? Am I not doing what you asked? Am I not taking you to your precious Amour?'

17

Maud draws the blue velvet curtains across the darkness pressing against the windows, puts out the monkey and the hound, and draws together the double doors to the dining room, closing out the sound of the birds twittering in their cages. She places swathes of blue chiffon over the lamps, turning the light violet, for it is known that spirits materialize more effectively in light that is at the blue end of the spectrum. (Did not the Celtic races meet their dead in the black-blue of November night?)

From a cupboard, she takes a bottle of Newgrange river-water and, while Willie lights incense, sprinkles its purifying essence on the furniture and into the air with her fingers. Then they distribute the consecrated implements that will help them to crystallize the astral plane around the room: a mirror, Enochian squares, a pyramid, diagrams of the elemental forces called tattvas . . .

The room set, Maud takes down cigarette papers and tobacco from a box on a high shelf and places them on the coffee table, then sits cross-legged and straight backed on the floor near his chair. It makes her a little stiff, but she likes the careless feel of the floor, and Willie likes her to sit so, beneath him, looking up. Today she is happy to give him that small pleasure. Maud believes the male admiration that is always, copiously, hers to be contingent, serving some need of the admirer; but to spurn the admiration would be ill mannered. And short-sighted. It takes so little to keep a man connected: an agreeable smile here, a well-chosen whisper there. Such regard can be a resource to draw on; she has furthered more than one cause on its reserve.

Willie Yeats is different: not predatory man but confused boy. His childlike and troubled soul leads him to be shy in manner, gauche in his lovemaking and odd in his ways, but is also what makes him a great poet. He will be great, of that she is sure: already, aged only thirty-one with, she believes, his best work yet before him, much is being made of his genius. And *she* is his muse. Through him, she is being immortalized. This would be heady, except that she never recognizes herself in his depictions. His poems about her are often a disappointment. That one he wrote of her dying in a strange land and the peasants nailing boards above her face: how offended he had been when she laughed! But she couldn't help it, because it is so obviously not about her at all but about what he likes to call his old high way of love.

It is when his strange fervour for her is merged with their desire to isolate and liberate the Irish national spirit that he writes his best work: 'Red Hanrahan's Song', 'The Secret Rose', 'The Two Trees'. Their intricate weave has a power that she cannot begin to unravel – she does not even try. She never spends time analysing such things; but, though she does not fully understand it, she knows it to be profound and good and intensely beautiful. Something of which she wants to be part.

He is sifting the tobacco evenly along the length of the cigarette paper with his long fingers. His fingers are beautiful, she has noticed that before. He strikes the match, lighting a corner of the lump of resin, and her nostrils fill with the sweet hashish scent. Once the resin has cooled enough to touch, he breaks away some crumbs and scatters them through the tobacco. Carefully, he lifts the open paper and begins to roll it around the tobacco to form a cigarette. With small flicks of a pink tongue, he licks the edge, moistening the gum. A twist on top, a small piece of board to stiffen the base, and it is complete.

He hands it to her, strikes another match, and she leans into the flame. She draws deep to keep it alight: one inhalation, down into her lungs. A second, then a third, and she hands it back to him. He closes his eyes. Why, he is wearing precisely the exact expression that her pious Aunt Judith makes at Holy Communion. He is indulging in the ecstasy of putting his lips where hers have been. This is why he suggested they should smoke the drug this time – not just because his friend Arthur Symons had declared it a more efficient mode of getting it into the bloodstream, but so they might share it, mouth upon vestige of mouth.

Today he seems especially desperate. Perhaps she is wrong to treat his love so lightly. He wouldn't do anything foolish, would he? Sometimes he has a strange look of his mother, that poor woman whom she saw only once in his home at Bedford Park. Sitting in a room with that family had been unforgettably poignant: the charming, talkative father offering his many opinions, the two polite and dull sisters, and, in the corner, the silent, black-clad, downcast invalid, ignored by all. Especially ignored by the intense, arm-waving son who looked most like her.

She has never spoken to him of this, but he suffers, she knows that. And she knows what it is to suffer. He has always been a good friend to her. She wants to be a good friend to him.

Her thoughts are disintegrating. It is the effect of the drug. The flowers on the wallpaper appear to stand out from the wall as if one could go over and cup them in one's hands, and smell a fragrance. Hashish is such a strange drug, making every object seem more complete in itself and simultaneously more connected to oneself.

They take a last moment of close-eyed silence before donning their robes, then, standing together on the hearth, they recite the words of the Banishing Ritual, to clear the space of all disturbing influences, including the personal emotions of the mundane personalities known as William Yeats and Maud Gonne.

She reclines upon the *chaise*, and he takes across one of the dining chairs and sits beside her, inches from her head.

'You are disturbed?' he asks. Her trances are often preceded by a moment of nausea or giddiness.

'No.'

'Ready to proceed?'

She inclines her head.

He places a fire wand in her hand to help focus her will and clarify their intention, and holds up a black-painted square of card. She gazes at the card, concentrating on the symbol, transferring the vital effort from the optic nerve to the mental perception, from eye-seeing to thought-seeing, letting one form of apprehension glide into the other. Her every movement now has symbolic meaning, of which she is fully conscious. Now, while manipulating an object in the physical plane, her God-form may be manipulating an entirely different force in the astral plane.

She hears him vibrate a word. *The* word, the Divine Name, Elohim. Inhaling deeply, she pronounces the name after him, silently first in her heart, conjuring up the white brilliance of the sephira Kether from the top of the Tree of Life. She sees each letter of the word written in brilliant white light. Then she speaks aloud, breathing forth the name strongly, sending it from her on a breath to vibrate throughout the entire universe.

He repeats the vibration. Elohim. As she breathes forth the word in repetition, she creates an image in her mind that goes with each letter of the name. From the sound of her own voice vibrating in her ear, she knows her sensations are intensifying. In this creation, she is neither the manipulator nor the passive receiver of visions but something between the two. In this state of balance, insight and judgement flow.

Willie begins to invoke Midir, one of the Kings of Fairy, in his mellow, musical Irish voice: 'Midir, Master of the Fairies, I invoke you . . . Midir, husband of Étaín, I invoke you . . . Midir, sweller at Bri Leath, I invoke you . . .' His tones rise and fall in a continuous flow of sound, lingering on some words, as if to avoid a hiatus. 'Midir, the clearer away of the stone out of Meath, I invoke you . . . Midir, builder of the way in the bog, I invoke you.'

Now he pauses, with deliberation, the invocation hovering in a silence still full of sound.

He says, 'Picture a square of yellow; perhaps it might be a door.'

The picture comes easily to her. All is clear and radiant. She feels ineffably well.

'Walk through it,' he says. 'Tell me what you see beyond.'

'I see a well, in a garden. Leaning over the well on the left is a mountain-ash tree, laden with red berries. They keep dropping, dropping into the water, like drops of blood reddening the pool.'

'Are you alone?'

'No. Midir is here.'

'How does he look?'

'He is calm. He shows me interlocking circles.'

'How many are your circles?'

'Three of each. Three interlocking circles of Heaven, my way to peace. And three of Hell. Midir is telling me that I am in Hell, but that some day I will be able to enter the three heavenly circles, though now I cannot.'

'And what do you see within them?'

'The first is a garden. The circle of almost fulfilled desire.' It is no effort now to see, all is bathed in light. The garden is very beautiful, with butterflies and bees, exotic and elegant flowers. As she focuses upon it, already it is fading into the second circle. Midir leads her on, and she is his willing vassal.

'The second is a place in a wood with a fallen tree. It is quiet, the place of peace eternal. This, Midir says, is very brief for any human soul.'

She can hear the scratching of Willie's pen on paper writing down what she sees. Near her ear but a long way off.

After a time he says: 'And the third?'

'A mountain with a winding road and a cross.' She pauses. 'The circle of labour from divine love.'

'And what of the hellish circles?' he asks.

The moment he says this, the light switches to dark grey. It is not night but the kind of light that precedes a great thunderstorm. Water swells. 'I see an ocean, a dark ocean, with hands of drowning men rising out of it.'

Her voice has changed and her body – she is still aware of it on the *chaise* while her soul takes this journey – begins to feel cold. 'This is the circle of unfulfilled desire. I can see a great precipice with dragons trying in vain to climb it – a continual climbing and falling.'

She would rather not go on. She knows she must.

'And again, the third circle?'

She has an urge to cry: 'A vast emptiness.' She can hear her own anguish forming the words. 'The falling petals of a torn rose.'

'What is this circle?'

'This is the circle of revenge.'

Silence falls, except for the scraping of the pen.

Midir leaves the circle of revenge and takes her along a path, towards a sprinkling of lights. Along the way, he hands her over to another, an old man with a long grey beard, who points the way to a castle on a hill. 'There is a castle and a wizard who –'

Ring, ring, ring! This is a sound from the outer world, not the inner. Her doorbell. The mind picture vanishes as she is snapped back to the material plane. She knows that signature ring.

'Somebody . . .' she says, jumping up. 'The door . . . Mr Yeats!'

'Miss Gonne, please. Do not strain yourself . . . Cannot Josephine take care of whoever it is?'

'No, quickly, get up . . .' She is throwing off her robe, rolling it into a ball, stuffing it under the chair. 'Please . . . help me set this place to rights. I think it is . . . It could be some of our Irish friends returned.'

She is almost running now to the door, snatching the blue cloth from the lamp as she goes.

A voice calls from the hallway. 'Maud? *Est-ce que tu là?*'

'*Ple-e-e-ase,*' she hisses back, opening the door only wide enough to slip through. 'Take off your robe. And get rid of what is on the table. Stick it into the box.'

'But –'

'I *beg* of you.'

The voice comes again: 'Maud?'

'Who is it?' asks the poet, getting up but oh so – slowly.

'I have no idea.'

She is gone.

It is not good for her to throw off her trance so quickly. He himself feels faint. He removes his robe, sweeps up the loose tobacco with his hands, throws it in the fire and puts the paraphernalia away in its box.

Voices in the hall grow louder. Is that a child he hears? Certainly he hears a male voice. And now hers, a furious whisper.

By the time they come in, the room has reverted to order. She and a tall Frenchman stand in the doorway, reflected in the mirror opposite, so that at first, to his dream-and-drug-befuddled mind, it is as if there are two couples, not one.

'Mr Yeats,' says Maud, leading the fellow in. 'You remember Monsieur Millevoye?'

The Boulangist journalist. A sensationalist. His name is one of those linked to hers by malicious gossip, gossip that has stirred a poem in him. It is as yet unwritten, but one line keeps recurring: *Their children's children shall say they have lied.*

'And you remember Mr Yeats?'

'Indeed.' The hand the Frenchman proffers is lax, almost greasy. He has the Gallic arrogance: his bow is conventional but somehow manages to be antagonistic too.

Frustration burns. Their work shall not resume tonight. Is this to be his life always, this endless preparation for something that never happens?

'We are just about to take tea, Mr Millevoye. You will join us?'

'Alas, I need to leave. I am here only to deliver Iseult.'

Maud looks about her. 'Where is Iseult?'

The Frenchman too looks behind. 'She was here a moment ago.'

Maud goes to the door. 'Iseult . . .' calls Maud. 'Are you there?'

A small bundle of energy charges in from the hallway and flings itself at Maud's legs. '*Amour.*'

'There, my little one. Why all the fuss?' Maud crouches down, so she is level with the child's face. This is a new mask. 'Did you have a nice time?'

'*J'ai vu un singe.*'

'A monkey? You mean Chap?'

'*Grand singe. Beaucoup des singes.*'

'The zoological gardens,' says Millevoye.

'How lovely. Now, Iseult, where are your manners?' She pulls the folds of her skirt out of the child's grasp. 'Come out of there and say *bonjour* to our guest.'

The girl peeps, suspicious. How should he address her? 'How do you do?' he attempts, holding out his hand. She disappears back into the skirts.

'Don't be shy, darling. Mr Yeats will think you most impolite.'

'Oh, no, I assure you. Assuredly not.'

'She is tired, are you not, my sweet?'

Maud whispers a long string of words into the small ear. Whatever she says makes the girl disengage herself and walk across to him with hand outstretched. '*Bonsoir, Monsieur Yeats,*' she says.

'*Bonsoir, mademoiselle,*' he replies, self-conscious of his deplorable accent.

Millevoye coughs. 'I must leave; I am already late.'

'Certainly, do not let us detain you,' says Maud.

Willie likes the edge he hears in her tone.

Goodbyes are made, and she leads the interloper out. The

child remains behind and is looking up at him, as if for guidance. Her eyes seem almost too large for her small head to hold. From the hallway comes an animated exchange in French that is somehow depressing.

'What age are you?' he asks the girl, in an attempt to be friendly.

'AMOUR!' she calls, turning towards the door. Even he, with his atrocious French, understands that word. What a strange moniker for her to give Maud Gonne. She follows her amour out to the hall, leaving him with his shame, struck once again by his accursed timidity, this quality of his that is so painful to experience. Timid with a child. Pitiful!

The hall door closes. Maud returns with the child in her arms. 'Mr Millevoye let himself in with Ghénia's key,' she says.

He feels an answer is required of him but what?

The child squirms in Maud's arms, much as the monkey did earlier. 'Bon-bon, Amour. Tu *dit*.'

'Yes, my little one. You shall have your bon-bon.' She sets her down and puts her hand in her skirt pocket. 'Now hold out your hands like a good girl.'

Yeats watches. He has seen her gay beneficence with the urchins of Dublin and London for whom she always has coppers or some fruit or nuts, but this is something else. All the child's self leans into those two greedy, grasping hands. Maud places a sweet in each: '*Un, deux* . . .', then another: '*trois* . . . quatre*. Now, go across to the table and when you have eaten them, you must go to bed as you promised.'

The child nods, crosses to the table and climbs up on to the chair. She sits with her back to them, her dark hair hanging down. Maud returns to the chair opposite him, drops her voice to a whisper. 'Her mother is a young girl to whom the world has not been kind.'

'When is the world ever kind?'

'Ghénia and I have taken pity on the little girl. I am thinking I might adopt her.'

153

The suggestion alarms him, yet he equivocates. 'A generous gesture.'

She smiles one of her beatific smiles. Yes, he has pleased her. One never quite knows what will please her.

'Adoption is much more common here in France than in England. The Civil Code allows a man to adopt as his heir any person who has saved his life, for example.'

'But would you not be concerned that such an arrangement might limit your freedom?'

'I should hire a nursemaid. Or make use of one of the convents; they are very willing to take in young girls for financial reimbursement.'

He nods, slowly.

'I sense you do not approve. I hope it is not for any reasons of false morality. These things happen in life, do they not? Are we to waste our time in condemnations? Why should this little one suffer for the sins of her father?'

'And her mother.'

'Her mother was only a young girl, too young to be condemned. But the man was a great deal older and married. But stop . . . I see you are shocked, none the less. You who are so indulgent of the far greater vices of your London men friends.'

'No, no. Not shocked.'

'What then?'

'A little . . . concerned, perhaps.' He waves his hands before him, helplessly. Something is slipping from him here, along with his hopes.

'Such double standards. Do you feel it is right that the woman should suffer so much more than the man in these matters, Mr Yeats?'

'Miss Gonne, I assure you, I did not mean to be in any way . . . My concern is only that you should not encumber yourself with a situation that is detrimental to your work.'

'You know my work will always come first, Mr Yeats. It was unfortunate that we were interrupted tonight, but we can resume. Once Iseult is in bed, she falls immediately to sleep and doesn't waken. She will not disturb us.'

Can she be serious? Can she really think the force of their work will be unaffected by the child's presence?

She has turned from him. 'Come, my little one. Time for bed. You are tired, *ma petite chérie*, are you not? *Dit bonne nuit.*'

The girl appraises him with dark eyes. '*Bonne nuit.*'

'Good night, my dear.'

Maud points to the sideboard, the decanter. 'Help yourself to refreshments; I shall return.'

As she is leaving the room, he calls her back. 'Miss Gonne?'

She turns, the child's hand in hers, and the smaller head turns too, eerily echoing her expression.

'Your vision . . . earlier . . . Did you see colour?'

'Why, yes.'

'Good,' he says, nodding. 'Good. The visions that come in colour are true.'

18

The world was back to work. I had a lawyer, a no-nonsense woman called Mags Halloran, hired the Irish way, through someone Pauline knew who knew someone who knew someone else . . . Mags was the only girl in a farming family of seven whose widowed mother had struggled and saved to put them all through college. Each year in August, three of them took a week off their high-powered city jobs in Dublin or London or New York to go home to Tipperary to help save the hay. This was the robust approach Mags took into the milieu of Dublin law, where she was known as 'a character'.

Short and squat, she wore calf-length skirts, flesh-coloured tights and flat shoes of the kind usually preferred by women twenty years older. Her dull-white blouses gaped under the bust, exposing dull-white flesh. I never met a woman who made less attempt to be attractive. Mags liked to be underestimated.

My case worried her from the beginning. She came to Doolough Barracks and sat opposite me at the table in the day room to explain that I might not get bail. The serious nature of my alleged crime, the strength of the circumstantial evidence, and the location of my home and business in another jurisdiction – all these were against me.

'Anything in my favour?'

'You tell me. Any previous?'

'Of course not.'

'So we'll go with good character, respectable, unlikely to offend again, yadda, yadda . . . They'll want a substantial surety, though. *If* they go for it.'

'If?'

'Not going to lie to you, Dotes.' Mags called everybody Dotes. 'We're fifty-fifty at best.'

'And if not? I'll have to stay here in the barracks until the trial?'

'More likely to relocate you to Mountjoy, I'd say.'

'What sadist decided to name a prison Mount*joy*?'

She shrugged. 'A more pressing question. Do you have the funds for bail? And for legal fees?'

'How much is it likely to be?'

She named the amount.

'You're joking.'

''Fraid not. They're going to want to be sure that you're not going to go skipadeedoo back to the States. And of course,' – this with a cheeky grin – 'the services of a good lawyer never come cheap.'

Months later, after it was all over, I wondered I *didn't* go skipadeedoo. It seems to me now that nobody would have cared, except perhaps Dr Keane. Not the Irish justice system. They knew that I was no danger to society.

Mags had brought a copy of the *Wicklow Gazette* to the barracks. I was their front-page story. MERCY KILLING? ran the headline and below, in smaller type, RETURNED EMIGRANT ACCUSED OF MURDER with a news story on page one and a large feature profile inside, complete with a photograph of me in my convent-school uniform. The reporter had talked to the police, who said an arrest had been made, to old schoolfriends, who said they just couldn't believe it, to a neighbour, who said I'd been estranged from my father for years before coming back a few months ago, to Dr Keane, who said he was confident justice would be done – to everybody except Pauline or Star or Zach or me, the people who were in the house that day.

'Could have been worse,' Mags said. 'They're going with the mercy angle. That's good.'

'Why? Why is that good?'

'We may need to use that ourselves.'

'I didn't do it,' I said.

'Right. Let's get you filling in these forms, then.'

She took them away with her. Eight days later I was climbing into the back of the Garda Ford Sierra on my way to Dublin. We arrived at the Four Courts to a glut of reporters huddled around the entrance. Beneath the roofline statues of Justice, Mercy, Authority and Wisdom they stood waiting, notebooks and pens, cameras and microphones at the ready.

'Your waiting party,' said Inspector O'Neill.

I shivered. I was wearing my most respectable outfit, as instructed by Mags, a brown linen suit, but it was too light for the Irish winter.

'Do you want me to try round the back?' Garda Cogley asked. The Inspector nodded, and Cogley swung the van through some narrow back streets, then pulled in by the kerb and got out to tap on a steel door. A guard opened it a crack, listened to him, looked across at me in the car.

'Okay,' Garda Cogley said. 'We're in.'

We were led through a warren of back rooms, and Mags was waiting for us outside Court Two as arranged. She led me through, her hand on my elbow. Pauline had come to the rescue again on bail, her bank manager cousin arranging a mortgage on my father's house and farm, and, after a twenty-minute sitting, bail was granted on condition that I surrendered my passport.

We tried the back way out again but this time we were refused. 'Prepare yourself, Dotes,' Mags said, as we walked down the long, narrow corridor that led to the round hall and the front door. 'They'll be out in force by now.' She was loving the whole thing, stomping up the corridor in her tough-cookie shoes, steering me through, her hand on my elbow, as the cameras flashed and the questions were thrown our way, like the barking of dogs: 'Is the trial date set?' 'Did you get bail?' 'What are your plans?' One of them called, 'Did you do it?'

(Could he really have expected to me to turn around and say, 'Well, yes, actually, I did'?) Some of the questions were for Mags. 'Did she get bail?' 'What's the plea?'

As we pushed through, they moved with us, all together like a multi-headed animal. Mags had her keys ready – these were the days before automatic locking – and as soon as she was in the car, she leant across and opened the passenger door for me but not before they had come crowding round, popping questions like toy machine guns. They pressed their faces to the windows, but it all had a forced feel, a going through the motions of what they felt they should be doing, or what they had seen journalists do in movies.

Mags revved the engine, not too gently, and they parted easily to let us through.

I took the 1.30 train back to Rathdrum and a cab back to Doolough. What I would have liked to have done, if I were free to, was sell my father's house. Not so much for the money as for the activity. Fixing it up, dealing with estate agents, the coming and going of potential buyers would have filled my days, but my bail conditions meant I had to remain, with only my writing as distraction.

As I walked from the cab to the front door, the windows looked down on me from under their fringe of eaves. Had anyone who'd lived in this house ever been happy, I wondered as I approached. Had groups of children ever played here, giggled and done tricks on each other? I couldn't imagine it, but maybe the lack was in me.

I went in the back door, into the kitchen. A blast of warmth from the Aga greeted me. The house was back in order, the broken furniture chopped for wood, all the rooms cleaned and vacuumed and polished. The kitchen seemed bare, since we had cleared it of my father's medicines and water bottles, but he was still there. Part of him would remain, for ever unburied.

I picked up the kettle. I would have a cup of tea. My mother's drink. My father drank coffee, a relic of his years in France, but tea was Mother's 'pick-me-up' between her endless chores. My mother tackled her work in the same way that she went at her prayers, steadily ticking off the tasks, just as she pushed each bead of the rosary through her fingers, all the way round till she was back where she had begun, only to start over again. Between each chore, like the little chains between the beads, were endless cups of tea.

How that woman loved to clean. The regimen she imposed on this house while she was alive would be considered an obsessive-compulsive disorder today, but in the 1950s it was commonplace. The oak kitchen table on which I was now laying a cup and saucer scrubbed three times a day. The oven and all its racks cleaned down and polished after every use. The undersides and insides of everything as pristine as the sides that were up or out. Nothing gave my mother more pleasure than the sight of Sunday's joint well roasted on a serving plate, surrounded by its subordinate dishes of vegetables and gravy and two kinds of potatoes. Except perhaps Monday evening's ironing stack – sheets and pillow cases and tea towels end to end, corner to corner – admired from across the rim of a nice cup of tea.

When I was younger, I feared this domesticity and all it stood for. After she died, my father and I lived in relative squalor. I did what had to be done, but I never gave myself over to the tasks, not until much later in life, when I came round to appreciating the virtues, the life-saving properties, of cleanliness and order. It took me until then to see my mother's housework for what it was – an expression of herself and her love.

Now my domestic routine, my entire routine, was slipping again. I knew I should stick to what Zach had taught me, what worked so well for me before. Eat and sleep well, balance work with play, meditate and walk, keep my environment ordered . . . but instead I found myself leaving the dishes in the sink, neglecting to hoover or dust and staying home, because going for a walk was like stepping on to a stage. All eyes were on me. I was the most exciting thing to happen in Doolough since the Civil War, when a shoot-out left a local man dead. The closest they'd got to murder since.

Not that anybody actually said so. It was all in the looks or the avoidance of looking.

I could hear Zach's voice telling me I was resisting what was good for me and I knew that was right. I was undereating and overworking, neglecting everything that was good for me. Except writing. All I could do was write.

Each day, I was alone in my father's house. Each morning, I went to his bathroom upstairs and took off my clothes and stepped into the same tub I used as a girl. Heard the same water gush from the taps, saw the same grey-green light falling in through the opaque glass. As I turned off the water and picked up the soap to circle it under my arms, between my legs, over my body, as I slid down to rinse off, as I felt the water close over my face, was it any wonder that it was a necessity, an imperative, for me to fill my head with things that happened to somebody else, somewhere far away?

19

Is it not the most splendid sight, Paris Opera, before curtain up? The men are all alike, so many penguins in their black suits and stiff white collars, but the women . . . Snow-white arms and shoulders rising from laces and satins and velvets in green or violet and carmine, cut to accentuate their curves. Hair piled and combed and smoothed away from the forehead, worn like a crown. Diamonds and pearls, opals or rubies or garnets, in loops or stars or butterflies trembling on wrists and throats and bosom corsages. Fans, purses and opera glasses held like garlands. Finery fine enough to rival the gilded stage and boxes and the arch of the vaulted ceiling.

Ghénia de la Sainte-Croix, recently married and now known as Madame Avril, sits in one of the largest boxes beside her dear friend Maud Gonne. Together they observe and comment on the sea of people below. Ghénia's frock is butter-yellow, her lightest silk, for it is a warm night, the warmest of the summer so far, and Maud looks splendid in a low-cut gown of deepest jade-blue, the fabric catching the glow of the gaslights as she twists and turns. Lucien leans over the balcony and calls down to his friend Romaine below. A coarse sound. They had earlier had to pull him away from the wine.

Maud feels Ghénia's attention upon her and smiles. 'I cannot wait to see Bréval,' she says, picking up her opera glasses. Wagner is Maud's favourite composer, and *La Walkyrie* her favourite of his works. 'A pity our Irish friends missed this treat.'

Such great efforts Maud made for these visitors from Ireland, who seem, to Ghénia, a little shoddy. None the less, she is glad to have met them: they have helped her to better understand her dear, complicated friend. Mrs Wyse Power, the most charming of the delegates, told her the truth about the national centenary celebrations in Dublin. Maud had not been invited to be on the platform, even after all her devotion to the nationalist cause. Little Mrs Wyse Power explained it by saying that many of the most powerful still believed Maud to be an English spy. 'Because she's quality,' Mrs Wyse Power had whispered, as if the Irish nationalists were behind her, listening. 'She's English born and Protestant, and they find it hard to believe that she is true.'

But the native Irish have accepted Protestant Anglo-Irish as leaders before. That Parnell man who ran the *scandale* with the English divorcée. And Wolfe Tone himself, the very man whose death they celebrate with this centenary. No, Ghénia thinks. It is not because she is Protestant or because she is rich, but because she is a woman.

Yesterday, on the way back home from the station, after seeing the delegates to the boat train, she questioned Maud, delicately, carefully, and the explanation was most convincing. She made no mention of not having been invited to contribute, saying it was she who decided not to speak because the organizers had allowed parliamentarians – 'milk-and-water fellows' who had previously denounced the more radical protestors – a place on the platform. The true soul of the Irish people was not to be found in Dublin, which was why she was organizing her own event in the west of Ireland, in two out-of-the-way places in County Mayo.

All plausible but . . . Ghénia knows how much sorrow her friend can hide. Look at her now, sparkling like the champagne they drank earlier, repaying Lucien's provocations with pure charm.

'I know a woman', Lucien says, 'who sings Brünnhilde's part far better than Bréval.'

163

'Unlikely,' says Ghénia.

'Lucien!' Maud is wide-eyed. 'Bréval is the finest diva in all Europe.'

'It is true, I assure you. But her talent will never be rewarded, because she will not give herself to the Directeur.'

The infamy! Maud has turned her head, presenting them with her fine profile. As if she does not perceive the insult. As surely she must.

'They do not generally employ café-chanteuses at the Paris Opera, Lucien,' Ghénia says.

He ignores her, keeps the conversation pointed at Maud. 'I shall bring her to see you, Maud. You would admire her, I am sure. She reminds me greatly of you, at that age.'

'You know I leave for Ireland soon, Lucien.'

'When you return, then.'

'I do not intend giving any parties in the near future.'

'She is most anxious to meet you.'

Just then the lights dim. The orchestra emerges, takes its seat and begins the overture. Wagner's driving rhythms sweep away thought. Ghénia glances across: Maud seems keenly attentive. Her opera glasses are up, her forehead has relaxed, and she leans forward a little, smiling into the music. Is it real, this pleasure? A distraction from her troubles? Or is she as ignorant as she appears of the trouble she is in?

At the interval Lucien leaves them to mingle and to enjoy another carafe of wine. Maud is lost in reverie, humming to herself. Ghénia lays a hand on her arm. 'You are too much away, my dear.'

Maud looks at her blank-eyed, her mind full of Brünnhilde. 'This is a most important year for Ireland,' she says.

'Always, Maud, you put work first. But it is not good to leave a man like Lucien so much alone.'

Maud pulls herself up to her highest height.

'No, my friend,' says Madame Avril. 'Do not rebuke me. I do not speak so for my own interest or amusement.'

Maud waves her hand. 'We both know Lucien. He is not likely to change now.'

'It is not of Lucien that I wish to speak but of you.'

'Oh, Ghénia, you know I never like to talk of myself. And on such a night, with such exquisite music . . .'

Ghénia sighs. 'It is not easy to speak frankly to you, my friend. You do not make it easy. But I *shall* speak. When you were young, you were unfeasibly beautiful and every man who met you wanted to marry you. Now you are still beautiful but –'

'Not so young,' Maud says with a shrug. 'That suits me fine.'

'Pah! You are young enough. But you have been compromised by your relationship with Lucien.'

'I am proud of our alliance.'

'That may be how you like to think of it, Maud. But to the unforgiving world, it is a dalliance.' There. It is said.

'Enough, Ghénia.' Her jaw is up. 'Do not say something you may regret.'

'No, I shall not be put off. I heard what happened at Comtesse de Piedemont's salon last week.'

'If we wanted to keep odious old women from indulging in gossip, we should never stir from our firesides.'

'Yet it cannot have been easy, to be so publicly treated.' The Comtesse had refused Maud's card, saying, 'We do not receive Mademoiselle Gonne any more.' And a hundred society ladies had now determined to say the same.

'You know I care nothing for such people and their clacking tongues.'

'My dear are you not tired of being brave? Would you not like to lay down your armory?'

'I want only what I have always wanted. To control my own life. To follow my own pathway.'

'As a married woman, you would not be such a target when you do.'

'You know I consider marriage an abomination. As, my dear, did *you* –' Maud smiles to take the sting out of her words – 'not very long ago.'

'Marriage can be made to work, even for women such as us.'

'Perhaps in your case that will be so. But how many husbands are as accommodating as Monsieur Avril?'

'Paris is a cold place without male protection. Even for Maud Gonne.'

'Is this my friend, *la féministe*?' She gives one of her tinkling laughs and flutters her fan.

'I am serious, my friend. I urge you to consider a marriage.'

Maud flutters her ivory fan and sighs. 'Let me tell you a little story, Ghénia. Last time I was in Ireland, I was travelling back from Donegal on a train when I looked out of the window across dark bog land. I saw a tall, beautiful woman with dark hair blown on the wind and I knew it was Cathleen ni Houlihan. She was crossing the bog towards the hills, springing from stone to stone over the treacherous surface, and the little white stones shone, marking a path behind her, then fading into the darkness. As I watched, I heard a voice say: "You are one of the little stones on which the feet of the Queen rested on her way to Freedom." I cried, Ghénia. It seemed so lonely to be one of those little stones left behind on the path. I wanted to be more than that.'

'You are more than that. Much, *much* more.'

'No, you misunderstand me. What I wanted to say is that afterwards, when I had time to ponder, I realized that I was happy to be a servant of my Queen. It seems to me the finest thing I can do.'

'Nobody is suggesting that marriage is to be the end of your work. You know I could not consider that any more than you. Thankfully, the days when a married woman had to give up her work are gone.'

166

'Marriage to another would break my alliance with Lucien, Ghénia. I thought you would have understood that.'

Ghénia shifts in her chair. 'How so, when he himself is married?' And, she thinks, when he makes a fool of you with every chanteuse in Paris? Can she dare express this thought aloud? It needs to be said. Her pulse skids. 'And when he is no more faithful to you than he is to his wife.'

Maud drops her head, as if slapped.

Moments pass.

When she looks up, her face is the colour of water just after sundown, both pale and dark. Remorse floods through Ghénia. 'Oh, *ma chérie*, I am so sorry. Forgive me –'

'I have always thought these matters were understood between us. I do not like to speak of such things, but let me explain and then let us put it away. Lucien's . . .' She stops, unable to find the right word. '. . . indiscretions . . . they make my position awkward, but our alliance is useful to Ireland. I, whom you know to be proud, perhaps too proud, am willing to sacrifice even my pride for Ireland.'

Ghénia speaks carefully, winnowing her words. 'I can perhaps grant you that, Maud, though I should wish more for you. But what of Iseult? She is now four years old. Soon she will be old enough to understand that she has no father.'

'She has a father.'

'Well, then, that she is illegitimate in the eyes of the law and of society.'

'Oh, *society*.'

'Would you consider the Irish poet?'

'Ghénia! Please.'

'His love is a true thing.' He has so long adored her. If only she could allow herself to be adored.

'He is only a boy,' Maud says.

'The same age as you, is he not?'

'A little older. But, none the less, a boy.'

'That can be an advantage in a husband.'

'After a man like Lucien?' She shakes her head. 'I could never be with Willie as a husband would expect.'

'If he is so immature, he might accept that. Tell him you think the sex act is justified only by procreation.'

Maud laughs, this time with real amusement. 'What a conniver you are, Ghénia. Is that what you tell Monsieur Avril?'

Ghénia shrugs. 'It is a man's world, my dear, and men have constructed the institution of marriage to suit themselves entirely. They have women at their service in the kitchen, the drawing room and the bedroom. We must use what ploys we can.'

'If I were to go to Willie, I should have to tell him about Iseult.'

'You will have to do that, whomsoever you choose.'

'It would shatter his view of the world and my place in it. And I fear that would be so bad for his poetry.'

'Then what about the Comte?'

'Ghénia, don't be ridiculous.'

'The poet, then. I am sure he would rather know about Iseult and marry you himself, than hear you are to wed another.'

'No, stop. Marriage I consider a major impediment to any woman who wants to make a mark on the world. If I were to give up my freedom in such a way, it could be for only one man.'

'Who is already bound.'

'I shall speak to him. I shall make him see my position . . . Shhh! Here he comes. Let us make idle talk. What did you think of the orchestra? And the divine Bréval? Was she not divine?'

20

In Samois-sur-Seine, autumn has begun its slow creep of colour through the trees. The day is crisp, pleasant in the mid-afternoon sun, though still cold. Frost glistens in patches where the sun's rays have not pierced. It is early in the year for such cold and it will make the winter long. Too long.

Iseult knows nothing of days to come. As always, she is delightfully present. Look at her kicking the leaves with her boots, sending them up into the air. She loves the crackle they make and the crisp lightness of them as they separate out from each other and fall back to the ground.

She stops, as if remembering something. 'Brother, Amour?'

Maud stops walking, squeezes Iseult's glove in hers. 'Darling, please. I don't want to have to tell you again.'

'Sorry. *Moura.*'

'Good girl. That wasn't so difficult, was it? So say it again: "What about my brother, Moura?"'

'What about my brother, Moura?'

'That's it. I am your own Moura: I know it's hard, but please, please, try to remember. For me.'

'Yes, Moura,' says Iseult, her little hand tugging as she trips into stepping forward again. 'And brother?'

'Yes, yes, we are on our way to see your brother. That is where we are going. Did Moura not promise?'

She smiles, content at the prospect. Good.

Maud's own feeling is that it is right and fitting for Iseult to meet her brother, now, while she is still young, but Ghénia worried her last night when she said, shuddering, that she thought it a mistake. Ghoulish.

Ghoulish? The word made Maud want to slap her, a most

unaccustomed feeling with Ghénia. What is ghoulish about death? Is it not merely the mirror of life? Iseult will have no more siblings – that much, if nothing else with Lucien, is certain – and if she is told of Georges now, at four years – old enough to understand but too young to grasp the full implications – she will grow with the knowledge of him. The other way he would become a secret kept from her: a big revelation at some later, more aware point of life.

'You know what a secret is, Iseult?'

Iseult nods.

'Tell me a secret that you know.'

'But, Amour, if –'

Maud stops in her tracks again. 'Moura, Iseult.'

'Sorry. Moura.'

'Please try to remember.'

Iseult nods.

'So go on, tell me a secret.'

'But . . . if Iseult tells it won't be secret.'

'Excellent!' Maud smiles down. 'Excellent. You have passed the test.'

The child gives a little skip. Through the shadows of the branches above, autumn sunlight splashes across her tilted-up face, adding to the beauty of her artless smile. She is a child whose loveliness never grows familiar: in different moods, under different lights, she can look startlingly altered, so that to catch sight of her is to experience all over again the shock of the new. Beauty like Iseult's *is* a kind of shock.

'Moura?' She is tilting her head to the other side now, her hair falling free of her ear.

'Yes.'

'Iseult hates England.'

This is something new. 'You do, my darling? And why, pray?'

'England is . . .' The little face squints up over the words. 'England is . . . a nation . . . of shopkeepers.'

A loud laugh swoops through Maud's throat, before she

has time to think. 'My sweet darling, did Papon teach you to say that?'

Iseult shrugs.

'You are delightful, truly you are.'

'Moura.'

Maud is still chuckling. 'Yes, Iseult.'

'Why is bad to keep a shop?'

'It is not the keeping of a shop in itself that is shameful. What is reprehensible is to care too much about the shop's profits to the exclusion of other, finer aspects of life.'

Iseult nods slowly, digesting. Is this a message sent from Lucien through their child, an imaginative attempt at making amends? 'Did Papon teach those words to you, Iseult? Did he ask you to say them to me?'

Iseult's face closes.

'Are you listening, Iseult? When Papon came to visit you the last time, at home . . . while Amour – I mean Moura – was away? Do you remember? Did he bring a lady with him?'

But the child turns a face as blank as a pickpocket's.

Lucien has grown quarrelsome again and most fiercely and wretchedly so. He published in *La Patrie* a detestable editorial, a sentimental and exaggerated appeal for Alsace-Lorraine, pointing to Germany as the one and only enemy of France. Nothing about England. It was a clear betrayal of their alliance, but, when she called his attention to it, he mumbled something about having only signed it, not written it. It was obvious that its flowery and sloppy language was not his. She had known as soon as she read it that it was the work of that singer he had wanted her to see – who, Maud had heard since, was swaying Lucien to support the *Entente Cordiale* with England.

When he saw this knowledge in her, he began to bluster about her Irish friends, as if the shortcomings were theirs: 'Those absurd Irish revolutionists of yours, they lead you astray; their schemes will come to nothing, I have seen them and judged them; they will never do anything. You should go work

171

with the Home Rule Party; outside Parliament you won't be able to do anything for Ireland . . .'

But it was not she who was deviating from the path they had laid for each other thirteen years before.

'So our alliance is at an end,' she had said to him.

'Don't be absurd, Maud. You know I will always help you.'

'How can you when we have different enemies?'

'England is not the threat to France that Germany is. Surely you must see –'

'And different *friends*,' she interrupted him.

He shrugged with a blasé twist of his shoulders that made her hate him.

A chorus girl. He would be taking them off the streets next and asking her to favour them.

Maud crouches down among the autumn leaves, reaches for Iseult and pulls her in, tight. She puts her nose in her daughter's lovely hair and inhales deeply. 'Oh, the smell of the outdoors on you, *ma chérie*. It is divine. So clean. *Ma belle animale.* You are so good with your secrets. But Moura would like it if you could tell her only this one thing. Do you think you can?'

Iseult looks up at the branches of the trees as if they are the ones who speak loudest to her.

'Please, Iseult, even if it is a secret. Moura needs to know. Did Papon bring a lady with him? He did, did he not?'

Nothing.

'Oh, my darling, I am sorry. Perhaps you are right. Perhaps it is not fair to press you. Let us talk about something else. Let us talk about your brother. I have not told you about him before, have I? I should tell you what a terrible loss he was to Ireland. He would have grown up to be a great hero and would have freed Ireland, if only he had not been taken by meningitis.'

'Men . . . i . . . ?'

'Meningitis. You have never heard of it, of course. It is the most ghastly disease.'

'Men . . . in . . .'

'Yes, yes, there's no need to keep saying it, dear. Listen to me. You know the bootees you found in my drawer that I didn't want you playing with? That is the reason why. Those bootees were his. Georges's. You see?'

Does she? Again, her face is blank. 'He passed away when he was only two years old. Younger than you are now, darling. It was all so sudden. In the afternoon, he was playing happily. By evening he was unconscious with fever. I hurried from Ireland, the moment I heard. I hired a hansom cab to take me immediately to the next boat. I didn't even take my belongings from the hotel. I came as quickly as I could, as quickly as ever I could. I couldn't have been any quicker.'

Iseult hand slips away. Maud grips her shoulders.

'Iseult, I know Papon had the lady there, so you don't have to keep the secret any more. Because I know. So you can tell me.'

'You're hurting my shoulders, Am . . . Moura.'

'Oh, my dear. Am I? What is wrong with me? What am I saying? Stop. Look at your little hands, blue with cold. I told you to wear your gloves. Where are they? Here in your pockets. And look, look at your fingernails. *Mon Dieu*, you have an entire field buried in here! Stand still, my little fidget, and let me wipe those grubby, grubby fingers with my handkerchief. You cannot go to see your brother with such nails.

'Dear child, don't look at me so. Moura does not mean to cry, truly she doesn't. Come closer to me again, Iseult, please. Come close. Here, let me hold you. Oh, yes, that is better. Hug me. Hug me tight with your little arms. There, yes, I knew it, see? You have made Moura feel so much . . . so much better, yes, you have, you clever thing. Yes. I shall stop now . . . in a . . . a moment . . . Just give me a moment. But look, I'm wetting your hair. How silly of me. How silly. Oh, Iseult . . .'

Meningitis. That is what Iseult remembers of that day. She forgets that she once felt Maud's weeping face buried in her neck, though the impression it left stayed with her. She forgets her months of childish fear that she too might 'pass away', taken by fever after a day of happy play. But she holds in herself always a memory, clear as a crisp photograph, of the boy who looked like an ugly doll. That, and the smell inside the vault, the smell she always thinks of as having come from him, from the illness that made him.

Maud Gonne to W. B. Yeats

My dear Friend,

How nice you are writing to me when I have been so lazy about answering, that is what I like so much about you, I am always sure of finding you the same – no matter what happens! I have been going through a state of mind I don't quite understand, for the last month I have been incapable of any sort of work, each time I tried something seemed to stop me. It was not that I had my mind full of other things, quite the contrary, my mind was blank and stupid. I thought it must be some of the forces that work for England that were paralysing my will so I have been imagining Celtic things with the water of the west and the earth from New Grange and suddenly feel as if the stupefying weight has disappeared and I can be active and useful again. Just when I got your letter about Maeve, *I had been invoking Maeve . . .*

I cross to London on the 24th Nov. and go to Manchester for a meeting on the 27th and shall be in Ireland by the end of this month. Write and let me know where *you will be and where we can see each other and talk over the things which interest us.*

In haste
I remain
Alwys your friend
Maud Gonne

21

January in Doolough, in the bedroom that is now my study. I stood by the window, looking down on the front garden, coffee cup in one hand and in the other, rolled into a scroll, a letter from Zach. Half a page. Seventy-five words and not one of them the word I needed.

Down on the lawn, a robin was digging up worms. The grass was green, but the rest of the world – the trees and the sky and the mountains and the slivers of lake through the trees – was grey, grey, grey. Although it was ten in the morning, the light was still on overhead and my desk lamp was also lit. Twenty years in California had eased my memory of low-hanging Irish winters – the fifteen or sixteen hours of darkness and the day so grey when it finally did arrive, damp and cloud-congested, as if the world had a head cold.

I tilted my head back to drain the cup. End of coffee break. How ordinary life remains, even when extraordinary things are happening. Breakfast, lunch, dinner, coffee; work, rest, exercise, leisure; family, friends, colleagues, acquaintances: that's all life comes down to – everywhere. Most days I struggled through, with loneliness ever knocking at my poor defences.

But I also had moments when the shadow of what lay ahead, the possibility of prison, concentrated my appreciation of daily things. A robin's bobbing head. The aroma of the coffee. A walk down the lane to the road and back.

And writing.

Time to get back to it. My fifteen-minute break was over. Time to forget Zach's letter. If the work wasn't done early, it wouldn't be done at all. Later in the day, my mind would wander, to my father's intentions in his last days, to the impending trial, to the whereabouts of Star, to this latest letter from Zach and what it might mean . . . As evening set in, my courage would disintegrate, as thoughts and memories congealed. But now good morning energy, the sense of connection that arises from not being too long out of sleep, would drive me through.

Zach was in the West of Ireland, a place called Ballyleagh in County Mayo, near a mountain he had 'befriended'. It sounded so phoney on paper, though I knew that in the presence of his six-feet-two of sleeked muscle, in the hold of his piercing eyes, in the force field of his presence, it would sound real and true.

Oh, Zach, I'm not just alone here, I'm incomplete. I get through the day, I put in the hours, I live out the minutes but I want to be who I was when you were here, when life lived me and I lived life.

Dearest Izzy

I have found a place where I can be. You were right about the West of Ireland. I spent the New Year on Inishmore and am now in this village in Connemara, below a mountain I have befriended. I climb it every day but never to the top. I hope all has come to pass as you wanted — that your father departed and your daughter arrived, and both are at peace.

Your
Zach

Just those seventy-five words. With all that had happened between us and all that he knew might have happened since he left. But why was I surprised? Zach had told me more than once that he had grown wary of words. I replied: 'The man who is wary of words is wary of life,' which made him sit up.

'Do you really think so?' he asked.

'Actually, I was paraphrasing the good doctor.'

'Who?'

'An English writer you Yanks probably have little time for. Dr Johnson.'

'Of dictionary fame?'

'Exactly. He once said the chief glory of every people arises from its authors. I happen to agree with him. So tell me what you mean: "wary of words".'

'I don't trust them. All they do is feed a false sense of self.'

I was thunderstruck. To the young me, words alone were, as W. B. had said, 'certain good', the lodestar of human achievement. Especially the written word that allowed us to reach across place and time to distant others. Only words could encompass it all, touch head and heart and soul, altogether, all at once.

'It's a matter of balance,' he explained. 'Words can be good, but what this world needs more right now is silence.'

Even when he was just a student, just setting out on life, long before he grew disillusioned with academia, Zach would say such things. I remember one day, very near the beginning – still early enough for me to be conscious of what others thought at seeing a thirty-year-old woman with this guy who was barely out of boyhood – we were walking in the park and came across a magnificent, flowering hibiscus and stopped to admire it and I was scraping my brain trying to remember what it was called.

'What does it matter what humans name it?' he said. 'Be quiet so you can look at it.'

On the long desk behind me, the papers and notes and jottings that made up my life and my father's and Iseult's were spread, in a fan of files and folders. I went across and placed Zach's letter with them. I couldn't afford to think any longer about his meagre words and what they might mean. I needed to sit back down and immerse myself in December 1898, when Maud Gonne decides she may have to settle for Willie Yeats. This was what would save me – from Zach, as from the rest. This was what would enable me to make sense of it all – him, as well as them.

I had been to Rathdrum to collect books I had ordered, books that contained photographs of the Gonnes and their circle. Maud prettified in Sarah Purser's portrait of her with the monkey, the one she disparaged as 'sweet one-and-twenty'. Iseult sketched by Maud, hair up, cheek to a lily. Willie, in black robes and pince-nez and poet's pose; and again, in later life, much more attractive, caught off guard, laughing, his hand to a tweed-covered paunch. Francis, the suicide's son, in handsome youth and in disintegrated age.

I had cut these photos out and hung them in a collage over my desk. There they sat, waiting, they and the files and folders, still not fully ordered, far from fully understood, anxious for my attention.

So why would my fixed feet not move in that direction? What was I resisting?

If you were here, Zach, you would order my days and soothe my nights. You would know how to cope with this trial that lies ahead. You would make it so I would find something other than grey in this deep Irish winter, something beside darkness in sixteen-hour nights. With you, night-time was my best time. Zach, soul of my soul. Come back to me.

It was no use. He couldn't. Not this time.

I put down the coffee cup, I sat back down at the desk, I picked up my pen, a dark green fountain pen full of dark green ink. I returned to the connections I had picked out earlier from among the files and began again to write.

22

Before Star was born, Brendan and I thought we would be able to live on as we always had. 'Babies don't eat much,' I'd said. 'And for a long time I'll be feeding him or her myself.' But of course it wasn't about food. Star needed all kinds of things we couldn't afford: a stroller, toys, clothes in ever increasing sizes. And then there were the needs marching towards us: bicycles, own bedroom, school, summer camp . . .

The drink and drugs and sexual shenanigans of the commune no longer looked the same to us either. As Zane said, we'd become a couple of downers.

Whether, and then how, we were going to leave began to occupy all our conversation. We'd whisper to each other about it, in bed at night, so the others wouldn't hear. We considered Ireland. We had both been away long enough to become nostalgic, not for our families but for the place itself: the ancient beauty and mystery of its landscape, the remembered simplicity of how people lived. But this homesickness was too flimsy a feeling to act upon, and anyway there were no more jobs in Ireland than in Taos. In the end, we settled on NYC. Brooklyn again. Brendan would get a job, and I would take care of Star. It wasn't what either of us wanted, but what we wanted for ourselves was no longer the most important thing in our lives.*

So one morning we drove away with Star in a cot in the back of our VW. We drove straight to NYC, no more meandering, into a two-room apartment, and a hasty ceremony at City Hall and a job for Brendan: selling advertising in the *Brooklyn Metro*. For him we bought two suits, some button-down shirts and a

* For a while anyway.

pair of shiny black shoes and an apron and oven gloves for me. Snakeskin and Lightning were put to rest, and I found myself with another new name: Mrs Creahy.

It makes me laugh, looking back. Was it our conservative Irish background reasserting itself, making us feel that this was the only way to be parents? Brendan would leave our tiny apartment at six in the morning, to be in the office for eight, while I clung to the mattress until whatever time Star woke me with her crying. Star always seemed to be crying.

This was due to a feeling of insecurity, according to my child-rearing manual. To make her feel secure, I should immediately answer these cries. So I did. I wrapped my time around her needs: for cuddles, for food, for sleep, for baths. Having brought this little scrap into the world, I was determined to do right by her. I bought a baby sling and carried her everywhere, her little body tucked tight on my breast, massaging my heart with the rapid rise and fall of her lungs. I would keep her there – *Look, no hands!* – even as I baked bread, up to my forearms in flour.

In the evenings, after she had been given her supper and her bath and her bedtime stories, I would lie down with her until she dropped into sleep. Often I fell asleep myself, to be woken by Brendan coming in, looking for dinner. Exhausted, we ate in crankiness or silence in front of the television, *The Andy Griffith Show* or *I Love Lucy*. I looked on at us, shell-shocked.

Brendan began to say things like: 'It was about time we grew up anyway.' Then: 'Everybody else has been working their way up. We're way behind.' Then: 'All those wasted years. I can't believe we stayed there so long.'

'We've had things other people have never known,' I would reply. 'I wouldn't change a day of it.'

For me, it was simple: up to 1961 we did that; now we were doing this. But Brendan had to keep comparing the two ways of living and in ways that made Taos the loser. So, in the way of life partners everywhere, we settled ourselves on opposite sides of the argument. I came to stand for New Mexico, its big skies and warm pulse, and whenever Brendan criticized something about our lives there, I would complain about NYC. How the cold was so damp and bitter. How my skin, which had been the colour of honey, had turned almost grey. How people were separated from each other in their little apartments and offices but mostly in their minds – bustling by each other on the street, locked in thought, all unseeing, with only the steam of their breath showing they had warmth inside.

I became the advocate for that other way of living. 'We would have been all right,' I'd say. 'We could have lived on like that, become crazies, dancing to the hum of the planet.'

He would look at me as if he never thought that way, but I understood. To get himself up and into his business suit each morning, Brendan Creahy had to reject Snakeskin, become a new man, with new expectations. Because he had been 'working' all day – doing activities that yielded dollars – while I was 'off' – doing activities that were unpaid, cleaning our home and playing, stimulating, feeding, training, walking, talking and minding our child – he expected, when he arrived home, to pull off his tie and his shoes and to be served dinner.

And at the weekends, or sometimes after work, he wanted to go for a few drinks with the boys. It was the least he deserved; he needed the break. As did I but, with him gone, I didn't get the option.

At home, he only wanted to watch TV – baseball, football, basketball. Crime dramas and comedies. The rest I could rationalize, but that drove me nuts. He'd never watched TV in his life, yet now our routines – when we could talk, have sex, go out – had to fit around the schedules.

What was that about?

23

So to Dublin, where the poet awaits his muse. He arrives at her hotel for breakfast on Maud's first morning. They eat together in the morning-room which has an agreeable view northwards over the cricket greens of Trinity College and discuss, across eggs and toast, with crumbs falling unheeded on to Willie's waistcoat front, their occult interests, careful to keep their voices low so as not to shock the respectables at the tables near by. Afterwards, they stroll together up Kildare Street to be at the National Library of Ireland when it opens at ten.

That day and the one following and the next, they pore for several hours over ancient tomes and recent research, progressing their work on their Castle of Heroes and the Celtic Mysteries that will sustain it. These rituals must, in their main outline, be the work of invisible hands, brought into being not by conscious thought but through invocation and meditation, a holding open of the soul. What this library research fills in are details: gods and goddesses, heroes and lovers, objects and symbols, which confirm their direction and add substance to the rites.

For days they work together. Mr Lyster, the Librarian, is a friend of Willie's father and permits them to work in rooms that are off limits to others. Thus they have privacy behind their library stacks. Maud is careful to be her most charming, and in the afternoons and evenings they go about very much as a couple, meeting friends and political and literary connections, and often, then, back to her hotel for a nightcap. Day, afternoon or evening: there is nothing to impede a declaration. Yet no declaration is forthcoming.

A week into her visit, Maud sits to her bureau after breakfast, the dilemma coming between her and her correspondence. Instead of writing, she sits staring out the window, the stub of her pen in her mouth, recalling the previous day when, in handing him a book, she allowed her hand to gently graze his. The touch reached its mark, for he blushed like a girl, but all he did was open the book at the desired page and point her towards what to read.

Contrary boy. So often, she has discouraged him; now that she wishes him to speak: nothing.

What is she to do?

She turns to the letters before her: quite a pile, forwarded from France. A bill for the house at Samois (she really should let it go; they never use it any more), a request to speak at a rally in Manchester and a selection of private dispatches, all unopened except for Ghénia's, which contained a dear little missive from Iseult. A picture fashioned in blue crayon of a tall lady and a little girl, *maman et fille*. They are hand in hand beside a bushy green tree with red apples. Underneath she has written in her dear, unformed hand: *Chère Moura, Je t'aime. xxxx Iseult.*

Clever girl.

Maud has begun her reply – a sketch of the seashore at Howth Head where she went walking on Sunday, complete with fish and seagulls – when a knock comes at her hotel-room door. At this hour it can only be him. Opening it, she sees immediately that he is greatly excited. His eyes flash, his fingers clutch each other and he looks more than ever like a skinny, dishevelled demon. Only one thing could bring about such fervour at this hour.

'I went to you last night,' she says, ushering him in. 'Did you find me in your dreams?'

'Yes, yes, that is what I have come to tell you. I woke with the fading vision of your face bending over mine. With the knowledge that you had just –'

'Just? Just what? Oh, do go on, Mr Yeats.'

'That you had just . . . kissed me.'

183

She moves a step closer, but still he talks, in his volatile, overexcitable fashion, of how he has often dreamt of kissing her hands, of how once in a dream she had kissed him but how this was the first time that the kissing had been mutual. She lets him talk and lets him finish and lets the ensuing silence grow as she feeds him a look, with eyes open and limpid, for as long as is seemly. Until such a look can be borne no longer.

The moment passes.

'Come,' she says, a little weary. 'Let us go down for breakfast.'

They spend that morning as they have spent every other morning, in the National Library, and in the afternoon they visit the old Fenian leader James Stephens. All day she is at her most charming and affectionate to him, even in front of others: another change in her that he disdains to notice. In the late evening, when dinner is finished and they are in her room, she moves to try again.

'Let me tell you now what happened last night,' she says. 'When I fell asleep I saw standing at my bedside a great spirit. He took me to a great throng of spirits, and you were among them. All at once, everything got very full of light and I began to see forms and colours more distinctly than I had ever seen them with my ordinary eyes and I knew that I was in the middle not of a dream but a vision. My hands were put into yours and I was told that we were married.'

She pauses, waits.

'Go on,' he says, with vehemence. 'Who told you this? What else was there?'

'I saw enormous multitudes of birds and in the midst was one very beautiful bird wearing a crown, a bird like a great white eagle. By now I was aware that I was out of my body, seeing my body from outside itself. I was brought away by the great god Lugh and my hand was put into yours and I was told that we were married. Then I kissed you.'

She leans forward in her chair, close enough to see the hairs on his face, a small tuft on the underside of his chin that he

184

missed in his morning shave. At least he has stopped wearing that ill-judged beard.

'I kissed you and all became dark. After that I remember nothing. I think we went away together to do some work.'

He assumes the air he always assumes in their most secret, symbolical dealings. 'What were you wearing in this vision?'

'Wearing?'

'Yes, when you came to me?'

'A white dress.'

He frowns. 'In my dream, you wore the dress with the red bodice and skirt of yellow flowers.'

'I don't attribute much importance to this, do you?'

'In my dream the flowers gradually grew and grew until all else was blotted out.'

She has had enough talk. The moment is come, and if he is too shy to initiate it . . . Well . . . She leans a little more out of her seat, stretches her neck to place her lips on his. There. There, Mr Yeats. Your dream come true. She strengthens the kiss, makes it full and unmistakable in intent. His lips are cool under hers, and unmoving. How much she has to teach him, about private and public ease. He makes life so difficult for himself and for all around him.

She sits back and opens her eyes to him, expectant, and finds his mouth shocked and slack, his eyebrows frozen into an expression of alarm. She has misjudged her move.

'You had better leave, Mr Yeats,' she says.

'Miss Gonne . . . Please . . .'

'I beg of you, do not speak. Go from here.'

'I must –'

'Please, I *entreat* you. Put all thoughts of me from you. If you care at all for me, go. Go now.'

Sleeplessness is a regular problem for Willie Yeats, but that night he welcomes the turning over and over in his bed, as if on a spit over a fire. He burns, he yearns . . . and yet. When she kissed him with her bodily mouth, he was afraid. That much he knows – but why?

He longs to tell her . . . what? That his body contains his steady, unwavering heart but also something else, something even he cannot find words or images to describe, something porous that shifts and breathes through his urges and haunts his memories, that is speckled with brightness like the night sky is speckled with stars but that is also as blank as the spaces between.

It was wrong of her. Of that too he is certain. But again, why? His thoughts go round and round as miserable thoughts do, without reaching a conclusion.

Next day he returns to her room and finds her sitting, with folded hands in her lap, staring gloomily into the fire. 'I should never have spoken to you in that way,' she says. 'For I can never be your wife in reality.'

'Why?'

'Mr Yeats, I have something to tell you.'

'I think I know it. You are betrothed to another?'

He has always denied it but, since yesterday, it seems the only explanation of her periodic cold spells, her physical reserve, the obscure look in her eye whose meaning he has so often wondered at (some journalist once said it contained the shadow of battles yet to come).

'Not betrothed. There is another. However . . .' Her voice quails at delivering these words, as well it might. 'It is . . . not as you think.'

So here it is, that which has been between them, always. That most banal of explanations. Another man.

'It is not as you think. I do not love him . . . I am forced to be the moral nature for us both.'

'You speak in riddles.'

'I know. I have something to tell you that is very painful for me. Before I speak, I want you to know that I do love you.

186

That I have loved you for a very long time. That for years now, your love has been the only beautiful thing in my life.'

He is at a loss to hear these words from her lips. Should he take a step towards her? It seems not; she is holding up her hand. 'No, please. Hear me out. I have kept you close while keeping a wall of glass between us. You have felt this, and it has been most selfish of me. When you know all, you will understand all and you will love me no more.'

'I assure you –'

'And that is as I deserve.'

He moves to stand.

'Please, I beg you, do not move, do not speak. You must hear me first.'

He sits back down, and she begins her story, her face all the while turned towards the fire. 'When I was a young girl, I longed more than anything for control over my own life. I read in one of Tommy's books of a man who sold his soul to the devil, and so desperate was I to be free of the terrible restraints put upon me by my English relations that I too prayed to Satan. I told him he could have my soul if I could have my freedom. I see I have shocked you, but I was very young, Mr Yeats. I wanted life. The afterlife seemed very far away and what happened after my death like a small price for freedom in this wonderful world.'

'I am not shocked so much as troubled.'

'As I made the pact, the clock struck twelve, and I felt of a sudden that my prayer had been heard and answered. But then, within . . .' She falters, lifts her handkerchief to her eyes.

'Miss Gonne, you distress yourself. There is no need.'

'But there is a need, Mr Yeats. A great need. I must tell all.' Her head drops, so she is speaking into her lap, the handkerchief twisting between her fingers. 'Then . . . within a fortnight . . . my dearly beloved father . . . dear dear Tommy . . . was dead.'

'Oh, Miss Gonne . . . Maud –'

Again she checks him. 'I know. I know.' She gathers herself, goes on. 'I was now an heiress, independently wealthy, free of my relatives as soon as I reached twenty-one. I had control of my life, but . . . I had lost the person I loved most dearly in all the world.'

She turns her face up to him, and he has a sudden vision of how she will look when old. Gaunt, haggard and still magnificent. 'The remorse, Mr Yeats. The remorse.'

He wishes he could rise out of his body and become vapour. Feel nothing of this heavy passion that weighs them both. Gather in around her, touching her lightly, with impartiality, as does the air.

'Thank you for not trying, as another might, to convince me that the two events were unconnected.' She rises from her chair. 'Shortly afterwards a Frenchman came into my life. I fell in love with this man. After some months, I . . . I became his mistress.'

Now her narration speeds up. She was often away from Millevoye, for yes, it was he, that nauseating sensationalist he once met at her apartment in Paris. Sexual love soon began to repel her, but for all that she was much in love. A little boy was born, a child she had once told him about, who she had said was adopted. Millevoye failed her in various ways and then the boy died – otherwise she would have broken with her lover altogether and lived in Ireland. She had thought of breaking with him and had engaged herself to someone else, but had broken it off after a week. (He thought he might have had that poor betrothal for *his* reward.)

She goes over and over the details of the death of the child and its effect on her. Here, her account becomes incoherent, and she clenches and unclenches her hands, and when he asks some questions she says it is not well to speak of such things. She had suffered nervous collapse and lost the ability to speak French. She had built a memorial chapel in a village outside Paris, using some of her capital – 'For what does money matter now?' – and had the body embalmed. She had gone back to

188

Millevoye in the vault under the memorial chapel where they buried the boy.

'It was *you* who made me return,' she says, explaining how he and Russell had convinced her that her lost child might be reborn. Except it was a girl who ensued. The child he had met that same day in Paris.

So why does she not leave him now, this man who has caused her so much pain, this man she deems so amoral? 'I have left him. But we are connected. He is the father of my child. And I am necessary to him. I do not know what would happen to him if my influence were not there.'

This is a troubled conscience speaking, surely. She thinks she can appease it by performing to the last tittle every duty.

'So now, Mr Yeats, you know all. And thus you know why, despite my love for you, I can never be your wife. I can never marry you or anyone, for my experiences have left me with a horror of physical love.'

She is finished. It is his turn to speak. He cannot. He thinks of the poem he wrote defending her, so recently published: 'Their children's children shall say they have lied.' What a fool he has been.

He is saturated with that feeling he most dreads: a conscious-ness of his energy, his transforming power, stopped by a wall. By something one must either submit to, or rage against help-lessly. It alarms him. Is it the root of madness? He wonders once again whether he has some nervous weakness inherited from his mother.

He cannot speak and he is careful not to touch her. Even when leaving he is careful to touch her only as one would touch a sister.

She, his Rose of the World, for whom his reverent hands had wrought passionate rhymes of beauty and despair, is the mistress of that greasy French politician.

She, whom he would beseech to tread softly upon his dreams, is the mother of two illegitimate children, one living.

She, who was once a priestess in a temple of the moon in Syria, who used to sit upon a throne and prophesy, now sits, a fallen woman, by a hotel fire.

She who used to gather herbs in a great wood under a full moon and burn them in the temple now speaks of a repugnance for sex while making pathetically plain sexual overtures.

He fears he *will* go mad.

24

Brendan looked back over his shoulder at me. 'We're not on the right road.'

'Oh, no,' I said, from the back seat of the car. 'Please don't say that.'

'It's not what *I* say that counts, Iz. What does the *map* say?'

'It says . . . um . . . Oh, shit, I think we took the wrong exit.'

'For God's sake.' Brendan banged his two palms against the steering wheel. 'What in God's bloody name are you doing?'

'My best, maybe?' I tried to keep the wobble from my voice.

'Jesus, no. Now the bloody waterworks.'

It was the day before Star's second birthday. She was sleeping serenely beside me in her little car seat while we drove her to a motel in Truro, Cape Cod, for her first-ever vacation. That's what we called it, though Star felt no need to be somewhere else. It was we who needed to get away from what we had become. I had chosen the destination, a village where a lifetime ago we had slept on the beach, under the stars, in two sleeping bags zipped together to make one. We both knew exactly what I was trying to resurrect, but it was all going horribly wrong.

'Stop shouting,' I hissed at him. 'You'll wake Star.'

It had taken me ages to get her off to sleep, sitting in the back beside her, reading to her, waving toys in front of her face, taking her on to my lap and rocking her off. I was exhausted myself. She had taken to waking in the night, and I had to go to her room each night to get her back off. The broken sleep left me stupid and helpless during the day. She walked around the house, jettisoning toys, juice, building blocks, clothing, toast, marbles, and I followed, half the time on my knees. Bending and picking, wiping and cleaning, tucking and clearing, like a servant.

No, servants get paid. Like a *slave,* one of those immigrant women who gets locked up in a house by tyrannical employers, except the tyrant was me. Us. The poverty that didn't allow me to buy some help was part of it, but, even if we had had the money, I wouldn't have considered childcare. While I complained about the housework and baby chores, another part of me was stunned that I had been entrusted with this child, this object of beauty, this precious treasure, this Crown Jewel of a daughter.

Look at me, driving her to the store, lifting her into the tub, feeding her in her high chair. *Me. On my own.* I was allowed. It didn't seem possible. It seemed like something bad must happen.

That must be why I was always issuing warnings. 'Don't do that!'

'Be careful!'

'No! Bad fire!'

'Get down, honey, get down NOW!'

'Mind the edge.'

'Come back HERE!'

We got back on to the right road and eventually made it to the hotel. In the bedroom, we closed the curtains against the glare of the day, spread ourselves on the big double bed and let ourselves play with her. Her favourite toy at that time was a letterboard that used to make animal sounds when she struck the right first letter of their name. It had been a gift that was too advanced for her, but she loved to bash the squares indiscriminately and hear the sounds. *Moo. Quack. Oink.* Her enjoyment and the half-dark, muffled peace of the hotel bedroom soothed us.

'I'm sorry, Bren,' I said, after a time.

'Me too. Give me a kiss.' So I did. A long kiss.

When we finished, he threw himself back on the pillows, body rigid. 'Ahhhh!' he shrieked, and I laughed, knowing what he was going to say next. 'Struck by Lightning!' Something he used to say a lot, before.

I laughed again and shimmied in close. 'Snakebite,' I whispered in his ear, and offered him my neck.

'Sssssssss!' went Star's toy. She had struck the snake box just as Brendan's teeth nipped my skin. She gurgled up into our surprised faces, not knowing why she suddenly had our attention, and we burst out in a duet of laughter.

'Who's a clever girl?' I said, though she hadn't done anything clever at all. And then we found we couldn't stop laughing – at the silly coincidence, at Star's adorable smile, at the satin coverlet so silky against our bare legs, at the good feelings now filling the room, at the daft names we used to have and the naive people we used to be. A laugh filled with tenderness for our daughter and our own younger selves. For youth itself, its carefree ignorance.

I was so happy in that moment, that's what I remember, as I sit here writing this. Parenthood might be tough, but we were surviving it. Beneath the squalls and storms of living, despite Brendan's dead-end jobs, even with my poor domestic skills, we still had love to give each other and our little girl. I was proud of us for that.

After a while we went down to the poolside. We had it to ourselves. The sun was low in the sky, the evening glowing orange and still warm. Brendan put water wings on Star, while I lay on a sun bed, watching. He swung her up on to his shoulders and climbed down the little ladder into the glinting water. This released a memory in me that I'd forgotten, of my father holding me like that on his shoulders, walking us both into the water at the beach. 'Ready?' he would ask me, his voice smaller in the wide outdoors than it was in the house; and, without waiting for an answer, he walked us in, me on top, him below, the roar of the waves in my ears. I held the sides of his head under me, unsure of my grip, frightened he'd go too far, that the water would come right up over his head and then up over mine.

I shook my head. This was 1962, I was here with Brendan, it

was Star's anxiety I was feeling. He was gently lowering her into the water, holding her out in front of him like the figurehead of a ship, and she was loving it. 'More,' she whooped whenever he stopped, and off he set again, her chubby little hands slapping the water.

Then: 'Aaaaargh!'

Not Star but Brendan, letting out a roar.

'Aaaaargh!' again.

Later it was discovered that Brendan had had a heart defect, never detected, but I don't want to recall any of that now, the story I repeated so often afterwards. How I saw him twitching in the water, then flaying, his face contorted. How I saw Star's face sinking under the surface, and, quicker than thought, was in the pool with them, water to my thighs, grabbing her, watching him.

Even now I can still feel her costume, wet and cold against my chest, and see Brendan thrashing forward, face down, spectacularly splashing until he was just as spectacularly still. And hear the silence that followed, and in it the slap-slap-slap of the lifeguard's bare feet on the tiles as he came running towards us.

The Action of the Storm

In the fable of The Oak and the Willow
these of the oak are broken, those of the other bend
but all submit to the action of the storm.

Iseult Gonne, 'Desire'

Christmas Eve, 1982
Zach

Dearest Izzy

We won't speak when I go downstairs in a few moments. Maybe you'll hug me goodbye, maybe you won't even be able to do that. I'm writing this now before I leave, so I can say it clear, no confusion. And the written word is always the best way to get your attention, isn't it?

You're always quoting writers at me, Izzy, but long ago I gave you the only words you need to hear. I wonder if you remember? It was a line from the Talmud: 'If you add to the truth, you subtract from it.'

I remember how you tried to understand. You tilted your lovely chin, the way you do. Your ear went down to nearly touch your shoulder and the other ear turned to me, really trying to listen.

Always trying. I love that about you. But, dearest Izzy, why is it so hard for you to hear?

If sacred words won't do it, here're a few of mine — nothing I haven't said before but here they are again: only two things are needed in this house, truth and forgiveness. Maybe now, after all we've been through, you'll be able to let them in? That is what I wish for you.

Izzy, it does no good for you to keep telling yourself you do not deserve this life that has been thrust upon you. Deserve has nothing to do with it. Deserve is an illusion. Deserve gathers nothing around itself but pain.

You have asked me to leave you here, between your daughter and your father. So be it. I leave you now, for the final time.

That is the truth.

And, yes, I do forgive you — for this, for all.

All love, always
Zach

25

In Mags Halloran's office on a grey January morning, we went over everything together again. She leant back in her reclining chair, her nylon-encased legs up on her desk, fingers interlaced behind her head, and fired a long list of questions at me. The pills, the pump, the comings and goings of Pauline. Zach's leaving, Star's arrival. At the end she said she believed I should change my plea to guilty.

'No,' I said. 'No way.'

'To get you off, we need an alternative possibility,' she said. 'Do you have one?'

'I think he must have done it himself.'

'Sorry, a DIY job won't do here.' No funeral home tones for Mags, no leaning forward with sympathetic eyebrows. 'A 93-year-old man doing himself in? And especially not when everything I've heard about this man paints him as a survivor.'

'None of us survives for ever, you know. And people change, even at ninety-three.'

'Very philosophical, Dotes. But not something I can take to a jury.'

It was hard to imagine Mags ever failing to survive. She liked to talk as if she were in an American cop show, complete with accent, though she had never lived in the US. The strength, though, was not an act. That ran all the way through.

'The way I see it,' she said, 'the best thing is for you to plead guilty. You gave him the morphine because he was suffering so intensely, couldn't bear it any longer . . . had to put him out of his misery . . . yadda, yadda. Go for the sympathy vote, and we might have you out in a few years.'

'No. I can't.'

'You can, you know.'

'I didn't do it.'

'Well, then, you're going to have to tell me who did. The neighbour? The daughter? The boyfriend?'

'I know this is going to sound ridiculously naive to you, Miss Halloran –'

'Mags.'

'Mags. But I can't bear to see this all wrapped up in a neat little parcel. It's far more . . .'

Her expression as she swung her feet down from the desk stopped me. She leant forward across the desk. 'Do you have *any* idea what you are facing? The prosecution's version of events is going to run something like this: you got tired of looking after your aged parent and killed him so you and your boyfriend – no, make that "lover" – could take yourselves back to California with the takings. They will push every prejudice the jury may hold about "foreigners". They will paint every action of yours in the most despicable light. You won't recognize yourself in the description, but you won't be able to do a damn thing about it, because none of it will be factually wrong.'

'All right, but –'

'Our only chance of salvaging something from this mess is to come up with a simple story we can hold up against that. The mercy killer is not superb, I admit it. I'd like it to be better. And I could do with your help in that.'

'But the truth is never simple.'

'When it comes to the law, it's not the truth that sets you free, Dotes. So tell me you don't like my story and let's work together to come up with a better one, but don't kid yourself. A one-line story is what we've got to give 'em.'

One line: the bad daughter, full of wild vengeance? Or the good daughter, full of forgiveness? How about neither, Mags? Or how about both? I was not the only daughter in the house that day.

I wasn't going to give her that. 'I'd just rather tell the truth.'

'That he must have done it himself?'

'It's the only possible explanation.'

She groaned. 'Oh, God. I got a right one when I got you, didn't I? I'm going to say it one more time. If you plead not guilty, saying your father killed himself, and the jury doesn't believe you, you're facing life imprisonment. Life. My professional advice to you is that they are unlikely to believe you.'

'Do *you* believe me?'

'That is completely irrelevant.'

'You don't.'

'What I believe – what I *know* – is that Mountjoy women's prison is not your kind of place. So I'm asking you to think again. Be your own best friend here.' She held up her hand as I attempted to speak. 'Before you say another word, think about it. Take an overnight on it.' She picked up the papers and knocked their edge against the desk. When they were all straight, she snapped an elastic band around them. 'We'll talk tomorrow on the phone. Okay?'

'Okay.'

'Right, then. Do you fancy a pint? It must be nearly lunchtime.'

'It's 11.37.'

'Come on so.'

On the way to the bar, we passed a news-stand. The evening paper was just out. 'Hiya, Mattie,' Mags said, giving the vendor some small change. She seemed to know everybody in the whole city.

'You're in this, apparently.'

'Me?'

'Yeah. Timmy told me this morning. Not news, features. Ah, here it is.'

EUTHANASIA: DEATH WITH DIGNITY? OR LICENCE TO MURDER? It cited a number of cases from abroad and then

200

mine, together with a photograph of me emerging from the High Court.

'Great,' squealed Mags.

'Great? *Great?*'

'They can't do this. You're innocent.'

'Thank you. I thought I'd never hear you say so.'

'I mean you're innocent until proved guilty. If they keep going like this, we'll argue that it's impossible for us to gather an unbiased jury. We'll be able to call a mistrial.'

'And that will get me off ?'

'Well, don't look so disappointed, Dotes. That's what we want, isn't it?'

26

Zzzzzzzz.

'Yes?'

'It's Iris Cunningham.'

'Come on up.'

I pushed the buzzing door and a tang of must assaulted my nostrils. The hallway had an old carpet, its pattern worn to grey in the centre all the way up the stairs. The banister looked sticky, and I avoided touching it as I climbed up, and up, round and round six flights. Beside a door was a home-made cardboard sign, inscribed unevenly with black marker: JEREMY PLOTKIN, *Psychotherapist*. The door was open.

I was about to turn and sneak back down the stairs when a voice called out: 'Com'on in.' A redneck Southern drawl. I hadn't expected that. My only exposure to shrinks was the movies, and I was expecting somebody urban and urbane. A dark beard. Specs. Instead I found a fat man with a bushy black unibrow and two bulging eyes set too wide apart, like that cartoon fish in Star's TV programme.

He was seated in an armchair with wooden arms and didn't get up. 'Miss Cunn-ing-ham?' His drawl made three separate syllables of the name.

'No, I'm –' I'd momentarily forgotten my alias. 'Er – I mean, yes.'

'Well, now . . .' He raised one half of the unibrow. 'Which would it be: no or yes?'

'It's Ms,' I said, recovering. 'Not Miss.'

The unibrow wilted, returning to its rightful place. 'Alright-y, ma'am. I'll try to remember that.'

He reached under his chair and brought up a clipboard with a plastic pen dangling on a grubby length of string. 'Maybe you'd fill out this here form for me.' A registration form: name, address, details of payment methods.

'I'd rather not sign up just yet. I'm . . . em . . . I'm talking to a few therapists before deciding who to go with.'

'Oh. Alright-y.' He returned the clipboard to the floor. 'So what appears to be the trouble?'

'It's not me,' I said. 'I'm here about my daughter.'

He nodded. 'Go on.' Go *aw-h-nnn*.

'She has taken to saving trash. Any scribbled piece of paper. Juice cartons from the playground. Her friend's discarded lunch wrappings. All sorts of garbage and junk. She keeps it in her bedroom.'*

'Uh-huuh.' He stares at me with his fish-like stare.

'That's it. I want to know why she's doing this. I want it to stop.'

He folded his fingers into a steeple under his chin. 'What age is she?'

'Six.'

'And how long has this been goin' on?' *Aw-h-nnn.*

'For months now. At first I hardly noticed. She just wanted to keep whatever she had touched. It started with price tags from new clothes, for example, or a piece of paper with a single mark on it, or wrapping paper torn off gifts. I didn't understand it, but it seemed harmless.'

'So you indulged her?'

'I ignored it for a while, but it's been getting progressively worse. It's turned into anything that has been touched by anyone she knows.'

'But you continued to indulge?'

'I don't believe I'd use the word "indulge". Somehow . . . For

* I have no memory of this.

some reason, it's painful for her to let anything go. But it's turning into anything she sees. Trash from the streets and school as well as home. It can't go on.'

'I see. A moment, please.'

He bent over his notebook and began to write. I looked about me. He had made some attempts to brighten the room with a pot plant and two scarlet velvet screens to corner off the interview space. I peeped past them at the counter kitchen, with miniature cooker and fridge, that occupied one corner and at the bed in the other. Did he live here as well as use it for clients?

'Do you think you might be able to help her, Mr Plotkin?'

'I do believe so, ma'am. But I'm going to need more.'

He wanted to know *everything*, not just about Star but about me. I answered all his questions, told him about Brendan and coming to live in Santa Paola. With Brendan gone, Brooklyn had nothing to hold me, and by 1964 it seemed like California was the place not just for beats, who were now being called hippies, but for all the assorted refugees from 1950s conformity. Artists and rebels and gays and outcasts and seekers and wounded soldiers: California was calling us all.

So I set out to go where Brendan and I hadn't reached. San Francisco was my destination, but when I got there it was too expensive for a single mother, so instead I went south to Santa Paola, a coastal college town. It wasn't 'the city that knows how', but it was sunnier and more child-friendly. I found us a roomy apartment close to the ocean on Westcliff Road, and Star and I settled into being Californian. Santa Paolan.

Immediately, I loved it. The Golden State is where you'll find the highest mountain in the US, the greatest bird, the biggest vineyard, the plumpest oranges, the hottest desert, the tallest waterfall, the oldest living trees . . . It's a waking dream of noise, smog, beach, sky, mountain, fog and open, golden light. It's nostalgia even while you're living it.

A good place for a widow and her child to draw together the

rents of a torn life. That was how I now described myself to strangers and how I described myself to myself. Poor, bereaved widow. Poor lone mother. Poor me.

At night, in bed beside Star, I lay still so as not to disturb her, my fingers clutching the mattress. If it wasn't for her, I told myself, I'd give up, throw in the towel, quit, surrender . . . What that meant, I wasn't quite sure, but I had to get up when she cried, even if it meant being tired. I had to produce healthy food for her, even if I couldn't care what I ate myself. I had to dress her up pretty, though any old clothes did me, and brush her hair when it was matted, though my own might look, in Doolough parlance, as if I'd been dragged through a bush backways.

Nothing in my life had prepared me to also be the provider. My choices were limited. I had a couple of part-time stints: stuffing packs to redeem coupon offers; ringing telephone owners to offer them complicated discounts; sitting at a table in a dark hotel basement, asking people what they thought of a chocolate commercial or an unnamed brand of margarine. For the most part, though, I cleaned and I served, the untrained female's fallbacks.

The worst thing about that kind of work is the management. Bartenders and waitresses serve, cleaners clean, bus boys fetch and carry, but all managers do is try to increase profits, usually through getting petty about ketchup bottles or some such. There's not much that's wholesome in work like that, even before you add the personality failings of those who think you're available for groping, or the ones who act as if your pay cheque comes out of their pocket, or those who get a kick from making you sweat.

At least, in those days, you could keep an apartment and a car and a kid on such jobs. It meant scrimping and saving, recycling and salvaging. It meant forgetting any dreams of going out of state for vacations, never mind back to Europe, a desire that was haunting me, but, unlike now, it could be done.

And I did it. I carved out a good life for us in the gentle town between the mountains and the ocean.

Never was a place more put upon by fantasy than California, but, for me, it delivered: the ever-presence of the ocean, the spectacular sunsets, the Redwood Pines, the mountains curving gently or absolutely sheer, sometimes wrapped in raiments of snow or mist, unmoved by storms or calms or anything going on above or below.

We moved there in November, and those first sunny winter days will always stay with me. Wind full of dust and dried-up leaves and the parched land seeming to listen for the rain that, when it came, was nothing like an Irish downpour but a gentle baptism, wafting in from the sea in mild and mellow veils, followed by days of softer sun and cooler air.

I didn't know it that first year, but this was Santa Paola's false spring, tricking plants into budding or even blossoming out of season and people into throwing off their clothes. In January the real rains came: in torrents, not from the ocean this time but as if the cloud directly above had been cracked open like an egg. Around us, dry river beds and arroyos raced with water, but, unlike Ireland, between each downpour we had blue skies and warmth again.

By the time the last rains came in April, in fitful squalls, real spring had arrived with its blaze of colour. Then it was the long, hot, dry season, greens gradually bleaching. In May, the first desert winds came sweeping down the canyons, as if somebody up there had plugged in a giant air heater. It ripped off palm leaves and sometimes even branches, and shifted the mountains closer. Inland was baking hot, desert hot, headache hot, but, in Santa Paola, we had our kindly fog bank. Throughout the summer it sat there, offshore on the water, about a thousand feet thick. As night fell, it would move in, filling the spaces between our homes, and in the morning, as the sun climbed, it would obligingly roll back out to sea.

It helped me make a good life for us. Star turned golden-brown and her hair lightened to gold.

Most of this I told to Jeremy Plotkin, the lead-up to asking him the question I dreaded to ask. Despite my efforts – ensuring she was clean and healthily fed, brought out to the hills on days off when I felt like sitting her in front of the TV, given all the extra-curricular activities I could afford – might this behaviour of Star's be a reaction to having a single working mom?

'Maybe, maybe not.' His unibrow frowned. 'I'd like to fill some gaps, ma'am. Can I ask you about your sex life?'

'I don't see how –'

'Oh, believe me, it's gonna be relevant.'

I felt the way I imagine any woman, alone in a room with an unknown man and a bed, would feel.

'Do you have a boyfriend?' he prompted.

'No.'

'But you have a history?'

I shrugged.

'Please, ma'am. I need to hear it.'

'There hasn't been anybody serious since my husband.'

'But there have been men?'

'Yes.'

'Women?'

'No!'

'How many men?'

'I'm not sure.'

'Approximately.'

'I've never counted. I really don't see –'

'Please, Ms Cunningham. If you and I are going to work together, you need to trust me to do my job. If you would . . .'

There had been a few. After Brendan, I really needed to see admiration in a man's eyes. Being attractive was as near as my life got to a sense of power. Flirting was the closest I came to fun. And casual encounters, slipped between work and Star, suited me well. Or that was the theory. In reality, it never stayed casual and straightforward. Sooner or later there was always a drama.

Jeremy Plotkin was waiting.

'Em . . . About eight.'

'How long again since you lost your husband?

'Four years.'

'When asked a question like this, a significant percentage of people lie or underestimate. It is important that you tell me the truth.'

'I have.'*

'Okay. Good. Now, tell me what sex is like with these men.'

'It depends on the man, I guess.'

'Can you identify any pattern?'

I shrugged.

'It's important, ma'am. Take your time.'

In the shopping precinct on the street below, faint voices were bidding each other hello and goodbye, having ordinary conversations, while I was trapped in here. After a time I said: 'Apart from the odd disaster, I've had better sex with all of them than I had with my husband.'

'Really?'

'I loved my husband; he was a very attractive man. But we were not very compatible, sexually.'

'Go o-on.'

'He enjoyed himself in bed, but I didn't. At least, not physically.'

'I see. Would that be lack of orgasm? Lack of desire? Or lack of pleasure?' He sounded like a laconic waiter listing the dishes of the day. Each syllable was drawn out until it was almost a word in itself: *or-gasm, dee-sire, pleas-uuure.*

'Maybe. I suppose. Sometimes.'

---

* She hadn't, of course. She also fails to convey the fact that this guy Plotkin was attracted to her, but I'm sure he was. They always were.

'Which, ma'am?'

'All, I suppose. I didn't think about it too much at the time. We were happy together.'

He nodded, as if he'd come to some conclusion. 'Ms Cunningham, I need you to come across to the couch,' he said. 'I want you to lie down and close your eyes and relax.'

'Why?'

'I want to ask you about your parents.'

'What have my parents – or my sex life for that matter – to do with Star and her problems?'

'A great deal, I'd say.'

'Look, I –'

'Ms Cunn-ing-ham, don't fight shy now. You are doing very well, very well indeed.'

'I really don't see –'

'If you don't feel able to continue, we can stop here and take it forward next week. But you do have' – he glanced across at the clock on the mantelpiece – 'twenny-five minutes left.'

The clock ticked at me. He stared at me with those baleful fishy eyes.

Tick tock. Tick tock.

'All right,' I said. 'All right. Let's do it.'

He led me across to the couch. I lay down. The bed smelt of body. He *did* sleep here.

'We'll begin with your father.'

'Really? I thought it was always the mother's fault.'

He didn't smile.

'So . . . Your daddy. Tell me all about him.'

'I don't know what to say.'

'He's alive?'

I nodded.

'What age would he be?'

I did a quick calculation in my head. 'He's seventy-six.'

'And you're fond of him?'

'I never see him. He's in Ireland.'

'That's not what I asked, ma'am.'

'Em . . . not especially.'

'What about when you were growing up?'

I hesitated.

'Did he beat you?'

'Only . . . Not . . . Just until I was thirteen years old.'

'What happened then?'

'I . . . I . . .'

'There's nothing to fear, ma'am. Please go on.'

'I was thirteen. I was just becoming conscious . . . I . . .'

My nostrils had shrunk to pinpricks. The room was airless. I was back in the church, the day of my mother's funeral. My father sitting beside my uncle Benny, the only member of his family who came, accepting expressions of condolence. His face like that of a child who's just opened a present to find a toy he already owns. Nothing said by the priest or any of the neighbours or friends who turned out for the day could console him in any way for the inconvenience my mother was putting him through by dying.

God, oh, God, what did I do in my past life to be left with the burden of this thankless child?

You get on your knees, girl, and pray to be forgiven for your holy ingratitude.

Jesus, Mary and Holy Saint Joseph, grant me patience to deal with this girl, this cross of mine.

'How far did it go?' Jeremy Plotkin asked. 'What happened between y'two?'

Between us? I shook my head, fiercely, against that.

'In-ter-course?'

'Look, there was nothing *between us*, as you put it. It was –'

'Feeling? Touching?'

The air has evacuated the room. I cannot fill my breath.

'Ms Cunn-ing-ham?'

'Yes.' It came out as a whisper.

'As if they were accidental?'

'Yes. Yes.' A flood of gratitude washed through me. 'Exactly.'

He was making notes. The scratch of his pen was loud in my ears. Outside lunchtime was upping the activity, voices and cars now bustling. When he had finished writing, I said, 'Tell me what's going on, what you're thinking.'

'I can say this, Ms Cunn-ing-ham. For a girl, her father is *the* primary male bond. Through him, she learns how to respond to other men.'

'What does that have to do with Star?'

'Just about everything, ma'am.'

Could this be true? Could my father's poison, despite my best efforts, have leaked through me to her?

'I don't understand how.'

'It is complicated, surely. We'll have to unravel the points of connection.'

'How?'

'Get you into a state of relaxation. Get you visualizin' and rewritin' your outcomes. First you'll be cured, then you're gonna find your daughter's fixed up too.'

'Really, doctor?'

'Well, now . . . I can't give you no guarantee. The mind is a mystery, Ms Cunning-ham, but, in your case, I'd be confident of a positive outcome. Yes, ma'am.'

I lay back down. He was not a doctor. Why had I called him doctor?

'So . . . you ready to go? Close your eyes there.'

Inside my eyelids was a night sky splashed with orange.

'You breathe deeply now. That's it. In through your nose, out through the mouth. Deep breath. Now relax your muscles, let your body grow real heavy. Yes, ma'am, that's it . . . very good. Now. I want you to picture in your head what I'm describin'. Your daddy has walked into your bedroom, and he's comin' close to your bed. You see that?'

'Yes.'

'Under those bedclothes, you're naked. You can see this in your mind, yes?'

I nodded through clenched eyes.

'Now your daddy is startin' to take off *his* clothes. He is climbin' into the bed beside you. He gets in on . . . Ms Cunning-ham! Snakes alive, Ms Cunning-ham, you can't jump up like that!'

The door. *Where* was the door? I couldn't see the *door.*

'Ms Cunning-ham, puh-lease. Lie back *down.* What you're doing here is dangerous.'

'No.' I stood, dizzy, trying to get my bearings. 'Sorry. Can't.'

'But, ma'am, you must, or you ain't ever gonna be cured. I know it is difficult but –'

'Can't.'

'You are overreactin', ma'am. Now I'm thinking this is likely what's causin' your problems. If you don't lie down now, it's over for you.'

I put my hands over my ears. 'Stop.'

'Yes, ma'am. For you, and for your girl.' His gimlet eyes fixed me in a stare, like the eyes on the dead fish my father used to catch in Doolough Lake. 'For y'all. For ever.'

My vision cleared. The door emerged. I picked up my bag, then did what my instinct had told me to do at the start. I fled.

27

In my files, connections unfold. It is now 1900. In London the chief business, as ever, is war. This time it is the turn of Boer farmers in the Transvaal in South Africa – Dutch settlers – to feel the long fingers of the Great British Empire reaching for their lands. On the principle that my enemy's enemy is my friend, a group of Irishmen in South Africa have decided to help the Boers defend themselves. They call up a brigade of soldiers from the Irish and Irish-American miners in the Transvaal to fight against the British. (None of them, British, Irish or Boer, recognizes that the native African people are the ones truly entitled.)

In Ireland this activity is milked for propaganda purposes by the great propagandist Maud Gonne. Leaving the six-year-old Iseult in the care of a convent, she spends a great deal of this year in Dublin, supporting Arthur Griffith, a journalist recently returned from South Africa, in publishing a nationalist newspaper, the *United Irishman*. In this publication Griffith burnishes the reputation of his old friend from South Africa, John MacBride, dubbing the raggle-taggle of pro-Boer Irish miners 'MacBride's Brigade', though his friend is, in fact, only second-in-command.

Maud sets up an 'Irish Transvaal Committee' and engages a subcommittee of young women to run an anti-recruitment campaign, discouraging Irishmen from joining up on the British side. Their most visible activity is following around Irish girls who consort with redcoat soldiers, crying shame. It is not unusual for this work to degenerate into screaming arguments, or even scratching and bruising.

Almost all of the women who follow Maud are younger;

some have only just put up their hair. Influenced by the suffrage movement and its slogan 'Deeds Not Words', they resent being excluded from nationalist organizations, so they form their own society: Inghínidhe na hÉireann (Daughters of Ireland). Their first big event is a Patriotic Children's Treat, to rival an outing for Dublin children sponsored by Queen Victoria. One of the children who turns out for the Patriotic Treat is my father, brought along for the day by his brother Benny.

'Dublin has never witnessed anything so marvellous as this procession of 30,000 schoolchildren who refuse to be bribed into parading before the Queen of England,' boasts the *United Irishman,* declaring it the largest peaceful demonstration the city has ever seen.

On the day, the children are marched through the city to the Phoenix Park, where they are entertained with games and dances, and fed sandwiches, ginger beer and patriotic speeches. They sing 'God Save Ireland' and the 'Transvaal War Song', and wave the flags and the green branches 'of hope' they are given, and listen or half listen while Maud tells them that they have washed away the stain put on Dublin by self-seeking bourgeoisie who vied with each other in an ignoble scramble for honours at the hand of the English Famine Queen.

Few of the children know what she is talking about, but my uncle Benny, older than the rest, is entranced, and pulls my father away from the lemonade to get closer to the stage and Her Ladyship with the big hat. When she says: 'Go home from here and talk to your fathers,' he feels as if she is talking directly to him. 'Tell them how in South Africa at this moment the English are trying to grab land that has belonged to Dutch Boer farmers for three centuries, just as they took the land of the Irish. Tell them that a contingent of Irishmen in Johannesburg fights side by side with the Boers against this injustice, led by the gallant Major John MacBride.

'Children, it is very possible that among you, another hero is being born, another Major MacBride, this time to act at home and show us how courage counts much more than numbers.'

Young Benny is stirred and he gets himself involved in the cause. Within ten months the attentions of the police have forced him to leave Ireland and exile himself in Paris. His doings, in turn, influence his younger brother, that small boy beside him at the Patriotic Treat filling his pockets with cakes, so that, three years on, he finds himself following in Benny's wake.

And in Paris, through their Irish compatriots, the pair will one day find themselves in the very drawing room of the woman with the big hat and the speechifying voice. Around my desk, the invisible presences press closer. As I write them down, my father's house creaks, seems to settle in around me.

Connections, connections. To read Griffith's reports, one would think that every Irishman in the Rand supports the Boers but, as Ireland's most popular song that year – 'How the Irish Fought the Irish at the Battle of Dundee' – makes clear, there are Irishmen on both sides of the conflict. Indeed, it is an Irishman who heads up the British troops there. A Sir George Stuart White.

Sir George has a niece called Lily, who is to travel to Australia to live on a sheep farm with her new husband, also a distant cousin of his. Sir George doesn't yet know it, but this cousin, Henry Stuart, is insane, full of a searing anguish about a great, unnamed wrong he committed at some time in his past. When Lily bears her first child (at the nearest nursing home, three hundred miles from the farm), a bat flies into the room during her labour. A bad omen that proves to her what she already knows, that the newborn boy in her arms is doomed.

Back home and suckling him one night, she hears a commotion from another bedroom and flees down the corridor towards it, to find her husband attempting to cut his own throat. She and his brother commit him to a lunatic asylum, where a short time later he succeeds in hanging himself in his cell with his bed sheet.

Lily takes her four-month-old boy back to Ireland and never again mentions to the boy or anyone else that she ever had a husband. But of course as he grows, he hears of him from whispering relatives and acquaintances. Through all the years of his growing, the blank of his father's suicide grows within him too. When he is an adult he will write novels that burst out of him, he says, 'as a shriek does from, say, a lone starling with a damaged wing left behind by the flock, or as a howl from a trapped wolf'. Until he dies, almost a century later, he will have a recurring dream of going into a ticket office and asking for a ticket to his father.

And when he is almost eighteen years old, this boy will meet and almost immediately marry a woman seven years his senior, a woman called Iseult Gonne.

Yes, yes, we will get to that. I look up at the collage I have framed, and in my mind I step into the picture to take Iseult's hands. Arms stretched as straight as they'll go, I lean back and so does she and we start to turn in a circle, slowly first, then faster and faster until we're creating a vortex that sets the others dancing round us. A wide and spinning circle held in place only by us and some unknowable, unseen force.

The Boers are defeated in Africa, and John MacBride, like Benny and Martin Mulcahy, is forced into exile. Encouraged by his friend Arthur Griffith, he decides to settle, for a time at least, in Paris, where that great supporter of the Irish movement, Miss Maud Gonne, will ensure he finds a placing worthy of him.

She organizes a group to welcome his train with banners and handkerchiefs, tins and spoons, and when he arrives she makes them all wait there on the platform at the Gare de Lyon, while she makes a speech about how he and the other Irish heroes of the South African plains have – with the Boer farmers – broken down the falsehood of England's greatness, that falsehood on which the British Empire has been built. 'The nations who accepted the legend of England's greatness – like Ireland – looked on in wonder, and some in shame, and all in admiration and delight as they held off the might of Empire.'*

They sing the new ballad now heard everywhere in Ireland.

> *. . . Eire watches from afar*
> *With joy and hope and pride,*
> *Their sons who strike for liberty*
> *Led on by John MacBride . . .*

'Speech,' someone calls as soon as the song is over.

He says, 'I'm no speaker. And what man would be able to follow the likes of that oration of Miss Gonne's? So I won't even try. I'll just say how good it is to be here, among friends. That you'd all come here like this . . . It's most kind of you all. I didn't expect anything like this. So thank you all very much. I . . .'

Everyone waits but he says no more. Then Arthur Griffith shouts, 'Tell us about the war.'

'Another time I will. But I'm sure people want to get away from this cold platform.'

The long shadow that is Maud Gonne looms in the corner of his eye. Whenever he flicks his eyes across, he finds as soft and kind a look as he has ever seen on a female face. He goes across. 'The flag you sent from the Daughters of Ireland,' he says to her. 'I can't tell you how many times I saw some young lad, thinking himself unseen in the big African night, go up and kiss its folds.'

* What dizzy heights would Maud's prose have reached if the Boers had actually won.

'Oh, I'm so glad. The women put such a deal of work into it.'

Not by one flicker does she betray to him or to anyone that she has just had the most disquieting surprise. In all the talk she had heard about John MacBride, nobody saw fit to tell her that the hero swelling her propaganda, the giant among men who points the way to Ireland and the world, was a mere five foot six inches tall.

What of it? Has she not spent her adult life crossing boundaries? Religion, nationality, class – none of these mean anything to her when held beside the soul of a man. Six inches of height, then, is really no barrier at all.

28

Star's face emerging from the school door chafed my heart. Her feet were dragging, and as soon as we got into the car she collapsed into tears.

'Did you not get the Molly Dolly part?'

'No,' she sobbed. 'No.'

'Oh, honey, I'm sorry.'

'I have no part . . . (sob) . . . at all.'

'What? But I thought everyone had to be in the school play.'

'Everyone . . . (sob) . . . does. Except I told Miss Rossi that I (yell) *quit*.'

'What? Why?'

Miss Rossi had given her the part of Mrs O'Brien. A silly old Irish lady. Not a doll or a pony or a doggie or even a tin soldier. The only grown-up in the play. Boring. Boring. She didn't want to do that. She wanted to be (wail) Molly Dolly.

The lead role had gone to Angelina Boyle, the prettiest girl in the class. I could see where Miss Rossi was coming from. At that time Star was about four inches taller than everyone else in her class. Dolly, she wasn't.*

'You said I was the best actress,' she cried. 'You said I was a *star*.'

I held her tight while she sobbed and tried to soothe her. When the storm eased a little, opening a space, I said, 'Won't you want to be in the play, sweetheart?'

'Not . . . (sniff) . . . if I'm not Molly Dolly.'

'But won't you feel left out, watching all the others practise and perform if you're not in it?'

* Why thank you, Mother. And I wasn't even fat yet.

219

Her chin dropped. She hadn't thought of that. She hadn't thought this through at all.

'You know it's not how big or small your part is that counts, it's what you do with it. How about you and I work together to make sure that your Mrs O'Brien is real memorable?'

'But I told Miss Rossi I didn't want it.'

'Well, why don't I ask her tomorrow to give it back to you?'

'Mommy, you can't.' She frowned.

'I'm sure she will, if I ask her.'

'I hate Angelina Boyle.'

Star got her part back, and for the following weeks she and I ran through her two lines over and again, as if we were rehearsing Portia for the RSC. We used our neighbour Mrs Quinn as a model. We modified her script, putting an extra word or two into the bare sentences to make them unmistakably Irish. We experimented with clothes, accents and attitude, and, by the time the great day arrived and the parents were taking their seats, Star could not wait to get backstage. I sat and watched while the curtain went back, and each mom or dad scanned the stage until they found their own darling. Star wasn't there; her entrance came later.

Dolls and soldiers and teddy bears came and went around a bewildering plot centred on Molly Dolly's lost teddy and her refusal to do her homework or chores until he was found. But where was he? The action was interminable, designed in time-honoured, school-play tradition, to give a speaking part to all. Bored parents fanned themselves with their programmes. When, three quarters of the way through, Star burst on to the stage dressed not unlike a drag queen, in a lime-green evening gown with matching high heels, I could feel the audience around me popping awake. Taller than the rest, she walked across to Molly and, with hands on her hips, delivered her line in a strong Irish brogue: 'Now, Molly Dolly, don't you be acting the rascal.'

Her timing and delivery were perfect. The audience hooted with laughter. Molly said her piece and Star delivered Mrs

O'Brien's second, final line. 'Little girls have to be doing what they're told.' Again laughter, not so much for what she was saying as for the look and bearing of her.

Molly said, 'But I'm so sad,' which was Star's cue to retreat and let Tommy Soldier step forward into the limelight, but she decided her appreciative spectators deserved more Mrs O'Brien than was scripted. She turned to the audience. 'Children these days,' she said, throwing her eyes to heaven. 'Begorrah!' At which the place broke up into a spontaneous burst of applause.

I cheered as long and loud as any of them.

For the rest of the performance she was on stage, and my eyes could look only at her, no matter what else was going on. She held her character all through, except for one small moment when she slipped and let her rosy pleasure and pride surface. That was my favourite moment of the night, better even than her accepting her due of compliments and praise afterwards backstage; or than the drive home in the car with her sharing all her thoughts, the purr of the engine beneath her small, delighted voice; or even than tucking her into bed after cocoa and cookies and receiving a special, solemn hug as I bent to kiss her goodnight, a hug full of gratitude and love and a thousand nameless things.

29

A carriage pulls to a halt outside the great gates of the Carmelite convent at Laval, steppers noisy in the silent street. The driver, who wears a fur cape against a bitter February wind, climbs down. Thrusting a card through the grating, he announces the name into the gate door. A pause. Bolts are heard to creak and keys to jingle and the big gates swing back and the driver climbs back on board and steers the carriage into the yard.

Sœur Rédempta pulls a bell chain thrice, three clanging peals, while the driver gets down again, this time to place a step at the side door of the carriage. Out comes an elegantly booted Maud Gonne, skirts held high, and, then, a younger woman bearing a distinct resemblance to her. Sœur Rédempta comes fluttering across, a cape thrown across her shoulder to run out into the cold, hands proffered: 'Welcome, madame. Oh, thank God you have arrived safe. Such frightful, frightful weather. Welcome.'

Maud bends to receive her kiss of greeting.

'How are you, sister, dear? And how passes life in the convent?'

'Passable, madame. We do what we can.'

'This is my cousin, Miss Eileen Wilson, lately come to live with me.' Actually not a cousin but Tommy's daughter, from a secret affair that came to light only after his death. For the past sixteen years, Maud has paid Bowie, her own nurse when she was small, to look after this girl but now Bowie has died and her half-sister – who bears an uncanny resemblance to her – has come to stay in Avenue d'Eylau. The latest link in the chain of change that began three years ago in the Gare de Lyon.

'Mademoiselle.' The old nun inclines her head. 'Come, come, let us get you inside, out of this fearsome cold.'

Inside all is shiny floors, the smell of cleaning wax, a sense of order and light. Maud releases a sigh. The convent always has that effect upon her: instant relaxation. It is one of the reasons she has so enjoyed the years Iseult spent here. Now that too is to change. Sœur Rédempta leads the way to the parlour, walking beside Eileen. 'You have always lived in England, mademoiselle?'

Eileen does her best to answer in French. 'Yes, in Farnham. But I have always thought of myself as Irish.'

Her accent is poor, but Sœur Rédempta shows no sign. 'And now . . . you shall live in France.' She says this with an air of someone who knows beyond doubt that France is the best of all possible countries in which to live.

Eileen bows.

'Aaaah, so young and so brave. God will protect you, mademoiselle. He protects you already, in bringing you into the care of your good cousin.'

Maud interjects: 'Have you ever been to England, sister?'

'No, indeed. I have never been outside France.'

The conversation falters. Maud is about to speak when Sœur Rédempta turns to her, eyes glowing. 'And it is true, madame, the news we have heard?'

Maud smiles.

'Glory be to God,' says Sœur Rédempta fervently. 'Glory be to His goodness. Our prayers are answered.'

Maud smiles. 'You are so kind to think of this poor sinner in your prayers.'

'Oh, madame, you must know that Canon Dissard and Mère Suzanne have long placed you in our intentions.'

'I do know, sister. It has been a great comfort to me during difficult times.'

It also made her fearful. In Ireland, in tiny cottages in the mountains of Mayo and Donegal, the rosary had been recited for years for the same intention: that she would convert to Catholicism. Was she really worthy of so many prayers? The plain Irish people would understand these decisions she has lately made. Her own would not.

'You must forgive me for taking so long,' she says to Sœur Rédempta.

'All happens in God's own good time, madame, and there is more joy in heaven for the wait.' She swings the door of the parlour open. 'I shall tell Mère Suzanne you have arrived. And Sœur Jeanne has gone to fetch Iseult. She is playing rounders, in the garden, with Sœur Thérèse. Oh, madame, she will be so excited by your news.'

'Yes. Yes, indeed. I cannot wait to tell her.'

Sœur Thérèse, a simple Auvergnate only seven years older than Iseult, has a trio of afflictions: a squint, a permanent scowl and a short leg. This might seem to make her a poor choice to play rounders with a child, but in the convent it is deemed good to do that for which one is least fitted. It pushes one's boundaries, and, if one fails in the endeavour, well, mortification is good for the soul.

Sœur Thérèse limps through the motions, and Iseult follows, slowly. At nine years old, she is settling into herself, and, though she still sometimes runs or jumps for the pleasure of running or jumping, or to vent the feelings pushing up and out against her skin, she has calmed a great deal in recent months. Partly it is her age, partly convent life. Here, nobody ever wonders where time has gone, as Moura is forever wondering at home. Bells announce the phases of the day, but nobody rushes. Each day and night has its full allocation of hours.

Iseult likes the convent, now she understands what is not permitted: running down the corridor, leaving one's hair uncovered at Mass, stretching one's arm at table to take food. All of this she accepts, as nine-year-olds do. It is as it is.

Sœur Thérèse's fingers are red, turning blue at the tips. She puts the bat under her arm to huff warm air on her nails. Iseult hasn't noticed the cold. She pays little attention to the weather, except when it turns dramatic, like the hail storm last week that battered the window with stones as big as hen's eggs. Winter means that outside the gate to the rounders pitch, the roses and lilies she loved in the summer have died, leaving a tangle of stalks, but they went so gradually that she failed to notice and now she has forgotten that they were ever there, let alone that they might come again. She is too young to think about seeds or blooms or pods. Time, for her, is still an open moment, not yet a line through years.

Sœur Thérèse bats the ball. Iseult watches. She is not a child who runs to order, and today she wants not to run but to dance, because yesterday Sœur Suzanne told her at breakfast that Moura was coming. Since then she has been eating the imminent visit at mealtimes, holding it in her pen during lessons, kneeling on it during prayers in the chapel, hugging it to sleep in her dormitory bed. Now, instead of giving chase, she decides to dance Moura's coming into the rounders pitch.

'Run,' shouts Sœur Thérèse. 'You're supposed to *run*.'

Moura's arrivals are always as sudden as a wake-up bell in the morning. Often Iseult gets no warning at all; she just appears wherever Iseult happens to be, at lunch or lessons or play, sweeping in, with laughter bubbling like fizzy water and Iseult's name tumbling from her lips, as if she has to repeat it over to make up for all the times she has not been there to say it. 'Iseult! Iseult, darling! Darling beautiful Iseult! Oh, my Iseult, how I have missed you!' She bends from her great height and swoops Iseult up, up, up into her arms to swaddle her in hugs and kisses and little whispers.

A bat and ball is pressed into each of Iseult's hands. 'All right, then,' cries Sœur Thérèse. '*You* do the hitting.'

Then Moura produces the gift. Always she brings something lovely: a scarf or pen or book or ring or a little animal friend. Once a Persian cat. Another time: a canary, smaller than Twee-Twee but just as yellow and lively. Once even a pet alligator.

'You don't want to play, do you?'

225

Iseult shakes her head.

'Don't bother, then. Go on, go talk to the grass or whatever it is you do.' Sœur Thérèse throws the ball as far as she can towards the far end of the pitch and sets off limping after it. 'Just don't go outside the gate, mind.'

On a blade of grass near her right foot, Iseult notices the shell of a ladybird. It is the wrong season for ladybirds, though she is too young to know it. She bends down. 'Moura is coming,' she whispers to the ladybird, by which she means crack your shell-body open, flutter out your wings . . .

It does not move.

A sound jangles out from the steps at the back door. The bell. Two short, sharp rings. She looks up. Sœur Conciliata is there, on the steps, waving. Iseult jumps up, ladybird forgotten. Sœur Thérèse, rounders game, garden, dancing, all forgotten. Now she runs, oh, yes, as though she has all the breath she could ever need, past the Virgin Mary, who smiles down on her from her pedestal, past the bushes and big trees and the fountain, all the way to the door, where she knows she must stop and walk.

In the parlour, tea is being served, Mère Suzanne meets Maud with a fond embrace, an assurance that her friend looks divine, better than ever, and an ushering towards the easy seats at the far end of the parlour. 'Sit, sit,' she insists, as if somebody has said they would rather not. Sœur Maria-Angeles plumps cushions, Sœur Jeanne brings tea and Canon Dissard arrives, leading to more embraces and introductions of Eileen.

How serene it is here, how quiet and comfortable and ordered, thinks Maud, as she settles back into the cushions, teacup in hand. It is women who have the truest sense of life. Look at this piping hot cup of tea, served just as it ought to be served: from shining silver pots in precious china cups. If you want your birthday remembered, your drawing room beautified, your clothes appreciated, your emotions soothed, it is to a woman you must turn.

It was this realization that led her to form Inghínidhe na hÉireann, her Daughters of Ireland. How is it that she was so unaware of it in her youth, the steadfastness and loyalty of women? Because her sister and cousins and aunts were so different from her, she had thought herself a complete exception, rather than seeking women who were of like mind. She must impress upon Iseult – and indeed now upon Eileen – the great importance of like-minded female friends.

The door bursts open. Two huge eyes cast themselves around the room, and, almost before they have landed on Maud, a small, fierce body is flinging itself in her direction.

'Iseult! Iseult, dear!' Moura laughs as the girl comes flying towards her, wrapping herself round her.

'Iseult! Is this how a young lady enters a room?' That's Canon Dissard.

And now the nuns are tut-tutting too, ashamed that Iseult's behaviour might cast doubt on their training. Iseult cares for none of them. She has Moura's dress in her hands and Moura's smell in her nostrils and Moura's arms coming round her. The fabric of the blue dress is scratchy on her face, but she burrows in. She did not expect the blue dress; Moura was wearing green when she went away. The clothes she wore on their last day together are what stay in mind, so that when she returns, Iseult is always surprised to find her in something different.

She doesn't like the laugh Moura is laughing either. A tinkling noise, not for her but for the others who are watching. Moura grips her by the upper arms, holds her away at arm's length. 'Let me see you, my beloved angel. How tall you have grown. How beautifully tall.'

Iseult wishes the others would disappear – Poof! Gone! – so she and Moura can make a little world of their own, the world where Iseult talks and Moura listens, as she never does when other adults are present. But no, they all circle about, standing and staring like gulls stare at the sea, holding something in their faces, something that presses against her. Why won't they go?

Or why can't she and Moura be the ones to go, out into the big garden, maybe, where she can dance and run again? 'Moura, you must wish to see Ali?'

Ali is the pet alligator brought from America, who now lives in the pond in the garden.

'Not today, *chérie*. Or, at least, not now.'

'We tied a ribbon round his neck,' Iseult says. 'Sister Beatrice helped me. Wouldn't you like to see him, Moura?'

'Maybe later. Iseult – Moura has something to tell you.'

'Sister Beatrice thought he might eat the fish. But he's too small. He's very gentle. All he does is swim and smile.' His alligator smile with the tough teeth.

'Iseult!' Canon Dissard's use of her name is soft and hard, both together, like Ali's body. 'Be a good girl, please. Today is a day for great rejoicing. Madame Gonne is to join our Catholic faith.'

Moura asks for Iseult with her eyes. 'Do you remember my new friend, the Major, Iseult? Major MacBride? Come now, don't make that face, of course you do.' Moura's eyes glint like wet pebbles after a rain shower. 'Well, I have the most wonderful news for you. The Major and I are to marry.'

Without moving, the nuns press closer.

'Why?'

'Why? My dear, what a strange question.'

'But why, Moura?'

'Because . . .' says Moura, smiling round. 'Because we wish to.'

Moura is pleading with her. Her words and her face don't say so – they cannot speak because of the listeners, the watchers – but Iseult can feel the entreaty inside her reaching out. She wants to give Moura what she wants. But . . .

'No, Moura.'

Moura laughs. The nuns laugh.

'I hate him.'

All the eyes jerk open, all except Moura's, which narrow.

'Yes. I do. I hate him.'

'Dearest, you barely know him.'

'He has the eyes of an assassin.'

The sisters' smiles are like small blades now. Everybody is acting as if something wrong is being put right by this idea of Moura's, but . . . no.

'We shall have such a fine time when madame returns,' says Canon Dissard. 'I believe we shall have a banquet in honour of the bride and groom, my little Iseult, and you shall be queen of the day. Wouldn't you like that?'

'Oh, darling, you would make such a lovely queen. And we are going to Spain for our honeymoon and I shall bring you home something very beautiful. The Spanish know what is beautiful.'

Iseult begins to howl. 'Noooooooooo.'

'Iseult, please. What a dreadful noise.'

'Nooooo, Moura. No.'

'Iseult!' Moura's voice is losing its purr of persuasion. She pulls Iseult close, whispers something in her ear. Iseult cannot hear because her own cries are deafening her. She stops to listen, and Moura repeats the words: 'It is for you, darling. I am doing this for you.'

'Nooooo . . .'

Iseult buries her head again in Moura's skirt. If she does not hold hard, she knows she shall start to do things that later shall make her ashamed. Pick up that tray of teacups from the table and smash it against the wall over the heads of the nuns and Canon Dissard. Fling teacakes and sandwiches into their faces. When she gets into a rage, she is capable of anything, Moura says.

Traitor Moura.

She is supposed to be learning to control this temper of

hers. So she holds her fury in her fingers and grips on to Moura's skirt.

'Come along, Iseult. Let Moura go.'

Sœur Catherine prises her fingers away. 'You'll tear it, you silly girl,' she says, as she drags her off. 'Come away now, come away.'

Mrs Honoria MacBride (his mother) to Major John MacBride

I have seen Maud Gonne. She is very beautiful; she is a great woman and has done much for Ireland but she will not make you happy. You will neither be happy, she is not the wife for you. I am very anxious. Think well what you are doing.

Mammy

Arthur Griffith to Maud Gonne

Queen, forgive me. John MacBride, after Willie Rooney, is the best friend I ever had; you are the only woman friend I have. I only think of both your happiness. For your sakes, and for the sake of Ireland to whom you both belong, don't get married. I know you both, you so unconventional, a law to yourself; John so full of conventions. You will not be happy for long. Forgive me, but think while there is still time.

To Major John MacBride from his brother*

You know of course what you are doing, but I think it most unwise. Maud Gonne is older than you. She is accustomed to money and you have none; she is used to going her own way and listens to no one. These are not good qualities for a wife. A man should not marry unless he can keep his wife . . .

* Mom wanted me to check whether this letter came from Anthony or Joseph MacBride. There is some biographical dispute, apparently. But I didn't know how, and it doesn't seem to me to matter much.

These letters represent just a fraction of the objections raised by friends and family on both sides to what is widely believed to be an ill-judged match, but Maud is determined. She might consider marriage an abomination, but, for Iseult's sake, and because she is getting too old and tired to be brave, what with her chest and her rheumatism and general decrepitude, she is resolved to make this sacrifice to convention. How could others, always so careful and constrained in their dealings with life, be expected to understand?

Only Willie Yeats makes her feel a little guilty. He too has written, telling her that she is at a moment of great peril, that with this marriage she is bringing herself down to the level of the people, that Maud Gonne, the great lady, is about to pass away. Poor Willie – always such a snob. This line has no influence on her. She has always told him that she is of the people.

Less easy to ignore is his appeal, in the name of fourteen years of friendship, that she, whose hands were placed in his by eternal hands, would come back to herself (by which he meant to him) and take up again the 'proud solitary haughty life' that made her seem like one of the golden gods.

But really, it is quite ridiculous to be made to feel guilty, for Willie had his chance. After that time, four years ago now, she allowed him to construct and continue his elaborate justification of spiritual marriage as the deepest expression possible between a man and a woman. She knows this is the only way he can align his rejection of her with his avowals of passion. For her part, it is face-saving, for it is never nice to be rejected and certainly not by one from whom one had every reason to expect acceptance.

She knows her marriage is going to shatter this fragile emotional landscape between them, but Willie needs to grow up. It is impossible to explain so she sends him a telegram.

W. B. Yeats is just about to give a lecture in Dublin when the telegram arrives, striking him, as he later writes, like lightning –

deafening his ears, blinding his eyes. So . . . she is impervious to his pleas. She is stepping down into a lower social and religious order, and rejecting that great work they were engaged upon together – that religion of free souls that would grow up in Ireland through the work of a few strong aristocratic spirits who believe the soul immortal. Just as he is coming to fully understand the work, she is gone from him.

Somehow, he manages to go on with his talk, recalling later, as he wanders the darkening city streets alone, that the audience had applauded, but he was unable to remember a single word he had said to them. With this marriage, she has done him and their great cause a great injury.

The burden of guilt that he has borne since spurning her in 1898 can now shift back to her.

30

'*Qu'est-ce que vous voulez?*' the woman says.

Martin Mulcahy stands blank, without a notion as to what she's just said – he hasn't a word of French, not yet. She goes to push the door against him, and the thought of another setback jumps tears into his eyes. Then the shame of that puts him into a fluster, so that she has the door nearly closed before he gathers himself and sticks out his foot to stop her. Only just in time. She looks down at the obstructive boot set between them and then back up into his face. A look he's never seen before. Is it fear? Fear, of him? He is nigh on six feet tall now, so maybe he looks a man to her, a male with dangerous intent.

The thought gives him a small thrill, but when he speaks it is in his softest voice, to show he means no harm. 'Please, missus,' he says. 'Please. I've come a long way.'

He shouldn't have pressed himself so hard to get here, stopping neither to eat nor drink. He sees that he was foolish to have expected Benny to be at home, waiting for him, in the middle of a work day, but it had kept him going, the thought of that bit of a welcome that would be his once he arrived: *Come in, come in, sit down by the fire, take off your boots, you must be tired . . .* Wasn't that, or something like it, what he deserved? *Here's a bucket of warm water and a soft sponge, a cushion for your head, some food for your mouth . . .*

Food! Dear God, what he would give for a morsel. A mile or so back, he had passed a cake shop with pastries in the window the like of which he had never seen in his life. One savoury tart, yellow, shiny, called out to him, but he was too shy to go in without any French. He thinks of its eggy sheen and imagines the sweet, darling taste of it in his mouth . . . Even a cup of tea, a sweet, merciful cup of tea . . .

The woman shakes her head at him. '*Non, monsieur. Je ne comprends pas.*'

He points to his suitcase and the space behind her in the hall, trying to make her understand that he'd like to leave it there. If he's going to have to walk back to the food shop, let him at least get rid of that burden. Not that there is much weight in it: his good suit, inherited from Jamsie, greasy-elbowed and the pants too short; a patched long-johns and vest; some wash things; his prayer book and a spare pair of boots that his mother got at the last minute from God knows where. No, it's not heavy, but the leather around the strap has frayed and the exposed rope has been digging into his fingers since he left home, scraping his skin.

'Please,' he tries again. Her English is about as good as his French, so he puts his heart into his face, trying to shrink himself in her eyes so she'll take pity on him.

To his own surprise, this time it seems to work. '*Irlande?*' she says, in such heavy French that at first he doesn't recognize the word. *Irrr-land-eh?*

'Yes,' he says, nodding energetically when realization dawns. 'Yes, yes. From Ireland.'

She opens the door, and he steps in. Inside, the house has seen better days. The plasterwork of a once fine ceiling is broken in large patches, like icing picked off a cake. The woman is beckoning him on, up a staircase that curves round and round as it rises. He follows. Three flights up, he finds breathing becoming a struggle for him, though it is no bother, it seems, to her. She stops in front of one of the doors.

'*Irrrlande,*' she says again, pointing at one of the doors with a scowl.

If that's her friendly face, he'd hate to see her crossed. But he makes his thanks to her, and she trips lightly away from him on her old legs, up another flight or two.

He turns the handle of the door, not expecting it to open, and it doesn't, so he sits down on the stairs opposite to have a think. Should he spend any of his remaining money – only seven francs and twelve centimes – on food? Or should he stay put here and wait? The relief to his feet and legs of sitting down draws a long sigh out of him. It would be nice to take his boots off, only he's afraid he'd stink the place out of it, so he settles for loosening his laces.

So this is it: his grand arrival in Paris. Not turning out quite how he'd imagined it, but he'll do better here than in London, the other choice he had. Less anti-Irish feeling here. And Benny has got on well, so no reason why his little brother – with a bigger helping of brains to his advantage – can't do better. Once he's picked up a bit of the lingo, he'll be grand. *Bonjour, au revoir,* and all that.

A shaft of sunshine comes slanting in through the big arched window above him, and he moves a little to put himself in the way of it. He leans back on the step, into it, and becomes aware, the moment he stops moving, of how his head is buzzing with tiredness, as if insects lined the inside of his skull. The air has a different feel here to home. What is it, that difference? It's drier and dustier, with a sweet smell, something between horse manure and baking bread.

Bread.

Oh, how hungry he is but also how tired. His limbs are scratchy. He finds himself turning, his arms folding together in the shaft of light, his eyes closing and his head, heavy, dipping towards the cradle of his arms. Before it has touched down, he is gone, carried off by sleep.

My father sleeps, a dead sleep, and nobody disturbs him. Hours pass, and he moves into the dreaming phase: feels himself to be on a farm, down the country, as when his mother once brought him down to stay at an uncle's house. Hay-saving time and he's down at the bottom of a field, atop a hayrick, hiding.

The sun-blue sky is above him and the noise of his family and neighbours below. A pitchfork comes nudging up out of the hay, disturbing his comfort, prodding into his back.

'Wake up, lad,' someone says. 'Wake up.'

He doesn't want to, but the voice insists on pulling him up out of the depths. He rubs his eyes with the heel of his hands and comes to, recognizing his surroundings with a jolt. He is in Paris! Not a field at all. That's no pitchfork but a gentle boot on his spine.

He sits up. 'Benny!'

'It *is* yourself.'

He stands, and nearly collapses back down again – his right leg is all pins and needles. He flicks it, gives it a stamp. Thank God, is his thought as he shakes the sleep out of his head. Thank God: food shouldn't be too far away now. His stomach is even emptier than before he dropped off.

'Jesus, lad, you've changed.'

'You could expect that, in three years.'

'But still a smart lip on you.'

His brother is holding out a hand to him, and, when he takes it, Benny brings his other hand round to grasp tighter. His eldest brother, shorter than him now, and thinner than he remembers him. His bright red hair has done a disappearing act, and the bit that's left at the back and sides has faded to the colour of muddy wheat. Hands and neck and face are very brown, except for a splash of red veins across his cheeks that looks like it would bleed if you touched it. His collar is caked with dirt.

Awkward with feeling, Benny pumps his hand up and down for too long. 'I can't get over you. You must be twice as long as you were. Do you remember me at all?'

He remembered a moon-filled night and a long donkey-and-cart ride out into the country, as far as the sea, and his brother appearing out of the darkness like a monster, with a beard and crusted in dirt and giving out that his mother shouldn't be there to see him like that and that she shouldn't have brought the young fella.

'Are you not going to introduce me?' interrupts a voice from behind and only then does he become aware of another man, standing back from them in the shadows.

Benny turns that way. 'Henderson, this is my little brother, Martin "The Mule" Mulcahy. Say hello to Mr Jack Henderson, late from the county of Cork.'

'Martin will do fine.'

'Hello, Mule.'

'Martin,' he says, withholding his hand.

'You can see he's well named,' says Benny, laughing.

'Go on, lad,' says Henderson, grabbing his hand. 'I'm only joking with you. Welcome to Gay Paree.'

'I can't get over you, so I can't,' Benny is saying. 'Last time I saw you, you were only that height.' He holds his hand out, level with his hip.

'Shall we go inside, before herself comes snooping?' says Henderson.

'Right you be,' says Benny. 'Come on, lad, we'll show you your accommodation. It's none too fancy, I'm afraid. A space of floor between our two beds.'

Inside the room it's dark as night. The bulky shadow that is Henderson goes across to open the shutters and then evening light floods the room. The space is a good size with everything in it: beds, wardrobes, gas ring for cooking, washstand, table and chairs. Beside one armchair, a stack of old newspapers is piled high. Henderson must be a reader.

Benny is bending under one of the beds. He hauls out a mattress into the space between the two beds. 'There,' he says, huffing with the effort. 'That's the best we can do you for.'

'It's grand.' My father puts down his bag and sits down on to it. 'Lovely.'

'We'll have to keep it under the bed during the day. We

237

haven't said anything to your woman upstairs about you joining us.'

'Would she mind?'

'Let's say that what she doesn't know won't hurt her. Was it herself let you in?'

'I think so.'

'Warm little piece?' asks Henderson. 'Knocking you out with a killer smile?'

My father smiles. 'That's the one.'

'So,' says Benny, leaning back against the wall and folding his arms, 'you've got yourself into a bit of trouble at home, eh?'

He shrugs, trying his best not to look chuffed. Benny will be proud of him, but not if he's seen to have a swelled head about it. 'A wee bit of trouble, all right. Best get out for a while, anyhow.'

'And as well off out, from what I'm hearing. Is it true that the whole place is gone soft, believing the Home Rule faddle?'

'It's true.'

'Jaysus, have we no shame? Any palaver out of the English and over we roll like . . . like . . .'

'Like a Parisian tart,' Henderson supplies.

Silence falls, then Henderson cuts in: 'Come on, we can solve dear old Ireland's problems later. It's time to get cleaned up. My stomach thinks my throat's been cut.'

'You must be hungry too, lad.'

'A little.'

'We'll introduce you to French food tonight. The best cuisine in the world. According to the French anyway.'

Mule looks doubtfully at the oil stove in the corner.

'We won't be cooking. We eat at the Frond.'

'The what?'

'Café Frond. What you might call our local.'

'Tuesday is not the very best, unfortunately,' says Henderson. 'On Tuesday the offering is a class of a horsemeat stew.'

Horsemeat?

'Don't look so frightened, boy,' Benny says, smiling. 'It's no different to eating a cow, if you think about it.'

'Jesus!'

They start stripping off their work clothes. 'You'll like it,' Benny says. 'The *patron* speaks English and is married to a girl from County Meath. There's always a good Irish contingent there. The famous Major John MacBride for one. The writer Arthur Lynch, have you heard of him?'

'No, but I've heard of the Major.'

'We've been back in his house,' says Henderson. 'A little palace of a place,' says Henderson. 'Like an Aladdin's cave. There's nothing they don't have.'

'Was she there herself?'

'Mad Gone? No. MacBride only doles out the invites when Mad-ame is from home. When the cat's away . . .'

'And lucky for the mouse MacBride,' says Benny, drying off his face with a towel, 'the cat's away plenty.'

'Aye. She'd prefer being in Ireland attention-seeking than at home looking after her children.'

'She's done great things for Ireland, all the same,' Martin says. 'And John MacBride too.'

'Maybe one time,' says Benny, 'but he only drinks for Ireland now.'

They step out into the Paris evening, Henderson leading the way through alleys and side streets out on to a tree-lined boulevard. The whole city seems to be abroad: couples arm in arm, friends greeting each other with handshakes, groups sitting beneath the striped awnings outside the cafés. The women wear elaborate hats, walking gardens of roses, laburnum and hydrangeas, and so many feathers that there can hardly be an ostrich left in the world with a tail. They pass pedlars of all sorts. A Negro, gaudily dressed in a turban and long flowing robes, offers nougat. A street later it's a Turk suggesting they buy Turkish Delight for their ladies.

In Ireland the streets are just thoroughfares through which

239

inhabitants pass on their way to somewhere else. But in France, especially in Paris, to walk the streets is to know the people.

My father stops in front of a church, entranced by Gothic angels and the grimaces of gargoyles looking down on him from above. The other two, well seasoned to Parisian wonders, laugh and pull him onward, but his heart rises to meet this awakening within, which is stronger than his wish not to make a fool of himself, stronger even than the call of food to an empty stomach. A sense of possibility is what he is feeling. A conviction that anything might happen, now that he is here in this place of carved and engraved stone, so very fine. So very far from what he left behind.

The way he feels, tramping through a passageway behind the other two, down a steep, curved archway towards the river, its steps worn in the middle by a million other feet, is that he doesn't care if he never sees Ireland again.

31

'Oh, Mommy, after you left this morning I dropped my lunch on the schoolyard ground and Mark Libovitz came over and he was going to jump on my sandwich except that Sabrina and Casey and Fred came around in a circle and stopped him and then we went in and we had Art first today, Mommy, instead of Science because Mrs Golightly wasn't in and Miss Cremona said my painting was good, except not as good as the one I did two weeks ago. Do you remember that one? Oh, look there's a dog crossing the road. Be careful, Mommy. It was boring during English and I was thinking about that programme that we saw last night, with the Monkees, do you remember, Mommy? It was good, wasn't it? Did you like it? I liked the sandwiches you gave me for lunch. I think that's my favourite now. Tuna fish. I used to prefer chicken but I think now I prefer tuna. What was I saying? Oh, yes, after Art, what did we do then? Em . . . Oh, History, that's it. Miss Cremona came in and she . . .'

Each afternoon now, when I collected Star from school, she launched into a frantic monologue, reporting to me everything that had happened to her that day, everything she had thought or felt or seen or heard, and whatever came into her mind while she was delivering her report. On it would go, compulsively, breathlessly, ceaselessly into the afternoon and evening.

'Stop, Star. Let it go. It doesn't matter.'

'I have to tell you, Mommy.'

'You don't, darling.'

'I do.'

'Why?'

'I have to.'

'But why? What would happen if you didn't?'

'I don't know.'

'What's in your head now?'

'Bertie, Mr Malvich's dog, and –'

'Stop.' I put my finger against her lips. 'Don't say the next thing.'

She stopped.

'Hold the thought. You got it?'

Another nod.

'Now let it go without telling it.'

'No, Mommy, I want to tell you. What I was thinking was –'

'No, no, wait a minute. You can tell me in a minute. First, explain something. *Why* do you feel you want to tell me? Why do you want to tell me everything that happens?'

'I don't know. I have to. Listen, Bertie was running up the road and her . . .'

Four years since Jeremy Plotkin, and things were worse, not better. I took it to her teachers, and then to the school psychologist, and then to another private counsellor. Four years of nobody helping much, while the problem pretended to fade or disappear, but was really only hiding, or mutating, before rearing up again.

Her relationship with trash – please don't laugh! – was not as intense as it had been, though she still clung to certain useless things with a strange anguish that now seemed almost harmless next to this compulsive sharing of every single detail of her life. By bedtime each evening we were both worn out by the torrent of her thoughts, and she would be crying at the idea of going to sleep, because sleeping meant not being able to tell me what was on her mind.

So now . . . psychiatry. Not gentle-sounding counselling or therapy but a doctor who had connections with a mental hospital, whose medicine bag included pills and injections and confinement and electro-convulsive therapy and other 'cures' that I couldn't believe in, and could scarcely bear to contemplate, except that not to give them consideration meant doing nothing, meant leaving things the way they were before or taking the wacko route, psychic healing or crystals or primal screaming.

So . . . a psychiatrist. Dr Amanda Aintree.

I blamed Brendan.*

'Ahh, Mrs Mulcahy, there is indeed a connection between all the different symptoms. They all point to her being a child who is out of control. Her symptoms, in my opinion, are a consequence of trying desperately to hold on to what cannot be held – whether it be trash or the events of the day. It could be the coming and going of her father, yes, but I suspect there's more. That in itself wouldn't account for how utterly unindividuated she seems to be.

'Yes, unindividuated. What it means, Mrs Mulcahy, is that your daughter doesn't know where you stop and she begins. Might I ask you a personal question? As a child, did you perhaps feel neglected or abandoned by your own mother, or indeed your father? Did she indeed? And what age were you when she died? Well, there, you see, that explains it.

'In trying to head off your daughter's troubles, Mrs Mulcahy, what you have been doing is mistaking your needs for hers. It's the little girl from long ago who wanted that kind of attention. What the little girl in front of you wants is entirely different.

'No, no, don't apologize, not at all. Tears are natural in this situation, to be expected . . .

'No, of course I'm not saying that it's all your fault. Please . . . There . . . Now . . .

'Don't worry. It's very straightforward. We'll take it slowly, step by step. I'll tell you what to do as each new situation arises. If I'm right, you should see a marked improvement very quickly.

'Of course it's not too late. With human beings it truly never is. For that matter it's not too late for you either. I'd recommend

* Did you? Well, Mom, I blame you.

that you consider talking that time of your life over with another therapist. No, not for Maya, for *you*. It can't have been easy. But it's your decision, of course. My focus will be on your daughter.

'Are you okay with that, Mrs Mulcahy? Is there something else you want to say?

'You're sure? Okay, then, here's how we begin.'

32

It is twenty past eleven, Martin is drunk. He has been drunk since nine o'clock, when the first stages sent delight surging through him. By ten, his brother's features had blurred over. By now he has to hold his gaze very careful or the room sets to spinning, leaving behind a strange fear. The only safe place for him is bed, and he knows it, but they are going on to John MacBride's house.

Sometime during the evening, Benny had pulled him over. 'Say how-do to the Major.'

'How-do, Major,' he'd said, the words all a-slur.

'How-do yourself, lad. Another exile, I hear, for old Érin's sake.'

Then he'd turned his back on him, but when the café was about to close Henderson said they were invited back, and now they're walking, stumbling, along behind him and his pal Victor Collins, while two other Irishmen, O'Brien and Finn, bring up the rear.

Benny says, 'I see our Major has another fine suit.'

'Isn't he lovely in grey?' says Henderson, like a girl, making them laugh.

Henderson nudges Martin. 'What d'ye make of his ten-dollar teeth?'

'Huh?' The nudge has set something in his stomach hurling.

'Purchased for him by his wife, on their American tour.'

'You, my son,' says Henderson, 'are looking at a man bought and paid for.'

'You mean he married Maud Gonne for her money?'

Everybody laughs.

'Ah, the poor gossoon,' says Henderson.

'Leave him alone; he's only wet off the boat.' Benny's defence doesn't make Martin feel any better.

'Yes, m'boy, that's what I'm saying. She got a name – and a patriot Irish name at that – to put on her bastard. So all were happy. For a while anyhow.'

'*Bastards*, don't you mean?' says Finn. 'Plural.'

'She has a girl of nine by the Frenchie,' Henderson explains. 'Now there's a new baby, a boy, said by the lady to be MacBride's but who knows?'

'Jaysus, pipe down! He'll hear you.'

'That's why he always looks so sour.'

'Cuckold's horns always hurt.'

Everyone laughs again, and MacBride turns. 'What's so funny back there?'

'This prize-headed eejit of a fella, that's what,' shouts Henderson. 'I don't know what we're going to do with him at all, at all.'

And Martin's too far gone to object.

MacBride leads them through a stout oak door in a high wall through a stone-flagged courtyard and across a well-clipped lawn. Inside, the apartment is like something out of the *Arabian Nights*. For a start, it would hold ten of the rooms Martin grew up in. Oriental-looking rugs are on the floor and carved wooden creatures around the walls. A floor-to-ceiling mirror takes him and the other six men and frames them. Makes a picture of them.

An enormous dog patters out, head turned in curiosity. Martin massages its ears. Its back is as tall as the table.

'That's a dog and a half you've got there.'

'My wife's.'

'She's an animal lover,' Henderson whispers, somehow making it sound dirty.

MacBride goes to a sideboard weighted with bottles. Every drink you could imagine. 'Whiskey for all?'

Martin would prefer stout or, better, nothing at all. The last of his legs will be gone if he drinks whiskey – but he can hardly refuse.

'Sit down, will you,' Benny shouts across at him. Benny always shouts when he's had one too many. 'Don't be shy.'

He goes to do it but pulls himself back when a heap of fur on the cushion reveals itself to be a cat. He shunts over and sinks into the softest seat he ever sat in.

The drinks go round. MacBride drains his glass like it's a draught of water on a hot day. He's so much smaller than Martin imagined he'd be. Crop of fading, thinning red hair. Head held high in the soldierly manner. A face burnt brick-red by the South African sun and something in the flinty bulge of his eye that makes you nervous to be around him.

While considering whether he might curl up like the cat and slip into sleep, he notices the door on the other side of the room move, open by itself. He stares. He knows he's in the grip of drink, but it definitely moved, he'd swear it. There's no draught in the room – all the windows are shut and shuttered and curtained, and anyhow the movement wasn't like that of a wind draught. Too nudging, too hesitant, too incomplete . . .

Look, there it goes again. Mystery solved. This time he sees a hand giving it a nudge. Look again. There's a head appearing round the door frame, a white face with two big eyes lighting it up like the headlamps on a motor car. A young girl, nine or ten in age, long, dark hair feathering a long, pale face. A looker, certain to break a few hearts when she grows up. Because of the dark of the corridor behind her and the way she peers round, she seems disembodied, as if her head were floating alone above the ruffle of white lace around her neck.

What a face she has. Her skin is like milky glass. If you saw her standing still in a museum, you'd mistake her for a statue. Though she doesn't stay still. She has the quick movements of a bird. Peep round the door. Pull back. Peep again. It must be *her*, he suddenly realizes. The b—.

The look on her face is impossible to read. It's not curiosity.

247

She looks stricken, as if she's been betrayed. Frightened, maybe? Why wouldn't she be, a crowd of strange men in her house at this hour of the night? He tries to think of how they must look to her, with their coarse clothes and boots, but the effort makes his head spin.

Still, they're as good as she is. What is she, only a little b—?

But when she pulls her head back and disappears, he has a sense of loss.

He pulls himself up and realizes that he has been looking at her through a mirror. The door, the plant beside it, the four small pictures of a lake, are all behind him. He turns his head but she's not there. The movement loosens his stomach, and he feels its contents shift sideways. He's going to throw. He'd better get up. There she is again, little girl-bird. Not a good girl. The sins of the father or, in this case, the mother. Sweet divine Jesus, help him. He's got to move from this sofa before the worst happens . . .

He can't.

He can't move. His arms are too long, longer than the longest drainpipes, his legs are gone. He is nothing now but a big stomach reeling and the effort of holding it down. Here it comes. Nothing for it but to turn his head and let it out. Not on the sofa. Not on the good carpet. Red. Oriental . . . from a bazaar . . . Bizarre. Caliphs and sultans. Cost a fortune. A fortune to clean. Aim for the floor. Here it goes. Aaaargh!

Cough. Splutter.

Aaaaargh! Up and out again.

'Oh, Jesus,' says Benny, in the background. Far away. 'The young fella's pukin'.'

Again, more in this one. A right gawk. Splashing on the table legs. The good carpet. Everywhere. Jesus, the smell.

And once more for luck.

Somebody is lifting him.

'You fucking eejit. Could you not have got up when you felt it coming?'

He doesn't care. He feels like smiling. His middle has lightened. He won't smile. He's not supposed to smile, not when he's puked in the Major's house.

'Would you look at him? He's out of his brain.'

'Get him out of here,' says somebody else.

'Easier said than done.'

Martin pretends to close his eyes, but he's peering towards the mirror that shows the door. She is there. She saw it all. In the mirror they meet, and her big eyes are even wider now. Disgust, he supposes. He's not the same as the rest, he's even worse.

She pulls her head back again, and this time he knows she's gone for good.

33

Iseult sucks. She draws her lips around the fat of her new brother's leg, pulls it into her mouth. She takes care, keeping the grip of the teeth soft and wet, so as not to hurt. Babies are beautiful and Bichon the most beautiful. He tastes of Chantilly cream. When she lays him along her forearm, his back, from neck to tail bone, matches precisely the length of her arm from elbow to wrist. His mouth pouts, as if he is kissing the air, and she kisses it back at him.

Bichon – it was her name for him first and now all use it. His real name is Seaghán, pronounced Shawn, Moura says, it being hard to make English approximate Irish, a more ancient language with a different, more sophisticated alphabet. Moura's attempts to learn Irish have floundered, but friends who are good Irish speakers assure her that Seaghán is the best spelling. But Iseult thinks Bichon a better name. Curly little lapdog.

Iseult sees. That MacBride is all red. Eyes like a lobster's, red-rimmed with the whites red-flecked. Crimson lips beneath a rust moustache. Brick-coloured complexion with blotches aflame on the skin of his skull. Broken veins across his nose and cheeks, making him look permanently *embarrasse*.

Iseult hears. Moura confessing her belief that Bichon is the reincarnated spirit of Georges. And MacBride's answer: 'Call yourself a Catholic? Belief in the transmigration of souls is blasphemy.'

He doesn't hear Moura, the truth of her, not unless they discuss Ireland. He doesn't hear what she is saying when she talks of art or nature or the gods. Or little Georges and his meningitis. *Men-in-gi-tis*: listen, stupid man, to what that word means in Moura's mouth! A word like 'Lucifer'. A word to make the heart tremble. If one had a heart.

Moura answers: 'John, each religion is a prism through which we look at truth. No one individual or religion sees the *whole* of truth, for, when we do, we shall have merged in the deity and we shall be as God. But that is not yet. In the meantime I look at the truth through the prism of the Catholic religion, my chosen religion. But I also look through other prisms.'

To which he says: 'Blasphemy is blasphemy.'

His mind is a labelled closet. If he found a sock in the wrong drawer, he would think it a scarf.

Iseult hears. 'I thought you were in jest, Maud. All of my family will be there, all the brothers and sisters and my mother. I've nothing against the girl. I'm not denying her, of course I'm not. Any other time would be fair enough. Any time but this. This is a christening, a Christian sacrament, in case you've forgotten. This is the baptism of Seaghán MacBride, son of John MacBride and Maud Gonne. You yourself said you wanted it to be a triumph, a surmounting of your old troubles. What do you think they'll be saying if you bring her? All the troubles of your life are down to such wilful flaunting.'

Iseult learns. That Eileen likes to see Iseult scolded and will always help that along. That Eileen likes to pinch her when others are not looking. That she, Iseult, is a bastard, same as Eileen, and so she has no call thinking herself any better. That they are both lucky John MacBride gave them a name. That he is the head of the household now and some think it's a shame how he gets treated in his own house.

Iseult sees. The big brown trunk being taken down. The christening gown going into it. A cloud of satin and lace billowing

251

beyond its folds. The gown that was Moura's when she was a baby, the gown that was Iseult's when she was a baby.

Iseult says: 'You *said*, Moura. You promised . . . you said that was why you were getting married, so I could be brought to Ireland and everywhere. You *said*.'

Iseult hears. 'You're right to stick to your guns, John. Maud can be so stubborn, but it's asking for trouble to bring hers. I know it might seem strange for me to say so, some might say it's the same for me, but in my case it's never been known the way it has with her. And maybe if she wasn't so strange. She draws such attention on herself. God knows what queer thing she'd do. And notice is just what you don't want in Ireland, with you avoiding the authorities . . .'
   'We'll have to find a nice Irishman for you while we're there.'
   'Ah, now!'
   'You could do worse.'
   'I'm not saying I couldn't.'
   'I'm telling you now, if I wasn't spoken for myself . . .'
   Eileen giggles.

But Iseult wins.

In Ireland, their house has fairies painted on the walls. The man who did them lives next door. He has a bushy beard and eyes that make her want to go to sleep. His name is only two letters, A and E. The fairies were a wedding present for Moura. He says Iseult looks like the fairy child needed to complete them.
   He visits, brings a canvas along to paint her.
   His son, Brian, is the same age, and when the sun shines they sit on the wall between their two houses. Iseult collects snails and Brian says they are bad for agriculture. He will not listen when Iseult explains how they are good and Iseult hits him for not listening, giving herself a fright.

She jumps down from the wall as the adults come protesting towards them. Iseult does not like Ireland or the people she meets there. Moura has too many friends in Ireland.

Iseult smells. Moura is away again, and, when she goes into their bedroom, he has a bottle by his bed that smells of him. Like rotting apricots. The bottle is half empty. He is sitting on the bed, not yet dressed. He is laughing. His eyes are pointing her downwards, past his wet lips, past his mottled neck, past the grey hair peering atop his vest, past the stomach . . .

She knows she should not give in to the silent command of his eyes. Assassin eyes. Before she looks, she has some knowledge of what she is going to see. She knows he means her harm.

But she looks.

Iseult screams.

And then? Then what? What then?

A gap.

Some references in later writings, other people's writings. Newspapers. Legal reports. Her mother's letters and later, much later, her husband's autobiographical novel. But from Iseult herself?

Nothing that I could find.

34

I met Zach in the spring of 1972 when I was almost thirty. He was on his college spring break. Yes, yes, I know. But, in my defence, Zach Coleman was no ordinary nineteen-year-old.

My job back then was waitressing at a bar-restaurant on the ocean front called Honolulu. A bead curtain inside the front door led to a bridge over a moving stream that dissected the building. The bartenders wore bright green shirts spattered with orange-and-blue palm trees and we, the floor staff, wore green halter-neck tops over faux-grass skirts and a yellow flower behind the ear. Being half dressed meant the tips were better.

We were having a busy evening, with too many Europeans who were spoilt by their high-wage, welfare states and unaware that we relied on tips to make up our pay. Jim-Bob, our manager, allowed us to 'grat' them, add a tip to the bill without their realizing.

It was Lindie, one of the other waitresses who was also a single mom, who saw Zach first. 'Mine!' she cried, elbowing me, as soon as he walked in. We had a mock rivalry running over good-looking punters.

I looked to the door. Tall, young, a small beard and dark hair, long and straight, like Jesus. 'Not so fast, missy,' I said. 'I do believe it's almost 8.30 and time for your break.'

She looked at her watch. 'So it is. Ah, he's only a tadpole anyway. You're welcome.'

When I brought him across the menu and he turned his eyes up to me, the joking stopped. They were the deepest grey I have ever seen on anybody, the colour of the sky on a new-moon night. He did look like Jesus, or that actor who played him in *Son of God*, and had a presence like I imagine Jesus must have had.

All through the requests from the other tables – a to-go box for Table 6; three more beers for 12; ketchup bottle on 8 is empty; high chair for the party of ten Europeans who wanted a variation on almost every order hold-the-gravy on the chicken and mash, extra cheese on the pizza, the burger without salad or pickle and one Coke without lemon and another without ice, thereby playing havoc with the order system that Honolulu used to keep communication between floor and kitchen streamlined – I felt him there. Whenever I looked across, he was looking at me. Each time I looked a little longer, but each time I was the one who drew my eyes away.

At last I was able to go to him. I went across and lifted his plate. He had hardly eaten.

'Was everything all right for you, sir?' Everybody over fifteen was 'sir' or 'ma'am' in Honolulu.

He nodded.

'Can I get you anything else?'

'Nothing, thank you.' Nothing but you, his eyes seemed to say. Or was that just wishful thinking?

'I'll get your check, then?'

He paid, his tip generous, and I watched him leave, the tallness of him swaying past tables, leading with his left shoulder and then with his right. Moving with soft, sleek grace, like a big cat. A dark, silken panther. Then he stepped through the beaded curtain and was gone.

I was never going to see him again.

Don't be silly. He'll come back in.

But what if he doesn't?

The thought was enough. I found myself running into the back and grabbing my jacket. I passed Jim-Bob's booth on the way out. 'Hey, where do you think you're going?'

'I'll be back,' I called, without stopping.

He came out to shout after me: 'Where're you going, I said?'

'Female emergency, Jim-Bob. I'll be back in no time.'

'Female emergency, my sweet Fanny Adam. You come back here, girl. You come back here now. If you go out that door, you needn't bother . . .'

I kept going. I needed only a couple of minutes. I had no idea what I was going to say to him, and by now he might well be gone, faded into the dark, never to return. The thought gave me a spur of panic, but, when I got outside, he was there, standing under the canopy, as if he'd known I'd follow. Or maybe just sheltering from the rain?

'Hey!' he said, as I drew close. 'It's you.'

'Seems so.' I was suddenly shy.

'That's so great. I was trying to work out whether to go back in to you or wait till you got off.'

That's how he was from the start. At first I didn't trust it, this openness of Zach's. I thought that he was doing the thing some guys do. The frank thing, the disarming thing that says you're safe with me, but usually means you're not. 'What's your name?'

'Iseult.'

'That's pretty,' he said, something Americans say every time. What they really mean is, that's unusual. 'I love your accent. You're Irish?'

I nodded.

'I'm Zach.' He put out his hand. 'Zach Coleman.'

I took it. It sounds so cheesy, but I felt something I'd only read about in books before. An energy, like electricity but gentler, as if the cells of our hands were dancing around each other.

'I'd love to go to Ireland,' he said.

'Really? Why?'

'Who wouldn't? Hey, maybe you'll take me?'

I laughed.

'Why not? It would be fun. You could show me round. What part of Ireland are you from?'

'Wicklow.'

Silence. He had no idea where Wicklow was. But again he filled the space, simply and directly. 'Do you want to go get a coffee?'

'I can't. I have to go back to work.'

'No. Don't.'

'Don't?'

'Come with me instead.'

'Except if I do that, I lose my job.'

'Maybe you will, maybe you won't. Anyway, there are other jobs.'

I laughed. 'This one suits me, actually.'

'It's not worthy of you.'

'Pardon?'

'Why do they have to dress you like that?' He made a face but with a smile that took the offence out of the words. 'I saw you, the way you did everything. You're too good for them. Don't go back.'

'You don't know what you're talking about.'

But he had taken my hand and was tugging me gently and I was letting him. We walked out into the rain, and for once, because of the small rebellion of running out to him and the way he was looking at me, the rain made me feel new and clean and lively. We found a coffee house and I started to talk and I told him everything, even about Star. I never discussed Star, certainly not with men I'd just met, but Zach knew all about her before we'd even kissed.

The kiss came four hours later, when I'd stopped talking and started listening and we'd left the coffee house and were walking aimlessly down a side street I'd never walked before, avoiding the rest of the world. I was drunk on the knowledge that I was doing something I shouldn't. Earlier, I had seen Star off to bed as I did every evening before handing over to Kate, the baby-sitter who slept at our house while I did my shift.

And what of Jim-Bob? Jim-Bob I'd have to deal with in the morning.

257

Zach kept staring at me. I haven't mentioned yet that in my day I was considered beautiful. I could give you the details – shade of hair (strawberry-blónde), span of bust, waist and hips (36–22–34), quality of legs (long, slim), texture of skin (tanned, peachy) – but it's nothing but cliché on the page. You have to see beauty to know what it means.

Beauty is in the eye of the beholder, they say, but what if you are the beauty? Then it can be a curse. It is the look in a man's eye coming at you from the youngest age, making you know more than you want to know. It is the hate they deal you for desiring you. It is a side show that doesn't pay the bills or raise the child or get the book written. It is for the beholder, not you.

One good thing is that it wises you up early to men and what most of them want from a woman, but, like everything about him, Zach's way of looking at me was different. His eyes were clear mirrors, and I loved what I saw reflected back at me. So, yes, the kiss. His lips were warm, tentative at first, then searching. I remember wondering how so young a man could know how to kiss like that, then recognizing that it wasn't him, it was him-and-me-together, then letting all thought go . . . It was a long kiss, with a fluctuating rhythm, like a finely drawn violin duet, and after our lips parted, we were locked into each other in a new way.

He ran the back of his forefinger gently along my jawline. 'My God,' he said, staring at me as if I were a newborn baby. 'You're stunning.'*

The kiss sent us swinging down the four blocks to his apartment and up his stairs. All felt natural and easy, even through the usually awkward bits like finding the keys and getting the right one to fit the lock. Once we were inside the door, it was

* It's so hard for me to read this. I can't believe we've got one third of the book in before she mentions the B word. Her beauty was the first thing everybody noticed about her, and, whatever she says, I know she was proud of her looks.

straight into the sliding off of fabric, the little tussles with each other's buttons and the first glimpses of each other's skin. I was in it, doing it too. Soon everything was off, and we were down to the clear, open bareness of each other.

It was too much for him. In minutes, he was gone. 'Oh, God,' he muttered into the base of my neck. 'I'm sorry.'

'Sorry for what? We're just warming up.'

I wasn't being kind; I was just pleasured by his pleasure. That was as much as I hoped for in any sex encounter and as much as I generally got. Until that night.

Zach's desire rose again quickly, as I knew it would, but this time he was determined to wait for me. He stayed my hand, he stared me down, he noticed everything and asked me questions and knew very little about what to do. So I had to get involved, to show him. And somehow, in the showing I found my own way with someone else for the first time.

Then we were off together, surfing wave after wave of astonishment, rising and dipping with desires and discoveries, until the first birds sang a false dawn and beyond, until the real dawn was almost rising and I really had to go.

I was sometimes late home from Honolulu but never this late, and I didn't want to meet Kate or Star, beginning their morning with the sight of me arriving back. One look at me, I felt, and they would know.

He drove me home in his car, a Ford Falcon, through black dimming to grey morning light. The streetlights were still on. Their flash and the hum of the engine and his sated silence made me drift. With the steering wheel in his hands, he appeared older, like a fully fledged man, handsome and solid. Someone I could stay with, someone whose kindness I could allow.

What had just happened between us seemed to hold out a promise to me that I hadn't asked for, wasn't even sure that I wanted. Yet I felt I could maybe grow to love this.

To love *him*?

No. I snapped myself awake. I did *not* hear that. I did *not* think that. A slip of the mind and a damnfool one. It was our very first night, I hadn't even known him twelve hours, and he was just a boy, nineteen years old, for Chrissakes . . . The car braked, we were outside my house. The lights were off in there, nobody up yet. All the houses around were in darkness, the whole world, except us, in the half-life of sleep. A question was pushing up in me and I had to ask it.

'That wasn't your first time, I hope?'

'No,' he laughed. 'What chance do you think an American male gets to wait till he's nineteen these days?'

'True.'

'But I have to tell you.' He brushed back my hair and touched my face, again with that tenderness that was half-frightening. 'It was the first time I realized what all the fuss is about. The first time it was so completely, fantastically amazing.' He whooped. 'Actually, thinking about it: yes, it was my first time.'

That was my Zach, charming and disarming, right from the start. What could I do but, there and then in the car, offer him seconds?*

* His must have been one of the cars that I saw her in around this time.

35

Major John MacBride to Victor Collins

Dear Vic

This is a letter I never expected to be writing. I learned on Tuesday last that my wife is seeking a divorce. The first thought that crossed my mind was that her wandering fancy had settled on some other man or that she had gone back to one of her exes but when I heard the charges she was bringing against me, I was simply dumbfounded. They are too evil and ridiculous to repeat in writing; suffice it to say that in addition to alleged drunkenness, they centre on her illegitimate girl, Iseult.

This is a terrible blow to me, hard to take after all the woman has put me through already. I left Paris for Dublin on 25th November, arriving in Westport on the evening of the 26th. Before leaving I left a letter for her. This letter annoyed her considerably. The contents in a nutshell amounted to this: that our life was not a happy one owing to her being unable to rise above a certain level. That it was painful to me to see that she was only the weak imitation of a very weak man. I also advised her that if I was hung or died in prison, she should get married again as she was a woman that cannot live without some man or other behind her and that it was better for her, if she was really interested in the cause of Ireland, to be married, even if she were a little unhappy, than to live an impure life.

I was probably foolish to write like that; but she had made life nearly unbearable by her complete lack of all womanly delicacy, by constantly lying, and by trying to force her exes on me.

In her first letter to Westport, she complained of the above-mentioned letter saying that she would have it out with me when we met. Notwithstanding she continued to send me friendly letters up to the 18th of December. On that day my brother Anthony in London received a note from her by special messenger asking him to call and see her on a very important business. He went to the house of Mrs Bertie-Clay, my wife's cousin (who is herself separated from her husband after being married about two years also), and she and my wife came out with their fairy tale to him.

She asked him to meet her at her solicitors the following day. He did so and my wife, Mrs Bertie-Clay and her English solicitor tried hard to make him believe their absurd and damnably false tale. Among other things they told him that they were drawing up a document which if I did not sign would lead at once to an action for criminal assault being taken against me. In this precious document I was to acknowledge that I was guilty of the offence with which I was charged, give over the control full and entire of Seaghán to my wife and her English friends, emigrate to America and never come back to my native land again.

No one but a devil incarnate could have invented these charges. I said immediately that I would leave for London, see my wife and refute the alleged offence face to face.

So here I am in London, hoping to see her. She has called on Barry O'Brien and told him a long tale of woe about my cruelty, drunkenness etc. most of which is absolutely false. The origin of all difference between us was her continual efforts to force her exes on me.

Forgive this long and confused missive. My head is spinning with thoughts, as you can imagine, and I had need to write them down. Say nothing of this to anyone else besides Nell.

Major John MacBride to Maud Gonne MacBride

My dear Maud

I learned on Tuesday last for the first time of the scandalous charges you and your English friends have been making against my character. They are absolutely false and of course I'll meet and disprove them. I'd prefer not doing so publicly for little Seaghán's sake and yours; but I cannot lie under any such accusations as I have been told you have been making lately. I can hardly credit you believe the charges yourself.

I went to see Barry O'Brien, whose judgement as an Irishman and a man of unquestioned honour can be relied on. He suggested waiting until he had a talk with you. After you have seen him, please send me word saying where we can meet to talk matters over without any heat. I had to tell him who Iseult was. I said nothing otherwise.

This is an awful blow to me as I was looking forward to a happy time in Ireland.

Please make arrangements as to where I can see Seaghán each day while I am in London. Any place and any hour you name shall suit me. His happy little face is always with me.

Maud Gonne MacBride to Barry O'Brien

My dear Mr O'Brien

By Mr Witham's advice, I cannot receive my husband. Also an interview between us would be very painful and quite useless. I would be grateful to you, therefore, if you would let him know three things which may influence his decision.

1st: That if you and Mr Witham can arrange a separation giving me entire guardianship of Seaghán, which shall not make public the horrible thing against John, no one shall ever hear of it from me and if he goes to America people generally need not know of our separation unless he chooses; it would appear quite natural that not having been able to find work in Europe during two years, he should go to look for it in America.

2nd: That, if by getting work and leading a sober, decent life for some years he proves he is worthy of it, I would not prevent him seeing Seaghán and having a share of his affection.

3rd: That there are other things concerning his conduct during our married life which took place at my house and which if made public as they inevitably would be, would injure the reputation of a woman who I should think he has every reason to wish to spare.* These things I only found out while inquiring into the other matter and it has been a great shock to me.

Please show this letter only to John.

I am very sorry to trouble you with all this and I thank you for trying for all our sakes to settle this matter as quietly as possible.

Major John MacBride to Barry O'Brien

Dear Mr O'Brien

You decline to hear me respecting the details of the differences between my wife and me. So be it. I shall not trouble you about them. But this much I must say. When I heard of the charges my wife made against me, I hastened from Ireland to London, wrote to her and called to see her, wishing to see her, to have this matter out face to face. She refused to answer my letter and she refused to see me.

Without consulting a single Irish friend (so far as I know) she went to an Englishman to take steps against me whom she would not hear or see. Assuredly, Mr O'Brien, that was strange conduct on the part of Maud Gonne towards John MacBride. In view of her conduct, I need scarcely say that I wish to see her no more.

She has shown me that she is dead to any sense of justice and that in a crisis she is ready to lean on English support regardless of the consequences to Irish interests. I think only of Ireland with whose cause my wife and I have been, however unworthily, associated and of my little boy and wish to be guided mainly by consideration for both in all I do in this unhappy affair.

* Eileen Wilson.

Barry O'Brien to Maud Gonne MacBride

Dear Mrs MacBride

*I think that both you and your husband should remain in London
for the present. Take care that you do not allow yourself to be
dominated by English political and family influences in a matter
where the interests of our country are concerned. This is no ordinary
case of differences between husband and wife. Were it so the charges
and counter-charges made by you and your husband against each
other would call for no interference from me. But this is a case in
which Irish national considerations must be taken into account.
Therefore I cannot regard with indifference the prospect of seeing you
and your husband made the subject of ridicule and contempt by the
press of this country.*

*You are bound to think of the Irish cause with which you have
been for so many years associated. Those who undertake public
duties have public obligations. Your husband recognizes this fact.
You shall recognize it too – if you are true to Ireland.*

Major John MacBride to Victor Collins

Dear Vic

*After the events of today I don't know where I am. I write, as
usual, to keep you posted of events but also to straighten my
thoughts.*

*Yesterday, Mr O'Brien met my wife at Mr Witham's office and
gave her my letter to read. She wept, acknowledged she did wrong in
not seeing me or letting me see Seaghán and wanted to know if she
could not see me now. Mr O'Brien told her that I did not wish to
see her now; but that if she sent the boy to his house with her cousin
Mrs Bertie-Clay on the following day at three o'clock that I would
be there to receive him.*

*So today I went to Mr O'Brien's at three o'clock and to my
amazement (and O'B's amazement), instead of sending her cousin
with the boy, she sailed into the room herself. I took no notice of*

her. I went to my child, and Mr O'Brien and herself left the room together. After some considerable time Mr O'Brien came back, saying that she wished to see me and that she expressed regret for not seeing me before and for not allowing me to see the baby. He said we must only talk about the terms of the settlement, that there was no good now going into the question of charges and counter-charges.

I said: 'If I see her, Mr O'Brien, I must deny this charge and ask her questions about it.'

He said: 'You can deny the charge, but there is no good in discussing details. You have agreed to separate – the only question is the terms.'

When I went into the adjoining room, my wife was sitting at one end of the fireplace and I sat opposite her with Mr O'Brien sitting between us. Mr O'Brien repeated what he said about charges and counter-charges and terms, but I said: 'I beg your pardon, Mr O'Brien, I must first of all deny these charges. They are absolutely false.'

My wife said: 'Oh, John, I fear they are true.'

'No, they are not, Maud,' I said, and moved up to a chair nearer to her. 'When is it supposed to have happened?'

'I can't give dates.'

'Was it when you were last in Ireland?'

'No.'

'Then why did you not allude to it before?'

'Iseult told Madame Avril and told her not to tell anyone.'

'That's very peculiar.'

Then Mr O'Brien interposed, saying there was no good in discussing these charges in the absence of Mr Witham and urged us to come to the question of terms. I turned to him and said: 'I beg your pardon, Mr O'Brien, but I must also speak about Eileen Wilson, as my wife accuses me of kissing her. I did kiss her, but it was all mostly done in my wife's presence. There was never anything between Eileen Wilson and myself that all the world might not know.'

Mr O'Brien again broke in. 'The terms of separation, please.
I must insist. This other discussion gets us nowhere.'

We then talked about terms, my wife wanting to have control of
the child for ten years, while I was willing to let her have control for
six years, after which time the question could be opened up de
novo. She wanted to let me see my boy four times a year, and
I wished to see him every day. After discussing the above for a long
time without coming any nearer an agreement, Mr O'Brien
remarked that there was no use in talking about it any more that
evening and advised us to go home and think it over seriously and
that we might be in a better frame of mind tomorrow. We both
agreed to do so.

Mr O'Brien led the way towards the next room. My wife walked
slowly past me, drawing herself up to her full height as I bowed
slightly without uttering a word. She got close to the door when she
suddenly wheeled round, stretching out her hand to me, which I
took, and then she fell weeping on my neck. This was too much for
my gravity and I commenced to laugh. However, we kissed each
other and she said to me: 'I love you now, John, but I shall hate
you before you go to bed tonight.'

I told her that the charges were damnably false and that I was
surprised she should believe the words of others in preference to
mine. She mumbled something in reply between her kisses. I swore
again in the most solemn manner that there was no truth in them
and she said: 'I can believe there was nothing between you and
Eileen but kissing.'

'It was you yourself that got Eileen to kiss me first and there
was never a word or thought of love between Eileen and myself.'

I then said: 'If you meet me tomorrow, Maud, we can talk it
over quietly, for, when all is said and done, you and I can settle this
matter quicker and better than any outsiders.'

She hesitated at this, saying that she would write me that night.

We all made as to leave, Mr and Mrs O'Brien going towards
the door, my wife and I lingering behind, and when they were all
out of the room, she flung her arms round my neck for the last time

and gave me a parting kiss. Mr O'Brien Junior assisted me in placing my wife, child and the nurse in the hansom, which had been kept all this time, and from there she shook us both by the hand in the most friendly fashion.

So there you have it. She is the most vexing of women. But I prefer to think of us sorting it among ourselves, rather than going into a courtroom, which can only damage the cause of Ireland.

I shall write again with the next chapter. Remember me to Nell and the children.

Maud Gonne MacBride to Barry O'Brien

My dear Mr O'Brien

I didn't thank you this afternoon as I should for your kindness in permitting John to see Seaghán at your home and for receiving me there – but I was rather upset. My nerves have been terribly overstrained lately and seeing my husband for the first time since I heard these terrible things was very trying.

I would like to have believed all he said. I cannot do so.

My nerves gave way and I began to cry at the end of our interview during the few moments we were alone at the end and I fear this has given John hope that I can be weakened in my determination about separation. He at once begged to see me today which I refused and this morning he writes again asking me to see him – which again I have refused.

In the arrangement which you shall make with Mr Witham it is useless to ask me to agree to anything less than ten years control of the child. I have already conceded too much. If John keeps from drink and does not otherwise annoy me, I am not selfish and would gladly increase the opportunities for him to see the child but it must be left to my discretion. I must have safeguards.

You know Ireland and you know how terribly it shall injure me, this separation without explanation. It is always the woman who suffers in these cases. The whole scandal coming out would be far

less bad for me than this shall be, which spares John, the guilty one.
If he were wise or wished really to atone for the wrong he has done,
he would accept your suggestion of getting a commission in the
American Army. Dublin is about the worst place he could be in
from the drink point of view.

It has occurred to me he might think of following me to Paris
with the hope of getting me to give up separation. The house being
taken in both our names I could not legally refuse him admittance
but I shall not see him any more. His presence in Paris would be
very dangerous as any indiscretion on the part either of my friends
or the servants who know that dreadful matter would get him
arrested for a criminal offence. Then the affair is out of my hands.
So if he says anything about going to Paris please advise him
against it.

Please give my kind regards to Mrs O'Brien and thank her for
her kind hospitality. I fear it must have been most troublesome to
her and to you.

Major John MacBride to Maud Gonne MacBride

I asked if there was a letter for me this morning Maud but was
told there was no delivery on Sunday. Did you write? It is very
important that you and I should have a few minutes talk before you
go to Paris and before I leave for Dublin. Send me word please,
saying where we can meet. I am going to Anthony's for lunch unless
I receive word from you before one o'clock and I'll probably remain
there until about three o'c.

I'd like to impress on you that we owe it to our country and that
it is only doing our duty towards little Seaghán to come to an
understanding.

The O'Briens were full of praise for the merry-hearted boy
yesterday. Please take him in your arms and whisper a New Year's
wish in his tiny ear for his father.

May I wish you a year of peace and happiness.

Maud Gonne MacBride to Major John MacBride

I cannot see you tomorrow. I have been through so much my nerves are so overstrained I should only break down foolishly as I did today. <u>I do not, I cannot,</u> believe what you say. Mr O'Brien shall see Mr Witham and draw up the terms of separation, the draft of which they shall send me to Paris. I shall write to you to Dublin news of Seaghán. In order to let the house in Paris I shall have to get a procuration from you taking off your signature or authorizing me to sign alone. The same applies to the property in Colleville.

What do you want me to do about your things in Paris – shall I get them packed and sent to you in Dublin or to Westport? If the house lets you would hardly care to have them there.

It is a sad New Year's Eve for us both. The years have been sad ever since our marriage. I hope the future may be more peaceful for both.

Major John MacBride to Maud Gonne MacBride

I am only afraid that in the present distracted state of your nerves, Maud, you are only too ready to believe any absurd story that may be told you. I would be very much obliged if you would have my things sent to Barry's Hotel, 1 Great Denmark Street, Dublin 1.

Major John MacBride to Victor Collins

Dear Vic

You above all others know I was not anxious for this marriage as I knew we were not suited for one another but nobody knows the hell I have been in since.

For eight or nine months I had been resisting her advances then one night she told me that she would place her whole future life in my hands to direct as I would wish if only I would make her my wife, that she had suffered greatly and wanted to try to be a good woman. I was moved by her tears, felt very sad for her, and

thinking I was doing a good act for my country and for her,
I consented to marry Maud Gonne.

It was when I was in the United States that I heard about her
other lovers and at first could hardly believe it. I knew she had had
an evil life before our marriage but did not know it was so bad as
I found out afterwards. By her own confession to me (around the
end of August 1904) she had been the mistress of three different
men! By one she had two illegitimate children and two miscarriages.

Since then, when she admitted her guilt, I could not warm
towards her at all and always felt unhappy and constrained in her
presence knowing how deceitful she had been with me.

The very day we were married she wanted to keep up a
correspondence with her ex-lovers and bring them to the house for
me to entertain. Of course I would not allow such a thing.

Once she had me talking to one of her ex-lovers at the Gare
Saint-Lazare for five minutes and got me to ask him to the house.
I did so, not knowing at that time the relationship that had existed
between them. To his honour, he declined to come.

Another time she got me to write to another of her ex-lovers
giving him an invitation to stay with us for a week, which I did
and which he accepted. Needless to say in this instance also I was
not aware of the relationship that had existed between them. Once
she told me that she had been in a house of ill fame in Marseilles
with her first lover. She wanted to hang her paramour's photograph
up in the house which I would not allow but she had the
photograph of another of her paramours on her desk in Colleville
and I, all unknowing of their relationship, left it there.

While she was enceinte *she was always complaining about the*
horridness of her condition. She had a French midwife and their
conversation was always on the one subject: namely the sexual
connection between man and woman and the different ways and
manners in which it was done. The woman was dead to all sense of
shame. She is a vile woman. Woman? It is a disgrace to
womanhood to call her by that holy name.

I gave her a name that was free from stain or reproach and she was unable to appreciate it. She had no conception of delicacy and no idea of truth and ever since has been constantly sending and receiving messages through Madame Avril and Iseult to her paramours

Iseult is a perfect specimen of a decadent, having no sense of right or wrong. However, it is better not to continue in that strain.

Forgive this confused epistle. I will write more clearly soon.

Best wishes to Nell and the boys.

Maud Gonne MacBride to W. B. Yeats

My dear Friend

I am glad you know all. Thank you for your letter and thank you for all the trouble you are taking for me.

My nerves are so shattered by all I have gone through, not only since I knew this horrible thing, but ever since my marriage, where insane scenes of jealousy, and an atmosphere of base intrigue have rendered life almost unbearable . . .

The French avoué *says I have quite enough evidence to go on without bringing in anything about little Iseult . . . I wrote to Mr Witham that as John was trying so hard to get political and religious sympathy to cover his vices and is making a great point against me that I have been to an English solicitor, it would be well to get an Irish barrister . . . Would you make enquiries and advise me on this matter. You might tell Mrs Bertie-Clay to see Mr Witham about it if you think well . . .*

Your kind letters are a great comfort to me and I thank you for your generous sympathy — but, Willie, I don't want you to get mixed up in this horrible affair. By my marriage <u>I brought all this trouble on myself</u>, and as far as I can I want to fight it alone. This is why I have spoken to none of my friends. Why should they who are engaged on noble work be mixed up with a sordid horror of this sort?

To have a really good counsel is necessary, and if you will help me in this you will do me a great service, but apart from this

Willie, for your sake, for Ireland's sake and for your own work as
well as for mine, try and keep quite clear of this affair, don't even
think of it too much. I know the generosity of your nature makes
you want to help me and to defend me but it would only add to my
trouble to know your life was touched in any way by this miserable
tragedy – That I have your friendship whatever happens is a great
comfort to me.

Victor Collins to Major John MacBride

My dear Mac

Your wife left a note at the Florence yesterday at 5.30 asking me to
see her at that hour today which I did. She said she and you were
going to separate and she wanted me to take charge of such of your
effects as she dared not send to you lest they might be seized.

She told me of some of your offences, coming home too drunk to
get out of the cab, going to bed in your boots, reading such obscene
books that the publishers' name did not appear, that no servant
was safe from your attentions, that you had gone to Margot, the
nurse's room at 3 a.m., and would not leave – <u>though fortunately</u>
<u>nothing worse occurred</u>. I pooh-poohed such tales, saying servants
were always ready to get up tales when husband and wife disagreed.
She said: it was not only with servants. I gave her to understand I
for one could not believe such tales; that I had known you
intimately and had never heard an indecent word from you nor seen
you drunk.

She said she was decided to separate and if you did not agree to
her terms by Saturday, she would apply to the courts. I said it was
a pity to make an open rupture as it would harm the cause. She left
it to you to avoid that by accepting her ultimatum.

She spoke of knowing of a scandal of yours before you left
Dublin. I said: 'And with your eyes open, you married him.'

'Oh,' quoth she. 'He had had time to reform.'

She had also heard from a girl that you had lately been drinking
in Dublin. I gave her to understand I put no value on that gossip;

273

*that no man of the world would believe such ill-founded charges;
that the best thing she could do was agree that the child should be
six months alternately with either parent.*

*At this she shouted: 'I have nothing to reproach myself with and
I shall never allow my child to be under such evil influences.'*

V. C.: 'He denies your charges.'

M. G.: 'Let my child out of my keeping? Never.'

V. C.: 'Mac shall say why should he be deprived of his child.'

M. G.: 'He would not be capable of looking after it.'

V. C.: 'But it could stay with his mother.'

*That she would not hear of and again referred to the Courts,
which evidently she thought had terrors for you, so I said: 'Well, my
dear girl, I'll tell you what I shall advise him to do. I shall tell him
to go to Court. Were I Mac, I would put a stop to all this
gossiping and character-blackening behind my back by having your
charge threshed out in court.'*

*She did not seem too pleased at my assuming this attitude and
the interview soon after broke up.*

*Once she put her foot in it, saying à propos of something or other
that when she left for London it was with the intention of getting
a separation.*

*'What!' I exclaimed. 'You had that idea when you were asking
me to urge Mac to go to America where you would join him on
a tour for the famished in the West. If you had that idea, you are
a good actress for you certainly seemed sincere when speaking to me.'*

*She saw her error but said something about not knowing the
procedure and that what she intended going to London [for] was to
consult her solicitor.*

*My reading of her is that she hopes to frighten you into letting
her have her way. I did what I could to disabuse her mind of that
by saying, 'If you don't agree to equal terms I, for one, should
advise John to go to court. You want the child, so does he. You say
you have nothing to fear; so says he. The child is as much his as it
is yours. The best plan is to agree to six months in turn.'*

She looked very white and upset when I spoke like this and

I put her in a cab for home, Collins' stock having gone down below zero in the opinion of Maud Gonne MacBride.

All here join in sending all good wishes

Maud Gonne MacBride to W. B. Yeats

One more hideous day [in court] listening to MacBride's friends perjuring themselves by saying he never got drunk . . . The strain of the last month has worn me thin as a shadow. It was such a nightmare work having to sit in court day after day listening to my witnesses describing the hideous things I knew of, I found myself feeling glad and relieved when they forgot some ugly detail and then I had to shake myself up to the fact that I was there to remind my lawyer to ask some question that would bring it out and that the future of my son depended on it. Day after day I had to listen to MacBride's witnesses perjuring themselves and contradicting each other and sometimes the fighting spirit in me woke up and it amused me to suggest questions that I knew would accentuate the contradiction, but all the time at the bottom of my heart was the sickening fear that the name of my innocent little Iseult would be dragged into the sea of mud. For though agreement had been come to between the lawyers on both sides in the presence of the judge that the affair was not to be alluded to on either side, I knew I was fighting a <u>mad man</u> who when he realized he was losing would do anything for revenge. As I expected, it came. The last day of the hearing of witnesses in spite of protest from the judge, in spite of remonstrance from his own lawyer MacBride insisted in calling his brother Dr MacBride to go into the whole affair. He ended by saying it was his belief that I and the British government had concocted this to get rid of his brother.

Nothing was left of me then but to ask for another day's hearing of witnesses and getting Madame Avril and the other witnesses to give evidence. As I had the calling of witnesses in my hands I refused to allow Iseult to be called and she knows nothing at all of the affair. The judge quite understood and appreciated the reasons,

*I think. It has damaged MacBride's case frightfully. His baseness
was so apparent that the judge spoke most severely to him when he
tried to put questions to my witnesses, questions which he knew
were groundless but which might perhaps leave a doubt in the
judge's mind.*

My lawyers say the case is certainly won now.

Maud Gonne MacBride to W. B. Yeats

The plaidoirie *of Maître Labori was infamous . . . Labori openly
spoke about Iseult as my daughter '<u>by a former marriage, I mean
union</u>' and said I had dared to accuse the 'chivalrous MacBride' of
having made an indecent assault on the child. That I had accused
him before members of his own family but knowing this accusation
to be false I had not brought it forward in the divorce suit. This
may mean that I will have to prove this horrible thing. I shrink
from doing it because it means that poor little Iseult will have to
appear in court and be questioned and cross-questioned on this
hideous thing which I want her to forget. She is a nervous child and
was ill for days after from the terror of it and used to wake at night
screaming that MacBride with his 'eyes of an assassin' was running
after her. Even now she hardly likes going upstairs after dark alone
because, as she told me last week when I was laughing at her for
being afraid, she is always afraid MacBride may be hiding and run
after her. Still it is possible it will have to be proved . . .*

*MacBride's friend Mr Collins was in a front row taking notes.
[With] every insult that Labori addressed to me he laughed and
rubbed his hands.*

Maud Gonne MacBride to W. B. Yeats

My dear Willie

*Here is the verdict as far as I can remember it not as yet having
received the written copy. MacBride has succeeded in proving Irish
nationality and domicile so that only separation and not divorce can*

be granted . . . The Court thinks the charges of immorality are insufficiently proved but that the charges of drunkenness are manifestly proved . . .

The Court grants Mrs MacBride judicial separation in her favour and gives her the right of guardianship of the child. It allows the father the right of visiting the child at his wife's house every Monday, and when the child shall be over six years old allows the father to have him for one month in the year —

I am very disappointed and I shall probably appeal . . .

Alwys your friend
Maud Gonne

The verdict was given at ten minutes after twelve today — I wonder if you could see anything in my stars for me on the matter.

36

Ding dong. I was preparing dinner when our doorbell rang. One of the things I don't like about myself is that I always experience the doorbell ringing as an intrusion. Maybe it's because a double-jobbing single mother is always busy and always has a plan for the coming hours. That evening it was the usual routine: dinner, Star's homework, TV, bedtime, Kate's arrival, go to work. Zach was gone, back to college, sending almost daily letters. He would be home for Thanksgiving. I had a calendar, like a schoolgirl or a prisoner, on which I marked off the days.

In the meantime, I was busier than ever. If he was going to have a college education, I thought maybe I should too. I had started to read again, to entertain notions of what I might do. I had written to UCSP for their prospectus and then to the English Literature Department and to College Administration about second-chance degrees.

I had started to swim in a sea of words. When I wasn't working or looking after the house or Star, I was reading. A great wave was breaking across North America and it was heady: the civil rights movement had been quickly followed by women's liberation, its bastard child. Unplanned and unwanted by its parent, it was sweeping into kitchens and schools and community halls, finding me and women like me, and giving us what we had never had. An understanding that what we had been told were private, individual problems were never just that.

It was handing me a whole new way of looking at my life, spinning connections I was only beginning to grasp.

That's why I resented the doorbell. I had been hoping to grab a half-hour between getting Star to sleep and having to go to work, for reading. If Star hadn't been watching, I wouldn't have answered the bell. Now, as I sit here writing this, I wonder what would have happened if I hadn't?

I guess he would just have come back another day.

I often played the same game with Zach, wondering what would have happened if he hadn't turned up at the restaurant that night. Or if I had been on my break? Or if I hadn't run out after him or he got fed up waiting outside and left? We might have missed each other for ever, I would exclaim, shivering at the thought, though we were snug under his quilt, in an envelope of body heat at the time. It all seemed so random, so accidental.

'I don't believe in accidents,' he said.

'Well, they happen, whether Zach Coleman believes in them or not.'

'Nope, no accidents.' He shook his head. 'No coincidence or happenstance, no such thing. No freaks or misfits either. Just things that we don't understand.'

'Oh, Zach. Tell that to the Bangladeshis.' Two years ago a cyclone and flood disaster in Bangladesh had killed thousands, and people had been starving to death there since.

That was the day I gave him the present. 'Here, today's our two months' anniversary.'

He was delighted. 'W. B. Yeats,' he read, taking off the wrapper. '*The Collected Poems.*'

'That Irish poet I told you about.'

'I know. I haven't forgotten.' He kissed me. 'Thank you.'

'You don't have to be nice about it. You think you're not interested but you will be, trust me.'

'Read me something. Read me your favourite.'

'I don't have a favourite. It's more like I have different poems for different days. I know exactly what I'm going to read to you but first you have to get into the right place to receive it.'

'Huh?'

'Think of it as watching somebody dance, okay?'

'Dance?'

'Poetry is language dancing. That's the way you have to take it in. As if you were watching a great dancer.'

'Okay, I'll try.'

'I'm going to start with the early stuff. His early poems are childlike in their belief in another world, and some people now find them too mystical and too naive. They're far less intellectual and formal than the later ones, but for me they are magic. The lines and phrases make me feel as if I've fallen into a dream . . . Anyway . . . here goes.'

I began with 'The Song of the Happy Shepherd', the poem that I've turned to again and again over the years to keep me writing. 'The wandering earth herself may be / Only a sudden flaming word, / In clanging space a moment heard, / Troubling the endless reverie . . .' I looked up at him as I finished the last line – 'Dream, dream, for this is also sooth' – and smiled to see how his eyes were shining. He got it. I knew he would.*

I moved on to 'The Cloths of Heaven' and 'When You are Old,' and told him all about the poet's hopeless, unrequieted love for Maud, the multiple proposals and rejections. 'That's enough for today,' I said as I was finishing 'The Two Trees'. Like any intoxicant, poetry needs to be taken sparingly.

Nineteen years old Zach Coleman might have been, but I was living the whole love cliché with him, feeling like a girl in a shampoo ad, ultra-smiley and glowing. At the time, I thought it was because of what I was receiving – the attentions of this kind and handsome (young) man – but I've come to believe it was the giving that left me feeling so good. When you're in love, you're so willing to amuse, to gratify, to charm, to pleasure . . . Later in a relationship, you become grudging again, but at the beginning you give of your best.

* Mom was always at this, asking us to *appreciate* poetry. Look at this *glorious* metaphor. What do you think the poet is *saying* here? What's your *response* to this? As a child I loved it. She was so often unreachable that when she turned her attention on me, I felt as if the sun were warming my face, but by this time in my life it was totally ticking me off.

When I recall that time, I always think of the big bed in his apartment, where we spent most of our time. For every true couple there is a quadrant of emotional landmarks: first sex; first 'I love you'; moving in together and marriage. We were stuck on Phase Two. The three words were not coming out of me, and I knew he wanted to say them but was being held back by the reluctance he sensed in me.

He kept pushing to meet Star. 'She's important to you, so she's important to me. I need to get to know her.'

'I don't introduce boyfriends to her. It's too confusing for her.'

A small flinch. He didn't have a history as long as mine and hated to think of me with anybody else.

'Zach,' I said more gently, 'in a few weeks, you're going back to college. You'll meet some preppy girl and that will be the end of me.'

He sat up, the sheet falling from his chest, and gripped me by the wrist. 'Don't say things like that.'

'Hey, take it easy.'

'You don't really believe that?'

'I . . . I don't know . . . It's what happens.'

'What do you think I'm doing here, Izzy?' His fingers tightened, making a mark. 'You know I've cancelled my summer trip to Europe to be with you.'

'Zach, stop. Let go of me.'

'Don't you know I'd give up college tomorrow for you, get a job, move in with you and Star.'

'I'm not asking you . . . I'd hate you to do that. It would be all wrong.'

'I wish you *would* ask. I want to give you something, I want to give you *everything*. But you won't even give me a meeting with your daughter.'

'I will but not just yet.'

'I'll know you're serious about me when you let me meet her.'

'I'm sorry, Zach, not yet. If you had a kid of your own, you'd –'

'You're just scared, Izzy, but that's okay. You might know more about poetry but I know more about us. I'll just have to wait until you know it too.'

'Know what, you crazy man?'

'That we were made for each other. That I'm not just a little boy for you to play with.'

'Is that what you think I think?'

'That we are *never* letting each other go.'

Next time, I promised. Next vacation, I would introduce them. In the meantime, while he was away, I would prepare the ground. Except I didn't. Every time I went to broach the subject with Star, I was at a loss. Maybe the best thing was for her to meet him first, then explain.

Ding dong, went the door again. I waved goodbye in my head to my reading half-hour and called across to Star, doing homework at the table. 'Will you get that, honey?'

I turned back to the cooker, heard her chair scrape back, and her footsteps, and the creak of the front door and then: his voice.

'Does Iseult Creahy live here?'

I turned too fast, dropping the pot I was holding. Bolognaise sauce spilled over the floor. *Creahy*. Nobody out here called me that. Before I came West, I had returned to using Mulcahy. And that voice. Its low timbre sent blood rushing into my skull.

The sticky tomato mess was oozing all over my shoes, and it might have been glue, because I found I couldn't budge.

'Mom?' My name fluttered in Star's mouth. She knew something was wrong. I couldn't look at her. The door creaked and his footsteps crossed the threshold. He was coming in. Coming into our house.

'Iseult,' he said, putting himself in front of me. My pulse butted against my temples. He looked bad, I saw that in an instant, though he'd done his best to dress himself up. Gone too far, in fact, with a suit and tie, but the suit was shiny and the shirt was faded and the shoes were bunched and knobbled. And no clothes could disguise the mottled skin and the red-rimmed eyes.

'Oh, God,' I said. And then noted, in that detached way that you do even while you're in shock, how people in moments of extremis always call to either God or their mother.

We were frightening Star. 'What is it, Mommy? What?'

'It's all right, baby.'

'Mommy, tell me.'

'It's . . .'

What could I say to her? She was beside me now, looking up at me, the false sophistication she'd adopted since turning twelve knocked off her. She looked skinned as she stood, tugging my sleeve, eyes full of accusatory questions.

'Mom! Tell me!'

How was I going to find the words to explain what I could see she already knew?

It was her father, of course. Who else but Brendan, returned from the dead to haunt us?

Lost as Soon as Won

Dance there upon the shore;
What need have you to care
For wind or water's roar?
And tumble out your hair
That the salt drops have wet;
Being young you have not known
The fool's triumph, nor yet
Love lost as soon as won . . .

W. B. Yeats,
'To a Child Dancing in the Wind'

Christmas Eve, 1982
Star

The Christmas Eve has tainted every Christmas of my life. Each and every year, I am forced to remember.*

When my mother took me in to see Granddad, he said: 'Well, well, look what the cat dragged in.' The same words he'd used the first time she brought me here. Did he know this? It was always impossible to judge just how much my grandfather knew.

I sat down in the chair beside the bed.

'Is she about to take herself off or what?' he asked.

'I don't know what you mean,' I said.

'Her boyfriend's done a runner.'

Mom stopped on her way to the door. She hadn't mentioned boyfriend to me.

'Boyfriend?' I asked, enjoying her embarrassment.

'Yeah. A long streak' – he pronounced it 'strake' – 'of a yoke with a baldy head. He's taken himself off, and she'll be going after him, just watch her.'

'Is that right?'

'Shocking it is, the way she throws herself at him and he half her age. A laughing stock she's making of herself.'

A burst of coughing seized him. When he came out of it, he said, 'Ah, I have it now. That's why you're here. I'm the great burden, of course. Well, I didn't ask any of ye to be here, so I didn't and –'

Again, he broke up into a fit of coughing. 'She needn't bother'

---

* This is not me writing but my mother's version of me – though, aside from her omission of the row we had on my arrival, it is not inaccurate. It is true that the events of those days tainted all the Christmases that came after – for us both, I guess.

– cough – 'playing Florence Nightingale. And you needn't' – cough – 'either.'

'I'm not,' my mother said, her voice as hard as gun metal.

'I'm well able . . . to look after myself,' he fired back. 'Always was.'

37

To Doolough Stores today, to stock up on provisions – a trip I'd prefer to avoid. I left early, while Mass was on, so the village would be quiet. I walked along, my shopping bag over my shoulder, searching for spring in the hedgerows and finding it in early primroses and snowdrops. The village itself felt small and closed and sealed tight, much as it was when I left, which was much as it had been for decades before.

Doolough Stores, McFadden's, is one of those shops that used to be common in the Irish countryside, stocking the most unlikely items alongside milk and bread and newspapers. Should you find yourself in need of a tea towel or fish bait or a primus stove, wellington boots or string or a plumbing U-bend, a tyre-repair kit or feather duster or drawer liners, you would find them in McFadden's, among thousands of pounds' worth of other stock, all snuggled together under a blanket of dust. My needs were more everyday: milk, orange juice, bread, tomatoes, pasta, sugar. As I was gathering them together under the eye of Mrs McFadden, the bell tinkled over the door.

'Good morning, Pauline,' boomed Mrs McFadden. I turned and yes, it was my only friend in Doolough, her too-blonde hair lighting up the dull morning.

'Hello, folks,' she said, her big, open smile including Mrs McFadden, Deirdre on the other till and the two strangers by the fridge, a pair of walkers in lace boots and wet gear, debating the merits of small bottles of water over large. And me too. No peering, prodding eyes from Pauline. 'Lovely day.'

It was, in fact, another dreary morning, but to Pauline most every day was lovely. I was glad to see her because I had something I had been meaning to ask her if I got the chance.

It was my intention to wait outside, to avoid embarrassing her, but at the till, as I took my change, she came across to me. 'Are you walking back?'

I nodded, aware of Mrs McFadden watching.

'I'll walk back that way with you.' She spoke in a deliberately loud voice. 'I'm on a day off, so would you like to come back for a cup of tea?'

'I'd love to,' I said. 'Thanks.'

I didn't just mean for the tea but also for showing our audience that I had at least one person who believed in me.

Pauline and I had gone to Doolough National School together, where I was the well-to-do sergeant's daughter and she was one of the Breens, the seventh of eight girls and a brother, the boy that Mr and Mrs Breen had kept on trying for. 'If Josephine had been a boy, they would have stopped then and I wouldn't exist,' she told me one day in school, all solemn-eyed at the thought.

Eleven of them lived, I can't imagine how, off a tiny patch of land and a couple of pigs that Mrs Breen used to fatten for the local bacon factory.

Around that time, a popular boy made overtures towards me in school by making fun of Pauline and the other Breens and their pigs. It made me uncomfortable to hear him talk like that, but I allowed it. We were overheard, and word got back to Pauline. I thought I would die of the sick guilt I felt and the certainty that she'd never speak to me again, but somehow, over time, she seemed to forget it had ever happened.

I never forgot.

'I'll have coffee,' I told her now that we were all grown up, sitting not in her mother's kitchen but hers, having walked the quarter mile or so from the shop, chatting about her children. Her movements were definite, almost sharp, bringing a little more energy than necessary to each action. Tap-tap-tap: the coffee into the container. Pat it down with the back of the spoon. Splash the water from jug to pot. Click the coffee canister shut. Watching her efficiency made me feel tired and inadequate. Her house was large and airy and as clean as the hospital wards she used to work in.

In the old days, I was the one with the material advantages, but Pauline and Mikey had, by hard work, bought a good life for themselves.

The room was filling nicely with the aroma of percolating coffee and we were having such an idle, easy conversation, that I pushed my question away again, to bask for another minute or two in these moments, to pretend that we were what we appeared to be, two ordinary friends having a coffee.

Before I came back to Doolough, Pauline had looked after my father, sent up by Dr Keane to monitor vital signs, a role she continued after I arrived. They were tough times, those months before Zach came. Only Pauline knew how tough. She monitored me too.

'It doesn't have to be like this, you know,' she said to me one day a week or two after my return, when I was complaining of being unable to get out for a walk or a drive. It was like stepping back to when Star was a child, a constant tie. 'I could organize some respite care.'

I shook my head. 'He wouldn't take it.' And I would have felt so guilty. Perhaps if I loved him more, I would have been at ease with doing less.

Now I was going to draw further on her good nature. I reached across her kitchen table for a biscuit and said: 'I was going to call you, Pauline. I wanted to let you know that my lawyer is going to ask if you would appear for the defence.'

The cup stopped on the way up to her mouth. 'Really?'

'You don't have to.'

'I don't know what it means.'

'To be a character witness. To say that you think me of good character and why. To talk about what you witnessed while you were nursing my father.'

'Oh.'

291

'Like I said, please don't feel that you have to. Think about it and you needn't even tell me what you decide.' I pulled a business card from my jeans pocket. 'All you need do is let Mags – that's my lawyer – know.'

I changed the subject then by telling her about a man from the Right to Die Campaign who had called, saying they wanted to take up my case. He was English, and he said he had heard about me from a member of their Irish group. According to him, I could be a symbol to the thousands of people in these islands who care for terminally ill family members. Carers were the ones who knew best what was right for their charges. Certainly they knew better than the courts or than doctors who wanted to keep them alive when they had no quality of life.

'Dear Lord.' Pauline's eyes seemed to swell over the rim of her cup. 'What did you say to him?'

'I told him I didn't do it, of course, when I could get a word in edgeways.'

'I wonder sometimes whether those people aren't right.'

A prickling sensation crawled up my back. Was she saying this to offer me an opportunity to confess? Did she not believe in me, after all?

'Is that not against your religion, Pauline?'

'It is, I suppose. But when you see the things I've seen . . . It would be hard to think certain people wrong if they decided to go that road.'

I topped up my coffee from her pot. 'I wouldn't let Dr Keane hear you saying that, Pauline. He might think you did it.'

'Oh, no,' she said. 'Nobody would think that.'

And they wouldn't. Not of her. But they thought it of me.

38

One reason why I said Brendan was dead was that I thought it would be better for Star (and yes, okay, for me too) if our new town thought me a widow rather than a deserted wife. Mainly, though, it was the truest explanation of what I felt he had done to us.

'Was there somebody else?' That was the question I knew people would ask if I told them the truth. A question I couldn't bear.

It undid me to know that while he and Star and I shared that weekend together in Cape Cod, while we fed her and put her to bed and then went downstairs together for dinner, a baby monitor on the table between us along with the candles and flowers and pre-dinner drinks; while we drank a bottle of wine and exchanged heavy, meaningful looks that had us all worked up long before we got back upstairs; while we made frenzied, wild, all-over love with Star sleeping sound and oblivious in her cot, that, yes, behind all that, there was somebody else. A girl from work called Jane, aged twenty.

My husband was dead, defect of the heart. That was the truth of it to me.

So why did I take him back? That is the question that flays me now. It wasn't as if he had improved with age. Whatever had happened to Brendan since I last saw him – most of his communications on the matter were long, circuitous rambles – he had become a man incapable of settling on anything for more than a minute. Watching TV meant flicking up and down through the channels; smoking meant lighting one cigarette from the last; telling a story meant losing his place and stumbling on to recount something else instead.

He spent the night he moved back in telling us an allegedly funny tale about what some guy had done to him in some motel, littered with cussing and swearing, each followed by an 'excuse me'. No matter how round Star's eyes grew or how often I said, 'Brendan, will you *please* mind your language?', he just excused himself and did it again, as if the apology cancelled out the use of words such as 'fuck' and 'prick' and 'mother-fucker' in front of a twelve-year-old girl.

I sat, offended by his careless talk and by the sprawl of him taking up way too much room. And fearful. When he tore a piece of laminate from a napkin carton and starting to pick his teeth with the edge of it, I thought: for this, for *this,* I am giving up my Zach.

Poor Zach. He had cried, real tears, forehead pressed against the steering wheel of his car. He had raged against me, calling me a liar, a cheat, and – ridiculously – a whore. He had tortured us both with his imaginings of me sleeping with this other man, this *husband,* and my assurances that I had no intention of sleeping with Brendan were rejected. What did such assurances mean from a liar?

I knew I was dealing him a version of what Brendan had dealt to me, but, trying to hold some dignity for us both, I kept bringing it back to one quiet line: 'He is Star's father, Zach.'

It was no good. Zach had made an idol of me and wasn't able for the real Izzy's life, all shimmers and shades and blurry edges. His hurt was sharp and certain and pitiless, and he said the most outrageous things. He'll learn, I told myself, pulling defences up around me as I looked out his car window. Just live a while longer, my dear boy, and you'll come to see it's not so simple.

After he was gone, the absence of him hurt. I missed his goodness and his youth, his caramel smell and the bright metal taste of him in his secret places but mostly I missed the true adoration that I had got used to, that had been turning me into something I wasn't before. I could have cried and wailed and ranted too, it would have been nice to have had the luxury of that, but I had to be shatterproof glass. Splintered into a thousand shards, splintered all over, but holding together.

Star would have a father again. Brendan and I would sync our schedules to ensure one of us was always there for her. We would become a proper family. Except the next thing was that Brendan wouldn't cooperate. He had lived the easy life for so long that he had become incapable of doing anything for anybody else.

'We're going to watch TV *again*?' he said to me one night not long after his return. I came down at about 9.30, groggy, having dozed off beside Star while trying to get her to sleep.

'Why? What would you prefer to do?'

'Couldn't we go out for a few hours? What about that bar down on the waterfront?'

'Of course we can't go out.'

'Because?'

'What do you mean "because"? Because of our twelve-year-old daughter.'

'She's asleep now, isn't she?'

Was he serious? It seemed so. 'You go,' I said.

'I think I will.'

It was 4.30 a.m. when he came home, stumbling and cursing.

I wasn't going to admit that I'd made a mistake. I had lost Zach in order to take back Brendan. I wasn't going to let him make nothing of that.

We stuttered on, with me forgiving the unforgivable and Brendan promising promises we both knew he wouldn't keep, didn't even mean to keep. Guilt made him lash out at me. 'It's so *bad* for Star, the way you indulge her.'

'It would be better to be like you, I suppose, and indulge myself.'

'Lying beside her every night to get her to sleep. At her age.

Never leaving her out of your sight when you're not at work. The poor child can't breathe.'

'Oooh, I'm so bad. If only *I* could be the person who can't last two evenings without getting drunk or stoned.'

'A man has to do something. There's no room for me in your little hothouse for two.'

'Oh, yes, that's it. I drive you to it. Like you never touched a toke or a bourbon till you fetched up here.'

'God help you when she grows up,' he said, his Irish accent strong in his anger. 'God help *her* even more.'

He loved to deal out suchlike to take attention away from his own shortcomings. I struck back, scoring my points, though I knew we were both losing the match.

It ended the night I came back from work at the restaurant and found a drunken mob there, three men and two girls. The thought of Star rising from her sleep and seeing their carry-on ... That did it. I gave them all their marching orders, him included, and he went, happily, he said.

I didn't tell Star that part. I just said he had to go away and I didn't know when he'd be back, but it hurt her, horribly. Thirteen weeks he'd stayed, just long enough for her to get used to the idea of a father and be distraught at losing him all over again. Just long enough for him to rend and wreck our lives a second time, in a whole new concoction of ways.

What a mistake. I see it so clearly now. What I should have done was bid Brendan good day when he turned up unannounced, stayed with Zach and slowly introduced him to Star. Let him grow over time into being her father. Zach would have risen to the role, and all that happened later would have been averted. With Zach, I could have gone to Europe, travelled the world, done whatever we decided to do ...

Now, I can see my taking Brendan back and letting Zach go for what it actually was: self-abuse. I made myself sorrier than any woman should ever be, not just for Star, which was what I told myself at the time, but because a part of me felt more comfortable with my flawed and floundering husband, or with being alone, than being with good, sweet, upright Zach.

Brendan, or loneliness, was as much as I deserved.

Star
2008

Sorry for interrupting like this but what has to be said here is too long for a footnote. It's not that my mother is lying, but that she's looking through a mirror. She's up front looking through the glass at the rest of us behind her. In her vision we're all back to front.

Or not in the frame at all.

Take that concern for me of which she makes so much. That was the burden of my childhood. She never said so, I grant her that, but I always knew that I was the one who was holding her back, who had brought her to small-town suburban life, who was keeping her in deadbeat jobs . . . I knew that without me, she'd be travelling through Europe, reading and writing poetry, dancing in the moonlight on misty Irish beaches.

As a child, that felt right to me. She was my lovely mother, so much younger than the other moms, so beautiful and desirable and free-spirited, that a scented kingdom of Celtic mists and shadows was just where she belonged.

In those days, I would sit on her bed watching her, adoring every gesture: the way she shimmied into or out of a dress, or twisted her hair into a coil, or kicked off her high heels. I would put the shoes on after her, feel her warmth through my soles, admire my feet and measure how I was growing into them. When she sat me down to look into her mirror, she would show me how alike we were – our long hair down, our eyes the same shade of blue, our freckles in the same spatter across both noses.

'Never forget we are of Ireland,' she would say. 'Land of saints and scholars and female fighters. Maeve, the warrior queen. Gráinnehuile, the pirate princess.'

It surprised me the first day she spoke like that. Until then, Ireland was that godforsaken country, that priest-ridden theocracy, that patriarchal hell hole . . . I knew she'd been reading something.

'Tiny little Ireland held out against the Romans first,' she said into the mirror. 'Then against the English. It kept the Celtic culture alive. In Doolough, the village where I grew up, they told stories and sang songs that were old when Homer was a boy.'

I liked this. I could see misted mountains and rained-out fields. I could hear the clash of spears, feel the strange, outlandish alphabet in my mouth. *Maedbh* (Mayve). *Gráinnehuile* (Graw-nya-wail). *Doolough* (Doo-lockh).

She fought hard always, my mother, to remain true to all that. I could feel her struggle, and I was the weight pulling at her flaxen-red hair, drawing her down. I tried not to make it worse.

Enter my dad. He was hopeless, I won't deny it. Even a twelve-year-old, bowled over by surprise that the father she had given up wishing for had suddenly appeared, could see that he was not good enough for her. He wore denim jeans and jackets and a long grey pony-tail. He was puffy and pale, from drinking and too much time indoors. He rolled his own cigarettes with a sweet-smelling tobacco that once, when I smelt it twenty years later in another country, brought him right back to me. His shirt buttons strained over his stomach, he didn't wash often enough, his manners were bad.

But I liked him. He had a lovely smile, which said, 'Sorry for not getting it right.' He was soft all the way through. He taught me to play poker. He introduced me to old movies, actresses like Barbara Stanwyck and Katherine Hepburn. He told me I was going to be a 'smasher', that the boys would soon be lining up. He was full of words like this, words I'd never heard, and the Irish lilt in his voice was much stronger than in Mom's.

And hers was stronger when she was with him.

The night after he came back, as we got the house ready

299

together for dinner, I knew that, for once, her thoughts were the same as mine. We were going to be three now. She would have help and everything would be easier. *Righter*. He would feed us and hold us and make us what we should be – a family – and she wouldn't want to go anywhere else.

I gave thanks as she lit incense – Nag Champa, the only one she allowed – and let her hair dry loose, walking barefoot around the house, in a white dress, humming.

When he came in – came home to us – we ate dinner together, the two of us listening to his stories, trying to laugh in the right places, and after I'd been sent up to bed, I left my door open and lay listening to the sing-song of their Irish voices in the dark, her soft laughter. I wanted to halt the moment and hold it for ever, shut it into a locket that I would wear around my neck.

That was the year I turned twelve. It was a hot summer, the winds blowing down from the canyons, shrivelling the grass. The TV news showed fires burning to the south. The hills closer to us seemed to smoulder, and the wind smelt burnt.

In the supermarket a man fell backwards over a trolley, looking at my mother. When out, she often invited looks, only to stare back with blue eyes fixed, until the man would grow awkward and not know where to look. I didn't like her doing it that day, with my father near by. It was wrong now, there was no need.

The man dropped his gaze and stepped backwards, only to be felled by the low trolley behind. 'Men,' she snorted, turning away with a sideward glance at my father that almost knocked me over too. The two brackets either side of her lips included him in her scorn, though I could see he didn't know it, not yet.

But I did. I tipped out the hope chest I was starting to build in my heart – a chest full of summer camp and a bicycle, new clothes and Thanksgiving dinner, and all the unnamed, taken-for-granted things that girls with fathers knew.

It hadn't even begun, and it was already over. After twelve years as Iseult Mulcahy's daughter, I could spot a condemned man a mile away.

In her book, in her looking glass, there are almost no men and I know nothing. Did she really believe that? Did she really think I was unaware of the tension always fizzing beneath her skin? I fizzed too, as I felt each wave of craving swell in her, watching and waiting until the air in our house crackled with static, until she chose whoever it was going to be this time.

Sometimes I knew them, my friend's father, or the man in the deli, or, once, one of the male teachers in my school, but mostly it was someone she met at the restaurant. Did she really think I had no eyes or ears with which to notice her absence by night, the strange cars appearing outside our house at all hours? How her clothes mutated and her voice deepened and her laughter flew higher? How all her gestures inflated? How her pupils darkened and she began to smell different, as if she were carrying someone else's scent?

How the atmosphere around us grew thinner and thinner as I watched, afraid each day when I was leaving for school, afraid each evening as she left for work. What if this guy did what the others had failed to do? Won her love? Swept her away?

Then it would collapse, suddenly and completely, and we would have our best times, when she read to me and told me stories. I loved them, those post-lover weeks when she was sated, when she was back with me and we breathed ordinary air again.

For a while.

Some weeks after the day in the supermarket, she brought me out on to the screen porch to tell me he was gone. It was dusk, the blue of the evening turning black, not wanting to leave, a lingering hope. She looked up at the stars, which she said were all wrong to her here in California, which we used to play at connecting into our own constellations – the Guitar, the Book, the Airplane – and told me he had left us again.

What she writes in this book of hers is not wrong, not exactly, but it was she who drove my father away. I felt it then, and I believe it yet. Her damaged heart, the padded cell at her core, the look of judgement in her cornflower eyes that would wither any living thing.

39

Lucien Millevoye lights the lamps in his den and arranges himself in his favourite chair, with all his preferred objects around him and Estelle, his cat, on his lap. Her purring fur is as delicate as a young girl's newly washed hair. He opens his book, then almost immediately puts it aside. From the corridor comes the sound of voices, and then a burst of laughter, the high laughter of the very young. They have arrived, then, precisely on time.

The door opens and he rises, Estelle jumping to the floor. But what is this? Girls no longer. The small swell of young breasts is unmistakable, even under their coats. The hair is up, the bonnets and boots and bearing thrust towards maturity. As he steps forward, hand outstretched, Iseult bends to the floor to stroke the cat, so he takes the hand of the other girl. He pauses mid-bend, her fingers held aloft in his, like a trophy. 'And who is this?'

Iseult looks up from her feline attentions. 'You know well who it is, Loup. It is Cousin Thora. I told you I was bringing her.'

His lips complete the journey, meet the crown of the girl's hand with a loud smack. '*Enchanté, mademoiselle.*' The dear thing blushes. Maud's niece, Kathleen's daughter. If someone had asked, he would have said she was six years old but of course Iseult is fourteen now and her cousin, he believes, a little older.

'You remind me greatly of your aunt, my dear.'

'Aunt Maud? Really?'

'Oh, not as she is now, but when she was a girl. She was

very beautiful then, the most beautiful woman in the world, some said.'

'She is beautiful still, I think.'

'Ah, but when she was young and frivolous ... Are you interested in politics, at all?'

Thora shakes her head.

'Good, good. Have a care not to distract yourself with intellectual matters, dear girl. It is a sure way to loss of looks.'

'Appearance being, of course, the only thing that matters,' says Iseult, rising.

'You see? Do not let your cousin lead you astray with her suffragist reproofs.'

Thora laughs, a little uncertain.

'I could understand if she were ugly. But she has the beauty and culture to be Aspasia to any man. As do you.'

'Aspasia?' asks Thora.

'The mistress of Pericles,' Iseult tells her cousin. 'Loup, you are showing your age. It is no longer antiquity. Girls no longer have to live on sex favours.'

'My dear girl, wherever did you learn such crudities?' He shudders. 'I cannot believe your mother permits you to say such things?'

'Aspasia was a sex slave,' Iseult tells Thora, in the manner of teacher addressing the brightest child in the class. 'With no rights or entitlements for herself or her children.'

'Aspasia', counters Lucien, 'was a beautiful and cultivated woman and her relationship with Pericles was closer and more harmonious than most marriages. So much so that it is still celebrated today.'

'He had his own name and his status. Hers rested entirely on him.'

'He gave her a life and experiences she would otherwise never have known.'

A silence drops. How stubborn Iseult is. Lucien catches Thora's eye and shrugs with a small smirk, as if to say, 'What a silly, wayward girl this daughter of mine is, be indulgent of her.'

While Thora frowns, wondering how to show that it is her cousin's side she is on, Iseult is off again: 'Well, Loup, it is the twentieth century now. If my husband turns out to have inferior intelligence to me, then I believe I have not only the right but the duty to take a lover with an intelligence equal to mine. And the same if he is not handsome enough.'

Lucien chuckles. 'I don't think you will find men so inter-changeable as all that.'

'Oh, I find one tires as quickly of a man as of a dress.'

'Come now, we are upsetting your cousin.' He rises to light the lamp. 'Pay us no heed, my dear. Iseult and I are old sparring partners. There is more sound than fury in our disputations.'

The gas hisses into flame, its glow chasing out the last of the dirty evening light. It is Lucien's favourite time of the day but not for the reasons of old. These days he likes to sit alone in his library, in a house as quiet as an empty theatre, perversely drinking in the silence. Ah, yes. Live as long as I have, my dears, and you shall come to know what it is to tire of wanting.

Outside, dark is gathering, a slow-growing blindness sucking colour from the sky, from the buildings and the flowers in his garden. Already the window holds nothing but the reflection of him and these girls behind him.

So here he is, with the scene of his old age set, the props carefully arranged. That which he most dreaded has come to pass, but he is comfortable – almost. So let his daughter, and her winsome cousin, thrust themselves forward, like their mothers. They too shall learn.

'Apologies, my dears. Where are my manners? You shall have tea, shall you not? Certainly. Let us ring for tea.'

Thora puts a foot out of the attic window, cautiously, and takes it back in as though she fears the roof may not be stable.

'Come on, little cousin, you are quite safe.' Though Iseult

is two years younger than her cousin, she always seems the leader.

'Take these first.' Thora shoves a bolster through the small window. 'Catch.'

Iseult pulls it through and her cousin follows with another bolster, some cushions and blankets. They are sleeping on the flat roof tonight, as they have done before. They love it out here when the weather is warm, where the air is cooler and the sounds of the city are theirs. The *clop-clop* of horses' hooves, the *meow* of cats, the diners at the restaurant down the street and the waiters taking in the umbrellas and cushions at the end of the night – all are louder up here, floating disembodied into their pocket of space. The blue of night is turned orange by the gas lamps or white by the moon, depending on where you look.

A rustle sounds behind them, loud and unaccounted for, making Thora jump. She snaps her head around. 'What is that?'

'Nothing,' her cousin laughs. 'Nothing at all. Come, Thora, we cannot do this if you are going to jump like a cat at every strange noise.'

'It is you who says we are two gutter cats.'

'Well, try to be a brave one.'

Iseult is always brave. All the virtues are hers: beauty, intelligence, grace and courage, and she is always so original and unique. For their last night together she wants to do something special, so as a nightdress she wears a shirt left behind by the poet on his last visit, and she insists that Thora should don an old vest of her father's. Which gives Thora a rather peculiar feeling.

How hot it is, as hot as high summer, even so late. London is never so hot as this by night. They settle the blankets and lie, side by side, close but not quite touching. Looking up at the stars.

'So now you understand my nickname for Loup,' Iseult says, picking up their conversation of earlier.

'Yes, he is a roué.'

He is so much older than Thora had expected. Much older than Aunt Maud, she feels sure, though she is uncertain what gave rise to that impression: he had no sign of an age stoop. Wrinkles, yes, and hairline receding. Women grow old, it seems, each in her own way, but men grow more alike, with their bald heads and paunches. Were it not for his handlebar moustache and his great height, he would look unexceptional. Surely the father of Iseult and the lover of Aunt Maud should not be unexceptional.

Perhaps it was his loamy eyes that made him appear older. They seemed debauched or perhaps she imagined them so, from listening to Iseult's tales of his depravity. Thora puts on a voice and an exaggerated version of his manner: '"You remind me greatly of your aunt, my dear. When she was young and beautiful enough to attract me."' She licks her lips and slavers, like a dog contemplating its dish, and is delighted when Iseult giggles.

'You each', she continues, in the same licentious tone, 'have the beauty and culture to be Aspasia to any man.'

'Ah, *that* I did not find so amusing.'

'You are offended?'

'It is offensive, is it not, that he thinks so little of the damage he did Moura, in allowing her to play Aspasia?'

It is the first time that Iseult has ever spoken of such matters.

'I don't know anybody with as much generosity and power for love as Aunt Maud,' she says. 'It makes me wonder how she chose –'

'Such a bounder? Do not worry that you offend me, Thora. My father is a bounder, you are right – though I have a certain affection for him. And when his treatment of Moura became too infamous, she chose another, the second even worse than the first.'

'Is it true that she keeps a revolver under her pillow in case Mr MacBride returns to steal Bichon?'

'Yes, but that is a touch of Moura dramatics. MacBride is unlikely to return now. He never really cared to have Bichon. He wanted only to hurt her.'

'At least in Ireland he can hurt her no more.'

'Except by keeping her away. It hurt her so when she attended that play at the Abbey and was hissed by the crowd.'

'How perfectly horrid.'

'And his friends have tried to have her blackballed from the Arts Club. Uncle Willie told her it would happen if she married MacBride.' Iseult props herself up, her elbow making a triangle. 'If only she had listened. Irishmen have such a rudimentary understanding of morality. Especially for women.'

'You do not like the Irish.'

'They seem crude, but Moura says I haven't met the right ones. She took comfort that there were others who set up a counter-hissing of "Up Madame" at the play. That is what they call her over there.'

'Poor Aunt Maud.'

'She has had to relinquish her beloved politics and take up painting. Yet this enforced quiet is good for her, I believe.'

'Poor *you*, then, darling. You – the most blameless in the whole affair – are left to suffer its worst consequences . . .' Thora lets her voice trail.

'It seems fanciful and more than a little self-indulgent, to attribute one's shortcoming to one's parents.'

'What shortcoming?'

'What I call the cockroach.'

'Oh, your melancholia.' What Thora had meant was her birth status. But perhaps the two are connected? 'Poor dear Iseult. Is it very bad, my darling?'

'It is as I told you before. Sleepless nights, with thoughts circling, that make me too tired by day to do more than languish.'

'What do the doctors say?'

'The latest one has recommended hot baths.'

'And have you tried this? Does it work?'

'The bath is broken. As is my belief in doctors.'

'I really think you could do with a change of scene. Perhaps Italy —'

'Oh, Thora!' Iseult sits up abruptly, dismissing Italy. She shakes two cigarettes from the pack in her shirt pocket and lights them, one after the other, in her mouth, handing across the first, a small apology for her sharpness. The smoke leaves her nostrils slowly and rises in stringy loops about her face. After a time she says, 'I have only one consolation, cousin, if consolation it is. To know that neither changing the occasion, nor my surroundings, nor my habits will change *it*.'

'I am sorry.'

'Please, do not be. What worries me most when it is upon me is my disdain for others. All about me seem so feeble.'

'Who? Not Aunt Maud?'

'All.'

'I should love to have had Aunt Maud for a mother . . . Mama is so distant.'

'Oh, she is a little egotistical sometimes. But she admires the Greeks.'

'That might redeem her in your eyes, Iseult, but not in mine.'

'Come, cousin, let us not talk of our mothers but of cheerful things. No, let us not talk at all. Moura is right, we talk far more than is necessary. Sing to me instead.'

Thora hesitates.

'Sing "*Des Animaux Merchanges*".'

So she does: *Il y a des animaux merchanges / Et nous sommes les*

309

pires ... Her voice sounds throaty in the night air, but her reward comes immediately as her cousin leans back into the song, and smokes to its rhythm, a small smile playing on her lips. . . . *hommes vous êtes fait pour souffrire / Et non pour jouir . . .*

40

What Dr Aintree set Star and me to do was simple but, as she said, not easy. I was to give her a list of all the things she could do to take herself to sleep and let her go to bed without me. I was to encourage her to have friends and wave her off with them when they went out together, knowing nothing more than where they were going and an agreed time for her to be back. I was to encourage her to do as much as possible alone but also to keep her routine stable and settled.*

She would ensure Star was supported with a weekly session.

We were lucky. Dr Aintree was an exceptional psychiatrist: kind, firm, knowledgeable, supportive, wise, and we needed her to be every quark of that. Each small change led Star into shrieking, sobbing fits of anger, me into fear tipping towards paranoia, and both of us wrung-out and wretched. Star was having her toddler tantrums now, the good doctor explained, and I was feeling classic separation anxiety. Stay with it. So we did. We rode the roller coaster of feeling, holding fast to Dr Aintree's instructions.

Change came slowly but was clearly change from the first. Little by little the compulsive talking started to fade. It took a couple of years, and even then, after it seemed to have passed, it would rear back up in her, unexpectedly, when she was under stress.

I remember best the morning I decided she was cured. She was in the kitchen, making flapjacks for the school fair and

* Mom implies that my problems were down to her over-parenting, but surely Dr Aintree must have mentioned Dad? And other stuff? Does she omit deliberately? Or is this what she thinks she heard?

talking to her friend Ginnie, who lived next door. They were fourteen, an age that fancies itself older than it is, and often high or low with feeling. I was in the dining room, having come in, in stockinged feet, looking for my shoes, and I stopped for the joy of listening, loving the camaraderie of their voices around the joint effort, the ten-minute fuss over measuring sixteen ounces of oats, the homely clunk of the baking utensils.

Ginnie was complaining about her mother and making Star laugh with stories of her absent-mindedness.

A burst of laughter was followed by silence while they cut butter, then Star spoke. 'When my mom gets cold,' she said, and I could hear the roll of her eyes, 'she puts a sweater on *me*.'

I was so shocked I gasped.

'Mom? Is that you?'

'Hi, girls,' I called in a breezy voice. 'Just getting my shoes. I'm heading out for a walk.'

I went up the hill, towards Turner's Point, the highest outcrop on the coast around there, two miles from our house. Some yards west of the public viewing point, I found a small pathway, concealed and overgrown. I took it and followed its winding way through grasses and dry spiky shrubs to a flat shelf of rock jutting out over the sea. A natural viewing bench. Above, the sky made a high ceiling of blue, and, below, ninety feet below, the swoosh of the waves closed over a small beach, over and over.

I sat and cried my latest outburst of tears. When you cry a lot, it sometimes feels like one big sea of tears, but in truth each crying bout has its own root and rhythm. Today it was loud sobbing in the outdoors, not silent weeping into my pillow, and today's tears held pride in Star and self-pity for me and relief and loneliness all erupting into each other. The detachment in Star's voice was exactly what Dr Aintree and I had been working for. How was it I hadn't realized that?

This was my second fright that week. I had also had a letter from Zach.

Dear Izzy,

I hope you are well. I can write that sentence now – and so I now can write to you. For a long time, I have to tell you, I did not wish you well. I wanted something to come along and hurt you like you hurt me. But now I am grateful to you and I wanted you to know that . . .

He had met somebody else. He was planning to go to grad school. And he did not include a return address. I had bid him goodbye; this was his goodbye back.

I hope it worked out for you with your ex, but I suspect it didn't. Maybe that's what you really wanted – to be alone? I don't know. This isn't coming out right, I really didn't want to go over all that – otherwise I'd have written long ago. What I wanted was to tell you that I am, at last, over us. And, now that I am, what I'm left with is gratitude. You opened me, the way Cummings said in that poem we used to call ours: 'as Spring opens (touching skilfully, mysteriously) her first rose'. For that I thank you.

The other thing I wanted to say is that my work is on the influence of Eastern philosophy on Yeats's magic and poetry. Whatever I might have studied, it would not have been that had I not known you. He and all the writers you introduced me to have led to a thousand good things for me, so for that too I am grateful.

Why why why had I let him go? What what what might have been? I turned dead to the day around me, full of brooding thoughts of where I had gone wrong.

After a time, I left my rocky perch, promising myself I'd go back again, and often, and retraced my steps back along the little pathway. As I walked, I cultivated my regrets until a point, more than halfway home, when I caught myself, stopped in the middle of the path, remonstrating with Zach, telling him what he should have done to rescue us from me, while he argued back with me in my head.

Pathetic.

A crazy old biddy talking to herself: that's what I had become.

That's what lay ahead. Star was going to outgrow me. Look at what she'd said to Ginnie. (And that was a good thing. *A good thing*.) And Mr Broken Hearted had already outgrown me. 'I can't live without you,' he'd said, and there he was, not just living but thriving. *He* wasn't in floods of tears on a rock, giving himself an emotional thumping. He was happy. He had enough happy left over to be grateful. *Grateful*. God, I could spit at him for that.

Okay, then.

Okay.

I could go to school too. I could study English and American literature, as I'd always thought I'd love to do. Study and write and see a thousand good things unfold for *me*. I restarted walking, purposefully this time, lengthening my stride.

There.

I tried a small jump.

Yes.

I gave a little skip.

Good.

Thus, on that June morning in Santa Paola, I took the first conscious steps that were to lead me back to Iseult and to Ireland.

41

It is Thora's last day at Aunt Maud's holiday home, and she is desolate. What a place is this Calvados coast, this beach at Colleville-sur-Mer, with its wide-open sky and flat horizon.

What a place is this house, Les Mouettes ('The Seagulls'), a Moorish-style villa so fitting for the Gonnes, being exotic and imposing and unique. Aunt Maud has furnished it simply, for very little money, with whitewashed walls – perfect against the Moorish blue tiles – and brass milk cans and carved Normandy cupboards and other quaint items from the locality that anybody else would overlook. Her good taste is instinctive and pure, not the acquired refinement of society fashion.

Oh, how is Thora to bear it, leaving this warm, embracing atmosphere for the desolation of travels with her cold and proper Mama – how *can* two sisters be so different? – and then back to her cold and proper finishing school in Lausanne. When she sits in the formal dining room there, she will pine for mealtimes here in Colleville, with all assembled together at the big old rustic table, everyone chattering happily and the birds and animals chiming in.

No wonder Iseult adores it so. 'I am sometimes a little ashamed of how much I love it,' she has said of this fantastical house and Colleville-sur-Mer itself. Town life is a disease, she says, and it is true that the seashore does seem like her true element. She is so wild and fey, like a droplet of sky or ocean that has taken human form.

At least this final day with her cousin has been perfect. Straight after breakfast, they struck out for a protracted walk along the beach, Iseult saying she had something she wished to show her.

As they passed the pine tree Iseult described as proud and troubled, she turned in one of her sudden outbursts of vehemence and took her hand. 'Oh, Thora,' she cried. 'It has been so good to have you.'

'Thank you, cousin. You know what it has meant to me.'

'*What* shall I do when you are gone and I have only Delaney's epic scenes about Bichon to entertain me?'

Thora laughed. Nobody was as amusing as Iseult.

'Oh, go on, laugh, you cruel-hearted creature, but how shall I bear it? That brogue of hers endlessly bleating. "Come here, my glory boy; what can I get you, my glory boy?" Ugh.'

'You know it gives you diversion.'

'It is so *bad* for him. Did I tell you that when he was born, she sent a telegram to the pope, saying, "The King of Ireland is Born."'

'Did the pope reply?'

'Through some official. She keeps the letter with Bichon's christening mug.'

'She is such an oddity. I wonder at Aunt Maud keeping her about.'

'Fie, cousin. And she so kind about you. Did I not tell you that she swore she would almost like you, were it not for your Protestant eyes?' Iseult grinned.

They stepped up from the shore, towards the caves that flanked the beach on the far end. The surf turned, but quietly, over and over, matching the gentle whirr of breeze in Thora's ear.

'Iseult, you know you greatly shocked Mama last night by telling her you winked at a young man on the street?'

'All these exasperating rules of what a young lady should not do. When a young man is handsome and smiles at you, why not smile back? It alleviates the boredom.'

'I hate you using that word. It sounds so sinister, the way you say it.'

'You are coming to know me too well, Thora.' She stopped

and took her hands in hers. 'Oh, my dear, our devotion is like that of the animals, is it not? Stern and solitary and upright?'

'Or like men's.'

'Yes. *Yes.*' She squeezed both hands before dropping them. 'Yes, let us be brothers and *refuse* to worship the false gods of femininity. I shall rename myself Maurice, after the saint whose feast day is today.'

'What did he do?'

'Refused to sacrifice to the Roman gods when ordered to do so by the emperor and so was put to death.'

'Very well, Maurice.'

'And you shall be Victor, who, when the emperor brought the belongings of the other massacred soldiers as spoils, refused to accept them and so was also slain.'

'Martyred knights of the moral realm.'

'Precisely. Arise, then, Sir Victor.' Iseult laid a hand on her cousin's shoulder.

Thora copied the act. 'Arise, Sir Maurice.'

They stood a few moments, the breeze flapping their skirts. Then Iseult said: 'The time has come for me to unveil my surprise. Come.' She turned and set off towards the caves at a great pace, Thora manfully following. Abruptly, at the mouth of a small, west-facing cavern, she stopped.

'Go in?' asked Thora.

'Yes. Of course.'

Thora hesitated.

'Come now, Victor, these are very poor sentiments for a knight.'

Stepping out of the sunshine felt like entering the great abbey Aunt Maud had brought them to see in Paris, except that the inside of the cave smelt of must and fish, and behind them the great white surf seemed to roar like an animal.

'Are you sure the tide might not turn and cut us off?' Thora asked, but Iseult only laughed. The cave took the sound and echoed it back at them through the dark: *ha-ha-ha.*

'You are quite safe.' Iseult took her hand, and coaxed her further and further into the gloom. *Safe-safe-afe-fe*. Underfoot the sand was soft and yielding.

Suddenly her hand was dropped. 'Iseult?'

'It's fine. I'm just lighting the candle.'

A match rasped, and then there was the little miracle of light. The wick accepted the flame with a small dip, like a curtsy. The wet walls of the cave caught the light, but Iseult was moving across to another area, where it was dry. When her eyes settled, Thora saw that it was covered in elaborate hieroglyphics and drawings.

It took a moment for her to understand. 'Yours?'

Iseult nodded, two great eyes glowing above the candle.

Thora knew she was being given a gift of great import. 'How wonderful. How simply wonderful. Show them to me, tell me what they mean. Show me all.'

That was their morning. The afternoon was spent flinging themselves down the sides of the tallest dunes, skidding down warm flanks of sand, then afterwards lying on their backs staring into the blue shield of the sky, laughing and out of breath and pricking with sweat. The sea, puckering a little under the breeze, called them in to feel the waves slapping against their calves, their thighs, their middles, a thousand icy needles at first, then warming to them. They spent hours in it, trying to store up some of its salt goodness to take away.

Now it is evening. Their shadows are twice the length of their bodies, and in the violet light all seems horizontal and vast and a little eerie. They lie on the sand just in front of the house, dressed in pinafores, their swimming costumes drying on the marram grass. The breeze has died and twilight is throwing its net over the flat sands, the flat sea-soaked meadows, the curiously flattened sea. The tide is coming to its fullness, slithering over the shingle to almost creep into the garden. Indolence has wrapped herself around them, like the haze that is swathing the water.

Iseult is trying to show her how to extract seeds from the dry heads of tall, scarlet poppies. 'Do you have some? Good. So now . . . you must eat them.'

'Tell me again how does it feel?'

'It is different for everyone. It is different each time. Last time, I had that exquisite sensation that one feels in dreams, when it is so easy to fly or swim or walk on water, like an ancient prophet.'

Iseult holds one up, and Thora opens her mouth, as if to receive Holy Communion like a Catholic. Iseult puts it on her tongue, then another. And another. Thora feels a little giddy. She asks the question she has wanted to put to her cousin all day. 'Iseult, what about poor Toby?'

'I am sorry, Thora, but I have decided your brother is not rich enough.'

'You'll have to provide a better tale than that.'

'Come now, you must admit that riches give one a certain independence.'

'Americans are rich. Perhaps you should marry an American.'

'An American would always be expecting me to bow down to the great importance of events. I suppose that is partly what gives them the "eternal youth" that Uncle Willie speaks of. Children also acknowledge nothing but events.'

'Oooh, Uncle Willie. What else does Uncle Willie speak of?'

'My dear Thora, what are you trying to imply?'

'I believe you know quite well.'

Iseult sighs. 'Uncle Willie. He is so old.'

'But in need of a wife, Mama says.'

'Marriage is too, too revoltingly down to earth. Let us take lovers, dear Victor, but *never* a husband.'

'Hmmm.'

'Unless we get married in order to cheat our husbands. That *might* be acceptable. Then, fed up with the two of them, we can go and sit in the Tuileries, pale faced, and think remorsefully of the enormity of our sins.'

'Either lover or husband would do me. Iseult, *naturellement*, demands both.'

'Indeed. And why just two?'

'Perhaps because it is hard enough to find *one*?'

'I do not think it so difficult to make a man love you.'

'Perhaps not, if one is as beautiful as you.'

'Nonsense. Beauty has nothing to do with it.'

'I notice how nicely you have avoided the question of Toby.'

'Oh, Toby. I told the priest all about him in confession.'

'No! Tell. What*ever* did you say?'

'Father, I accuse myself of having kissed a young man on the lips.'

'And did he cast you for ever to suffer among fire and brimstone?'

'He was most understanding. I have told him much worse before. I am always inventing sins to please him.'

'Iseult, no! Truly?'

'Life is very dull without embroidery, is it not?'

'Is that not sacrilegious?'

'My dear Victor, you have a very dramatic understanding of Catholicism.'

Thora suddenly sits upright. 'Iseult, look!'

A cloud of yellow butterflies has risen to hover over the flowers and all along the edge of the water. Each one flutter-flutters, but the whole together moves in a smooth undulation, as if one body.

'Yes, it happens sometimes on such days. Is it not remarkable?'

They watch for a time, then Thora says, into the quiet, 'Iseult, why not Toby? Then we should be sisters.'

'Toby pleases me very much, and he is very brave and very companionable.'

'But?'

'Alas, as with almost everything, there is indeed a but.'

'So alas poor Toby.'

'But really, Victor, is it any use to come out of the demi-slavery of one's parents to fall into the same thing with a husband?'

'Are you sure you have told me all? Are you sure he has not been displaced by another?'

'Indeed not.'

'Ah!'

'Ah? What is this "Ah"?'

'No clever refutations. No circular sophistries. Just a simple "indeed not". This naturally makes me suspicious.'

Iseult picks a good-sized pebble from the sand and aims it at her cousin's abdomen. It lands like a small punch.

'Oy!' Thora picks up a handful of sand and flings it. Iseult shrieks and returns the favour, and then they are once again laughing and yelling and rolling about in the sand.

Later, as the sun approaches the horizon line, Iseult rises and goes down to the edge of the water to dance her dance. Thora watches her movements, her twisting and turning with the wind and the waves, her feet bare, her long hair blown back. She is lost to her now, part of another realm. Iseult has told her of how, when she dances like this, she undergoes an ecstasy in which all boundaries recede into infinity. 'Who is at one with one thing in nature is at one with all things,' she said. Thora senses the truth of this but has never experienced it for herself. Her cousin seems to have a direct relationship with what she calls the irresponsible wind, and with nature in general, that Thora is unable to enter. It is another thing of which she could be jealous, if she were the jealous type.

As the darkness imperceptibly deepens, the breaking waves shine brighter, like ribbons of silver: the splashes that rise up under Iseult's feet are fountains and her footprints in the sand shine too.

Night is thick around them by the time she returns. 'Oh! The moment of the sun setting, it is the most beautiful moment of the day.'

'I love it too.'

'In that moment we are almost gods, who could fly far away into the golden clouds.'

'Iseult?'

'Yes.' Her breathing is husky.

'You know earlier, when you spoke of embroidery . . . I am just wondering what you have "embroidered" for me?'

Iseult throws herself down on to the sand beside her and brings herself close. 'Oh, no, little cousin Victor. You are as myself, you know that. And, though I sometimes tell lies to other people, I do not lie to myself.'

'So if I ask you something you will give me an answer.'

'That is not quite the same.'

'A simple question: do you have thoughts for Aunt Maud's poet?'

'Oh, my niggardly knight, what a question.'

'And your answer?'

Iseult pushes herself away, flat on to her back, and sighs. 'Thora, why must you talk always of love? You know it is the essence of my soul that is everything to me.' And then she smiles, the glint of the moon on her teeth.

Next morning, the poet comes down for early breakfast, as arranged, to see the Pilchers off. He stands for a long while in the middle of the hall, as wide-eyed as an insect and just as ineffectual, watching while various items are retrieved from various rooms, and trunks and suitcases and hatboxes are brought below, and everybody runs in and out of rooms, fetching and organizing, while Bichon nearly steps on the parrot, which has decided to climb the stairs at the wrong time.

During an Aunt Kathleen commotion over a dog-chewed

slipper, Maud loses patience with him. 'Well, really, Willie, if you can't do anything useful, just go into the dining room and *wait*.'

This he does, theatrically closing the doors behind him, locking himself in with the birds. Iseult has noticed it before, this ability of his to fall into a great abstraction and withdraw from the world when it comes to matters like suitcases and taxicabs – a characteristic she would rather like to emulate.

Once all the bags are packed on to the donkey-and-cart and the Pilchers are coated and behatted and waiting, Iseult is dispatched to fetch him. She has one hand on the door handle and the other raised to knock when she hears from within a pacing of the floor and a strange, monotonous murmur. She knows what she is hearing: what Moura calls 'Willie's booming and buzzing like a bumble bee', the essential alchemical moment when something comes of nothing.

In response to many questions – not this time, while Thora was here, but before – he has explained to her his method of composition. First come fragments, lines, rhymes, beats, occasionally whole stanzas, along with the inner tug of an idea that he knows to be somehow related. That thought he usually shares. He is unusual, Moura says, in exteriorizing his ideas before writing them out. He tells his plans for the poem, discusses the challenges, even asks for advice . . .

Then comes the most important phase. *This*: what is happening now behind the door, when he hums and chants such words as he has, until he is almost in trance. He is like a miner's pan, sifting for the gold that is the rhythm of the whole.

Once he has pinned that on to a page, the tortuous process of revision can begin. He has shown her twenty pages of scratch-outs and rethinks for a single short poem. Alternative words, tenses, rhyme schemes: nothing that goes in first time round is essential to the outcome. Yet, reading the finished product, one would never guess. His poems always read so instinctively and spontaneously and *right*, as if they flowed as unbidden and unhindered as a spring of cooling water on a mountainside.

It takes great toil, he says, for it to seem so natural.

Poetry is more important than goodbyes, even to the Pilchers. She takes her knuckles back without knocking and tiptoes away.

'He is composing,' she says to her mother, out on the front step. 'I did not like to disturb him.'

Maud shrugs. That's Willie, her shoulders say. And what is Kathleen's departure to him? If they are friends at all, it is only for her sake.

Now all is ready, and there is nothing for it but to say goodbye. Nobody wants to part, yet everybody wants it over. Iseult and Thora stand opposite each other with tall, almost soldierly bearing, each a firm image of the other waiting, while Moura and Aunt Kathleen finish effusive hugs and kisses. Aunt Kathleen steps away towards the cab, smile locked in place, and Thora accepts kisses from Moura and Bichon and felicitations from Delaney before, finally, they have only each other left.

No kisses for them, not here in front of others. Instead the gestures and words that have become their prescription but that have nothing of formula in them. The grip of her cousin's right hand placed upon her left shoulder and her reciprocation of the manly gesture.

'Ah, my dear Victor,' she says. 'It was so good to see you.'

'Dear Maurice,' her cousin returns. 'I'll come again soon.'

A strong handshake and she is gone, stepping with grace into the carriage. The cab-man cracks the reins, and they are off, handkerchiefs fluttering all the way. A cough comes from behind: Willie arrived for the send-off, his hair askew, reading spectacles on his head.

'Too late, Willie,' Moura says. 'They had to leave. They were beyond their time as it was. How did you get on with your poem?'

'It is finished.'

'That's marvellous. What is it about?'

'I shall read it to you, later. I shall read it to you both, and you both shall tell me what you think.'

Iseult lies in bed, telling herself tales full of formal drama, that take her from the dreary and sordid things of life. In these stories, chronicles of ordered sadness and ceremonial tragedy such as might be found on a Grecian frieze or an Etruscan urn, Thora is always with her. She calls it the land of Maia, the place they go together in her head, where they live the most wonderful adventures and always manage to do finer deeds than anybody else and to be the object of everybody's admiration.

Sometimes, when the feeling engendered by these imaginings threatens to burst her skin, Iseult writes. Now that Thora has gone, she has only her journals to confide in and, despite her avowals to her cousin, to her journal she is more candid. She takes it from her nightstand and begins to write again of he whom she considers the only person 'of her own race' that she has met. A French expression by which she means that he too puts the religious impulse and all that flows from it – prayer, meditation, art, culture – above all else.

She weaves a possibility. A time ago, he said he should like, if he married, to live in an old house in some out-of-the-way place like Bayeux. Next time she was in Bayeux, she saw the perfect house. It was during that Easter when she had experienced God's ecstasy, days and days on her knees, in bursts of love crying to God of her hatred of sin and of other times sinking into stillness, believing then that the calm of her soul would never leave her.

How different now, trying to get back to Christ. (Always this feeling of being alone, abandoned, this vague, strange terror that something mysterious and unseen is menacing her, even while praying.)

To shift it, she writes, imagining the poet in the house, a medieval town house with a courtyard, within sight of the great cathedral, and she with him, both of them writing and reading. Like everybody, he tells her she should be a writer, but it seems such *labour* and to require such certitude. Sometimes, especially while at Colleville, she is moved to write, but more often she sees all the beautiful thoughts of her soul come like lightning and then go, nudged out by her selfish and stupid boredom.

Uncle Willie – Willie as she is allowed to call him now she is old enough to discuss literature and magic and astrology and art, to share books on Plato, Pindar, Loyola, Keats, Shelley, Pater, Voltaire – is most encouraging of her writing. She has told him she dislikes plays in modern dress and that she prefers the *Iliad* to any other book, two facts she knows impressed him. He has told her that she has a delicate feeling for words and what may well grow into a very great literary talent.

He has much to teach and – this she likes best about him – he is open still to learn. His is an explorer's soul.

So . . . they could live in Bayeux and write together, and if her own writing was not good enough, she could devote herself to . . .

Oh, stop. What did she care for all that? It is true, as she said to Thora, that she can make any man love her, but she can do without a man. All she asks of God is quiet and seclusion, the company of one or two dear friends, a wild and beautiful bit of earth to live in and a life devoted to religious and poetic rapture.

Iseult listens, from outside the breakfast room door. Seaghán is crying at being taken by the nurse. 'There there, little Bichon,' Moura says. 'Nurse shall take you for a lovely walk and then I shall play with you again.'

When the crying has faded away, Uncle Willie asks, 'Why do you call him Bichon?'

'It was Iseult who started it. You know her penchant for nicknames. She is calling herself Maurice now and Thora,

Victor. She says she will never be taken seriously with a feminine name, especially one so resonant of love tragedy!'

'She wishes to be taken seriously.'

'Even when she was a child, she had a wonderful imagination and a remarkable love of art. She would always rather go to a picture gallery or to see beautiful things than to the circus. I think she will do good work some day.'

'Yet you worry.'

'Always, Willie, always. She is much too lazy.'

'She is very good with the boy. I heard her yesterday, chattering away to him. I could not understand what was being said – she spoke rapidly, in French – but I could hear the affection in her voice.'

'Yes, everybody loves dear little Bichon.'

'Do you still fear MacBride might come for him?'

'Of course. But I don't hate any more, Willie, and that is such a relief. Underneath now I have a great calm I would not want to disturb. So, unless MacBride makes more trouble for me, I shall not go after him again.'

'Even though to do so might clear your family of him entirely?'

'Ugh, that horrible courtroom. No, I cannot go back there by choice. It was hate that brought me to that room. For years I wore blinkers, so as never to cease working for the cause and only to see one end and object. That is what I felt John betrayed. He put drink before decency, before his wife and child, and, what seemed even worse to me then, before Ireland. Now I have taken off my blinkers and I find so much to look at. It is a great thing to know one can never suffer again as much as one has suffered already, Willie. It gives one great calm and great strength and makes one afraid of nothing.'

'Iseult, what are you going to *do* with your life? Your Uncle Willie was asking and I was at a loss to inform him. You know, you really should go in for literature. You could do such interesting things, darling. But you must *finish* something.'

'Iseult, you know you are destroying your health by the endless smoking of those cigarettes and inhaling the smoke *so* deep. The doctor was most urgent. Your heart is weak. You must give up smoking, you must eat meat and keep your windows open.'

'Iseult, in this wonderful, troubled world, with so much good work to be done, only imbeciles and lunatics get bored.'

'Iseult, I'm sorry. I do understand why you are so tired and restless. You must apply your will to that intense imagination of yours, darling. It is your lack of *will* that makes you restless.'

'Iseult, such simple instructions, why do you refuse?'

'Iseult, *please*. Why will you not take care of yourself?'

'Iseult, sometimes I think you are a little mad.'

'Uncle Willie?'

'Yes, my dear.'

'Are you going to ask Moura to marry you again?'

His spectacles fall. 'My dear child –'

'Oh, I do wish you would stop "dear childing" me. I am almost as tall as you. And at fifteen, I am old enough in French law to marry myself.'

He bows from his shoulders, with exaggerated gallantry. 'A thousand apologies. So you are.'

'And the question does have relevance for me too, you know.'

'Moura's religion does not allow her to remarry.'

'Ah, the question avoided. Perhaps you consider her too old to marry now? Men are so heartless.'

'On the contrary, it is you who is heartless. For if Moura is "too old", then so am I. We are of an age.'

'Ah, but it is different for men.' She reaches across and closes over the cover of his book. 'Perhaps you should marry *me* instead.'

An uncertain sound catches his throat, something between a laugh and a cough.

Ah-ha, thinks Iseult, *now* he listens. 'We should make a fine couple. On holidays we would visit the beach, to draw pentagrams in the sand, or to discuss whether there is only one perfection and whether it is best expressed through the artistic life or the religious life, or else what on earth we are going to have for dinner . . .'

He laughs outright then, a big belly laugh. 'It's a fine idea, my dear. But . . .' He tries for insouciance, but she is not deceived. Excitement flares in his eyes. He turns from her, seeking distraction, reaching for his spectacles with ceremonial care and looping the black ribbon around his neck.

'But?' she echoes, perhaps a little too saucily.

'I'm afraid you have far too much Mars in your horoscope for one such as me.'

42

You will agree that my life thus far has been chequered: a menacing father, a feckless husband, a dearly departed lover, a troubled child and not one absent mother but two . . . It's not self-pity, I hope, to say any one of these events would be considered unfortunate but I've come to know that everybody suffers, that if I didn't have all that big stuff to worry about, I would have fretted more over the small.

At the time that I've now reached in my history, I was happier than at any other, except the early days with Brendan and Zach. I had the single-parent complaint of loneliness, and I was overworked, but on balance I was, in that great word of the politicized, forward-focused 1970s, surviving. Some might even say thriving, since I'd signed myself up for a BA in English and American literature at UCSP, availing myself of a funding programme especially designed for single mothers that gave me a fees waiver and a small stipend.

While my classmates – mostly fifteen years younger than me – were enjoying the camaraderie of UCSP's small campus, I was juggling classes and assignments with work as dining manager at a new restaurant-and-nightclub venue called O. The increased wages (now called a salary) had helped me overcome my scorn for management, but it still wasn't enough to support me and Star. Without my student aid, I couldn't have managed. Being busy always brings extra costs, and I was in a perpetual time-and-money squeeze. Looking back, I don't know how I did it, but at the time I was mostly aware of how lucky I was to be there at all.

One night, I was sitting in my living room excited after a lecture, brain buzzing, finishing homework for the next day. Light stuff, part of the personal development work that our director deemed essential, the personal being political. Casting about me, I was to enumerate all the things I liked in my life. I started thinking it wasn't much to show for twelve years in Santa Paola – a modest three-bedroomed house (one bath), and its mostly well-worn possessions; an eight-year-old car outside the door that I used only rarely – but instead of pondering what I didn't have and trying to work out how I was going to get more, my usual standpoint, the task was to stop and give myself credit for what I *had* achieved.

So I listed them in my head, all the things I was grateful for in my life. The new Philips record player I had only been able to afford by doing overtime on Wednesdays for seventeen months. The rug on my easy chair in the hall, my favourite thing to wrap round me. The stacks of books that were building into towers in rooms all over the house, evidence and source of the new knowledge I was acquiring. My job, my house, my yard full of flowers, my daughter, my friends ... Looked at through this lens, I had to admit that it did feel different. Everyone – father, mother, husband, lover – might have left me and Star, but we were doing okay.

It was an important moment for me, and it's an important memory. Golden. I look back on that short period in my life the way Iseult's generation used to look back on the years up to 1914. Suffused in sepia tones that shade out so much. Far from being a tranquil, rosy time, Edwardian Britain was racked with strife: Ireland boiled; the army mutinied; suffragettes burnt and starved and threw themselves under racehorses; labour unions learnt the power of the strike, and the House of Lords forced a constitutional crisis. You'd never know any of that to listen to the war generation.

I am the same about that me who sat so tentatively dispensing her pride upon the things she loved. She seems so poignant, I could cry just to think of her. So unknowing of what lay just ahead, waiting in ambush. Star's Adolescence. Oh, yes, capital A.

*

It arrived suddenly and complete, as if a light switch were turned off. One day Star and I were on the same side, tackling her childhood problems together; the next I was fumbling in the dark, unable to help. Somehow, suddenly, the enemy.

Photographs of Star as a child show her always with a golden tan, dressed in whites and blues and pinks. Once into her teens, it's as if the pictures have reverted to the days of black-and-white photographs. She stopped growing at fourteen and during that year a tall, skinny, golden-fair child turned short and fat and dark. She dyed her hair the colour of soot and cut and gelled it so it stood up straight from the crown, except for bangs that were so low I wouldn't have been able to see her eyes, if it weren't for the kohl rim around them.

She started wearing what was to effectively become her uniform: black lycra t-shirts with a wide elasticated belt pulled tight so her flesh bulged above and below (bulges that grew and shrank, multiplied and melted, depending on what stage she was at on a diet). A skirt not much deeper than the belt. Tights in – what else? – black, and chunky boots. Clothes that simultaneously called for, and shunned, attention. A body that wanted to claim space and also to disappear.

And beneath, a devouring drive that I called 'It', that I felt would not give her rest until she was entirely consumed. She wanted to eat but she didn't want to eat but she wanted to eat but she didn't want to eat but she wanted to eat but she didn't want to eat but ... The fatter she got, the more comfort she needed and so the more she was driven to eat and the more she yearned to stop. Today, 210-pound teenagers are common in the US, and, as US culture spreads, becoming more usual everywhere, but back in the 1970s Star was an anomaly.

At first, I stifled my knowing. I told myself it was classic teenage territory – bad crowd, drinking, smoking, overeating – and I was being the classic worry-mom. Hadn't I done all this myself in my own way, learnt and grown from it? Wasn't this sort of self-fracturing essential for a child to crack open and mutate into a functioning adult? Hadn't we already come through tough stuff? If I stayed vigilant in the wings, doling her enough love and care and attention of the right kind, she'd be okay. Sooner or later, she'd put herself back together in a shape that fitted.

Underneath, I was frightened. Food, the stuff of life, had for Star become a dangerous substance. To see her standing at the kitchen counter, throwing down four or five slices of buttered bread while waiting for the toaster to pop, was frightening. To go to put something in the trash can in the kitchen and find her eating out of it – something she had earlier tossed away in self-disgust – was frightening. To find a suitcase crammed full of empty packs of cookies and potato chips felt like finding an empty syringe.

And when she was out with her friends, was there heroin too? Food was the home habit, but out of the house she was vacuuming up great quantities of cigarettes and alcohol and, I suspected, speed and, perhaps, other drugs I'd never heard of. In the sixties, drugs had been about expanding and exploring our psyches and our perceptions. For Star and her friends, it was opposite: they just wanted to get 'out of their minds'. At night, I'd lie in bed and hear her stumble in, the unsteady fall of her feet just like her father's.

By this time she was bringing only one friend home: none of the others were willing to abide by the house rules of no drugs, no alcohol. Ginnie was clean (an alcoholic mother), and she and Star were linked by music, being two members of a four-girl band called Vixen. Ginnie's stage name was Veno, short for Venom, and she wanted Star to take one too.

'Something anarchic, something *frenzied*, girl, instead of that hippie-dippie handle.'

Star refused, saying two names were enough for anyone.

Veno, as we were learning to call her, was another big girl. Not one for real connection, she had an approach to people that consisted of finding a theme and keeping a running riff on it. With me, it was scoffing at my generation's music. Pleased to be communicating at any level with somebody who was important to Star, I held up my side.

'You kids are still listening to our songs. Can't see that happening with any of your lot.'

'Yeah, I've heard that when you get to a certain age, you don't see too good.'

Star snorted.

I said: 'All I'm hearing in your music, Veno, is just the same note, over and over. Anger, anger, anger.'

Star curled her black lip into a sneer. 'Don't talk about things you don't understand, Mom. Go listen to some . . .' She looked at Veno and they both said – spat – out the biggest insult they could think of: 'Disco!'

Then they collapsed into giggles at the line they had obviously prepared against me. Their trump card. Not only was I held responsible for the musical and political shortcomings of my own generation but also for those that were following and crumbling our idealism into glitter dust. Which didn't seem fair. Our generation had done its best to change the world – a lot more than Star and Veno's seemed set to do – but we hadn't understood what we were up against. We thought we were an inexorable move forward; instead we had found that action brings on an opposite reaction. Tit for tat, ebb and flow, lash and backlash . . .

By that time, my mind was knotted with such thoughts. I had been drawn to college by the English and American literature course but had begun a women's studies component that was turning out to be far more significant. My literature lectures always reminded me of my old Biology teacher, standing in front of the class having dissected a rabbit, with the animal's eyeball on her index finger, pointing out the parts. I know we need (good) critics, just like we need (good) doctors, but the act of dissecting a poem or story still makes me feel faint, as if something is being violated.

It was women's studies that was teaching me what I needed to know, bringing me to politics and economics as well as literature, bringing me to all of life. As I read and worked on my assignments, as I jotted down notes and mapped plans and explored ideas, a fuzziness around my understanding of the world cleared. Few of our ideas about gender, it seemed to me, served us well. I saw how my experiences – of sex, of work, of money – had been determined by an invisible weave of beliefs. I saw how these beliefs had been as binding on me as any law of the land. I saw the potential for my own transformation if I could unpick them. I saw the potential for social transformation in understanding that what was true of me was true of many.

But now here was my daughter and her friend, two intelligent, educated and anti-establishment young women, belittling all that, writing us out already.

'Do you honestly think they didn't listen to us in the sixties? We had far more political impact than you guys are having.'

'Political impact!' sneered Star. 'Ugh! Pretensho!' This was their word to deflate anything more serious than sex or drugs or rock 'n' roll. 'At the beginning, maybe. But all that peace and love.' She stuck two fingers in her mouth and made a vomiting gesture.

'Yeah, Mrs M. You can't win a fight against anyone, especially not the establishment, with peace and lurve.'

'Ah, girls,' I said. 'You can't win anything worth having with anything less.'

When Star and I were alone together, of course I tried to help her.

'Darling, should you . . .'

'I don't think you really need to . . .'

'Couldn't you just . . .'

I organized a nutritionist. A gym. Each time she got slim, though never as slim as she was the time before. Then, after a while, she got fat again. Fatter than ever. Naturally, I turned to my women's studies course for answers.

I read books that told me food was a language, and fat a metaphor, a message to be interpreted.

I read books that explored the hidden messages: the desire for protection, the desire to remain unseen, the desire to rebel against imprisoning social ideals.

I read books that urged girls and women to stop dieting and instead to seek to understand the patriarchal culture that wanted them thin.

All of which drew Star's complete scorn. 'It's a *candy bar*, Mom.'

I tried not to preach, tried to appreciate that it had taken me thirty-three years of living to be ready to hear this stuff. But all the understanding I could muster didn't stop my eyes from wanting to close whenever I saw her reach for another cookie, didn't stop my foot from itching to kick the refrigerator closed whenever she opened it, didn't stop my hand from wanting to reach across the table and stay the food on its way to her mouth.

'Whatever happened to "Mother knows Best"?' I said one day to Marsha Blinche, a new friend and one of the most articulate women in our class.

'Forget that. It's all "A mother's place is in the wrong" these days. It's a pity you've only one kid. If you had more, you could point to her brothers or sisters and say, "Look at them, they turned out fine, it must be you."'

Marsha was another single mom who had come in on the same programme as me but her child, Dan, was in his twenties, all grown up, so she had more time for socializing. Marsha was one of those people who have time for everything, who manage to squeeze their days full but never seem hurried. She adopted all the younger women in our class, doling out care and attention and advice – and delicious, home-made cakes. She proofread my dissertation before I submitted it, and the revised version that I turned into 'A Child Dancing' before I put it forward for possible publication.

'So well written,' she told the others in the class, until I squirmed in my chair.

I was embarrassed but it also warmed me, I admit it, to have this intelligent woman pressing my vanity buttons. I had never had a true friend before and had always put it down to not having enough time, but here I was, busier than ever with home and work and writing and essays and a dissertation, and still with time for Marsha.

I wasn't somebody who blurted in the Californian way, but nobody could be with Marsha even for the length of a cup of coffee without spilling a neurosis or two. So, somehow, a few months into that summer, after we'd completed our papers and exams, I found myself one morning in Decies Coffee House listening to her story of having been raped by an uncle when she was seven and then – astonished at the sound of my own voice coming in at my ears – telling her some stuff about my father.

She listened, one ear angled towards me, forehead bobbing in encouragement, eyes on my face the entire time. I cried, familiar hot tears of shame, and she took my hand and we talked it all through, her experience and mine, knowing that all over America women were having similar whispered conversations, the unspeakable being given voice. That feminists, pulling back the rug of what they called patriarchy, had revealed a silent slime beneath.

As for Star and me, we were back with Dr Aintree, who said she could no longer talk to me. If she was to take on Star, it had to be as her client, and what happened in session would have to be confidential. It would be up to Star if she wanted to tell me any of it. Surprise, surprise, she didn't. It would be up to Star to keep going. Surprise, surprise, she gave up.*

One evening when I arrived back from lectures, a package was waiting for me in the hall. I dropped my book bag off my

* At the time I thought it was going nowhere. Later I went back to her.

337

shoulder and picked it up from the telephone table and immediately recognized the handwriting. My heart clenched, as if an ice hand had thrust itself inside and squeezed.

Star looked up at me, bangs falling into her eyes, hangover obvious in her mussed hair and face and clothes and poisonous expression. 'What's the matter?' she asked.

'Nothing.'

'It's that mail, isn't it?'

'It's nothing.'

'Aren't you going to open it?'

'Maybe later.'

'Why? What's in it?'

'Nothing,' I said. 'Have you done your homework?'

As soon as I could, I took it into the bedroom. Inside I found a book and a letter but, again, no return address.

For a minute, the room started to spin and black dots appeared before my eyes. When they cleared, I read the title – *Words Alone are Certain Good: W. B. Yeats, Religion and the Occult* – and the inscription on the flyleaf: 'For my first love, Iseult Mulcahy. I will not in grey hours revoke / The gift I gave in hours of light.'

Dear Izzy

Yes, it is me. I hope you're still at the same address. I wanted to send you a copy of my book (enclosed). I teach English Lit. now at UCLA. This book is based on my M.Phil. It tries to show how Yeats combined the myths of ancient, heroic Ireland with a belief in Western magic to create a new mythology and a new religion. It purports that Yeats's writing, including the poetry, was the medium through which he disseminated his belief system.

Will you read it? I'd like to think you might try. Will you enjoy it? I doubt it. I'm not sure any lay person can even finish it, but I wanted you to have a copy because it was you who introduced me to Yeats. Also I wanted to say to you that I've come to think of him as being like you in a way. Oppositions tormented him and at the same time spurred him on.

Perhaps none of this is of any interest to you. Then how about this? That famous line he used to describe his beloved Maud: 'I had never thought to see in a living woman so great beauty.' That's precisely how I felt about you. Are you still beautiful, Izzy? Still breaking hearts? I am older now and able to hope that it has worked out for you and your husband and your little girl, who I suppose is not so little any more.

Be Happy
Zach

Not so little any more, no. And not in need of help either, so don't go asking. If people couldn't handle her appearance, that was their problem. She didn't have a problem. Or rather, she had only one problem: that I wouldn't leave her alone. 'Just leave me alone': that's the one you can't argue with or defend yourself against.

Poetry helped. I watched television but that was good only for passing the time. I read novels, sometimes poor ones that passed the time a little better, but more often stories that were more than just that, stories that were also voyages of language or detection or recognition. The Brontës for passion. George Eliot for intellectual fervour. Jane Austen for wit. Henry James and Alice Walker for their, each very different, outsiders' eye. Toni Morrison for compassion.

Stories took time to digest; poetry was a quick hit. So long as I avoided love poetry, on good days it gave me what I wanted; on bad days what I needed. After Zach, I wasn't able to bear the love stuff, Rumi or Cummings or Neruda. Except for W. B. His was so specific and his love position so insanely subordinate that he didn't salt the wounds like those whose ways of loving were more like my own. To read Willie's poems for Maud or Iseult is to see a man dazzled by his own soul and the desire to

339

make it heard, by his own passion and the need to fashion everything, including – no, especially – the beloved, to fit.

As I moved out of youth, the lyrical age, I was coming to prefer his middle and late periods – the songs of Irish politics, culminating in 'Meditations in Time of Civil War'; the rages against old age; the longings to escape the body, to sail to Byzantium and be taken out of nature and hammered into Grecian gold and set upon a bough to sing. And the poems to Iseult, less other-worldly, a little more cognizant of the person behind the beauty.

On my course I discovered a tranche of new poets. Walt Whitman. John Keats. John Donne. Sylvia Plath. William Wordsworth. Emily Dickinson. Percy Bysshe Shelley. I lay out their names, a list you'll find in any canon. Nothing original or pioneering about it, but these were the people whose words held me through all that was to come. Held me up and held me open – to other worlds and other ways of being.

Just as I told almost no one about Star, except my new friend Marsha, but I freely tell all here, in the private whisper of mind to mind that is a book, so I want to acknowledge in print how writing – my own and others' – has been both the roof on my house and the gap in my fence.

43

Iseult needs her sketchbook, which she left last night in Moura's room, while borrowing a little face powder for her walk with Willie. It is early, too early for Moura, a late riser, to be up, but Iseult will tiptoe in. She knows just where it is, on the floor beside the dresser.

She hopes her mother will *not* waken. Moura is so tiresome these days, forever implying sadnesses and sufferings to which Iseult must – *please* – not add.

She who was so daring in her young life, who valued independence above all things, has turned traditionalist, given to incessant and unnecessary fretting. When Bichon's master wanted to put him in a higher class, as he was racing ahead of his classmates, Moura chose to see this progress as alarming and argued strongly against his advancement, recalling how at his age Iseult was just the same.

'Don't you remember, Iseult? It nearly resulted in meningitis.'

Her dread of dreads. Thus is Iseult imperceptibly blamed, once again, for something that is surely not her fault.

When in France, she insists on acting the chaperone and, when away, asks her friends to take the duty. (Luckily the friends are not so vigilant as she.) Of course Iseult rebels and hints towards Moura's past – a hint is all she dares – her mother's excuse was that Iseult should benefit from her mistakes, and anyway that *she* could not afford to be bohemian. Having no father, she must compensate by being ultra-respectable.

Rather a low blow.

And yet ... How could one hate a mother who has just sold her diamond necklace, the last of her jewels from the days when she was an heiress, to provide dinners for starving children?

And yet . . . how can one not hate her, for making one feel mean-spirited and inadequate?

A floorboard creaks as she crosses the landing. As always, before entering her mother's room, she registers the memory of waking frightened in the night and all changed to right by going to Moura's presence, of being pulled into the sweet night warmth of her touch and slipping back to sleep inside the rightness of all things.

She pushes open the door. Under the white coverlet the shape is wrong, bigger than Moura, and across the covers and on the floor is discarded clothing. A jacket, a white robe, a nightdress, a pair of trousers open to the ceiling, boots with stockings hanging out. Male mixed with female clothing.

For a second, time warps. The smell of sour apricots fills the room. A wave of shame rocks her stomach. Maud, seeing her there, says 'Oh!' Not loud but in such a strangely startled tone that it stirs her companion. The shape moves. Iseult wants to turn and run but she is fastened to the floor. From the depths of white the top of a head surfaces, dark hair grey-speckled and tousled. Maud places a hand on it, pushes it back down under the covers but not soon enough.

Uncle Willie . . .

'A moment, Iseult,' Maud says, her voice cracking around the words. 'Give me a moment, *chérie*, and I shall be with you.'

Iseult retreats backwards out the door, pulling it quietly closed. As if that soft click is the starter gun in a race, she turns and runs, slippered feet flying along the wooden floor, down the stairs, through the double doors into the dining room, where she is brought up short by Minnaloushe, who jumps into her path as she bursts in. The cat miaows, slant eyes peeved. Iseult picks her up, hugs her warmth to her face. 'Oh, Minna, Minna . . . Oh.'

The flesh under the fur, the life in it, fills her hands and her nostrils. She is drowning and darling Minna is a float.

A noise on the stairs. Does Moura follow? Surely even Moura is not that insensate. Iseult needs time. In time she will be able to meet her – meet them? Oh, how? With composure. Not yet. The back door. Minnaloushe cradled, she slips through to the kitchen. Josephine is in the scullery, poker rattling in the stove. Thora told her that Josephine had a reputation as a drunkard when Moura hired her, and she was taken on with the stern admonition that if there was one incident with alcohol, she would be dismissed. There had been no such incident. Josephine would do anything for Moura. She adores her.

So many people adore her and why would they not? Moura does not indulge herself in selfish and stupid boredom. She is a live fountain, springing unbounded from the earth, full of primitive life-giving power, whereas Iseult . . .

Iseult makes a joke of Josephine and Moura and everyone because of her disdain for herself.

Last time Thora was here she had confessed as much to her. 'If you have a great secret that makes you unhappy, Thora, don't share it with me. I would probably keep it for a day or two, then suddenly I would make fun of it with the first fool who came my way. I wouldn't do it out of wickedness or because I can't hold my tongue, but just because I would be in a light mood and feel everything was good for a joke. Then the next moment I would almost kill myself for having done it and feel an awful beast. In the old days each time I thought it was quite an exception and that I would never do it again. I had faith in myself. Now I know better.'

Where does this blinding sense of disdain and failure come from? It makes her feel so old, as if her life were already as good as over.

Oh, to be in Colleville now, dancing by the seashore. Bathing in the odour of the sea, that salt odour that is incorporated with the wind and almost of the same nature. She can feel it on her skin. Yes, yes, she can all but taste it. The rhythm of nature is all embracing, a belt around eternity. If she were there now, she would dance into safety, to where she is held within the in-breathing and out-breathing of the waves. Dance, as she used to before last summer, before she learnt that the poet was watching from his window.

44

'Have you ever considered', Marsha asks, 'that there might be more?'

'More?'

'Locked away? Repressed? I had only the vaguest memories of what my uncle did to me until I went into therapy.'

She invited me to go on what she called a rebirthing weekend, a two-day session that used breathing techniques to bring about recall of lost memories and thereby transformation. 'You'll remember something you've forgotten, guaranteed. It might be your birth, it could be some other grief or trauma from way back when.'

'Forget it, Marsha. I'm Irish. A feed of booze and a two-day hangover – that's our idea of therapy.'

'You don't even drink,' she said.

'You know what I mean. I'd rather let sleeping dogs lie.'

'Even if they're yowling inside you?'

'Is that what you think?'

'You tell me,' she said, looking at me too hard over her coffee cup.

Over the weeks that followed, I found myself thinking about the word she used. Rebirth. The idea of that appealed, but I was nervous. Marsha offered to come with me, to be 'my second', the partner that every participant had to have during the rebirthing, to look after them.

'Like a duel,' I said.

'Not a bad metaphor. The better part of you will be slaying a weaker part.'

'With breathing!' I laughed.

According to Marsha, she had been a mess before this

rebirthing. Chronic pain in her lower back. Disappointed with Danny, her boy, and generally with the hand life had dealt her. Eaten up by negativity. This description of herself bore no resemblance to the woman I knew and admired. Negative was the last word you'd use for Marsha, whose slightly protruding teeth were always rushing towards a smile. Not just her teeth, actually. When Marsha smiled every part of her was gathered into that beam of white, brilliant as a photographer's flash.

She was the most engaged person I knew: in her work as a classroom assistant; in her voluntary activities for the hospice that eased her mother's death; in her exercise routine – swimming and yoga, both daily; in the projects she was forever taking on behalf of the needy – fundraising or second-hand-clothes collecting or event organization or . . . All this (not to mention the degree she had just completed) and yet somehow when she was with you always seemed to have enough time. Marsha was totally with you, giving you full, unhurried attention. And when she was alone, she was apparently complete – not fretting over Danny, or restless for other places or experiences, or yearning or mourning lost love. Marsha was a doer as energetic as Maud, a thinker as deep as Iseult, a giver of the type I most wanted to be – while avoiding the flaws of us all.

I went to the rebirthing weekend but not for the reason I told her – that she'd give me no peace if I didn't. I knew if I genuinely asked her to back off, she would. I went because I wanted something of what she had found for herself.

The routine was to sign in on Friday morning at the Rebirth Center and stay until Sunday evening, accommodation and meals included. Our facilitator was a woman called Frankie in a pink tracksuit, and we were sixteen women and two men in loose, comfortable clothing, each with a partner, all of us believing we had been mistreated – the word to use was 'abused' – as children.

Marsha sat on a beanbag as I took off my shoes and lay down

346

beside her on a mattress. Frankie ordered us to close our eyes, and a soft male voice came across the sound system telling us to relax, to breathe softly. Some New Age music started up, Celtic-style pipes. 'Breathe as though your breath is liquid,' the voice said, sounding like melted butter itself. 'Let your breath make a noise in your throat as you breathe in and out.'

I did as he said. Now that I was there, I would do whatever I was told to do. The lights were slowly dimmed all the way to darkness. As I continued to breathe in this very deliberate way, sensations of numbness and tingling rose in my limbs and face. The music changed. A drum sound entered and the beat picked up.

'Now breathe fast,' ordered a voice, female this time. 'Breathe as though your life depends on getting as many breaths inside you as fast as you can.'

The drum sound became louder. Lights flashed on and off and the heavy drums rose another few decibels and now wild music poured in on top of the relentless beat. Distress came welling up in me, brimming over, drowning my heart. I heard a prolonged, agonized shriek. Interference on the sound system? The slide of a violin bow? A screech from one of the others? From me?

All sorts of cries and moans and screams were thickening in the room, adding another layer to the strange music. I knew that Marsha was there beside me, that I could ask for her hand, or for a drink of water, or to help me get up and leave – Frankie had said we could do that any time – but I had moved into a different dimension, with new and urgent rules that made hand-holding or water or Kleenex or escape irrelevant. I had to keep breathing hard and fast, breathing like a madwoman, had to . . . wanted to . . . I felt the distress inside shape itself into an out-loud scream. This time, definitely me.

Time warped, folded over, with me inside. At one point I broke to ask for a tissue, into which I blew my nose, then matter of factly I returned to the breathing, in and out, in and

347

out, and a memory pushed up out of my centre. I had come here expecting my father, but I also got my mother. Specifically, her funeral. Her body in its coffin in our front room. The room hot, so hot, and me, my face boiling red from being in there too long, praying and talking to her in my head. A fly was crawling up her face from her lip towards one of her eyes, the one that was not quite closed; it had a small opening at the inner corner, as if it might come apart.

I couldn't take my own eyes away – if I did, the fly was going to crawl up along there, his skinny leg was going to slip in and touch the innards of her eye. The thought made me frightened, panicky, but, around me, everyone was saying how well she looked, laid out in her Sunday-best suit and heels.

'She's dead, for God's sake,' I wanted to shout at them. 'What are you talking about?'

It was so hot, I had taken off my new and scratchy jacket. As I passed my father on the way to the food table, he caught hold of my arm. 'She's as flighty as a feather, this one,' he said to his brother sitting beside him.

'I can see that,' said Uncle Benny.

Daddy pulled me down on to his knee. 'What's this?' he said, lifting my arm out. 'Jaysus, would you look? She's getting hairy.' He pointed to the down that was forming in my armpit and started to laugh. Uncle Benny laughed too, loud and false: *ho ho ho*. I sprang from his grasp and ran off, with their laughter chasing after me.

I found I was screaming: 'I cannot do this, I cannot do this, I cannot do this.' The ache in my chest hardened and swelled, a boulder that might burst. I was clutching my rib cage and whimpering with pain. Marsha, growing worried, called Frankie over to check, but I was fine, apparently. I was aware of these events, but they were behind gauze. All the other people who were in the room were in a different pleat of time. In mine, I was alone.

*

348

Next day, after a deep night's sleep, we sat in a circle in a sunlit room and wrote down the memories that the process had 'resurrected' and then 'shared' them with each other. Nobody – including me – got to the end of their story without crying. Part of me hated this, turning into a B-movie character, crying at my catharsis in a roomful of strangers, but I had given myself over to what was happening. It was bigger than me, and I didn't understand any of it.

In any case, weeping wasn't what Frankie had in mind. Once everybody had fessed up, she gave each of us a tennis racket. It was not our experiences that had damaged us, she explained, (was I damaged?), but our repression of the appropriate response to those experiences. What we needed to do was to feel our anger (was I angry?), because when anger is suppressed – here she pulled out a screen and showed us some multi-coloured slides and charts and diagrams – toxic amounts of endogenous neurochemicals accumulate in neurons in the brain. The neurons periodically eject these toxins during other crises in our life.

She was going to teach us how to give ourselves an 'anger detox'. Holding the most painful part of the memory in our heads, we were to take our tennis rackets and beat our anger out on to the beanbags. Any questions?

'What if we don't feel any anger towards the person in our rebirthing?' I asked.

'Honey, I saw you and I saw your tears a moment ago. You are angry with her, believe me.'

'Am I? With *her*?'

'With her, for sure. Don't shake your head. What happened yesterday didn't come from nowhere. It came from deep in you, a part of you that knows more than surface you. So why don't you ditch the tears and give in to a good old tantrum?'

We were each assigned a beanbag, and Frankie and her assistants came up behind us and encouraged us to beat harder and faster if we seemed too slack. Then we were sent home with a list of suggested activities to do whenever we felt anger rising.

I have that list still, I referred to it while I was writing this. 'Select one of the following,' it says.

Pound on a bed with your fists and yell. (Use a tennis racket to spare your fists if you prefer.)

Take a pair of jeans, hold it by the ankles, and whack the hell out of your bed.

Tear up a phone book. Yell while you tear. (Put work gloves on to avoid paper cuts.)

Yell, scream or shriek into a pillow in the closet.

Pound on the wall or hit a punching bag. (Put on heavy gloves.)

Throw things at the wall (not random things, safe things such as pillows).

Take pages out of a magazine, tear them in half and throw them around the room.

Do a dance of anger.

Stomp your feet when you walk.

Kick a rock down the street.

NOTE: The use of knives or dangerous weapons is to be avoided.

One spring morning, Star made a pronouncement over breakfast. Her official breakfast of the day, the bran flakes and fruit she shared with me before moving to a day of resisting then succumbing to doughnuts or pastries or muffins or rolls or pancakes or blinis before moving on to potato chips or corn chips or fries or sweets or chocolates or . . . or . . . or . . .

'You know, Mom,' she declared, after a week of being particularly obnoxious, 'we need each other. We're the only family we've each got.'

'Is this Jeffrey's latest theory?' I asked.

Star's best friend now was Jeffrey Keeler, who wanted to be a psychologist when he grew up. He was Star's age but nerdy and small, so they made an odd couple: she in her black, bovver-booted outfits, he by her side like a little brother, head at her shoulder, turned in towards her, talking, talking. Always talking. Jeffrey had opinions on everything and was particularly wide-ranging on the subject of my shortcomings.

That wasn't why I disliked him, though. Jeffrey had a nasty streak. He was a cynic and supremely good at pretending to be on Star's side while actually undermining her.* A benevolent controller, Marsha called him. I lived in fear of her falling for him.

'I thought you'd approve. You would if it was anyone else who said it.'

Perhaps I'd have been more enthusiastic if I hadn't felt that next week she'd be quoting him saying the opposite.

'It makes sense,' she said, shovelling a heaped spoonful of cereal into her voracious mouth. 'With no aunts or uncles or grandparents, no other family, is it any wonder that we're too much for each other? After all we . . .'

She spoke on but I wasn't listening. I was stuck on those two words: each other. *Each other?* What had I done to you, Star, that weighed, even in the smallest way, against your insults and aggressions and rejections? Made your food? Washed your laundry? Paid for your education and the extra-curriculars that you decided to skip as often as not? Tried to protect you from a father who was never going to do anything but hurt you?

---

* Jeffrey did do this, though I didn't realize it at the time. He was also the funniest person I ever knew, with the blackest sense of humour. And we were close. He showed me the suffering he hid from everyone else.

Each other: that stuck in me, irksome and impossible to leave alone, like a sliver of food between the teeth that the tongue can't shift. She was all in earnest, and I would have thought I'd welcome her saying such a thing. Instead I found myself turning my back on her, to get up and go over to the sink to rinse my bowl. I wanted to deal her back a slight, an insult, an act of disrespect, just one in return for the countless numbers I'd swallowed. (Oh, yes, I was bitter and full of self-pity. Years of rejection and abuse will do that to you.) I thought of doing one of her favourite tricks: covering my ears and singing *la-la-la* so I couldn't hear what she was saying. I thought of – somehow I know this would be the worst – ignoring her, changing the subject, pretending I didn't understand that this was her big effort.

You'd want to be a saint, an outright saint, to resist.

Horrible, isn't it? I didn't want to be thinking like this, to be holding such twisted thoughts about my own daughter. Neither did I want the tension that had become a living component of my body, a throbbing resident deep down in the pit of me. A perpetual anxiety that was like an acid, corroding the fragile ropes I'd spun to keep a hold on myself. It panicked me to think I could no longer trust myself to do the right thing by Star. To be . . . not a saint – let's face it, you didn't have to be a saint – just an ordinary tongue-holding, time-biding mother.

I let as little as possible filter through. That it wasn't our differences that counted but how we handled them. That I needed to back off and let her be who she was. That I needed to stop fretting and nagging. That I needed to give her space. That, again, we were too much for *each other* because we had no other family.

I let her speak on and on and let her finish and when she was done I said, 'Okay, honey. Fair enough. I'll think about what you've said.'

But that was wrong too.

'Is that *it*? Is *that* all you're going to say?'

The items on my counter-list, all the things *I* felt *she* did wrong, banked up behind my teeth, banging to get out. But where would they take us? Only down a pathway we'd already worn away: me trying to help her see how she created her own misery, she resisting all the way, hearing advice as nagging. She (Jeffrey?) was right, something needed to change.

That's when I, not knowing what I was doing in choosing this less travelled road, not knowing all the difference it would make, the terrible places it would take us, said instead: 'Star, if I tell you something, will you promise not to be mad?'

'Go on.'

'No, you have to promise.'

'I promise.'

'Really. Will you promise to look on the positive aspects, like Dr Aintree said?'

'I promise, Mom. What is it? You're scaring me.'

'We do have other family. You have a grandfather. In Ireland. I'll take you to see him if you want.'

I'd been thinking a lot about Ireland. A version of my thesis – 'Speaking with a Different Tongue: Yeats's Love Poetry to Iseult Gonne' – had been accepted by Barricade Books (pardon me, barricade books), a small publisher in Dublin, for inclusion in a book of essays about overlooked women in Irish literary history, and they had invited me to the launch. Since hearing this news, I got it into my head that Iseult might be leading me back. Back to the home I'd escaped from as a teenager on the back of a Honda C100. Back to my father, my mother, my birth mother. Back to sort out the mess of my past, so I could find myself a future.

London. Paris. Dublin. Just the names were enough to send a shiver of excitement through me. And Star saying what she had said about not having any family, felt like another sign pointing me in that direction.

To get there, I would have to work a double shift twice a

week and take on any other overtime that was going, then see if I could wangle three weeks off. She would have to get a part-time job. What did she think? Could she bear to be away from Jeffrey for that long? Was it something she would like to do?

Yes, was what she thought. Yes, yes, yes.*

Five months later, under the false, bright lights of Los Angeles airport, I watched her heft her bulk down the long corridor towards a transatlantic flight to Dublin, via London. Tried not to notice her too-loud breathing. Averted my eyes from her waddle under the weight of her backpack. I was intimately, overly sensitive to every pound of her flesh, and her fat felt like an onslaught here, under the relentless lights, as if a layer of skin had been peeled away. The back of her head banked from ears to neck with flesh, held taut as far as the chin by the skin of her skull but from there settling in rings, like doughnuts. Her breasts were now an indiscriminate pillow of flesh, captured but not contained by her bra, inverted and drooping, overlaying quilts of flesh beneath. Each of her thighs now the size of an average waist (mine, for example).

You thought an end point had been reached, it seemed to scream. Hah, were you wrong! This will go on and on! This will get worse and worse!

When you're fat, people see everything you do as fat. So Star walked her fat walk down the airport corridor, feet splayed, making too much effort. She toted her fat suitcase on to the check-in platform, perspiration breaking on her fat forehead. Most fat people wear fat clothes, loose, baggy, unincriminating, but not Star. Tight layers that ignored her bulges were her style. From the knees down she was encased in lace-up boots, not boots I would have chosen, being spiky and studded, but I

---

* I was so surprised and delighted at the idea of Europe that I never stopped to imagine what the reality of three weeks alongside Mom's disapproval would feel like.

354

understood the intention – is there anything more poignant than fat-woman feet in high heels, bulging through their straps?

We boarded the plane and loaded our carry-on cases in the bins above our heads and our accoutrements for the journey in the seat pockets in front of us: crossword books, notebook and pen, *The Sea, The Sea* and *Dreamscape* for me; *Scruples* and *Sass* magazine, potato chips, peanuts and candy for Star. Our air stewardess eyed Star's hips with anxiety, and I showed nothing of my relief as they barely squeezed between the armrests.

Showing and saying nothing was becoming my forte. I didn't tell Star of my fervent hope that my father might have mellowed with the years, become what W.B. called 'a comfortable kind of old scarecrow'. I had told her so little about him but didn't kids almost always like their grandparents? Even when – maybe especially when – the parents didn't?

We fastened our seatbelts and leant back in our seats, silent, as we waited for take-off.

She of Dancing Dreamed

On the grey rock of Cashel I suddenly saw
A Sphinx with woman breast and lion paw,
A Buddha, hand at rest,
Hand lifted up that blest;

And right between these two a girl at play
That, it may be, had danced her life away,
For now being dead it seemed
That she of dancing dreamed.

Although I saw it all in the mind's eye
There can be nothing solider till I die

W. B. Yeats,
'The Double Vision of Michael Robartes'

Christmas Eve, 1982
Pauline

Witness statement of Mrs Pauline Whelan, Doolough Upper, County Wicklow

'I went to look in on Mr Martin Mulcahy as I had been doing for some years, since his second wife died. More recently, I was hired by the Mulcahy family, namely Mrs Iseult Maria Creahy, née Mulcahy, to give nursing care five times a week. On the day I visited at twelve noon approx. I found the victim in good form, considering his health status, though perhaps a little more tired than usual. He complained of a number of ailments but that was not unusual.

'After seeing the patient, I spent some time with Mrs Creahy in the kitchen, as I usually did during my visit. We had lunch and talked about many subjects, including the care of her patient. She was tired and under strain. Her father needed constant care and she was very devoted.

'She told me that the man who had been staying with her in the house, one Zach Coleman, lately of Santa Paola, California, had left the house earlier that day and would not be returning. She was a little upset at this, as she was fond of this man. He had left because her daughter was expected at the house that afternoon. She gave me to believe that it was for this reason she had asked Mr Coleman to leave. I left the house at approximately 2 p.m. and went directly to my own home.'

It is a dream. I am dreaming. It is an image that I am imagining. It is a memory too. I remember drifting upwards, through murky lake water, curving like a fish through the loops of previous risings. Strands undulate. I circle through them, round and up, up and round, holding my breath until I break the surface.

My eyes open. I am awake.

Awake, in Doolough for the first time in eighteen years. Light leaks in at the edges of the curtains but early light by the look of it. No more than 5 or 6 a.m., I reckon, pulling my wrist out from under the covers to check. Yes, 5.42 and the sun's up already. The short Irish summer night.

I hoist myself off my pillow to look around. It's all so familiar and why not? I woke in this room for sixteen years of my life, in Santa Paola so far only for fourteen. The wooden ceiling and rafters above, the big mahogany wardrobe and dressing table stand out, sharp and new, vibrating for me as they never would have if I'd stayed here. This must be how it feels when the bandages are removed after a cataract operation, when you see again as if for the first time but also remember what you used to look at before, the two at once.

The air is as familiar as the room: a chill, a damp in the nostrils that is always in the atmosphere in Ireland, indoors and out, summer and winter. Doolough Lake is in it, and the mountains, and woodland, and the unfeasibly green grass. It beckons me outside.

I slide from the bed and pad, barefoot, across the chill, wooden floor to pick up yesterday's clothes from the chair. Suddenly, I cannot wait to be gone, to grab a slice of this early morning and make it mine. A quick brush to my teeth, then I look in on Star. I don't want her to feel abandoned, not on our first morning. I stand over her in the dim light, listening to her breathing. Deep and even and likely to stay that way for hours. I scribble a note, leave it beside her head on the pillow. Then I tiptoe down the stairs and out the back door, through the gate, and round the pathway towards the lake.

Doolough Mountain oversees my path and also the ring of mountains behind. Ballinedin. Cloghernagh. Corrigasleggaun. Slievemaan. Lugnaquilla. Old friends: I hadn't let myself miss them, except once when I met Iseult's lines about the presence of mountains, 'blue hills in the distance that sigh faintly, / "Come! In our distance, in our vagueness, / A God is hidden!"'

This morning, I feel it again. I become aware of the birdsong, and the sound of it makes me skip along the woodpath into a tunnel of trees. It is spongy underfoot down here and everything is soaked. I pick a sprig of pine, and a shower of dew, or yesterday's rain, spatters my head and shoulders, making me laugh. The lake when I reach it is impassive, quiet waters lapping against the shore. Flitters of my dream come back to me. The fish. The feeling of being fished.

My father used to bring me down here in summer sometimes. Fly-fishing, of course, the only kind that warranted the name in his book. Coarse fishing was for boot boys; any eejit could do it. Fly-fishing took skill, because a fly weighs almost nothing, so how do you propel it twenty or thirty feet into a lake? He showed me how: a complicated combination of the weight of the line itself, the flexibility of the rod and the casting action that sent the line into a perfect horizontal U behind your back, then forward on to the water.

'The whole thing is in that pause between back' – he cast the line behind – 'and forward. The rod flexes behind – see? – and gathers the energy. Like that. Here, you try.'

I tried. I failed.

'Stop snapping at it like a fairy wand,' he said, but not cross.

Down here he was a different Daddy. He showed me how to hold my wrist unnaturally straight. He showed me a variety of flies. He showed me how to tie knots. He showed me how to 'play' a fish.

I must have been about eight then, I think. It's hard to be sure. I never liked fishing, but I did like how concentrating on those square feet of water brought him an ease he never had anywhere else. You don't succeed at fishing until you calm down and accept what the weather and the water offer. You are in the hands of the unknown, of things that you can't see.

He caught a trout. It jerked and bounced at the end of the line. I had never seen an animal fighting for its life before. I wanted to shout at him to throw it back in, but I knew that if I did, I'd never be brought again and I would lose this new father I was just – maybe – finding. As it was unhooked and priested on my behalf, I fought the impulse to cry, and as soon as I got back home I went up to my room and sobbed for the fish. Even then I think I knew that I was also sobbing for me, and for my mother and, yes, even for my father.

On our return to Doolough yesterday he stood at the fire-place, in the very place he used to stand eighteen years ago (somehow, I had known that's where he would be), with the same bald, blotched head, same thick neck spilling over a too-tight collar, same trousers pulled high over his paunch by metal-clipped braces, same hefty posterior warming itself by the fire, uncaring that it blocked the heat for everybody else. I had expected the serge navy trousers of his policeman's uniform, the cap on the mantelpiece beside him, medallion shining. But of course he was long retired by now.

The furniture and decor were just what I had left behind, too full, nothing touched. Aside from a few accessories and the new bulky television in the corner, it could have been the year I'd left. Except, of course, for the new wife, standing beside my mother's fireside chair.

It was she who had answered the door to us. Rose was her

name, an O'Leary from Carrawood. I heard afterwards that he had advertised in the local paper for her. *Widower, Garda sergeant, own house and land, seeks* . . . And it was she, I knew, who would have added the few bits of colour and comfort that had found their way into the living room. She welcomed us and ushered us in, gladiators into the den.

He looked up from the job he was making of stuffing tobacco into his pipe, rested his eyes on me for a second, then moved them across to Star, to give her the full treatment, from crown to feet and back up again, with eyes that hadn't blunted with age. 'Well, well, well,' he said. 'Look what the cat dragged in.'

The trees draw in around me. The sky is growing light as the sun climbs out from behind the eastern hills, drowning out the stars. The lake is a mirror this morning, allowing Doolough Mountain to admire itself. So very quiet, almost attentive, as if it had been waiting for me all this time. I sit on a log and listen, as I did when I was a child. I breathe deeply, sucking in air, as if I could suck in its peace through my pores. The lake is blameless.

Such a thing for him to say. Oh, what had I done? Delivered myself and my daughter unto the enemy, forgotten what it took to leave and lock that door on him. His refrains after Mammy died came colliding towards me again, down the tunnel of time.

How would you like to be packed off to the orphanage? Oh, no, that wouldn't suit you, no, because ones like you always know what side their bread is buttered. The nuns wouldn't put up with your carry-on for a minute, they wouldn't be long putting manners on you.

'Would you listen to him?' Rose cut in, all bustle and distraction. '"Cat dragged in" indeed. And he so looking forward to you coming.'

'It's good to see you, Daddy,' I said, anxious like Rose to move us off the insult. 'You look well.'

He looked the same. Exactly the same. How could that be, eighteen years on?

He didn't answer me.

Rose said: 'Come in, girls, come in now. You must be dying for a cup of tea.'

Tea: one shilling and six. Butter: two shillings. Eggs: one and eight. Sausages . . .

'Could I have coffee?' Star asked.

Rose's hand fluttered to her chest. 'Coffee. Oh, dear. Do we have coffee? Do you know, I don't think we do.'

'Then tea will be fine,' I said.

'No, no, let me check. There might be a jar at the back of the press.'

'Really, there's no need –'

'But, Mom,' hissed Star to me, as Rose was gone and my father had bent to putting coal on the fire so he wouldn't have to talk to us. 'You know I don't drink tea.'

'Try,' I hissed back.

Rose seemed kind, and I was immediately drawn to shield her. She was very like my mother; he must have had a nose for women who could take what he doled out. The sin of my leaving was still rigid in him, as hard as the fire iron he was clattering around the grate, as hot as the day I left. Somebody was going to suffer. I feared for Rose and for Star, who had no idea what it was like to be so treated. What had I done?

'I'm awful sorry now about that,' said Rose, coming back in. 'I never thought of coffee. We don't take it at all. Will you have a glass of minerals . . . em . . . Star? I got some in especially for yourself.'

'Soda,' I said to Star.

'That would be lovely,' I said, smiling at Rose.

Star folded her arms, stretched out her legs and yawned, making me tense. He wouldn't like that. In his presence young people sat up straight. Rose returned, and we sat with the drinks, the two of us upholding most of the talk. The length of the journey. The couple of nights we had in London. How you couldn't beat a musical for a good night out. The size of London and the business of it and how did anybody manage to live there at all. The journey from Dublin airport. The beauty of Wicklow.

A couple of times a silence fell, and the clink of spoons and tap of cup on to saucer grew loud between us, but we made it safe to the far side of tea. Once finished, Daddy, still silent, went up the fields, and Rose saw us upstairs.

'My old room,' I said, as she led us in.

'Your daddy thought that would be nice for you,' she said, but I knew it was she who had had the thought.

I walked into the room. Same windows looking out on the front drive outside. Same dressing table. Same bed. Could it actually be the same bedspread? Except that there were now two big mahogany wardrobes in the room instead of one, nothing had changed.

'And, Star,' she said, leading her on. 'You are here, next door to your mam.'

I put my bag on the bed and opened one of the wardrobes. It was full of old clothes that smelt of mothballs and the past. One dress wrapped in cellophane, jade-blue, my favourite colour, stood out. I pulled at it and with it came memories: of my mother, bent for days over her sewing machine, taking in the seams on this dress, of her and my father side by side, smiling down at me, dressed up for a rare night out. The Garda Ball? Was that right, or was I inventing? His neck, too red, bulging over a white collar and tie I certainly remember, and the shock of my mother with bare shoulders and hair piled on top of her head, looking like somebody else.

'What do you think?' she'd asked, turning slowly around so I could admire her, but the dress showed a part of her that I'd never seen and something about her half-naked back frightened me and I started to cry.

'Oh, now,' she'd said. 'What's that about?' She was laughing down at me and up at my father. Happy, for once. Happy with him.

Where had this memory come from? I was sure I'd never had it before yet already it felt like part of me.

'That old wardrobe was put in from the other bedroom,' Rose said from behind, making me jump. 'I hope it won't be in your way.'

'Of course not.'

'That's a lovely dress.'

I looked down at it, then back up at her, the ghost of its owner hovering between us.

'You should bring it back to America with you, get a bit of wear out of it.'

'Oh, I couldn't.'

'Why not?'

I looked at it. Indeed, why not? It was beautiful, a tight, strapless bodice covered in tiny, worked detail over a full skirt. The sort of detail you rarely get in dresses now and far too beautiful to be left to rot here. But where would I wear such a dress?

'Just don't say anything to your daddy,' she said, dropping her voice to a whisper. 'You know how he likes to hold on to everything.'

So that was how she played it, us against Him. Fair enough: you'd need some survival strategy.

'All right, then, I will. Thank you.'

'Not at all. So, tell me, have you everything you need?'

'I'd love a shower,' said Star, coming in behind us.

'Oh dear, I'm afraid we don't have one of those.'

'You don't have a –' Star's face would have made me laugh but for poor Rose's discomfiture.

I cut across her incredulity. 'Maybe a bath, darling? I'll show you the bathroom.'

'A bath?' said Rose. 'Oh, dear me, yes, of course. I'll just need an hour or two to heat up the immersion.'

Quietly, slowly, trying not to disturb, Iseult eases back the curtain of her cubicle. Her cell, as Dymphna, the nurse who

366

sleeps beside her likes to call it, although Dymphna is here of her own free will, not brought along by an avid aunt and mother, and does not feel this war encampment is like a prison.

She takes her journal from its place under her mattress and slips it into her regulation green bag. The keeping of a journal in wartime is forbidden, but many of them do it and for her it is a necessity. A last look around the cell to ensure all is in order – bed made, locker tidied, washing jug and basin rinsed and wiped – then, hitching the bag on to her shoulder, she tiptoes past Dymphna's cell on the right, Moura's and Kathleen's on the left. The part of her that wished she was still abed is shrinking, and gone completely as soon as she steps outside, into the lovely shock of cool air on the face.

She stands for a moment, smelling the dawn wind and the moist, clean smell of earth and grass. The ambulance turning circle has a puddle at its heart like a small lake, filmed in petrol. In the distance the guns thud, the usual early morning bombardment.

Oh, to escape to somewhere, a blessed island, like the Kingdom of Maia, where she and Thora and a few others who have escaped the war infection could give their attention to the things that matter: individual affections, the beauty of this world and the search after the other world . . . if there is another world. Well, today she will. Today she will forget ambulances and guns and all the cacophony of modernity and conflict in a return to sand and sea.

Her boots pick up their pace, tapping down the waste ground towards the shed that holds the common room, to retrieve something to read for the journey. What a deprivation she had thought it when she had to hand over her books on arrival for storage in the common area, but, as it turned out, it hadn't mattered. After ten hours of nursing, her brain finds it impossible to yield to the solace of words, or to the mind of another.

So much has happened in such a short time. In August, they were in the Pyrenees on holiday, when war was declared. They

367

heard the village church bell ring the tocsin that called the men in from the harvest fields and were awed by their quiet acceptance. No protest, not in that village at any rate, just the murmur of *ma patrie* and a bundling up of their small possessions for a quiet leave-taking.

In England too patriotism conquered. Their boy cousins volunteered, Aunt Kathleen's golden sons, and she and Moura followed, which brought them to this particular hospital at Paris-Plage, on the Normandy coast (not many miles but a thousand worlds away from Colleville), to be near their English brigade. As close as Kathleen could get to where they were serving, hoping, with the illogical hopes some women bring to war, that she would be the one to nurse them should they fall.

Fall they did of course, Tom first, one of 24,000 lost at Neuve Chapelle in the first big British attack. Kathleen was not near by. Nobody but she had ever thought she would be. Now she and Moura and Iseult tend his memory by nursing the sons and nephews and cousins of other women.

Gathering her nursing cape around her, Iseult enters the common room. Its smell is a mixture of damp and eucalyptus and that faint tang of disinfectant that hangs around everywhere. A group of medics gathered in the corner, huddled around a joke that one of them is telling. They take no notice as she goes to the trunk where her books and mementoes are kept. She chooses Pater's *Marius the Epicurean*. A little philosophical romance from the time of the catacombs should be the perfect accompaniment to a day's escape. What joy to have some hours to give to it. In this place, one has little room for any interest besides one's duty to the latest charred and blackened soldier arriving with a label tied around his toe. The pleasures of a book are faint light to hold beside the next batch of horrors concealed beneath the next wad of sodden bandage.

When she started, she had truly thought she would not survive the rigours of this life. Assigned to watch a soldier who had just come, that moment, from an operation, she panicked when he started to bleed suddenly and profusely, and ran – for he seemed very bad – down the corridor looking for a qualified nurse. On finding sister, she explained breathlessly and to her great shock was given a box on the ears for leaving her patient.

Iseult had never before had her ears boxed, and the injustice stung as much as the blow. 'I cannot do it,' she had sobbed to Moura at the end of that shift, her head on her mother's lap as if she were twelve again. Moura had not told her why she must prevail, nor invoked the memory of Tom nor said anything trying, just patted her hair until she was cried out and ready to sleep.

A moment of closeness between them, rare now.

Now they were both hardened nurses and Iseult had all the firsts that war nurses speak of behind her. The first time to glimpse the inside of a human body (it had seemed to her sacrilegious). The first time to peel the clothes off a man and wash him (she had to force her eyelids not to close). The first time to remove a dirty dressing (she panicked again: did you ease it off, slow and gentle, or flash it away, firm and fast?). The first time to see a man cry (she almost cried with shock herself). The first time to cut a trouser clear to reveal a leg gauzed black with congealed blood (her jaw ached from holding her face blank).

Moura and Kathleen are to be moved next week to another hospital, and Iseult and Dymphna are on a new ward, where all is different, where the wounds are of the mind, not the body. Hysteria and disorientation and limb paralysis and loss of speech, altogether making up a condition they are coming to call shell-shock. In some ways her new charges are more disturbing than the gangrenous feet, slime-green and scarlet, or quivering stumps of fresh amputated bone she has left behind.

As she exits the common room, a guffaw breaks behind her. The joke has reached its climax.

'You're looking chirpy,' says one of the porters, seeing her on the way out. 'A day off, by any chance?'

Iseult nods. 'My first in five weeks.'

'Well, you just make the most of it, y'hear. For us all.'

Oh, she would, she would. The lay of the land out where she is going reminds her so much of Colleville. The flat sea and sky and water all melded one into the other. What a comfort it will be to go out there by the shore and breathe, breathe naturally, after the long disease of hospital routine. She lengthens her stride at the thought.

On her way, she has to pass the pathway towards her new ward. Should she call in to say goodbye to that Irish boy? Mulcahy. He will be awake, and if she does not tell him, he will spend all day wondering. She imagines him asking one of the other nurses and being told and not accepting the answer and asking again, the same nurse or another. Pestering, as is his way.

Since he made his terrible request two days ago, he was much in her mind, this tenement boy who was handsome, yes, but no more than many others, and really rather coarse. Intelligent, yes, but wholly unread. The story told of him was that he'd suffered a mild concussion when knocked out by the flying limb of a blown-up friend, an experience that had wounded mind more than body.

What an appalling admission he had been, all blood and dirt and curses and apologies. She had soaped along his limbs, felt his bones long and thin and tough beneath her sponge. His unbroken white skin was a wonder after ministering to so many gashes and wounds. If a man's body could be a thing of beauty, it would be of this type. Tall and thin, with shoulder blades of the angels and hip bones of Christ. (She averted her eyes from the penis curled like a conch between his legs.) His left arm and leg take fits of spasm, as if they were creatures independent of him – but the cause is mental.

She was washing away in silence when he asked her, outright, with no lead up or introduction: 'Is it true you girls will help a man out if he wants to go?'

She knew immediately what he meant, though she pretended otherwise. 'Go,' she repeated, in a silly, airy voice, as if he might be referring to discharge. Or holidays. Or the lavatory.

He had clutched her wrist. 'Help me, nurse. You know how. I can't go back out there.'

It was being understood by them all now, soldiers and medics alike, that the war was not going to be over by Christmas. Or maybe next Christmas either.

'I'm afraid to go asleep,' he whispered. 'You can't imagine what that's like.'

Oh, but she could.

All the time she said nothing, just wrung out her cloth, carried on soaping, as if he were talking about the weather.

'I'd rather go quiet, with pills. In a bed.'

She pitied him but she couldn't give him anything. Certainly not pills but not even a word, because if they started that, if the nurses let go of bravery and cheeriness, where would it stop? They would all unravel.

He sighed. 'You're not going to, are you?'

'No.'

'You think me a funk.'

'No.'

'It's disgusting to you that I'm in here, that I'm saying that, while other boys are out there, doing their bit.'

'You are ill, that is why you are here.'

'The regiment thinks I'm a funk.'

'I'm sure they do not.'

'Captain Rogers said as much. He told me not to come here, said it would look bad for the regiment and be bad luck for me.'

'I see you are down for this new electrical treatment. I believe it is quite miraculous.' A military medic had come from

371

Besançon to show the doctors how to use it and made the most startling promises.

On night shift, the week following, when the rest of the ward was asleep or pretending to sleep, he shattered the quiet by sitting up in his bed and screaming. 'Mam! Mammy!' His eyes were open, but he could not see her and would not be quieted. Eventually he fell into an awkward sleep, hunched over on one side. In the morning, before she went off duty, he asked her if he had done anything untoward.

'No.'

'I did, didn't I? Don't lie to me, nurse.'

'All the soldiers call out in their sleep. We take no notice.' And many of them call out that word, the first they learnt.

He told her how he never knew when it would strike and that one of the soldiers in his regiment used to call him Mummy's Boy. 'Enjoy your holiday,' another had said to him when he was being transferred to hospital. No one said anything now, and that was worse. That let him know that things were really bad.

'I'm sorry about the other day, nurse.'

'Please. Don't apologize.'

'Moment of weakness and all that.'

'No need. Please.'

'I'm no coward. It's my aim to be back in business in no time.' His hand and leg jerked under the blanket, a huge spasm, which made him bite down on a quivering lip.

Her new ward is even worse than the old. Suffering of the mind is harder to endure – or cure – than suffering of the body but at least he has her pity. She has not yet become infected with the experienced nurse's bright immunity from that emotion. She is happy to suffer over his fate and the fate of them all. Rather that than to become indifferent to pain, her own or another's.

Poor soldier Mulcahy. She knows what it is to be afflicted with that terrible blankness of mind that knows no repose, that sees doubt withering every hope. How many more of them now roam the earth because of this conflict? This war that is not the denial of their European 'civilization' but its supreme achievement. Not an eruption of unaccountable madness but the rational crowning of its mediocrity.

But no, no thoughts of mediocrity or madness or suffering soldiers today. Today was for pacing water-softened sands and leaping brooks and letting her soul run through all the untamed things it has been craving. She veers away from the pathway towards Private Mulcahy, turns towards the exit instead. Only in the country are things pure and simple, for there they exist in their natural essence from which one is free to fashion truths or lies or nothing at all.

I needed a vacation: that's what I was realizing on my break in Ireland (which was turning out to be anything but that). I was tired. In Santa Paola my hours were budgeted with care: the minutes between the end of one meeting and the beginning of another; the time to eat a meal as well as to prepare it; the commute to college as well as the lecture hours. I allocated time for studying and completing term papers and picking up the shopping on the way to or from work but was caught out by a caller at the door, a broken tap, a flu or surprise invitation, the small things, the unexpected that every life can expect.

My days were packed as full as those of any overachiever, as planned as those of any executive – but I had neither the support nor the rewards. At thirty-four, I was still working at the restaurant, making Barney Fudrow rich. Now I wanted to be rich myself. Or what I thought of as rich. I wanted to be able to afford good clothes for Star, not to wince when I saw Dr Aintree's bill, to drive a car that was fewer than eight years old, to travel to Ireland without dreading what might be left unpaid when I got back.

There was more, I realized as I walked up the mountain trails around Doolough, my first time to stop and think for years. The routines of parenting, study and work had been the scaffolding of my life but of parties or picnics, of travel and adventure, of friends for dinner and walks that were not solitary, of midnight conversations and shared bottles of wine, of kissing and sex, of movies and dancing – of all kinds of play, I had had too little. I had never gone rollerblading, or scuba diving, or poetry slamming, or cycling through Amsterdam, or flamenco dancing, or moonlit swimming . . .

I want, I announced to myself to the tune of my shortening breath as I climbed, to do *all* of that. I want to change my life. But first I had this vacation to survive.

Vacation was the wrong word. There was too much tension flying around to call it that. My father. Rose. And now Star. She was refusing to go to my launch.

'Who would I talk to? It will be full of whiny critics and up-their-own-ass professors.' She shuddered.

Star loathed critics ever since our local paper's music column had savaged Vixen, with a line about their particular sound of fury signifying nothing and picking out Star for special opprobrium. ('The drummer was a big – let's be honest, fat – girl in Spandex and combat boots, with a sense of rhythm as idiosyncratic as her sense of fashion.')

My moment of glory wasn't exactly scintillating for a sixteen-year-old, I did realize that. For anyone, really. It was only a small essay in an ancillary volume by a subsidized press but it was publication, recognition that what I had to say was worth hearing by *somebody*.

I tried another tack. 'What will you do here, while I'm gone? I'll be staying in Dublin overnight.'

'I guess talk to Rose.'

That's what I'd found her doing quite often these days when I got back from my solitary drives or walks, but, if I came in and settled down beside them, Star always slipped away.

'What on earth do you two talk about?' Daddy, I suspected, from the few snatches I had managed to overhear. 'I didn't think she'd be your choice of company.'

374

'I feel sorry for her; she's on her own all the time.'

'So am I.'

'Oh, Mom, don't start.'

'It's natural that I'd want you there, surely you can see that.'

'Granddad says he'll take me fishing.'

'If you don't go to Dublin with me.'

'Yes.'

Star had by now gleaned a sense of how I felt about my father. On the plane across, realizing that she had an image of him as a kind of Dan Rather, I thought I'd better brief her as to what she could expect, but in the telling I had somehow ended up in tears. She had to call the stewardess to bring me Kleenex and a glass of water, and we'd both been shaken by that.

Since we'd arrived, we'd had more than a few whispered exchanges about his carry-on. And silent communications with eyes and eyebrows behind his back, forming a bond of sorts around his perverseness.

So she knew precisely what she was doing to me with this talk of going fishing with him. It spliced me in two to hear it. After all the years of her tirades and her tantrums, of trying to be the best I could be, of keeping what shouldn't be said unsaid ... I felt something split open inside me. I paused, teetered, but only for a moment, then every mean thought I'd ever had about her came surging up: that she was ruining the vacation with her self-centredness just as she always ruined everything at home; that she needed to get her act together and realize that she was not the centre of the goddamn universe and stop making life so hard for everyone around her; that she was picking the one way, above all others, to be mean to me and why, when I always tried to be good to her; that she was coming to Dublin and that was that . . .*

* It was a relief to hear them spoken. I always knew they were there. And she said a lot more than she lists here.

375

'You actually think I'm going with you after *this*? You can go to hell.'

Since starting to work at the hospital, Iseult has taught herself to breathe through her mouth, and she reverts to this habit now as she enters the shell-shock ward, the feel of country air falling from her as she arrives back. After her blessed, beautiful day out, the soup of smells that is the hospital ward – of blood and festering wounds, of dirty clothes and discarded boots, of sweat and disinfectant and gangrene – feels more offensive than ever.

As soon as she closes the door behind her, she sees someone is already there, sitting at the end of her soldier's bed. Moura! What is she doing here? Why does she always think the Irish ones are hers?

Iseult turns to slip back out – she does not wish to speak to him alongside Moura – but it is too late.

'Iseult! *Ma belle!*'

Iseult turns back and goes to them. As she approaches the bed, she sees his hand has taken on a mind of its own, jerking and twitching under the blankets.

'Ah, here comes my niece,' Moura says. His glance slides across on the word in a way that tells her he *knows*.

'Did you have a good day off, nurse?' he asks her.

'Thank you, yes.' She keeps her voice distant.

Moura says, 'This is Nurse Gonne. *Ma belle*, this is –'

'We've met. She admitted me.' His Irish accent is as strong in English as in French.

'But, Iseult, *wait* for the news we have. Private Mulcahy here was present at a treat day for Dublin children that I organized against old Queen Victoria back in the old days.'

'Oh,' says Iseult.

'Yes, isn't it astonishing? It seems such a long time ago, Private. The war has opened such gap between now and all that went before. But I remember that day so well. A wonderful day.'

'It was that, madame.'

'I hope some of those little ones grew to understand what we were doing.' The boy is struggling to get his arm to stay put, but Moura disdains to notice. 'I hear from home that England's difficulty may once more prove Ireland's opportunity. Pray some brave lads may make it so.'

'You wouldn't want to say that too loud around here, madame.'

'Of course not. But we Irish must stick together.'

She leans in close to him, in full dramatic flight. 'War does strange things to us all, Private. In my sleep, or the sort of waking sleep I have here, I have been seeing . . . I think I have been among masses of spirits of those Irish who have been killed in this war. They are being marshalled and drawn together by waves of rhythmic music . . . the thousands of Irish soldiers who have been killed are being drawn together in this wild reel tune I have been hearing.'

This is strange talk for a nurse, but the boy looks at Moura as some people do. As if hypnotized. As if she might be answering the question his unruly arm is asking.

Really, this is not good for him.

'They are dancing to this tune, some with almost frenzied intensity and enthusiasm, while others seem to be drawn in unwillingly not knowing why, but the rhythm is so strong and compelling that they have to dance.'

Iseult thinks to interrupt. 'Did you hear what happened on Ward 11?'

'So you mean the Senegalese?' says the Irish boy.

A Senegalese soldier had brought the severed head of a German from the front in a cardboard box. It was discovered under his bed only when it started to smell.

'It is leading them back to the spiritual Ireland from which they have wandered,' says Moura. 'Where they would find their self-realization and perfection. And in so doing they bring to Ireland their strength.'

377

'That was something else all right,' he says, smiling at Iseult. The arm jerks like a fish at the end of a line.

At last Moura notices. 'I think it's time you got your rest, Private.'

'I'm fine, madame.'

'Rest, that's what's called for.' She gets up from the chair. 'Come, Iseult.'

Iseult pauses, looks down on the boy. His eyes are upon her, entreating. She knows what he asks. Just her time. No euthanasia requests on this occasion. Just a talk with the only person around here who understands. Behind them in the ward are the sounds of other, soothing, medical voices, pierced by occasional groans. Her mother taps her foot, impatient.

'You go ahead, Moura,' Iseult says. 'I think to stay a little longer.'

'Ladies and ladies,' I said, beginning my talk, for there wasn't a single man at the book launch. A titter broke round the room like a wave. Looking down from my podium at the faces turned towards me put a nervous wobble into my voice. 'In 1889, the year that W. B. Yeats first met Maud Gonne, he was moving away from the influence of the older men who had been so predominant in his life. Men such as his Pollexfen grandfather and uncles, the old Irish Fenian John O'Leary, the magician MacGregor Mathers and, of course his father were ceding their place in his life to a number of strong-minded and unconventional women. These women – the Gonnes, Madame Blavatsky, Olivia Shakespear, Florence Farr and Augusta Gregory in the 1890s and many others from then on, most notably of course his wife, George Hyde-Lees – were, variously: emblems, muses, providers, literary and mystical cohorts, mentors, friends and sometime sexual partners.'

My eyes floated back to a couple of kindly faces near the front.

'Of all these women, none were more important to his poetry than the Gonnes, and it is them I'd like to talk about tonight, most particularly Iseult Gonne, whose influence is so often overshadowed by the poet's unrequited love for her mother. Maud Gonne, the radical Irish revolutionary, the celebrated beauty, the unattainable muse, would – I think – have loved to know that we are here tonight, discussing her. Iseult, her daughter, would have hated it. When I started my biographical work on this subject, I had a disconcerting image of her watching me with a cool, disapproving gaze as I scoured dead books and papers and letters for meanings they were never meant to bear.

'Iseult's light is a subtler, softer one than her bedazzling mother's but she . . .'

On I went, talking to a room of strangers with nobody I knew there to hear me. Before leaving for Dublin that morning, I'd looked in on Star, who was sleeping with her head under the duvet, like a bird with its head tucked under its wing, only her quiff showing, collapsed across the pillow.

'Star,' I called gently.

Silence.

'Do you want breakfast before we leave?'

Silence.

'You are going to come, aren't you? Please come, darling. We can talk in the car.'

Silence.

I went in, sat on the side of the bed. 'I know what I said the other day was wrong and I'm sorry. But I'm not asking you to forgive me. Only don't let it stop you coming with me today. Today is a big day for me, the biggest day in my life since I had you. I'd love you to be there and I think if you don't come, you'll regret it later. Don't let a row stop you. Star? Please? Star?'

After my speech, there was a wine reception at which most people, except me, knew somebody. We stood around, eighty or ninety of us, holding long-stemmed glasses between our fingers and our copies of *Between the Lines* under our arms, saying what we hoped was the right thing to each other. I can do it – restaurant work is training school for small talk – but I don't ever enjoy it. It feels more like performance than connection to me, and, that night, I'd had enough performing on the podium. I wanted to get away, consider how it had gone and what I was feeling. Failing that option, I should have liked to be with people I could really talk to, to ask them what they really thought and tell them how I really felt. Star or Marsha or – stupid thought – Zach, instead of these strangers coming across to congratulate me.

And then I was tapped on the shoulder. I turned around to a pair of aquamarine eyes that I recognized immediately even though I hadn't seen them for years, not since my mother's funeral. I had expected the habit and wimple she'd worn then, but it seemed they were gone, replaced by a sensible navy skirt and jumper. 'Sister . . . Auntie . . . Catherine!' I said, delighted. 'You came!'

'Came? Of course I came. Best invitation I've had in years.'

I hugged her, taking a moment to settle the emotions that leapt in me at the sight of her. She was my mother's sister, long-time principal of a girl's school in Dublin, and I had sent her the invitation unsure whether, being a nun, she would prefer to ignore our flawed connection to each other.

What age was I last time we visited and took tea with her in the convent parlour? Ten? Eleven? My mother had wanted me to go to her school, but my father hadn't seen the point in paying fees to send me boarding in County Clare when there was a perfectly good convent in Wicklow.

'So, the prodigal daughter returns.' She cast her lovely smile around the room. 'And on a wave of glory.'

'Not exactly glory,' I said.

'Now don't go making little of it. I hate people who play

down their achievements. It's a fine book. Very interesting work. Very *important* work, excavating all those untold stories. And your contribution is so well written. Tell me, about Iseult Gonne . . .' And she was off. No small talk now. We had so much to tell and ask each other. She was lovely, as kind as my mother but with a stronger core. My mother's life had withered her sense of self; her sister's had nourished hers.

After the launch party broke up, we went back to my hotel on her Honda motorbike. She had brought a spare helmet along, thinking we might do just that. We sat in the lobby drinking tea and talking, talking. She knew so much about me and my past, and nothing, it seemed, was out of bounds. Towards the end of the night, when we were both overcome by yawning tiredness, she spoke of my adoption. 'I hope you won't be offended if I say that at the time we thought it a hard thing to do to poor Martha. The whole family was outraged on her behalf.'

'I understand. I would have been too.'

'But it turned out well. She loved you like her own. You were lucky to have each other.'

I nodded. 'My father wasn't easy,' I said. 'For either of us.'

'I remember trying to talk to her after she got engaged, but she wouldn't let me near it. It wasn't until the day of the wedding, when we were getting ready, that I got a chance to ask her if she was sure. I made light of it, saying something like, this is your last chance now to change your mind.'

'What did she say?'

'That he was a good man, a guard, with land and prospects, and she knew what she was doing.'

She hesitated.

'Go on, sister.'

'I don't know if I should be telling you this, but it's always burnt a hole in my memory of her. She said to me, "Isn't a bad marriage better than no marriage at all?".'

'Oh, God.'

'She was twenty-five, and her time was running out. That's the way it was then. Marriage was everything for a girl – job, status in the community, the lot. Women weren't allowed to work at much else, remember.'

'Unless you became a nun.'

She bowed her head, as if in prayer, and when she looked back up she said, 'It was on Martha's wedding day that I knew my own calling.'

Next morning, driving back down to Wicklow, I thought about Sister Catherine the whole way, about how different two sisters can be. I'd told her about my wish to trace my birth mother and the stonewalling I'd met from the adoption agency. She'd probed, but gently, careful as a cook checking a soufflé, and after hearing all she promised to 'make enquiries' for me, in a tone that told me I'd have my information soonest.

I left her chugging off on her motorbike into the Dublin night.

Funny how life works, I thought, driving up the lane at Doolough and parking the car. If Star had come to Dublin with me, I wouldn't have been able to speak half as freely to Sister Catherine.

I walked into the kitchen, where lunch was being served. As soon as I crossed the threshold, I felt the tension in the room. Something was wrong. The smoke of anxiety I remembered so well from childhood immediately swirled in me. I stopped, afraid to speak, knowing any word or action would unleash the menace that was waiting to pounce.

I looked at him sitting there in his place at the head of the table, chin against his chest, and wondered what it must be like to be him? To rarely speak anything but scorn or dislike, always to be quarrelling with something inside your head?

'Oh, here she is,' he said. 'In time for the food. And arms swinging, of course.'

I looked at my hands, not knowing what he meant.

'Not so much as a loaf of bread to contribute to their keep.'

Our keep? We had brought presents when we arrived. A book, handkerchiefs, whiskey for him. Flowers and chocolates for Rose. He wanted a contribution to our *keep*?

'Nothing but complaints from the moment yez arrived. Coffee, how are you. And showers. It's far from the likes of that you were reared but in you come as you please with your notions and your nose in the air, snooting around the place.'

Star's eyes were white circles all round her irises.

'And all your talk about America, America. If America is so damned fine, what are yez doing here?'

His face was swelling, like a red party balloon. I tried to keep my voice calm. 'Are you saying you want us to go?'

For the first time in my life, I held his black, blazing gaze. A familiar throb began to beat in the space between my eyes, but I didn't drop them and I wouldn't have, if I'd had to stand there looking into his hatred to this day. He was the one to break off. His eyes dropped to contemplate the toe of his boots, and I felt my heart surge.

From the side, Star said, 'We should go, Mom. It's obvious we're not wanted.'

'What about you, Rose?' I said. 'Do *you* want us to go?'

Rose looked from us to Daddy, panic-stricken. He flicked his wrist, a wave that dismissed us. Maybe her too. 'You can leave Rose out of it,' he said. 'Ye're not her people.'

Star stood up, a loud scrape of her wooden chair on the tiles. 'Let's just go, Mom.'

'That child needs the strap taken to her,' he said.

'You lift one finger to her,' I said, 'and I'll call the police.'

'I am the police, you little fool.'

'Not any more, you're not.'

'Oh God, oh God, oh God,' wailed Rose. 'Stop. Let's all be friends.'

'Come *on*, Mom.'

My father let out a guffaw. 'Would you listen to them? Should

383

they stay or should they go? It's our house you're talking about, or have you forgotten? So, yes, go. Go on. The free hotel's just closed its doors.'

Star was in my room, waiting for me to finish packing, when Rose came into the bedroom.

'Oh, no,' she said, seeing what I was doing and Star's case, already packed, on the bed beside us. 'Please don't leave. He doesn't mean it, honest to God he doesn't. You should have heard him before ye came. He was all excited. Come back and let's sort it out. Or let him sleep on it. He'll be grand in the morning. We'll try again tomorrow.'

Star looked at me as if to say, don't you dare. But she needn't have worried.

'I'm sorry, Rose. I left here because I couldn't put up with the likes of that. I'm certainly not going to let him turn it on my daughter.'

'This is terrible, just terrible.'

I zipped my bag closed. 'I'm sorry. Goodbye, Rose. Thank you for everything.'

'I better go back down, so,' she said.

'Of course.'

'He's not as bad as he makes himself out to be.'

'I know,' I said.

Star snorted.

'Did you take the dress?'

'Dress?'

'Your m . . . The blue dress, from the other wardrobe.'

She saw from my face that I hadn't.

'Please, take it,' she said. 'I want to think of you having it.'

After we hefted our cases down the wooden staircase and outside to the car, feet crunching on the gravel, we stood on the doorstep for a little while, but my father did not appear.

'What should we do?' I said to Star.

'Let him go to hell,' she said. 'Come on.'

I thought of the last time, eighteen years ago, sneaking away by night. 'No, I'd better say goodbye. I'll regret it if I don't.'

'What did you ask for, if you didn't want my opinion?'

I pushed open the door and stuck in my head. He was in his seat at the head of the table, where we'd left him, his back to the door. 'We're off, then,' I said, my voice grating with falsity even to my own ears. 'Goodbye and thanks for having us.'

'Goodbye and good riddance.'

Rose moved towards us.

'Stay put, you!' he growled at her.

'Goodbye, Rose,' I said, a sort of apology, and left.

As I drove away, looking through the rear-view mirror, my vision was split. I saw the house as it was now and also as it was when I was small and my mother was alive. The years fell away and into the chasm tumbled all the years I should have had – saying goodbye the first time, returning afterwards every year or two for a visit, to warm hellos and sad goodbyes, observing the changes in the place, little on little, year on year, giving me smaller pangs of loss. Bearable pangs. Shakespeare's sweet sorrow of parting, not this wrench that must be endured again in order to survive.

Star said, 'Are you all right?'

'Not really. But I will be. You?'

She nodded. 'I am now.'

A moment of accord. A silver lining. Next to what went on in that big old farmhouse, our little three-bed in Santa Paola seemed a model of family feeling. At least now she understood what he was like and why I had kept her from him for years. It wasn't quite the reunion I had hoped for when we were setting out, but it was something. A bond of sorts.

'*Go up and hide in your rooms and wait until tomorrow,*' Star said in a silly voice, a bad imitation of Rose. '*When he's had his sleep he'll be a pussycat, a little lamb.* Is she crazy?'

'I know. Poor thing.'

'How does she bear it? He's absolutely awful to her. And she never says a thing to his face . . .'

'I'm sure her answer would be that she loves him.'

She did, poor Rose, but only because she did not love herself. She was able to live with my father, to – in Star's words – bear it, because beneath his bad behaviour she sensed the torments that drove him. Her antennae were more attuned to his suffering than to her own.

Whenever somebody started to tell Henry James an anecdote that ignited his storytelling instinct, he'd stop them before they were finished, saying, 'Don't tell me too much.' I know why. He wanted the freedom and insight that can come only from the imagination; too many facts would constrain him, inhibit his ability to shape the tale.

I understand. Truth above facts is my motto now as I sit in this study, before the window that throws a greenish light across my hand, working through this reworking. I use the tools of fiction to tell the story – selecting incidents, reordering time, plotting and orchestrating, representing speech, winnowing the chaff words and chopping and changing others – but I also must do justice to what is known to have happened. Pulled between the biographers, who stand in the territory of what was, and the novelists, who care most for what might be, I cross and recross the frontier, like a demented double-agent.

It is still winter. Will it never end? February 1 is the official start of spring in Ireland, but it is well into February now. Three days ago a relentless wind got up. The trees outside groan as they are blown this way and that. The windows rattle and whine, making me shiver, though I am not cold. I sit here, trying to make decisions. So much has already been written about the Gonnes and their entourage but so little about my family, on either side.

I am drowning in detail about Iseult, but all I seem to hold from my own early years is an intense but undefined embarrassment, a sense of blushing and shuffling through my days, especially in the presence of others. I was ashamed, but of what exactly? I rummage through my child's mind and find nothing but a swirl of feelings. Only Pauline stepped into the haze I had sprayed around myself and forced me to see her face. I do have memories of this house, of course, especially of the kitchen. I can conjure up the border of walls, the solidity of the big kitchen table as I rode around it on my tricycle, the warmth of the fire, the grey light coming in the low window, everything tall and looming. And walking out, up to the mountain or down to the lake when the house was too full of feeling for me, face burning, feet tripping over the stones.

It's like stepping into a finger-painting, trying to remember my childhood. The strokes are too broad, the lines too erratic.

My father suffered none of these difficulties. His early life seems to have always returned to him in clear, bright lines. Marbles in his pockets, games on the streets, dinner on the table, devilment with his brothers: a happy boy, by his own account. It's idealized, it has to be – my father grew up in a tenement house in what was then the poorest city in Europe – but I can feel a truth in it. When he recalled those early days, his words softened, his sentences lengthened, it was as if he let out a breath. And so I can imagine that as a boy he was different to the man he became.

He never spoke out loud about the war, just as he never spoke about the tenements. It all went into the notebook, and I find it hard to read through what it tells me, to take the decisions it asks me to make. I find it hard to put him and Iseult Gonne together into a hospital ward. Yet it happened. I have the fact of it here in my hands, though I don't believe it was quite the way he tells it.

Outside the wind blows and howls as I try to decipher the map my father drew in his diaries. To bring each of them to that shared time and place, I have to pull back and squint through the words and imagine how it really was.

A moral shock, that's what Moura called it, but it wasn't moral, it was medical. The boy was sick, much sicker than he seemed. The old and kindly orderly had said as much. She could feel his hand on her still, as if he had left a permanent print on her skin.

Dymphna would not be so precious, Dymphna would have slapped his hand, laughed it away. Dymphna loved to go to the wards at night with some of the other nurses. They waited until the night sister had completed her visits and then they sneaked down.

'It's not serious,' she said. 'It cheers them up. Where is the wrong in it?'

Nursing is largely a matter of providing small vitals like water or comfort. Many of the men – and not just on this ward – could have no better comfort than the sight of a woman. They sucked on it as helplessly as their mouths sucked water from the little jug she took round to them in the mornings. 'Please hold me,' more than one had whispered.

Or: 'Give me a kiss.'

Sometimes Iseult held their heads in her lap, like Bichon, to feed them the water, but kisses? Never. She is glad of the rules that forbid it and despises the uninhibited lovemaking that goes on around her, between other nurses and officers. Under beds, in cupboards. Today at the beach, as she topped a sand dune, she had seen that Canadian nurse and her French officer. They were too far gone to notice her, and she had watched them a while before diverting to another path. A most perplexing spectacle.

Perhaps Dymphna is right, perhaps she is overscrupulous. But from the boy, one did not expect such treatment: that much is true.

Once Moura left, she had sat down in the chair beside him, its surface still warm, and he made her tell him all about her day off. The dark came down; she was aware of it pressing in around the huts and tents and of the guns, which were loud tonight. Every so often the glass of water by his bed shuddered. They chatted a while about sea and fields and the great outdoors, and when the cocoa trolley came round, she was offered a cup and she took it, not quite knowing why but wanting to prolong the day and enjoying this quiet, companionable finish. As the patients around them slipped, one by one, into their drugged sleep, he began to talk of his family. She had noticed before how patients – and the medics too – open up at night in a way they wouldn't dream of doing by day.

He had seven siblings, he told her. 'When I came to filling in "next of kin" on my conscription card, I misunderstood and squeezed them all in.'

'Do you miss them?' she asked him.

'I moved to France years ago, so no. You wouldn't miss my father's belt. I miss Dublin, though, sometimes.'

Her eyelids were drooping over the cocoa. Afterwards, she could not remember what she was thinking about when it happened. She was in that in-between place, her mind blank and busy, both at once, and next thing, he had lunged forward and one of his hands – his quiet hand, his good hand, his writing hand, was on her breast, cupping it.

The other had grabbed hold of her wrist and was jerking her hand in under the covers. She opened her mouth to shout at him but no sound came, and she tried to pull her hand away but he was too strong. His fingers on her wrists were like too-tight ropes, cutting into her skin. She could feel the heat of him, in the direction he was pulling her. She curled her hand into a fist, struggled to pull it back, but the bulge brushed against the back of her knuckles.

'Please,' she whispered. 'Have mercy.' What a thing to say, why had she said that? It made no difference what she said, he was fixed, avid in his intent.

She felt him shudder – was it a spasm of his arm or something

389

more sinister – and released a scream. The orderlies came running. She heard the shouting of voices behind, felt his arms being pulled from her. 'What do you think you're doing, you scoundrel?' one of them said.

A grey-haired kind man with a face like an elderly hound.

'Say sorry to nurse.'

'Sorry?' the Irish boy said, his voice loud and rough, so unlike the voice that had whispered secrets a minute before. 'Where's the sorry? She loves it.'

'Stop that talk, you!' the orderly said, sharp. Then to her: 'Sorry, Nurse Gonne. We'll sort him now.'

'Sorry? Sorry? Don't you know who you're talking to?' He is shouting now. 'Niece, me arse.'

Sister arrives on the scene. A proper nurse with years of experience, unlike Iseult and Maud and the other lady volunteer. The professional status she wears as a hard skin is bristling. Sister is a cliché: efficient, detached, energetic, immune to pity and frivolity and weakness. And so utterly effective.

'That's *quite* enough out of you, Private. Medicine trolley please, Nurse Collier. Thank you.' She reaches for a syringe. 'Nurse Gonne,' she says, opening the package and holding the syringe up to the light of the candle to check it, 'you can leave now.'

He has stopped prattling, but his eyes are still on her, black with choler. Why? She has been nothing but kindly to him. Yet she somehow feels responsible for his fate. His bad arm is back under the covers, jerking.

'You are officially off duty until tomorrow, Nurse Gonne,' sister says.

She takes a few steps away. When she turns back to look, he is rolling around the bed, muttering again. 'She wanted it . . . can't you see that . . . don't you know that? You too, . . . all dying for it, pretending not . . .'

'Roll up his sleeve, Nurse Collier. Not that one, we'll never get a vein on that, the way it lashes about. The other one. Hold still now, Private, and hold your gabble. There. That's it. Now, that should do it.'

And, indeed, his voice begins to fade almost instantly. 'They all pretend . . . too good for it . . . all . . . All aw saw her shhh . . .'

'He's gone, sister.'

'Thank heavens for that. You'll tidy up, Nurse Collier, thank you.' She turns around, slow and stately as a ship. 'Nurse Gonne, what are you doing here still?'

Iseult's mind is full of scattered thoughts, like a pin box overturned, each one loose and thin and sharp.

'I thought I told you to go? Be off with yourself, this very instant.'

Sister's tone is what is needed to make one realize how to put one foot after another. Like Moura.

'That's it. Good girl. A sleep is what you need now. A bit of a rest and you'll be right as rain.'

Ribs of Time

... To clutch life's hair, and thrust one naked phrase
Like a lean knife between the ribs of Time.

Iseult Gonne, 'The City of the Soul'

Christmas Eve, 1982
Star

'Pass . . . that, would you?' My grandfather's bony finger jabbed the air.

I gave him the glass of water from the bedside locker. A moment's silence, then, 'It's Pauline Whelan I blame. Interfering auld biddy . . .'

'Shouldn't you rest?' I said.

'Rest, is it? Oh, that's what you'd all like to see.' Cough, cough, cough. 'Me . . . going . . . to my rest . . .'

'Daddy, stop that old nonsense,' my mother said. 'It's time for your meds.'

'She's poisoning me,' he said. 'You'll be my witness now if I go early. You make sure you tell the world . . .'

Mom cast her eyes heavenwards behind his back. 'Star, would you hand me across that vial of pills, honey. Thank you. Now, Daddy, here you are . . . come on now, sit up.'

'I can do it myself.'

He took the tablets from her and, with a sudden change of mood, docile as a child, swallowed. She settled him back down and, when leaving, offered me escape: 'Do you want to come through for lunch, Star? You must be starving after your flight.'

'No,' I said. 'No. I think I'll stay here with Granddad for a bit.'*

---

* Again, this is Mom's version of me. Though accurate, as far as it goes.

45

Moura looks up from her newspaper and says, almost wistfully, as if telling one of her dreams: 'MacBride has been shot.'

They are in the drawing room, Iseult and Mary Barry Delaney answering letters, Seághan reading a book, Moura an Irish newspaper. Since the Irish Rising, she has been beseeching friends in Dublin and London to send her newspapers. The rebels surrendered to the British Army at the end of April, and many of her best, and most noble, friends, have been imprisoned – and some executed. She is overwhelmed by what she calls their sacrifice and can speak and think of nothing else.

The papers come, bearing news of another of the ringleaders, or signatories to the Proclamation, to be shot by firing squad. Willie's great friend, MacDonagh. Pearse and Heuston and Plunkett, all fine men with whom she had spent so many happy evenings at Russell's house next door in Rathgar. Her old friend James Connolly, badly wounded and suffering from gangrene, tried in bed and strapped to a chair to face the volley.

The French are horrified by their ally's brutality – and their folly, for what effect will this have on Irishmen at the Front?

Con Markievicz, who is like a sister to her, and Arthur Griffith, almost a brother, were also in jail, waiting. As was her husband.

Moura reads the report aloud. It seems John MacBride had not been privy to the plans for the Rising. That morning, he was on his way into town to meet his brother, who was getting married the week following, when he met the volunteer troops on the march. He immediately offered his services. At his trial he said he considered it his duty to do so. For this, and maybe for old offences, he too was shot at dawn. Iseult imagines the scene: the assassin, assassinated. He would have gone bravely. Physically he was brave. That she could admit.

A concoction of emotion assails her. She hardly knows what to think. Moura, of course, has no such trouble. She sits for a moment with her hand on her heart, then rises and takes Bichon away from his book and sits him on a chair. With her hands on his shoulders, she says in her most dramatic fashion: 'Your father died for his country, Seaghán. He did not behave well to us, but now we can think of him with honour.'

Poor Bichon does not know what to think, as until this moment his father was the bogeyman who might come in the night to steal him away.

Moura straightens and looks round at the adults. 'He has died for Ireland, and his son will bear an honoured name. I remember nothing else.'

Nothing else?

Delaney takes her cue and begins to howl. 'They've never killed him, no, oh, no.'

'Iseult, *ma belle*,' says Moura. 'This means we can return to Ireland.'

Iseult ignores this and says, 'Delaney, don't talk such nonsense.'

'Oh, no, it is a tragedy. A terrible tragedy. English scoundrels to do such a thing. May the soul of an Englishman be lost for every hair on his noble Irish head . . .' Delaney continues thus, working herself up, until Iseult takes her by the shoulders and shakes her.

'Nonsense, I tell you. Nonsense.'

'You have no heart.' She starts to sob, and Iseult has to walk away before she goes too far, for of course it is really Moura she would like to shake.

Nothing else.

Oh, what it is to have such a mother who never takes a moment to consider or to understand.

*

397

Evening in London, though one might not realize it, for it is May and the study is awash with orange light, angling beams full of dust and mystery on Willie's new wall hangings. A satisfactory effect. For twenty years Willie has lived in these rooms. Some months ago, the drunken woman below set fire to her sitting room, getting herself evicted, and he took over her rooms too and attempted to tie the two apartments together into a space fitting for a man of his age and inclinations. He had the walls scraped and repapered in an effort to remove insect life, the stairs painted blue and the woodwork in a variety of colours.

In the pantry, Mrs Old is cleaning about, catching up on work she wasn't able to do at her usual time because of a doctor's appointment. From outside the window come the voices of children playing, unselfconsciously enjoying the length of the day, the warmth of the sun. It is one of those moments he so often longs for but so seldom wins, a moment of quiet.

The doorbell rings.

He looks up from his book. He expects no company. From the hallway, Mrs Old cries, 'I'll go.' Mrs Old does so love a caller. Down she treads, and from the door comes the sound of voices and of four feet treading back up the stairs, Mrs Old's heavy gait dominating. 'Here's a nice surprise,' she says, coming in. 'It's Miss Gonne.'

Maud? How long since she has called like this? He puts down his book, Keats's 'Lamia', as it happens. In the old days, when she used to come in her carriage, the urchins would call her his Irish princess and gather round for the coins she always carried for them. He hadn't seen her since . . . when? The war makes travel so difficult. So he has not had a chance to tell her about Mabel. Or his increasing desire to be wed.

He rises to greet her, and as the door swings back he sees that it is not Maud but Iseult. Of course. What was he thinking? Maud would be Madame. Madame Gonne MacBride. Miss Gonne is Iseult, looking even more beautiful than when she impressed all London back in 1913. Beautiful but also pale and drawn. A distinct look of her mother about her now. Same height, same carriage, same dignity, same hint of suffering, tight as a bow, beneath.

'My dear, this is a surprise.'

'Moura sent me. Did you not receive a letter?'

'No. The damn censor, like as not. Come in. Let Mrs Old take your coat. You would like some tea?'

'Actually, could I be very forward and ask you for a whiskey, Willie?'

'Whiskey?'

'We developed a taste for its healing powers in the hospital,' she smiles. 'I only ask because I know you keep it. And after a day at Cousin May's, I am sorely in need of something stronger than tea.'

'Well . . .'

'Dear me, don't look so shocked. It is eight thirty in the evening, not the morning. And I am not a child.'

'Of course you are not. Tell me your age now.'

'I am almost twenty-two, Willie.'

He laughs. 'Mrs Old, when you return, would you bring the whiskey bottle?'

Iseult drapes her coat on the back of a chair, sits down opposite him.

'Your cousin is as trying to you as ever?'

'Worse. The war effort brings out all her jingoism. And I am not allowed to so much as walk to the garden gate without a chaperone for fear I should elope with a soldier.'

'Being more conventional, she is bound to allow you less freedom than Moura.'

'Oh, Moura is as bad in recent times, but she is more occupied than May and therefore easier to deceive. I had to invent a great number of tedious lies to be here this evening. And tomorrow you shall receive notice of an official call from us both, so you shall have to pretend not to have seen me at all.'

399

He frowns. 'My dear, I do not –'

'Your home is delightful now,' she says, turning away to consider the room. 'I saw you had painted the stairs. Didn't it used to be black and red? And here too. Everything looks awfully nice.'

'I've taken over two rooms downstairs.'

'Isn't it fun making plans for the arrangement of a house?'

'In my case, it is rather foolish, as the lease expires in a few years and a local hotel has its eyes on the building. But I was driven by a compulsion.'

'A good one.'

She smiles that smile of hers, fey, wan, ethereal. Does she have any idea of its effect? And what a strange mixture she is, so childlike one moment, the next as insouciant and self-possessed as her mother. No 'Uncle' now, just Willie this and that. And that smile.

Mrs Old hands him the bottle and two glasses. 'Are you quite sure this is what you want?'

'Pour, my dear man, before I burst into tears.'

'Should Mrs Old remain?'

'Dear God, Willie, don't be a dowager.'

He chuckles, then nods to the housekeeper.

'There is no danger here, Willie, you know that as do I. Just a small taste of life. Please grant me that, for a small hour, then I shall hop back inside the strait-laces of a well-brought-up young woman. I promise you.'

He sits in the armchair opposite her. 'Come, then. Let us talk. Tell me what has you looking so very pale.'

'Too much responsibility.'

'Moura? Ireland? The executions?'

'Oh, Willie.'

'Has it been very bad?'

She raises her glass to him, takes a sip of the amber liquid. The tip of her tongue flicks into view. 'Only you, I believe, can imagine how bad. Moura is consumed by plans since she heard.'

'Ah. Plans.'

'Her life of quiet is over. She is like a woman possessed. She must get to Ireland.'

'So she can play her new role. Widow of the martyred hero.'

Iseult's pale skin flushes. What must the poor child feel when the man who molested her is now glorified? 'And what of you, my dear?'

'I do understand why Moura is distressed. And why she wants to leave. France is impossible at the moment –'

'You cannot be so sanguine, surely, at leaving the only home you have ever known?'

'I do have an objection, but it is not one I feel I should voice.'

'Be frank, my dear. You have few enough opportunities.'

'It is a confession that is reprehensible, but it is the truth. I don't care. I don't care about the Rising or the war or any of the things that so engage Moura. Yes, of course I am saddened when I see small children beg, but the minute I no longer have them in my sight I forget that some feet away sordid misery and distress rumbles in their ignoble tenement houses. Or, if I remember, I say to myself, "Life is a dirty trick," and I mean for me, not them.'

'That is certainly frank.'

Her face is compressed, as though she is trying not to laugh. 'You see, Willie, what egotistical mediocrity hides beneath the exterior of a young lady with enormous, compassionate eyes?'

'It is good to hear somebody speak something that is not wartime cant.'

'Oh, how I loathe it, this disgusting war.'

'The most expensive outbreak of insolence and stupidity the world has ever seen. I give it as little thought as I can.'

'I wish Moura could hear you. She can think of nothing else. You heard about Tommy? We were so worried for Kathleen, we thought she might actually die too, of sorrow.'

'And you were fond of him, were you not?'

'He was a fine person, incapable of a low or mean trick. I

miss him, terribly, though he was not really a part of my daily life.'

'And what of that life? You are still nursing?'

'No. It became too much for us all. I have taken a job as secretary with the French Army's committee on aviation.'

'*Secretary?* To an *aviation* committee?'

'Yes. It is dull, but one must do something. It is that or go to Moura for pocket money – which is rather humiliating at my age.'

'And your writing? Does it leave you time to write?'

'It's just a few hours in the afternoon, writing business letters. I really cannot claim it as an excuse.'

46

'Cat's piss and porcupines!' says Ezra Pound. 'People need to wake up to a few SIMPLE facts.' He leans forward to spear a potato with his fork from the dish in the middle of the table. 'And they'd better hurry up if they don't want to wake up too late to DO anything.' He lolls back to munch his capture.

Iseult is trying not to stare, though there is much to observe about Mr Pound. Ezzzzzzra, as he insisted she must call him. His attire: a most outlandish garb like motley robes and an earring in one ear. His demeanour: when he came in, he extended his hand to Willie in an American handshake, two hands around one, letting his ebony stick clatter to the floor. His marriage: his wife Dorothy mincing behind him, carrying herself delicately and apart, as if she feared the sudden movements of her husband might damage her. His energy: pacing the room while they had their pre-dinner drink, rattling off his elliptical sentences with their bombshells of emphasis. It has him up out of his chair every five minutes, arms waving like an out-of-control windmill, declaiming the flaws of the contemporary world, this 'bitched mess of modernity', as he styles it.

He is appallingly brash, a man with the worst traits of the world's worst race – the Americans. According to Arthur Symons, her closest ally among Willie's friends, Pound pursued Willie for years, wormed his way into his life and so took over that Arthur, and other old friends, no longer attend his Monday night at-homes. And that is how he is here now: topping up the wine, as if he is host.

Iseult has been invited to dine with this group at Woburn Buildings before. The first time, her cousin May, Mrs Bertie-Clay, was also in attendance, a thoroughly awkward mix.

Thankfully poor May couldn't endure the thought of subjecting herself again, so convinced herself that Pound was too obvious to be dangerous and that Iseult was sufficiently chaperoned by the presence of Mrs Pound.

Tonight is less excruciating than last time, but is still largely a matter of listening to Ezra. He has an opinion on everything, and, like Moura, seems quite incapable of introspection. Iseult would much rather hear what Willie has to say, though there is satisfaction too in seeing this younger man challenge him. 'It is like the Irish rebels,' he declares now, twitching and clearing his throat before throwing one of his pronouncements in his nasal American twang. 'The Eagle's Irish theatre had developed a wide sympathy for the country that they have now wiped utterly away.' The Eagle is his nickname for Willie.

'Please let us talk of anything but that tiresome rebellion,' says Dorothy.

Her husband looks at her as if she is a bug he should like to squash. 'Very well, my dear. Do you wish to propose a subject for conversation? No? Then shall we ask our guest of honour what it is she writes?'

Iseult blushes. 'Me? Writes?'

'Indeed. The Eagle tells us you are a fine writer.'

'I have written very little of late.' A small shake of her head signifies to them, she hopes, that that line of conversation is closed. She shall have to speak to Willie. This must cease, this going around telling all and sundry that she is a writer. It is too embarrassing.

She takes another sip of wine, keeps her eyes down. A claret, Willie said. She feels giddy, thinks maybe she has had a little too much. Ezra has launched himself upon a treatise that she finds hard to follow and, coming out of thought, discovers he is laying upon her the most kindly look. He is giving her time to recover from her embarrassment. Perhaps she has misjudged him.

How he talks. How much and in such a manner. Like no one

else. His accent is American but overlaid and mingled with what seems even to her, with her French ear, a dozen assorted English society accents. He inserts London Cockney in mockery, and makes French, Spanish and Greek exclamations, and made-up words and strange cries and catcalls. All oddly inflected and set off by dramatic pauses.

At a point of comparison between writers and artists, he turns to his wife, who is a Cubist artist of some note, for concurrence. 'Is that not right, my dear?'

'But of course, dear, you are always right,' she says with a shrug.

They all laugh, a laugh that sounds habitual to Iseult, as if they have had variations of this conversation so many times that they know just when the laugh should come. She is laughing too, though her amusement is less knowing than it sounds. Still, she is a part of something. It is a long time since she felt a part of something.

A momentary silence follows. Then Willie says, 'You did not think him so right when he volunteered to fight the Germans.'

Iseult wonders if this too is a joke. 'Truly?'

'Guilty as charged,' Ezra says, throwing up his hands. 'It was as Rilke wrote: "Into everyone's breast, suddenly no longer one's own, leapt a heart like a meteor. An iron heart, like an iron lung."'

'Yes, the war so swallows our own lives that one ceases . . .' The two men are leaning in towards her. 'I should say *almost* ceases to have personal experiences or emotion.'

'That is exactly right,' says Ezra, and something about the way he says it makes her shy.

Yet she asks him. 'You have not been to the Front, have you, Mr Pound?'

'Call me Ezra, won't you, for pity's sake.'

'The War Office turned him down,' says Dorothy, making the WO sound like a sensible parent handling a recalcitrant child.

'I think that was just as well,' Iseult says. 'Physical work is not good for the mind. I don't believe in it, though once I did.'

'Miss Gonne has been nursing,' Willie announces. 'At a military hospital in Normandy.'

Willie is beginning to irritate her with his Miss Gonne this, Miss Gonne that, all evening. She is grateful to him for having these dinners and bringing her about London and including her in these conversations about poetry and art as if she were an equal. But he claims her with a possessiveness that chafes.

'*Nursing*,' says Dorothy, as if Iseult had been in the front line of combat. 'Was that too dreadful?'

'It gives one a dangerous feeling of activity and energy, but it's only an illusion, for it requires no real effort of will. While I was there, I lived just like a machine.'

'With no time to work,' Willie says, meaning no time to write.

'No time even to wonder. No desire to.'

'Or read, me supposums,' says Ezra, dropping a slice of potato in under his moustache with his fingers.

'No. It is an – how do you say? – *abrutisement* life that leaves no room for the intellect. I kept a copy of the *Iliad* close, though was almost always too distracted to read it.'

'Miss Gonne has an admiration that borders on adoration for the *Iliad*. For all the gods of antique Greece and Rome.'

'Have you, b'God?' asked Ezra, looking her over anew.

'For all that is pagan,' she admits. 'When in Italy, I kept thinking that the country of Scipio and Caesar should have more respect for their gods instead of celebrating so heartily the religion that destroyed their culture.'

'But this fellow led me to think you a papist. He has been praising the French Catholics and persuaded me it was your influence.'

'Yes, Catholicism is my faith, and when I pray it is in front of a crucifix. My interest in the gods of antiquity is intellectual, but I believe we should have perfect beauty if we could only unite the ideal pagan and ideal Christian –'

Iseult runs out of words, the attention of the two men and the sound of her own voice making her suddenly shy. Six eyes rest upon her as she closes her knife and fork together on her plate, unable to finish. Torment. When she dares to look up, she finds Willie is beaming at her from across the table, as if she were a poem he had just completed. From the side of her eye she sees that Ezra is looking not at her but at her plate. He leans across, picks up the rind of meat she left over and pops it in his mouth with a wink.

She smiles, despite herself, at his antics, then remembers her mother's teaching that good manners mean ensuring nobody feels left out of a conversation. Men are easy to please but women, apart from Thora, are always a challenge. 'Which poets do you like to read, Mrs Pound?' she asks.

'I rarely read poetry,' Dorothy says. 'I don't really care for it.'

Can this be true? Or is it part of the baiting that goes on between a husband and a wife? She has a profile that is clear and detached and utterly lovely, yet she is part of the great movement against beauty that seems to have gripped the arts in England. The consequence of the war, perhaps? But if art does not add to the beauty of the world, is it art at all? She and Willie have spent much time since her arrival debating this question.

Ezra throws his wife another look like a gunshot, then he is off again, this time outlining the connections between the writings of the Romans and present-day Europeans. 'The Roman poets are the only ones we know who had approximately the same problems we have: the metropolis, the imperial posts in all corners of the world and so on. From them we can learn, if only we wake from our MASS DOZE, and . . .'

Dorothy looks at the clock above the mantel and suppresses

a yawn. Iseult looks out of Willie's window at the smoke of a summer cloud drifting high. In another few months, the sky will thicken again, but for now it is light and wispy and clear.

47

Chekhov says that writers lie most often at the beginnings and endings of their stories, but where I am most tempted to fictionalize, to improve and alter, is here, right in the middle. Good stories demand reverses and turnabouts, so I should like to be able to say that after our trip to Ireland Star's bad behaviour improved. That our moment of connection as we fled my father's house heralded a new way of being together.

Too bad for narrative twists. The turbulence and tribulations continued, and – as it is impossible to stand still in life – because it wasn't getting better, it was getting worse. I was reminded of how it was when she was a small child, of the way in which I'd just get on top of one phase as she was already in the act of launching herself on to another. Trotting behind her, all I could do was note the latest barrier to be breached. No longer out till 3 a.m. in the morning but now five or, sometimes, not home at all. No longer just refusing to pick up her things or help out in the house but calling me names for daring to ask. No longer finding 'Cow!' or 'Idiot!' released her ire but moving on to 'Bitch!' and 'Retard!' and 'Fuck off'. It was the drink and drugs talking, I knew that, but it didn't make it any easier to hear.

You shouldn't stand for it, people said. No child of mine would speak to me like that. It's disgraceful. I knew it was disgraceful, I tried not to let her get away with it, but it was what I got anyway. Reason, sanctions, kindness, punishment: none of it made any difference to Star if she decided to play the tyrant. Spoilt, I was told. A bully. Selfish. And yes, all of that was true, but it was not the whole truth. Other words described what lay beneath. Lost. Troubled. Lonely. Confused.

I saw less and less of her, as she spent more and more nights with friends. Along with worries about her welfare, there were financial burdens. Soon – how had it come round so *fast*? – she was going to start college. (If she managed to get a place; she was a bright girl but her grades were slipping.) College or work, soon she was going to be launching herself upon adult life. Leaving home and living without me. The thought crammed me with fear. I was so uncertain of her ability to cope – no, that's wrong, so certain of her *in*ability to cope – that I had to visit a doctor and get chemicals to put in my own body each night, so I could sleep.

For some reason my daughter had a very fractured sense of self. She felt the need to armour herself with fat and belligerence to get through life. But why? Yes, she'd grown up in 'a broken home', but it wasn't as broken as some of the ones I'd seen with the Daddy still firmly *in situ*.

'You're barking up the wrong tree,' said Marsha one night over a late-night glass of wine. 'She's had nothing but love in this house. It's our toxic, sexist, over-sexed society. Girls are falling apart all over the place.'

'But is that not our fault too?'

'Come off it, Izzy. You don't believe that.'

'We're the ones who yanked off our tops and danced around maypoles in the People's Park. *Drop the hypocrisy*, we had cried. *Make love not war. Let it blossom, let it flow.* Oh, innocent us.'

'No way, Izzy. It was the corporates.'

'Huh? The corporates?'

'Yeah, their most successful takeover bid, *ever*. They are the ones who cheapened and degraded sex, not us. They are the ones taking porn mainstream, moving it out of fantasy land and turning it into a paradigm for all women.'

'Paradigm. Jeez, Marsha, this isn't women's studies class.'

'You think of a better word, then. You know I don't have a problem with porn, per se. To me, the sexism there doesn't seem any worse than the sexism anywhere else. And too many anti-porn feminists are prudes or wimps. But porn's been –'

'I know she's doing things she's going to regret,' I said, trying to bring the conversation back to Star.

'Of course she is, poor love. And telling herself she's finding freedom all the while.'

'Oh, Marsha.'

'I know. It's terrible. People who work with child abusers call it "grooming". Using porn to convince their victims what they want to do is dandy-o. Well, that's what our society is doing to girls. No two kids come together now without a woman-despising blueprint of sex already in their heads. Star is a victim of that. Don't tell me she isn't.'

Could this be right?

'And that girlfriend of hers too.'

'Veno?'

Marsha nodded vehemently. 'She looks like Bambi Woods.'

'Who?'

'You know, *Debbie Does Dallas*.'

'No, I don't know,' I said. 'And, frankly, my dear, I'm shocked that you do.'

I knew what she meant about Veno though. She had kept her pugilist-punk name but had adopted a completely new look – peroxide hair and false eyelashes, low-cut tops and push-up bras, polished nails and fucked-up eyes. In the late 1970s a girl like that was unusual. Now you see them everywhere.

Marsha was still talking. 'Don't tell me it's any coincidence that this is emerging in the wake of the women's movement. It's like the woman haters are saying, "You want out of the kitchen? Okay, honey, get into the bedroom, then. Here, look at this magazine, at this TV show, at this music video. This is all you're good for."'

'Oh, Marsha.'

'It's true, Izzy. And it's damaging us all, men as well as women.'

'Marsha, *please*.'

'Sorry, I'm ranting. I know. But I hate to see you beating

yourself up about poor Star when you've done everything – *everything* – a mother could do.'

Summer brought flaming hoops of fire to the hills. On a day of scourging heat we heard that Star had, despite my fears, secured herself a place at UCLA.

I sat on her bed watching her do her final packing. She was scared, I was scared, and neither of us was admitting to it. *Snap, snap*: she closed the clasps on her suitcase and looked about her. Clothes in piles, all over the floor and on every free surface. Another fight I'd relinquished.

'Don't change anything while I'm gone,' she said.

'I'll have to clean it.'

'You're not to.'

'Star, if I don't, we'll have vermin.' I picked up a broken cookie from the floor and a glass circled with stale milk. 'You're not supposed to eat up here, remember?'

'Jesus, Mom, can't you drop the nagging, like, *ever*? Even when I'm just about to leave home?'

'I may have to do some fumigation, that's all I'm saying. But I'll keep it to a minimum. You're right, let's not fight.'

'Only if you promise not to throw anything out.'

'Nothing. I promise. Pinky swear.'

We picked up a suitcase each. At the door, I put my arms around her. One thing about loving a fat person, they're nice to hug. I sank into her and of course broke the vow I'd made and started to cry.

'Mom, don't.'

'I won't.' I let her go, blew my nose. 'I'll miss you, darling. Write me as soon as you land.'

'What will you miss – cleaning up the mess?'

'Star, honey, come on now. You know I don't know what I'll . . .' The sentence wilted into the shrug of her shoulders and her turn towards the door.

Had she overheard what I had shared with Marsha the night

before: that I looked forward to coming home in the evening to peace and tranquillity after work, instead of another unnecessary drama? That I might miss her less when she was away than I had for the past years while she was right there under my roof? Was she senstive because she knew that I was only in part, really in quite a small part, crying for what was ahead and mainly for the loss of all we'd already suffered, all those years we would never get back?

I followed her out to where she was waiting beside the passenger door of the car. The morning sun was climbing, shining at us through the tree in Mr Connors's front yard, throwing our shadows in front of us, Star's all spiky-headed and bulky, serrated along the leafy ground.

Calling all mothers! Some advice for you. If you have a little girl, don't be the kind of mother who says: all I want is for her to be happy. No, no, no. Want her to be top of her class. Want her to become chairman of the board. Want her to marry a millionaire. Want something negotiable, so she has room to fail you. If all you want is for her to be happy, that's all she can use to separate from you when the time to separate comes.

The doctor said that I had to turn my attention from Star's life to my own. Worry might be the mother's lot, but it was not to be indulged, and my fretting was bad for us both. With the help of her little pills, I resolved to take myself in hand.

Like Iseult, I had decided that my life should be devoted to a noble end, though at thirty-six I was considerably older when I made that decision and so in more of a hurry about it. My noble end would be writing. 'Words alone are certain good,' as my favourite poet had put it, but of course woman could not live on words alone. I still needed a day job, and now I had one I enjoyed. Weary of working for others, Marsha and I took a leap into business and opened a little coffee house down near the boardwalk called Better World Café.

The name, the concept and the start-up capital came from Marsha, and I brought the catering experience. The café would be a hub, a place from where we would encourage what she called 'meaningful and creative connections' as well as good food. Our coffee would be imported directly from a non-profit project run by a friend of hers in Kenya. Our food would be mostly vegetarian, without announcing itself so. Our staff would be valued with a share of our profits. Our tables would be dressed in (recycled) paper tablecloths with a big light-bulb outline in the middle labelled 'Big Thoughts and Ideas' to write within. Our napkins would be smaller versions of the same, labelled 'Neat Thoughts and Ideas'.

We'd provide coloured pens and pencils and cover our walls with thought-provoking and inspiring pictures and quotes. We'd also provide, twice a month, a cultural event: a poetry reading, or music, or storytelling . . . 'The great thing about being on the boardwalk,' she enthused, 'is that we won't just attract the converted. People will drop in, all unknowing, for a cup of coffee and leave with a little more than that.'

I look back now on our audacity and smile. We hadn't a clue what we were getting ourselves into. Over that first year, we had so many crises, especially with staff, but eventually we settled down with Stella and Toni on the floor supporting me, and Mercedes and Laine in the kitchen, helping Marsha turn out her delicious breads and cookies and cakes and soups and salads.

Now it's not the crises I remember but the accomplishments and the daily small sensations, sometimes so small as to seem almost like nothing. The smell of Marsha's mushroom soup (my favourite) bubbling in the urn. The glint of a good Merlot in one of our lovely glasses. The sound of our customers talking and laughing, in what was for many of them the happiest hour of their day. Small moments that I used to rest in, that helped me believe that yes, everything would be fine, everything was fine already, before being thrown again by a brainwave flitting up to the surface, cutting through my peace with worries about Star and why things were the way they were.

Stop, I would admonish myself. Return to the sunlit murmur of now, the clink of two glasses, the froth on a coffee mug, the shine of dressing on the salad you're serving . . . Beware the voice in your head. Don't live by it. Be careful. Pick up that finished plate. Smile at Stella. Tidy up the newspapers into the rack. There, that's better.

We only seem to be planted in time. Wherever you are now, stop what you're doing and look around. Observe those people not so far away. No matter how intact and how present they seem, just behind the face, there's a fissure, a separation filled with the crackle and fizz of regretted pasts and anticipated futures.

48

The French train crawls slower even than the one to Dover. At first Iseult hadn't minded the pace, the stops and starts, the delays and waitings in line. The carriage is comfortable, and she and Willie have it to themselves, allowing them to doze between the long strings of conversation they have been enjoying since leaving Euston at 7 a.m. yesterday. When younger, she was intimidated by his curiously mannered speech. Then, for a time, irritated. Now she knows that the kind of chant in which he talks is a way of seeming. It allows him space to live in this unforgiving world.

She is noticing other things about him. His trick of tossing back his head, as though to shake his hair back from his eyes. How pale his face is beneath the black hair. How the dreamy look in his eyes is attributable to nothing more esoteric than short-sightedness peering through pince-nez. How his feet are too big but his hands quite fine.

They are talking of Ezra and Dorothy. 'I liked them so much more than Lady Ottoline and that set,' she says.

'You know Dorothy is the daughter of one of my dearest friends?'

'Mrs Shakespear. Yes, I met her with you. She is very beautiful, is she not?'

'The daughter or the mother?'

'Both. But I meant Dorothy.'

'Her face appears to be made from Dresden china. I look at her in perpetual wonder, it is so hard to believe she is real, yet she spends all her daylight hours drawing the most monstrous pictures. It is the same with Ezra. Is it not mysterious that a man so distinguished in his poems should in real life be so uncouth, so jarring?'

'He holds a view of the writer as a besieged minority,' she says.

'Oppressed and victimized by false morality all around.'

'Which is forgivable if he is a bad poet and excusable if a good one. Which is he, Willie?'

'I think he *will* be great, but that the very keenness of his intellect will make his apprenticeship a long one. And he does nothing to help himself. He is so violently American.'

'I think he is not made for compromise.'

'London has even less time for the Americans than for the Irish. It is quite wonderful how people hate him.'

'But not you?'

'No, he amuses me vastly. And, as a poet, he is full of the Middle Ages and helps me get back to the definite and concrete, away from modern abstractions.'

'He has taught you to fence, Dorothy tells me.'

'Indeed. I need something to keep this under control.' He pats the swelling paunch that underlies his new tweed waistcoat. 'And he appreciates you, my dear, which confirms my faith in his taste. He told me you were worthy of a troubadour's romance.'

Iseult casts up her eyes and folds her hands together under her chin, female submissiveness in the medieval model.

He laughs, a deep rumble, with lips closed. 'Ezra does not take to many people. But of course he has a connoisseur's eye for beauty.'

She inclines her head, acknowledging the compliment. Or is he giving her a warning?

'It is not just he, as you know. I told you about Lady Cunard saying she had never in her life seen such a complexion. And Rothenstein so keen to do your portrait —'

'Have a care, Willie. With all your talk of Lady This and Lady That, you are beginning to sound like Cousin May.'

'You know if you lived in London you would be a reigning beauty in no time.'

'Ugh. Please, desist.'

417

'You should not be so dismissive. What do we writers labour for except to create a thing of beauty?'

'Willie, would you really want me to become the type who makes a to-do over swallowing a miserable petit four when it would be much simpler to swallow the whole plateful?'

He chuckles again.

'I did try, you know, for a little time. Following Thora, I set myself the task of leading the carefree and gay life of a young female snob who thinks only of being fashionable. I paraded down the street in a costume with a very tight skirt in which I could hardly walk and a big white jabot to complete the effect. But, having spent half the day doing my nails, and an infinite amount of time trying new ways of doing my hair, the resistant old beast that is Time still refused to be killed.'

'Because you were engaged in the wrong activities for you.'

'So thought I. I then set myself to read books that would perhaps make me blush – *The Double Mistress* and others of that kind. For five days this killed time better than the occupation of a little female snob, and I was beginning to imagine some joy in vice, but then, on the fifth evening, lifting my eyes from my sordid book, I saw a picture of Saint John looking down at me. His mysterious smile gave me to understand that virtue is more beautiful than vice.'

'These do seem more appropriate thoughts for a circumspect young lady.'

The door slides open. It is the ticket collector, clicking his punch and seeking tickets and travel documents to check. Since they left, they have had to endure a succession of wartime red tape, first at London Bridge, then Dover, then Le Havre, and here, once again, Iseult is submitted to a litany of questions. After much squinting scrutiny and flipping of pages, the guard takes the documents away.

'What is he doing with your papers?'

She shrugs. 'Not having a father's name on my passport makes them suspicious.'

'Do you mind not having a name?'

'No. I often think how much most girls would mind. I only mind when it is inconvenient like this.'

'Can you not take your father's name?'

'I should not wish to. He is impossible, Willie. Quite *impossible*. I do not know if you heard that Henri, my half-brother, was killed at Ypres?'

'I had not. I am sorry . . .'

She shakes her head. 'Not for me, we were not close. But the news made me feel I should go to see Loup.'

'Loup?'

'My father. Le Loup, the Wolf.'

Willie's eyes widen. 'Gracious . . .'

'Moura must have explained him to you?'

'Not rea– He was rather a painful subject between us.'

'He is a painful subject to us all. When I arrived at his apartment, he was sitting by the fire staring into the flames, tears pouring down his face. I felt such a pity and flood of affection for him that I rushed to his side. "So you know?" he said, and I answered that Moura had told me. Then he said: "I thought you would disapprove," which puzzled me, but I thought that perhaps he felt the guilt old men must feel towards the young being sent out to fight. "We spend so casually the gifts of the gods while we have them," I said, which made him weep even more copiously. "So all of Paris knows," he said, which again I thought peculiar. "All of Paris suffers," I said. "Nothing is as it was." He replied: "You are right, *ma belle* Iseult. Our Belle Epoch is over." Then he started to speak of some mademoiselle and of how he should not have minded so if she had moved on to a younger man but to have chosen that oaf, who must be close on one hundred . . . And so on until I knew we were not speaking of the same sorrow.'

'Oh dear.'

'I said, "I came because of Henri" – which made him ashamed.'

'I should think.'

'He really is quite pathetic.'

'Like all of us who are growing old, he must watch a world managed by other men, men who no longer stop when he passes in the street. He thought he would leave his mark, but instead, the world has marked him. It is called age, my dear, and it will come to you too.'

She sighs and stretches out her legs. 'Indeed you are probably right. And Loup at least devoted himself to what he believed in. Perhaps he did not make a great task of it, but it looks like I am going to utterly waste mine in sordid futility.'

'Come now, perhaps while I am in France, we can set out a schedule of work for you.'

'Willie, it is so kind of you to take such trouble on my poor behalf.'

'It would be my pleasure. Moura tells me what you write is unusual and very beautiful, very living and sincere.'

'But no doubt complained that they were only fragments, all unfinished. And she is right. I never have the will to finish anything. I long to do something big with my life, to devote it to an idea, to an art, to a god, yet the days pass and what I have done is nothing – through sheer weakness of mind. The tick-tock of the clock seems to say to me, "You are twenty-one years old. God who created you did not put you in the world in order to contemplate whether you should have been. Wake up. Work." Yet still I idle.'

'But why? That is the question you must answer.'

'In France we call it *le cafard*.' She makes her hand crawl across her lap like a giant insect. 'The cockroach.'

'You have a talent, my dear, and to flex it will drive away the devils of despair. Work has saved me many times.'

She nods. 'My brain has got very rusty from lack of use, but I would do my best to work on any line you traced me. Moura says only imbeciles and lunatics get bored in this wonderful world, which has so much work to be done.'

He puts aside the book he is holding. 'I should perhaps tell you . . . Your mother has been much in my mind of late.'

'Are you going to propose to her again?'

He starts. He does not realize how transparent he is.

'Do you think she would accept me if I did?'

'I cannot know this, Willie.'

'I have been writing my memoirs, and they have prompted many memories of the past. And this is occurring at a time when Moura has been widowed and by a fateful event that seems a culmination of our long-ago work together. I am coming to think of her as, in a sense, Ireland itself. A summing-up in one mind of all that was best in the romantic Ireland of my youth. It may be that there is more work for us to do together.'

Iseult looks out. The countryside is rain drenched. This June has been uncommonly wet and cold, but one cannot complain, for as soon as the grumble is made, one's thoughts or those of one's companion turn to seeping uniforms in a trench, or marching boots churning up mud.

'However,' he continues, though she wishes now she had not asked, 'I have decided that I can make her an offer only if she gives up politics.'

'Willie, you must know that is not a proposal at all. Not to Moura.'

'I would gladly see her work at charity, such as her movement for feeding the children or any such.'

'She would like to work for peace, she says, though she is not sure how. Her thoughts for the moment are mostly for the Irish in prison. Prisoners of war, she calls them.'

'I include the amnesty work. Any work directly on behalf of the rebels would be a problem.'

'Then perhaps it might be wiser to wait, Willie. I don't know why you are so keen to marry. Marriage is so revoltingly down to earth.'

'There is an astrological imperative.'

'An astrological imperative. Ooooh.' She squints her eyes like a bug to tease him. 'Explain, pray.'

'I have a poor horoscope for marriage,' he explains, 'but a weekend next year has a stabilizing pattern. Transiting Saturn is conjuncting Mars in the Seventh House of Marriage while trining both my Neptune and transit of Venus. This forms a Grand Trine in Fire, a most beneficient aspect which would give me discipline and inspiration for my poetry. This pattern is spiritually augmented by transiting Jupiter opposite –'

'Stop, Willie. Speak English, I beg you.'

'In summary: marriage next autumn would bring me stability, luck, philosophical harmony and creative inspiration, as against poor indicators for any other time. And in case I was to be in any doubt of this, another predictive system is equally affirmative.'

His right hand is gravely raised, as if in benediction, such as Hector might have given in Troy. She understands how, to some people, he is a drawing-room act. The demonic mage.

'Autumn 1917, thus, is my time for matrimony. If Moura is to refuse me now, I shall need time to find another potential bride.'

Iseult nods slowly.

The train rolls on, cutting through the sky that is everywhere reflected in furrow-floods and puddles, as far as the eye can see.

49

Summer 1916 is the summer of the Allied warlords' 'great offensive'. A massive onslaught to break through German lines on the Western, Eastern and Italian fronts and put a finish to this increasingly horrific war. To the generals and marshals casting clay soldiers into battle on the sands table, the strategy is well conceived. Foolproof, according to more than one. That is their sincere hope, because if they are wrong then this war is truly out of their control.

In the last week of June, the campaign commenced: a ceaseless artillery bombardment of German positions along a five-mile stretch. Many of the shells were faulty and failed to explode, but it made little difference to the Germans, one way or the other, for their fortifications and subterranean tunnels had been designed to provide protection against just such attacks. In seven days, more than one and a half million shells were fired, to little avail. So now men must be ordered to follow the bombardment across No Man's Land to take out German defences.

Thus it is that on 1 July, the day that Willie Yeats proffers his final proposal of marriage to Maud Gonne, my father – long discharged from his ward – is summoned by a whistle out of his trench, to march across open grass, rifle cocked. He knows as he climbs up and over that he is part of a line that includes Irish, English, Scots and Welsh, Australians, New Zealanders, Africans, Indians and Canadians, all faithfully or resentfully plunging across similar acres. Mule was his family's name for him, and it stands to him now, as he leaps out and roars forward, straight into the worst the Germans can do.

Rat-a-tat-tat. Clusters of hot bullets burst into shins and knees and thighs and hips and stomachs and chests and necks and cheeks and eyes and brains and hearts all round him. Men fall beside him and before him and behind him, urged on by their captain, 'Come on, lads. We'll be all right. Come on, then.' Men are mangled by bullets and bombs, some sent up by their own side, missiles that fall short or long. The explosions tear at the earth and the skies, as if trying to bring down the heavens. Men are killed instantly but cleanly, by concussion or blown apart by direct hit or sliced into segments, as if by an evil butcher. Somehow, through it all, he is missed.

Forward he marches until given the order to retreat, then back across a carpet of the dead, their flesh plucking at his boots, their smell thick at the back of his throat, like a foul medicine he'll never be able to swallow. The next day they start it over again, and the next and the next.

Day after day, fired by rum and adrenalin and shouts from his captain, he hurls himself over the top, offering his body, the only thing he owns, to be hacked like a blade of grass. Day after day, on and on, for months, knowing it is happening in all the other regiments too, boring place names on to the map with blood. Ypres. The Somme. Salonika. Suvla Bay.

My father doesn't remember. He doesn't remember. Between the moment of flinging himself forward to the moment of his – always panting – return to the trench, only fragments stay with him. Floating limbs, hands, feet, arms or legs torn away. Helmets and gas masks, forsaken. Rats, which always make away first with the softest tissue of the dead, the eyes and lips. Heads, with exposed teeth grinning beneath the hollowed-out sockets of evacuated eyes.

He finds God in the killing fields. A harsh disciplinarian God, the One that's fashionable at that time. A God who believes in discipline, like a sergeant major or head corporal, who holds out no promises of rewards in this life but only of bliss in the next, for those who do their duty. Who do what is right.

All that's in his journal now is prayer to this new God. That when his time comes, it will be in the form of a bullet somewhere vital. Heart or head, please. Not dismemberment. Not pulping. Please, God.

He does not pray to be spared. He expects now to die.

Then a lucky injury. His leg is broken by a piece of shrapnel, and he waits out the rest of the summer in a hospital bed. Through all this activity, the Allied Front has slid only five miles forward on its wave of blood.

He comes to know that war is a thing with its own life, living off him and the officers and the newsmen and the politicians and the women too, with their goading and cheering and flag waving. He remembers Maud Gonne and looks back through his pages to see what it was she said in the hospital, about the Irish soldiers' dancing, and he writes it out again, a second time, without being sure why.

If he remembers Maud Gonne's daughter, it's not something he notes. Not at this time.

In Colleville, they can hear the guns but they do their best to put them out of mind. Maud is delighted to have them back and grateful to Willie for chaperoning Iseult to safety. They take tea together, the three of them with Bichon, who Iseult swears has grown two inches since she left. She has brought him a rubber mouse with which he tries to torture Minnaloushe, but the cat refuses. 'Dear Minna,' Iseult laughs. 'What a beautiful look of disdain. One is so adored by one's dogs that it is good for the soul to have cats.'

After tea, Willie invites Maud to take a walk by the seashore. If Moura knows his intentions, she gives no sign.

Iseult longs to be out in the air herself. It is blustery this evening, and the sea is streaked with light and dark shades of green, like that Connemara marble that Moura is so fond of. It has been so long since she breathed free. London's acres of brick and concrete and smoke are so depressingly vast.

She will go out, but in the opposite direction: up over the

425

cliff-face and down into the cove, where she will not meet them, where she can be alone and breathe in rhythm with the waves. First, she will just go upstairs and watch a moment from her bedroom window.

She snatches Minnaloushe up into her arms as she goes, the cat squealing a startled miaow. By the time she gets up, they are already a way along the sands. She lights a cigarette and settles Minnaloushe, purring, along her arm. Moura wears full-length widow's weeds, black veil fluttering over the collar of an ankle-length coat. She has declared her intention now to wear black from top to toe for the rest of her life. As a clothing decision it is convenient, she says, making shopping easy, doing away with time-wasting preparations and decisions in the mornings. As symbol too it is effective. Black will keep her husband's martyrdom in people's minds. And Ireland, of course. She mourns for Ireland.

Iseult watches them and watches on, stroking Minnaloushe and blowing smoke against her fur as they walk into the distance, growing smaller with each stride.

'Come in. Oh, it is you, *ma belle*. Is everything all right?'

'May I borrow your hairbrush, Moura? It appears I left mine behind in London.'

'Of course.'

Iseult picks up the brush but, instead of leaving, she begins to stroke her hair while looking at herself in her mother's mirror. 'Did you and Unc . . . Willie have a nice walk?' she asks.

'It was a little sad. We talked about all our friends who have been imprisoned or executed. Willie marvelled at how Con Markiewicz burst into tears when told that her death sentence had been commuted to life imprisonment. But of course she did. What else would she do?'

'What did he say about our getting to Dublin?'

'He doesn't think there is much hope of it. He will help us, though. Thank you for fetching him here, my dear.'

'He needed no persuasion.'

'No, he wouldn't. He is the dearest friend when one is in need.'

'I believe,' Iseult says, turning around, 'he still wants to be more than a friend.'

'He told you? But of course he did. Poor Willie, he cannot keep a thought to himself. When we were young, in Dublin together, he was always telling me things in the greatest secrecy that I later found he had told to countless others, all sworn to silence.'

Iseult comes across to sit on the bed. 'I cannot imagine having Willie for a father. Now that I know him, he seems more like one my own age, or younger.'

'I know. I have always felt ten years older than him.'

'So you refused him again?'

'Of course. You hardly expected I should say yes?'

'Not once he told me he was making his offer on the condition that you would give up politics.'

Moura snorts. 'His English friends in London and his Unionist friends – especially Lady Gregory – have twisted his thinking. Willie so loves the lords and ladies.'

'He would like a child, he says. Did you read that poem of his addressed to his ancestors?'

'No, he is going to give me a number of poems to-morrow. But I hardly think he expects me to give him a child. Not even Willie could be as ignorant of female biology as that, surely?'

They meet each other's eyes fully for the first time in months – or is it years? – and laugh.

'Did he explain to you about his astrological deadline?'

'This is not really nice of us.' Iseult's hand is guiltily over her mouth. 'Poor Willie. I think he is lonely, Moura.'

'Perhaps then I shall change my mind tomorrow and say yes after all. Just to frighten him as he deserves.'

'Moura!'

427

'He is not sincere, Iseult. His proposal was *comme d'habitude*. No, Willie will never marry.'

'Do you really believe so?'

'I do. He has spent a lifetime making poetry out of what he likes to call his loneliness and unhappiness. He will never propose to anyone likely to say yes.'

Next day, Maud and Willie sit on the terrace overlooking the sea, top clothes discarded. The sun has finally emerged, tipping the temperatures up, and between the two old friends the heat is also rising.

'Those who die for Ireland are sacred,' Maud says, leaning up out of her deck chair to make her point. 'And those who enter eternity by the great door of sacrifice atone for all. Are you listening, Willie?'

'Yes,' he murmurs, pretending to be sleepy. He began by offering his views, but Maud turns opinion to tyranny.

'You do not seem to realize that this is the moment we worked for all those years ago. The great sacrifice made by the men and women of the Rising has raised the Irish cause again to a position of tragic dignity.'

Willie stretches out his long legs. 'It is not so long since you described such work as blinkers of hate.'

'That was before the Rising. How can anyone remain unmoved by what is happening in Ireland? Don't you understand? They have done more with this one action than you and I would have achieved in decades.'

'Every word you say makes it clearer. If you go back to Dublin, you shall have no peace in your life.'

'You may be right, but it would be cowardly not to. I dread how changed it will be. So many that I loved are dead and gone and so much dissension is building there but I have no choice. I must be there to do whatever needs to be done. And Seaghán must be brought up in Ireland. That is his destiny.'

'And Iseult?'

428

'Oh, Iseult. She is such a worry, destroying her health by endless smoking and, with it all, so unhappy and bored. I fear that is how she will be, wheresoever we live, and certainly she has no tie to France of any importance. No, we shall return to Ireland. At the very least I can make sure that the school meals bill, which took three years' work to win from the government, does not remain a dead letter. School meals will be hideously wanted this winter.'

The thought of that good work eases her, and she lies back into her easy chair. After long silence, she says: 'Were you not very much relieved that I refused you yesterday?'

'Hmmmm.'

'Is that yes or no?' She goes on without waiting for his reply: 'Though I dare say it might be better for the children if we were to marry. Iseult spent all yesterday afternoon and again this morning writing, instead of floating by the seashore. You are the only person who seems able to get her *moving*.'

'I have set her some small tasks.'

'And it would be very fine for Seaghán to have *two* illustrious fathers.'

She does not speak of those in Dublin who already believe that Iseult is his daughter. Now they are to live there, marriage to him would have the great advantage of stopping their tongues.

'But alas no.' She shakes her head regretfully and sighs. 'I do not think it would work.'

'There might be another way,' Willie says.

'Another way to what?'

'To offer my protection to Iseult and Seaghán.'

Something in his voice makes her sit back up again to look at him. He is lying with his face up to the sun, closed of eye and devoid of expression. Yet he is up to something, something that makes him sheepish. 'Go on, Willie.'

'I could ask Iseult to marry me instead.'

A laugh bursts forth from her, a loud cackle that sounds too raucous, even to her own ears.

His eyes are still closed.

She stops her laugh. 'You are serious?'

'It may not be possible but would it not be a fitting outcome?'

She opens her mouth as if to say something, closes it again.

'You and I should be bonded in the outer world as in the inner. Not in the way we once imagined but . . .'

She is shaking her head, but he cannot see that.

'I should of course not do this if it were to give you any offence.'

'Offence?' She laughs again, more naturally this time. 'No, Willie, it does not give me *offence*. You may ask her if you wish, but I hardly think –'

'Thank you, Maud.'

'You know, you are thinking dangerously much about a wife. Are you sure? Think how she would disarrange your life and your things.'

Still he does not open his eyes to her. 'I may not ask her at all. But I am pleased –' and here he smiles behind his closed face – 'to have your blessing.'

50

'Imagine,' Iseult says to Willie. 'A beautiful woman you would be in love with. Her frowns would make you sad, and when she smiled you would feel like smiling too, you would be keen on the sound of her voice yet hardly notice what she said, and you would love more the manner of her walk than where she went. That is the way I feel towards *life*. She moves me far more by her expression, by her manner, than by what she says or does.'

They are supposed to be working. The dining-room table is covered in books. The poetry of Jammes, open at the dialogue between poet and bird; Iseult had read, and translated, it for him earlier, making them both misty-eyed. Péguy's *Le Mystère de la charité de Jeanne d'Arc*. A French–English and, for Willie, English–French dictionary. Willie is helping Iseult towards translating these works, mainly by engaging in discussion of their aesthetic value and encouraging her to keep to a schedule.

He has written to Lady Gregory explaining why, as July passes into August, he will miss his annual visit to Coole Park for the first time in nineteen years. He stays on in Normandy for Iseult's sake, he writes. His feelings towards her are not love or desire but the kindness and affection natural to his years.

Lady Gregory's reply, brisk and pointed as always, refused this interpretation and insisted on reading his decision romantically. Yet it is true that Iseult has need of him.

This morning he has allowed himself once again to become distracted from the work, and they have retired to the easy chairs, one opposite the other, where they discuss the ongoing, intractable problem of her unhappiness. 'To look at you dancing on the shore at the edge of the sea,' he says, 'or coming in with your arms full of flowers, I would think you the most joyous of creatures. It is only as I get to know you better that I realize you are not joyous, that you have this blinding and, might I say, most inaccurate sense of failure.'

'It makes me feel my life is already as good as over.'

'Come, my dear, have we not agreed that bringing the French Catholic writers to English is valuable work?' He waves his arm towards the desk. 'The thought of you civilizing Dublin almost reconciles me to Moura's scheme of taking you all to Ireland.'

'It is so kind of you to take an interest in my work and to worry yourself as to whether I am going to waste sordidly my life in futility or make a great test of it.'

'But?'

'But . . . I find that most thoughts end for me now in a point of interrogation. And then, soon after, a yawn.'

She strokes Minnaloushe, who purrs contentedly on her lap. The cat usually snoozes under the table while they work and is always pleased by the extra attention she wins when they are diverted.

Willie faces the window and in the darkening evening light he sees himself and the back of her head reflected in the glass like a tableau. Beauty, with head tilted, smoking a cigarette. Beast with white hair and high, wrinkled forehead, looking admiringly and pityingly on. The montage set off by the spines of books – along the shelves and stacked upon tables and chairs and floor.

'You kill yourself with self-analysis, my dear. You make everything food for self-accusation. These metaphysical sins of yours – not enough love for God, for others, and so on – have you ever thought that you might be mistaken? That it is the consequence only of silly, oversubtle thought?'

'Yes,' Iseult pronounces, stroking the cat. 'I know there is no poetry in it, no bitterness or sadness even; just a dull knowledge that I will never achieve anything. I have come to know that I am not reliable to others, nor even to myself. I don't think it is possible to realize anything more disheartening than that.'

She shifts in the chair to reach for another cigarette, and the cat jumps to the floor.

'It is the peril of sensitive youth. I too made myself suffer to illness with self-analysis.'

The changed timbre to his voice makes her look up, and their eyes meet with a jolt, like walking into a clear pane of glass.

'I hear a voice always,' she whispers. 'Saying "worthless, worthless, worthless".'

This is it. This is their moment. The deepest moment of William Butler Yeats's love life, outside of his long infatuation for Maud, which carried within it much of the same emotions. Indeed for him, it is the same emotion, replayed over. None of the many other women who came before or after ever touch him again as he is touched this day in Colleville, as he was touched by Maud long ago. With the others, love was a matter of receiving, of taking what the latest beautiful, sophisticated, intelligent, complex woman had to offer. With Maud, and now with Iseult, he is stirred to an emotional giving that he never manages for anybody else. Pity is mingled within it and so is pity's opposite – his highest regard.

'Oh, my dear.' He moves toward her, removes the cigarette from between her fingers, cups her hands in his. 'When I was younger and tortured myself with such thoughts, Lady Gregory offered me a formula. If you do not love so and so enough, do something for them, sacrifice something, and you will love them. You might try it.'

She nods, biting down on a trembling lower lip.

'You must find a way out of this unhappiness, Iseult. You are so very young and –'

'Please, Willie, stop saying youth and young every half-minute.'

'I say it only because when I am with you I regret my own age.'

'Willie.' She looks up at him with dewy, tremulous eyes. 'When I was in Dublin four years ago – the time I met Lady Gregory – I wanted to marry you. I can show you the entries in my diary. I remember your saying that you would like, if you married, to live in Bayeux, and I took it so seriously I chose the house and would imagine us in it.' She takes her hands away. 'I had that wish for two years.'

'You know you might marry me, if you would.'

'But what of your great age?'

'In exceptional cases, even thirty years' difference might not prevent happiness.'

'I have vowed to myself that I shall not marry, except for love.'

'Love takes many forms, my dear, as you will realize.'

'Ah, if only you were a young boy. I feel sure I should have loved you then.'

He takes this as an invitation to act as a young boy would. He leans forward in his chair, puts his hands on her shoulders and kisses her.

She permits it. His lips are dry, papery, and the kiss is chaste. It is she who pulls away. After she has left a seemly pause, she says: 'It is very tempting, and I am very flattered, but I think I must decline.'

'I would make you a fine life among artists and writers. You could act as my amanuensis when not engaged in your own work. You would escape this impossible life you live now.'

'I –'

'Think upon it, my dear. There is no need to rush an answer.' He stands, quick as a knife. 'I am going to leave you. You can continue with the work on Chapter 2 and I shall check it later. I have some letters to write.'

'To Lady Gregory?'

'Among others.'

'Do not tell Lady Gregory it is quite certain I am not going to marry you. For, if you do, she will not be kind to me when we move to Ireland.'

'I shall tell her that . . . that nothing is decided.'

The main work that Willie has brought to Colleville is his memoir. In the mornings, after he has sat Iseult down at what she calls that dreadful table, with two hours' work in front of her and three cigarettes doled out with a grudging hand, he works on this manuscript in his bedroom, recalling his youthful pursuit of Maud, his devotion and repeated proposals. They lunch together, often with a bird in a cage beside Maud, a white rabbit beside Seaghán, the black Persian cat at Iseult's feet and a white Japanese cock that perches on the back of the chairs while they eat. In the house also are thirty-three singing birds, the green parrot, two dogs, two guinea pigs and two rabbits.

Yet it is peaceful. Their worst anxiety is how to limit Iseult's cigarettes. In the afternoons, while Maud sketches flowers in the garden, Willie presses his affections on Iseult during their long walks together, and in the evenings he reads instalments of his memoir (which Iseult is typing for him) aloud to the household.

As I sit here working on my own memories, I am brought to wonder. Which instalments does he read aloud? Which does he give to Iseult to type? The passages in which he describes first meeting Maud? Their arguments over her revolutionary zeal? Her grief at Georges's death from meningitis? His brave description of his first experience of sexual arousal and masturbation, included so 'some young man of talent might not think as I did that my shame was mine alone'? The closing passages, with Maud's revelations of her secret life, her undisclosed children, her agonies of guilt?

Surely even for Willie, it would be a step too far to read these aloud to the Gonnes, or to have Iseult type them up?

Whatever Iseult learns about the man who wanted to marry her mother and who now wants to marry her, she is pleased to get this close to his writing. This is what Ezra said she should do, take the work of a writer she admires and examine it as a model.

As for Maud, she cares little about technique, but is much exercised by the content, objecting vehemently to his interpretation of the national movement at that time. If he does not modify it, she declares, she will have to add a political appendix to set the record straight.

51

Clearing up. Sometimes, most times, a satisfactory winding-down ritual to the working day, but, when you're tired, hard to face. At Better World Café each evening two members of staff, one front of house, one back, stayed behind to leave the place spotless for the early start next day. Marsha and I have made it a maxim not to ask them to do anything we don't do ourselves, so tonight, as we did one night in three, she and I worked together after everyone else had gone home. Mopping out the floor, dusting the shelves and ornaments and pictures, emptying the vases of old flowers, clearing out the newspaper tray . . . We ticked off the routine tasks between us without discussion, a silent minuet.

Above, the ceiling fan whirred like a song of secret loss. Marsha was about to sound me out. I knew it, she knew it, though I hadn't said anything yet about how I was feeling and all her talk so far was about takings and stock and the day's doings. But soon we would sit opposite each other at one of the tables, probably our favourite one down the back, cup of tea or glass of wine in hand, and this time it would be my turn to talk and hers to listen.

That's how I found myself talking again of loneliness and saying that one day I would love to go to Europe, to do it properly this time.

'Why don't you go now?' she said.

'I couldn't. How would you manage here?'

'We're doing okay, you know that. We could hire someone to fill in. How long would it be? Six months? A year?'

'Six months would be enough. More than enough.'

'Well, then.'

'It would bring our profits down.'

'We've plenty of profit, Izzy. What's it for, if it doesn't get us the things we want? No point in just stacking it up.'

'You're serious.'

'Why not? Star's well settled at college, now she's in her second year. Go between her vacations.'

Now that I had no excuse not to go, I had to ask myself was it really what I wanted? I searched myself. It seemed that it was.

'So long as you don't go leaving us for some sexy Frenchman.'

'*Mais, non!*' I indulged my atrocious French accent. '*Je te promets.*'

'And you have to send me a postcard from everywhere you go. I'll put them up where all the customers can see them.'

She made it sound so easy.

'Are you sure, Marsha? I can't help feeling it isn't fair.'

'It wouldn't be fair *not* to. I'm going to want to head off myself some day soon. Do it, so I can have my turn and you'll hold the fort then, for me.'

That was the clincher, as she knew it would be.

'Will you go to Ireland?'

'Oh, yes.' Sister Catherine had sent me a package, full of leads and information.

'See your father?'

'No, not this time.'

'So what, then?'

'I'd like to do it properly. No daughter, no father, no family visits, just experience the place.'

'And?'

'France too. And London. I'd love to see London properly.'

'And?'

'Marsha, stop.'

'There's something else, isn't there? Come on, Izzy, you can't fool me.'

'Maybe.'

'Your birth mother?'

438

That walloped me. 'How? *How* do you know these things?'

'Just a feeling,' she said, smiling. 'For what it's worth, I think you're doing the right thing. Nobody I know who made the search ever regretted it.'

So I told her about Sister Catherine and the string-pulling she had done to get me the details I needed. I don't know why I hadn't told her before.

'You'll see her while you're there, then.'

'Definitely. She's great.'

'And family too, your mother's sister.'

'And family too.' Yes, blood or not, the woman who raised me was my mother. Blood or not, her sister was now providing me with something my father hadn't got to give. Without my having to spell it all out, Marsha understood.

She had a gift for true friendship, that woman, for knowing what you needed and helping you to get it. In our culture, *amitié* is very undervalued compared to *amour*. I hadn't expected, in my late thirties, to make a new, true friendship, and in all my life, before or after, it never happened to me so thoroughly again. I would like to put it on paper here that Marsha has meant as much to me as any lover, even Zach, and far more than my (admittedly hopeless) husband.

Marsha is always saying, 'I love you,' to me, but I am Irish of a certain age. We don't say such things face to face, not easily. I hope I've said it enough in other ways, but, just in case I haven't, Marsha, I say it here.

My trip to Europe was a multilayered pilgrimage, and Marsha had persuaded me to take my time. My route was mapped. London. Sligo. Coole. Thoor Ballylee. Paris. Colleville. Étaples. Paris-Plage. Argelès. All the places where Maud and Willie and Iseult and my father and the rest had lived and breathed. And Dublin, where my birth mother lived with her husband.

It was during this time that I also launched myself upon another journey. Iseult's life was like a novel, everybody said

439

so, and I finally embarked upon writing it that way. Instead of telling people what happened, I'd just let them see and hear and taste and touch and feel what happened for themselves.

Just! From a series of hotel rooms, with their desks turned to face out the window, I launched myself, uncertainly, as a novelist. Dimly, I felt my way. Blindly, I took wrong turnings as I followed any hunch. Slowly, over the weeks, as I travelled around London first and then Ireland and then France, ideas and facts and summaries yielded to a world into which a reader – if they had the inclination and the concentration – might sink.

Now I revisit the scenes I wrote at the beginning. Some began with an image of something that really happened: a girl dancing by the seashore. Some began with a line. 'You would not dare be so tender to a young man.' Some with a question. 'What made Iseult [me] so unhappy?'

I go back over what I wrote, chopping words here, adding them there, and marvelling at the way in which the book knew more than I did as I followed it into being.

That was my grand tour of Europe. I spent my mornings with characters I would have liked to have met, people whose lives were fired by the pursuit of virtue and knowledge and truth. I admired them, for all their flaws, and was happy hitching my life to theirs. In the afternoons, after a short nap, I headed out at around 3 p.m. into the streets and bars and cafés, the museums and theatres and art galleries, the attractions of culture in the cities, or into the woods and seashores and mountains, the attractions of nature in the countryside.

I went to find Woburn Walk and read its blue plaque commemorating Willie. I went to look at the houses where May Bertie-Clay and Kathleen and Thora Pilcher lived. I had grown fast during my college course but I never felt such an explosion in capacity and possibility as I did in those days in Europe where I shuttled between the early twentieth century of my imagination in the mornings and the late twentieth century of my experience in the afternoons.

Every meal and every excursion, every sunrise and sunset, every art gallery and performance, every lake and tree, seemed significant. I pitied the poor tourists who could come and stand in the Tower of London or the National Portrait Gallery for only an hour before moving on. Having seen it this brief once, they'd hoard the postcard for the rest of their days. I, however, had all the days I wanted. I could return to any venue every day for a week if I wished.

Had I travelled more earlier in life, I might not have been so intense. Being alone was also part of it, the attention I had time to give from a position of solitude. I can recognize that, now that I am alone again.

Those were the ups of my trip. I had downs too. When thoughts of my failed relationships – with Brendan, with Zach, with Star – assailed me. When past and future both looked broken, and nothing seemed worth the energy it demanded. These feelings were exacerbated when I left London for Dublin.

Sister Catherine had rung my London hotel with the news that there was a funeral Mass for my birth mother's brother – my uncle – in two days. I called the airport and booked a last-minute flight.

I knew her the moment I entered the Church, knew her from my own features. She was obviously an Irishwoman but as unlike my mother or Rose as it was possible to be. Tall, well dressed, hair once the colour of my own, I imagined, now highlighted to a tasteful ash-blonde. Enough looks preserved to see she was a beauty when young.

This was not a woman to welcome disruption, you could tell that just by looking at her, by seeing how she was with the other mourners and the sympathizers. I had thought it would be straightforward enough, because I didn't expect her to turn her life upside down. My intention was simply to open a door to some communication, but, with her there in front of me, I could see she was not the type to walk through. She would have

441

been too frightened of that equally striking husband of hers finding out about her murky past. I could tell his type too from one look at his well-cut coat. Business, golf club, drinker of fine wines and fifteen-year-old whiskeys. I was sure he had no idea that I existed. I could see their whole, settled, comfortable life of antiques and art and dinner parties and bridge, the kind of life I'd never had, and I knew the last thing they would want was a human bombshell imploding in its heart.*

So I let it go. Did the rest of my business and got out of Dublin as fast as I could.

The experience unsettled me, so that I started accepting the attentions of men I was meeting. Up to then, I had been ignoring them. I knew a hotel-bar encounter was never worth the effort. The sex-to-go is too much trouble for too little reward, and the ones who want more are worse. I wasn't able to take on anybody else's loneliness. I was sodden with my own, like a sponge, and adding somebody else's would make me leak. Yet I still would catch myself searching for my lipstick, unable to face another night in another beige or grey hotel room, turning up my TV to drown out the muffles of other people's voices. People who had others to talk to, or even at. Couples and families, doing what couples and families do.

Those were the days before the internet and emails, when the price of a telephone call to the United States from Europe would have bought you a small chateau. To keep in touch with home, I wrote letters, supplemented with a weekly telephone call to Star from freezing phone booths or hotel lobbies. I was in Paris, in a phone booth in Passy, when Star told me her big news, her voice bouncing out of the telephone. 'Mom, I have to tell you. I've met someone.'

The words took hold of my insides and squeezed it. *Don't*

* Good old Mom, always projecting her feelings on to the rest of us. It was she who was scared, who cut and run, not my grandmother. By the time I got a chance to go there, she was dead.

love him, hissed the inside of my head. *You are mortgaging your life. He will hurt you.*

'That's wonderful, darling.'

'Isn't it? Oh, Mom . . .'

Normally our conversations entailed me describing what I'd seen or experienced that week, knowing the details of these places she had never seen were boring to her but that, without my babbling, the conversation would collapse.

'Well, well,' I said. 'Tell me all.'

'His name is Shando.'

'Shando?'

'Yes.'

'Mmmm. That's unusual.'

'He's a Buddhist.'

'Oh.'

'What else? He's twenty-six and . . .' (*Twenty-six?* But, my child, you're only nineteen.)

'. . . and he's a yoga teacher.' (Yoga? How could he expect to support a wife and family with *yoga*? Wife and family? What was I on about?)

'We met a good while ago, before you left for Europe, but I didn't want to say anything . . . till . . .'

'Are you' – my voice as casual as I could make it – 'seeing a lot of each other?'

Tadpoles of rain swam in wavy lines across the glass of the booth during her silence.

'I guess.'

She was sleeping with him, this 26-year-old. This father figure. Oh, Star.

This stranger was now intimate with her body, all of it, every portion. Just thinking about that – not going so far as to imagine it, I couldn't even imagine imagining it – brought on a glut of panic. My darling Star, be careful.

'I don't know what else to tell you, Mom. He's a really sweet guy.'

443

'That's wonderful, darling.' It didn't sound any more convincing the second time.

There was a silence, in which I felt like I could hear her eyebrows draw together.

'I hope he's not making you neglect your studies.'

'Mom, for goodness' sake! But listen, guess what, I've lost weight. I don't know how. He's always cooking.'

Love, my darling. Filling up that space you used to cram with food. Filling up the space that my love couldn't fill.

'Does it mean something, his name?' I ask. 'What was it again?'

'Shando. Yes, it means "New Way". He's a –'

Beep, beep, beep.

'Oh dear, honey, there are the pips. I'll call again on Saturday. Have a great time with . . . er . . . Shando. Tell him I said hi.'

'I will Mom. Thanks, Mom. I w–'

But she was gone.

I stood with the receiver in my hand, until I noticed what I was doing and put it back in its cradle. If he was putting healthy meals in front of her and making her happy, I should be pleased. I *was* pleased. And how ridiculous to be thinking of marriage, of family, of inevitable hurt. Any guy able to see beyond her body shape couldn't be all bad.

Or did it mean that he was dysfunctional too?

No.

Stop.

Star had her first boyfriend. And high time too. It was a good thing. *A good thing.* I stepped outside the phone box, into the rain. The street lamps shone at me, their orange glows diffused, a row of blurry suns. I bent my head and pressed on. I was hungry and my restaurant table for one was waiting.

52

Iseult Gonne to Thora Pilcher

Dear Little Brother Victor

*. . . between us, the Great Poet has proposed to me. Thirty years'
difference is, all the same, a little too much, so of course I said No
and it didn't seem to affect him much, he lost no appetite through
this; so I came to the conviction that he had merely done it to follow
a mad code of politeness which he has made for himself, he often
told me: 'I think that a proposal is the myrrhe and the incense
which every beautiful young woman has the right to expect from
every man who comes near her.' I think Alas that the myrrhe and
the incense are not the compliments or the love that we receive but
the love which we give. That alone would be happiness and a real
homage to oneself. I wish I could fall in love! But I am almost
afraid I never will.*

Maud Gonne MacBride to W. B. Yeats.

*. . . No I don't like your poem, it isn't worthy of you and above all
it isn't worthy of the subject – Though it reflects your present state
of mind perhaps, it isn't quite sincere enough for you who have
studied philosophy and know something of history know quite well
that sacrifice has never yet turned a heart to stone though it has
immortalized many and through it alone mankind can rise to God
– You recognize this in the line which was the original inspiration
of your poem 'A terrible beauty is born' but you let your present
mood mar and confuse it till even some of the verses become
unintelligible . . .*

. . . you could never say that MacDonagh and Pearse and

Connolly were sterile fixed minds, each served Ireland, which was their share of the world, the part they were in contact with, with varied faculties and vivid energy! Those three were men of genius, with large comprehensive and speculative and active brains. The others of whom we know less, were probably less remarkable men, but still I think they must have been men with a stronger grasp on Reality, a stronger spiritual life than most of those we meet. As for my husband he has entered Eternity by the great door of sacrifice which Christ opened and has therefore atoned for all so that praying for him I can also ask for his prayers and 'A terrible beauty is born'.

There are beautiful lines in your poem, as there are in all you write, but it is not a great WHOLE, a living thing which our race would treasure and repeat, such as a poet like you might have given to your nation and which would have avenged our material failure by its spiritual beauty –

You will be angry perhaps that I write so frankly what I feel, but I am always frank with my friends and though our ideals are wide apart we are still friends . . .

Maud Gonne MacBride to John Quinn

. . . I am writing this hurriedly in all the confusion of déménagement. We are changing from our apartment where you saw us to a smaller one in the same house on the 7th floor. It is nearer heaven and has a roof terrace from which the sunset on the chimney tops of Paris looks wonderful. I hope to live chiefly in Ireland now, so am only keeping a pied-à-terre here.

I still have the same opinion about the continuation of the war. No one but England and possibly Russia stands to gain by it. The exhaustion of Europe is so great that unless you [the US] save us, we shall be eaten up in the end by Japan who is sharpening her teeth threateningly. After the mess Europe is making of civilization, we deserve anything. Already every idea of liberty and of generosity and truth has been trampled by all the belligerents' *satires. Nothing is left standing but the insolence of ammunition manufacturers, ship owners — and still the grim massacre goes on.*

I have decided on going to Ireland with Seaghán and Iseult. I do not know what I can do but I feel it is cowardly to remain idly outside Ireland. I can at least organize the children's food in the schools, which in my absence has been let to drop. Though that will be very hard this year for I hear that potatoes, which form the principal part of the school meals I used to provide, cost over £10 a tonne when formerly they cost no more than £3! . . .

Iseult Gonne to W. B. Yeats

. . . I received two days ago only your letter dated 29th of October; the censor has evidently been pondering some while over it, and I did alike for it is a letter to read and to reread; for me it was like a strong handshake and a kind greeting smile . . .

I am in a talkative mood so I will probably speak a lot of pompous rubbish, but you won't look too stern will you? You will only smile and pass your hand through your hair, and pinch the tip of your nose (remember not to do that too much by the way) and say: 'Her Knighthood wanders, but then knights always wander.'

Willie, you are wrong to say that I shall gradually forget that I am your pupil (and your teacher??). You cannot think that; you know as well and better than I do that absence means nothing or rather means a very great deal.

Thus it is that now you are nearer to me than when we were together, for, from all our common memory I have kept but the best and I can shut myself up in a small but very dainty treasure room and play with my gold like a miser. It's a good game and the best of it is that the gold goes on accumulating . . .

I am reading Initiation *by Steiner. His philosophy seems to me very honest and healthy and his absence of paradox is very reposing. As time goes on, I want more and more subtlety in poetry and less and less in philosophy. Theories should be very simple, because the realization of any theory is so very hard and intricate.*

447

Every evening before going to sleep, I say: 'Tomorrow with God's help, I will be good.' And goodness and God's help seem delightfully easy then, but tomorrow comes and I find that God's help is to be found nowhere, and goodness everywhere just like wickedness; and it all seems altogether too complicated. Oh, you are right to say that spiritual life is both more simple and difficult than one can imagine!

... You speak of the winning of Quiet, it is the key of simplicity and charity and the battle cry of all holy war in the spirit, isn't it? It is to be found in meditation and it is also to be found in action. I think the secret is this: make duty a game and game a duty; bring fancy into work and seriousness into play; then both play and work seem good for they hold each other company and are no longer lonely in their tasks ...

Now I must dress and go out for dinner. I think of the shore. And I am always your,

Very affectionate Maurice
Iseult Gonne
PS It seems such a waste to leave a bit of white paper at the end of a letter that I must really add something. Here are two thoughts of Heraclitus that I am translating into English.

The harmony of the world comes back on itself like the lyre
    and the bow
The Daimon of Man is his destiny
It's an awful bore to have to go out to dinner

(That last isn't from Heraclitus!)

Maud Gonne MacBride to John Quinn

I had got rid of my apartment, packed up everything, got my passport signed at the English consulate, countersigned at the French Prefecture, my tickets bought and places reserved, when the day before we were to have started I was officially informed by

Major Lampton, head of the British control bureau, that he had received telegraphic orders from the English War Office to inform me that I might go to England but that I would not be allowed to go to Ireland. No reason was assigned.

In the meantime I am stranded here in Paris, living in a tiny attic on the 7th floor which I had taken to store my furniture in. I would go to London to agitate the question there, but unofficially Major Lampton told me he thought it very doubtful if, once I was in England, the English authorities would allow me to return to France. Such is the liberty of the world we live in!

Iseult Gonne to W. B. Yeats

. . . I am writing to you in bed with 8 blankets over me, 2 woollen coats, a hot bottle on one side and Minnaloushe on the other. The frost makes on the windows a lovely arabesque pattern of palms and acanthus leaves and each breath one takes feels like a knife prick; A good weather to dream of a garden packed with flowers and grasshoppers in some sunny corner of the south.

Oh, I wish I could sleep all through the winter like a dormouse.

Our friendship with the Rummels has become very close. We see each other almost every day; one day we come to their house and the other they come to ours and we sit by the fire speaking of art and theosophy. This is the sort of discussion Rummel and I are always having; its aimless absurdity may make you laugh:

Rummel begins for instance, to speak of bringing spiritual reality into Art. Then I say: 'Begin by bringing sensuous reality first; that's more important.' Then he answers: 'If you don't first bring spiritual reality you will never get your sensuous reality.'

I: 'Not at all, you must first shape the plastic world before you can give it the fluidic impulse of life.'

R: 'This is altogether wrong. You must bring the spirit down into the matter, while the matter is yet shapeless and let it work through it. Think of Michel Angelo . . .'

I: 'What about Leonardo da Vinci?'

449

R: 'What about Villon?'
I: 'What about Anacreon?'
R: 'What about Wagner?'

Here he gets a mean advantage over me for I never dare to venture on musical grounds.

Yet to be quite honest, I think he may be right. In fact I am almost sure that he is right, but that really matters little so long as there is plenty of wood to feed the fire and keep the cold out in a friendly company.

Oh, I wish you were here too!

I have not been writing at all lately, for directly I try to think actively I feel my thoughts frozen and hard like blocks of ice; and expression becomes more and more difficult. I feel entirely in a receptive state of mind, so I read and study a good deal.

. . . I should so love to hear what you think about Steiner. Initiation *is really not the best book; you should read* Science Occulte. *I think it has also been translated into English. I have also been reading with exquisite pleasure Shelley and Keats lately. In spite of all its beauty there is something metaphorical and abstract in Shelley that I feel alien to, whereas Keats altogether delighted me.*

Oh, Willie, I do need you badly, my thoughts are running wild and poor; our beautiful world, the sheltered aromatic garden of thoughts we had planted together is now far away, and the shadow of the abstract is over everything — even an innocent tulip becomes an idea to me now before I have taken in its lovely shape.

Maybe this is an aspect of the Dark night of the Soul.

Now I have no more room to write any more. I will write you again shortly.

Affectionately
Maurice

Maud Gonne MacBride to John Quinn

. . . Paris is very unhealthy at present, life is difficult. We are often without coal, for at times it is impossible to get and thinking all should be in Ireland by now, we had no supplies laid in. We have cards for sugar (3 lumps a day or 3 teaspoonfuls of soft sugar per head.) Butter is often impossible to get. Vegetables have trebled in price. Only stale bread is allowed to be sold and soon we are to have cards for that also. Gas and electricity are also rationed and only a very small quantity allowed and travelling is rendered hideous by the suppression of the express trains. So we have come back to Colleville by the seashore.

We have been busy turning our garden here into a potato and bean field, for from what I can see bread will soon become a luxury and a plentiful supply of potatoes and beans will help me to help ourselves and others – if only we were in Ireland. Things are going badly there – as usual all the food is being sent out of the country and in the towns, the people are starving. The cattle are starving for want of fodder, as for want of hands a good part of last year's hay crop was lost. Little milk or butter to be had. Every able bodied man has been conscripted, the one Belgian refugee in the neighbourhood is in great request. The farmers here have asked for war prisoners to work on the farms but [are] told none are available at present. My potato field was dug and sowed by women . . .

We have torpedoed fish sometimes and coal, wood etc. washed up treasures brought by the sea. We hear occasional big naval guns from here but otherwise all is peaceful.

Iseult Gonne to W. B. Yeats

. . . We left Paris a week ago for Easter and are now in Colleville; it is very different in this time of the year to what it was last summer, so different in fact that you would hardly know it for the same place. The fields by the sea are under water, it's all a long lake from the cliffs to Vierville. The little hill behind is the

strangest desolate sight; it has been all burnt to get rid of the dried grass and is now perfectly black, the shore itself is changed; do you remember that grey slippery stuff, the remnants of a prehistorical forest, that used to be only before Saint-Laurent, it has been cut bare here too and there are miles of it to the cliffs.

I am writing to you like a baby but those are great events for me; you who know the all absorbing interest of country life, you will understand.

. . . What you said on those little fragments I sent you has been very useful to me and I am trying to apply it in some things I am trying to write now. I think also that a kind of second-rate archaïsme is a pretentious and suburban vice in style; but it is a great danger and temptation for people who have but a poor knowledge of a language, as is my case with English. But I will try in future to avoid it.

I am most thankful to you for those criticisms you have made on my scribblings. Yes, they <u>are</u> bad. I knew it all the while and I am glad of what you say about truth and beauty. I will try and put it into practice; but just now I am still too tired to work.

Moura all day weeds and digs at the garden; it suits her, she looks strong and contented. You will not know Seaghán when you meet him again, he is nearly as tall as we are, speaks with a man's voice and has at last acquired some smoothness and grace of manner.

I have brought here a trunkful of books, and when I see them close packed, all in a row, they make me laugh, for when will they ever be read? Seaghán and I are repainting your room in white; it's quite hard work as we have to scratch off the wallpaper before but it will be much improved.

O do come soon; this land will be good to you also; there's much to tell and much to listen to . . .

Affectionately
Your old Maurice

53

And so Willie comes to Colleville with a trunkful of new clothes bought in Dublin and, according to his friend Lady Gregory, in a great excitement at 'being fetched in so romantic a way!' Iseult is sent with Pierre to collect him off the Bayeux train at Saint-Laurent, then they travel by cart over the fields to the edge of the sea.

They quickly slip into a routine. Mornings and evenings are spent indoors, in literary and spiritual investigation. He flaunts his erudition, she her beauty, and each admires the other's display. In short, everything is perfect, if they ignore – and they mostly do – Maud's withering gaze.

The afternoons are spent outside, walking and running and swimming and bathing in sunshine, all to the backtrack of a sea that is what Iseult calls 'pleasingly untidy' for days, blue in some places, green in others, black in the hollows of the waves and white at the crests, with little streaks of foam all over. Willie is a powerful swimmer from his boyhood summers in Sligo. Iseult says he moves like a pelican on land but is like a swan in water.

After a swim, she often runs fast and barefoot across the sands, sometimes with a kite, sometimes just for its own sake, for the feeling of wild delirium it can induce. As Willie watches her run and watches the rise and fall of her panting ribs after-wards, the movement of her tremulous breaths in and out as she lies beside him, he begins to think of her as a hare.

'Yeats is in France feeding young rabbits with a spoon,' is how Ezra Pound describes them to John Quinn, the American philanthropist who is friend to them all. A warm, bright, benign, protective circle is how it feels to the two partakers. Outside are pressures: the war, Moura's baleful eye, Iseult's looming emigration to Ireland, but here at Colleville is the purest safety, within an orbit of two.

There are privations, of course – they live mostly from the vegetable garden Maud had the foresight to plant at Easter, but, after London and Paris, Colleville feels free of the war, except for the occasional green-glass globe washed up on the shore, buoys from the nets that catch torpedo boats. Daily they walk for miles, across the beach or the cliffs or the dunes, four long legs striding strong. The weather is perfect, blue above and below a faraway horizon, a cooling breeze puckering the waves, soothing the beat of the sun.

On their walks, Willie is much taken with elaborating his system of occult philosophy and astrological patterning. 'You are in Phase 14,' he tells her, marching the dunes towards home.

'But what does it mean?' Iseult has trouble attributing spiritual significance to some of Willie's theories, most particularly this 'system' of his, which seems more like his attempt to codify and control the world than something of real spiritual merit. She has an instinctive suspicion of anything that gives a psychic result without inner effort, such as seances or spiritism or fortune telling. Only the purifying fire of love can burn its way into the spiritual world, she believes. A disciplined mystical training, a reshaping of self, a constant working towards transformation, appears to her the only way to get into communication with that which she prefers to call God. Willie has made these his life's effort but always too he is attracted to the surface and the immediate.

Or perhaps it is just her poor brain unable to grasp the subtleties of his thought?

He says, 'Phase 15 is complete subjective or antithetical beauty, where all thought becomes an image and the soul becomes a body. The characteristics of Phase 14, your phase, are a delight in certain glowing or shining images of concentrated force. And an element of frenzy.'

'*Frenzy?* And I thought I had made upon you a good impression.'

He does not smile. The system must always be taken seriously.

'Who else belongs there?' she says, in an attempt to mollify him.

'Blake, the great English mystic poet. Rabelais. Helen of Troy. Many other beautiful women. The women of Burne-Jones but not those of —'

'Psshh, Willie! You and your beautiful women. Have women without beauty no place in your system?'

'This from she who would be a poetess. Dear girl, what book's insight can approach that granted by high female beauty? I should like to slay that half-dead dragon that is your thought in order that —'

'In order that *your* thought should win over.'

'In order to have you turn your true eye upon your looking glass. In an instant you'd have all the wisdom of the ages.'

'So no beautiful woman can be learned like a man. My thought is a half-dead dragon beside my face. You sound like Le Loup.'

'Perhaps she *can*. But if she has beauty she has no *need* of learning.'

'Fie, my dragon slayer! This is the twentieth century.'

'Look at the artists you admire – Paul Veronese, Michelangelo . . . Does their work not prove that in the end all must come to sight and touch and sinew?'

She widens her eyes. 'But, Willie, do not the wise men say that there is great danger in the body. Surely it is in the mind, in thought, that our highest self is found.'

'When Jesus distributed bread and wine, did he give man His thought or His body?'

'Hmmm.' She squints an exaggerated, quizzical squint. 'Now my wretched dragon is perplexed.'

This makes him laugh, as it is meant to, his lovely hearty chuckle, with his shoulders up around his ears. She thinks of it as Irish, or at any rate most un-English, this laugh of his. When he settles, he says: 'Blessed souls are not complex. A beautiful woman lives in simple blessedness and may lead us to the like – if we banish thought.'

'They say such different things in school.'

He laughs again, but quieter this time, and they fall into a companionable pace, he slicing across the head of the grasses with a stick as they walk. At the crest of the cliff, he stops. 'We had better turn back if we do not want to face Moura's ire again this evening.'

'What a temper yesterday. Poor Moura, she is frustrated. She so longs to be in Ireland.'

That is one reason, but there is another that they do not name: Maud's displeasure at the turn their friendship has taken. A sour milk under the cream that neither intends to unsettle.

No, so much more pleasant to be out here together on the dunes and the sands, under the skies, walking, swimming, lying about in bathing suits, folding thoughts over ideas and passing them across to each other. Body and mind, beauty and knowledge, forward and back – what middle-aged bachelor would not be captivated, what young maiden would not be flattered? And there is much in Willie, even yet, of the blushing virgin and much in Iseult of the world-weary recluse.

Which is the rabbit? Who holds the spoon? Does it matter, so long as they give sustenance to each other?

54

'Mom . . . Oh, Mom.'

I knew at once, the second I heard her voice.

'Darling, is it him?' The ridiculous name stuck in my throat.

'Mom, I want to *die*. Just die.'

So it had come to pass. Already, within months, he had let her down.

'Darling, don't say that. Of course you d—'

'I do, I do. I don't think I can bear it. I just want to die, that's all.'

I felt blame gathering in me against this unknown boy. Any hopes I had settled on him jumped back inside me, flattened themselves around my heart. 'Star, listen to me. Don't do anything, just wait. I'll be home on the next plane. I'll ring tomorrow with the details.'

Once I had made the decision, of course, my loneliness vanished and I began to instantly think of all the things I would have liked to have seen and done. I had been to Europe, yet, too many times on this trip, I was not in Europe at all. I had walked the streets, crossed the bridges, gazed at the churches, admired the art, eaten in the restaurants and for half the time had only half noticed it. Why did I not write about it as I travelled? That would have forced me to pay attention.

It frustrates me now, as I sit here, trying to remember, not to have written details to draw on. The sun rose and set on me there for fifty-six days, and I retain so little of it all. It was a sin, one of Iseult's sins of omission. The sin of preoccupation. Had I known that the trip was to be cut short, I would have visited France before England, the war memorial at Étaples before

Paris. I would have moved considerably faster, done more of what I set out to do.

Held beside Star's need, however, this was nothing. It never occurred to me to stay on for an extra few days, never mind leave her to recover alone. The tremor of her voice on the telephone had been like a finger jabbing into a bruise, reviving the days after Brendan left. I hated to think of Star stumbling around the black well of rejection, drawing its walls in around her. Oh, I remembered. I remembered.

Fear. That was the sensation firing me as I packed my bags and hurried a cab to the airport. My little girl, so fragile. I prayed I would be in time to save her.

I went to her student dorm. Unwashed dishes stacked themselves on the table, along with three half-empty glasses of milk, one with a solid yellow head on top. Unclean clothes lay in heaps on the floor and over every flat surface. Sprawled across the bed, face down in the recovery position a paramedic would put you in if you'd had an accident, lay my unkempt daughter. Her ample, quilt-draped bottom facing me.

'Star, it's me.'

'Mom, you came . . .'

She sat up, she let me pull her close. A hot spurt of tears stung my throat. I sent thanks forth to this . . . Shando. For the first time since she was – What age? In how many years? – I was allowed to properly hold her. I felt her soft shoulders under my fingers, sunk my chin on the pillow of her neck.

'My poor darling,' I murmured. 'My poor poor darling.'

After a time we separated, though I held on to her hands. I asked, 'What happened?'

'He dumped me.'

'Why? Did you guys have a fight? Maybe –'

'No, no, no fight. Just . . . he doesn't want me. Too fat, probably.' She detaches from my hands, pulls a pillow over her face, grinds into it and wails: 'Knew he wouldn't. Knew it from the start. Out of my league.'

'Star . . . Honey . . . Don't . . .'

I made her get up and dress and brought her out for dinner, and she told me all over a plate of food that she fiddled with while she talked, talked, talked, as she used to talk years ago, when she was afraid to let me go. I brought her to my hotel room, and she spent the night in my bed, and next morning I encouraged her into the shower and then onwards to her lectures. To my surprise, she obeyed. She didn't know what else to do. By the time she went back to her dorm room, I had it sparkling clean, everything in its place and a bunch of sprightly daffodils in a new vase on the table. 'You shouldn't have,' she said, shrugging her book bag off her shoulder.

I brought her to dinner that evening, but, again, she barely ate. At the end of the meal, she said: 'Mom, I want to give up college. I want to come home.'

'What about your degree?'

'I'm not studying anyway. I cut two classes today. I can't concentrate. I can't stop crying.'

'You'll get through it, sweetheart. You're not going to be like this for ever.'

'You don't want me either.'

'Of course it's not that.'

It would actually have been one of my own silly fantasies come true. Star asleep in her bedroom, home with an illness. I hadn't imagined a love sorrow, more a physical complaint. Nothing serious: a flu or suchlike. Nothing that a few days in bed and a little tender mother-loving wouldn't fix. In my mental movie, I brought her books and magazines, of the kind I despised but she liked. I set her up with pillows and the TV remote control. I fixed her lemon remedies and a little food, nothing heavy on the stomach. Soups, custards, plenty of fluids. 'You do know it's not that, don't you?'

'Yeah, Mom, sure. Whatever.'

I left her, with money and presents and a promise to take a phone call every night. I left her because I was sure it was the right thing to do and had, in a stronger moment, won her agreement on that. I arrived back to Santa Paola, seven weeks early. Marsha was disappointed for me but pleased for herself, she said. She had missed me.

So I slotted back into my life, everything the same, except a nightly phone call from Star. She was not coping but she was managing to force herself through her days, often giving me a hard time on the phone but always calling again the next night. Everything the same until – just when it was most awkward for me to be in a relationship with a man – Zach came back to Santa Paola.

Early one Wednesday afternoon, during that lull time in the café between lunch and afternoon coffee, I headed out for my break. I had two chores to do: to the library to exchange my books and to Brown's Deli. Both were on Ocean Avenue, close enough to walk, so off I swung, out into the sunshine with my book bag over my shoulder, heavy but not weighing me down.

All along the street, I greeted and was greeted. On Fade Street I crossed to talk to Mrs Hawkins, whose husband of forty-four years had died two months ago, unsure of what to say but certain of the need to say something. For sixteen years now, I had lived in this college town, population 50,000, swollen in term time by the student population to almost double that. Sixteen years of basking in its sunshine (325 days a year is its boast), of tending my house, raising my kid, living out my life . . .

Here was where I knew best, and where I was best known. I was Izzy Mulcahy, the Irish woman. I lived on Westcliff in the smallest house on a lovely road, almost in view of the ocean, and in that little house, it could be said, I lived the life I chose sixteen years ago, negotiating its clear spaces and islands of homely furniture, nurtured by its books and music, comforted by its cushions and blankets. I was one half of Mulcahy and Blinche, the business that owned the (fairly) new café down on the boardwalk, one of the minority (only 25 per cent) of the town's businesses that were run by women. Nice eating spot if you didn't mind things a bit hippie-dippie.

I was also Mrs Mulcahy, single mom, mother of Maya, more commonly known as Star. Such a sad case, that girl . . . They remembered seeing her around town as a girl, riding her bike along the boardwalk, or strolling the stores with her friends, such a pretty little thing before she put on all that weight and started wearing those awful clothes. Drink and drugs, it was said. So overweight. And my, so aggressive. Remember her walking down this very street with that friend of hers? One hand held inside their leather jackets, some sort of affectation. Stomping like a pair of off-duty soldiers, angry eyes up front.

Tough, raising kids these days, especially on your own.

That's what the best of them said, and those who said worse didn't bother me, not any more. I was steadied by the presence of my neighbours. Their 'Hi, Izzy' or 'Afternoon, Mrs Mulcahy!' or 'How is Star?' seemed like a small, everyday gift and reminded me of what I had opted for when I moved here. Domesticity, suburbia, a place where I could fight free of my past. A place where I, and my daughter, could feel safe. I held on to those small connections, valuing what I still had, though much was lost.

Freedom and safety aren't external, I knew that even then. A man won't keep you safe, a trip to Europe doesn't set you free, but as I walked up that street I still yearned. *I wish, I wish, I wish.* Those dangerous, soft-footed words still formed the backing track in my head. I never said them aloud, not even to Marsha, but I was thrown forward on them, tossed up the road on their swoosh and slice. The flounce of desire prodded by the rod, the cane, the wand, of I . . .

Tsk! I gave my head a shake. Self-indulgent claptrap.

461

To the library, where heads looked up as the wooden double doors swung closed behind me. We were lucky in Santa Paola with our old-fashioned library. Here too, I was well known. It was quiet today: no students from the high school as there were last time I was in, coming up to exam time. I didn't have to ask for my books. Jenny saw me and bent for them behind the counter. I always rang ahead, a relic from busier days.

She slid them across the polished wood. The new Edna O'Brien, especially ordered. A how-to on writing fiction. *The Bell Jar*: I was rediscovering Sylvia Plath. I fished in my bag for my library card, grateful as always for the gift of free books. Tonight, after we closed the café, I would take them home and choose which one to read first. The O'Brien, I reckoned. I could do with an injection of her luscious, overripe sentences, her sense of the hidden dilemma within the obvious conflict. I would turn the key in the lock of my front door and sit immediately down at the work table I had set up in the hallway, delaying the pleasure of reading until after I had written something myself.

I thought of it as a room now, my hallway, since Star was so rarely there. Big enough to take an easy chair alongside the work table, another telephone table and the big blocky bureau in the corner, where I kept my accounts and business correspondence. It faced west and was the place to sit at that time of day, catching the evening sun.

I continued, despite everything, to work away on my book. I was still integrating the information I had gathered in Europe. At this stage of her life, Iseult was propelled by the mating drive, but, oh, how she overcomplicated everything – just as I did, just as Star does. I grow a little impatient with us all.

Tonight, I would work until I grew too tired or hungry, whichever came first. A break to eat would mark the end of work for the day. The O'Brien would come out of the book bag and be taken to the kitchen and laid on the pine table while I prepared supper. Bean stew brought home from the café, accompanied by a robust chunk of bread and a glass, or possibly two, of red wine (never a third). The bright new cover of the book would gleam in its plastic library jacket, catching the light from the lamp overhead and, food warmed, I would sit and open it.

Page one.

A new story.

After eating, my reading would continue in the living room. It would be dark by then and I'd put on the reading lamp and the soft table lamp in the corner. Plumping the cushions, I'd sink down, pulling a coverlet around me. After reading my fill, I might watch the late news. The medfly outbreak that threatens California fruit farms has put an end to Governor Jerry Brown's bid for election to the Senate. The nation is sinking into its worst recession since the Great Depression. More than nine million Americans are now officially unemployed.

Watch is the word, with all the distance that implies. I won't be engaged by these news stories as with the novel. I'll let their information wash across me only because I feel I should. It's important for me to be informed. Tomorrow in Better World Café, earnest students and academics and activists will debate the detail of the latest developments, with passion and rigour. Marsha – forever skipping with feeling about some injustice or another – will come out of the kitchen to join in, with her always intelligent, always probing opinions.

I will join in in a way that facilitates others to talk. My opinions are too watery to survive in Better World. The unfolding of political events feels inconsequential to me. I know millions of people are affected by these decisions, but they don't feel real. People enter and exit the world, and their own life story unfolds to understanding. Or not. That seems to me to be where the news starts and stops.

I admire the caring of Marsha and all the others who do care. I provide a place where they can work out what they think and share it with each other and make a difference, in the way they want. They are so taken with their own thoughts they never notice I don't offer mine.

After the news, I will prepare for bed. Tidy the house, iron whatever I am going to wear next day, undress and go through my night-time routine. Cleanse, tone, moisturize, tweeze, brush. Tonight is Wednesday, so I may also manicure. Shiny and polished, I will take myself to sleep with some more reading, another chapter of the O'Brien or a different book, something lighter, or maybe the *Santa Paola Sentinel,* which comes out on Wednesdays. Then to sleep, in time to get eight hours before rising at seven.

That's what I thought was ahead for me that evening. Instead, I left the library and walked on to Brown's, Santa Paola's famous deli, and bumped right into Zach.

As soon as I walked in, I noticed him from behind: an eye-catching back, tall and broad under a white t-shirt. For a second maybe two, I was unaware that it was him but then realization dropped. I could feel it falling inside me. He was pointing towards the cheese. As I drew nearer, I heard his voice – '. . . and six slices of Swiss . . .' – and I knew for sure.

'Zach?' I said, from behind his back.

He stood stock still for a second, frozen, before turning around. A splinter of something as our eyes collided, then I saw him settle himself into himself. I felt it again, what I had felt the first time we met. An intense presence, stronger than before, I thought, or maybe I'd forgotten how strong it was. A word from my childhood floated into my mind. Charismatic.

'Well, well,' he said, voice breezy. 'If it isn't Izzy.'

He wore a smile that said, I am pleased to see you but I am just as pleased to see this cheese I am being handed. You are no more special than anything else. Instantly a thought rose in me: *You can drop the nonchalance, my friend. You are mine, I'm getting you back.* The sensations that swirled around that thought flooded my entire body – with him, with us, with what it had

464

been like to be with him and what it had been like to be without.

I flicked a quick look at his left hand. Naked. Zach would wear a ring, I think, if he were married.

'It *is* you,' I said.

'Me indeed.'

'Home for a visit?'

'Maybe a bit longer than that.'

'Really? That's great.'

'Yeah?'

'Of course it is. It's great to see you.'

He turned back to the assistant behind the counter. 'And a large slice of Camembert,' he said, bestowing on her his beautiful smile.

Mine.

'Your hair,' I said to him. 'It's so different.' It was short, very short, practically shaven. He ran his palm across the skull and stared at me, as if he didn't know what to say. Didn't have anything to say to me. No, no, unthinkable thought but words had also evacuated my head. Silence grew and grew like a big, invisible balloon pressing against us.

It was he who rescued us: 'How is your little girl?'

'Not so little any more. She's in college.'

'*No!*'

'It's been ten years, Zach.'

'I still think of her as a kid.'

'Yeah, it's the kids who bring home what ten years means.'

I was now facing forty but until this moment, had not found that milestone oppressive. Sure, I had more awareness now of what was going to happen when the ageing stopped, but the American obsession with looking younger has always seemed ridiculous to me. All that running and bending, all that cutting and slicing, just to pretend you're a few years younger than you are. Grow up, people. Being unlined or gym-honed won't save you. You are not as young as you look, or as young as you feel: if you're forty, as I almost was, you are forty.

That day in Brown's, all this reason flew away from me. Under Zach's eyes, I was conscious not only of the lines around my eyes and mouth, the sag that was developing in the skin behind my chin, the wedge of padding that lined the top of my waistband, but also that I wasn't wearing any make-up, that I was in my second-best jeans – only half as flattering to what was left of my figure as my best – and that my hair colour needed a retouch. For the first time, I felt the impulse that drives women under the knife. If in that moment a surgeon or shaman were to promise that he could restore me to what I was at thirty – the age I was when Zach and I first met, the age Zach was nearing now – I might have chosen to allow him.

It didn't help that Zach was not less but more beautiful than he had been ten years before. He had filled out in the shoulders and filled out internally too: come into himself.

Looking at him was giving me the strangest feeling, as if time were tunnelling in around us from all sides, cutting out the girl behind the deli counter, the two people now standing in line behind me, the shop and all the people in it. There was only us two. I knew not to approach him as I would another guy. The light swapping of banter, the game of the tip and parry you play so you don't expose too much too soon wouldn't do for Zach.

'Would you like to get a coffee?' I asked.

He laughed. Was that a bitter note? Was he still hurt? That meant I had a chance.

Mine. Mine.

'Unless you'd rather not. Unless there's somebody else?' I said.

His eyes widened, surprised at my directness. 'No, it's not that.'

'Will that be all, sir?' asked the deli girl from a long way off.

'Come on, Zach, this doesn't need to be so hard. Just say yes or no. Your call.'

As soon as the words were out, I regretted them. Too blunt.

Yet if I played it as cool as him, he'd let me walk away. I played my last throw. 'Zach, I'm so sorry about what happened. Not just for what I did to you but also to myself. It was the biggest mistake of my life.'

'You think I don't know that, Izzy?'

'Then let's not make a second one.'

His silence stared me down, face full of so many saids and unsaids. I held his eyes and would not let them go.

'That will be $6.40, sir.'

'*Please*, miss,' I said, without turning my head. 'Can you give us a second?'

Still he didn't speak so I had to. I put my hand on my heart. 'I forgive myself, Zach. I forgive me even though I put myself through the wringer by leaving you. I forgive me, because if I don't, I'd only be doing the same thing all over again to myself. And to you. Zach? Do you understand?'

'Sir, ma'am, I really must ask you –'

'So don't forgive me if you don't want to, but know what you're doing, okay?' I felt as if I were fighting for the life of a child. 'Know that it's *you* making the mistake this time.'

Still he stood.

'*Sir?*'

I took one of the business cards I always carry in my purse and wrote my home number down on the back of it. 'Call me,' I said.

He looked at the card. 'Better World Café?'

'Or call in there if you'd prefer. Any time. Come and meet my friend Marsha. You'll like her.'

And she'd love him. I could imagine them, having long intense talks about how to save a world that didn't think it needed saving.

'Sir, I really have to ask you to –'

'Just *wait*, will you?' I turned on her, hardly knowing what I was saying.

I turned back to him. 'Zach?'

467

'Ah, go on, son,' said a man from the line.

'If you don't, can I?' shouts up another voice.

'Yeah, man, you crazy, turning down a chick like that?'

'I'm out on a limb here, Zach. Look at me.'

He looked, he let himself look. A spark jumped in his eyes, I saw it. Time tunnelled in closer. 'Help me,' I whispered.

He reached out his hand

'Oh, thank God,' I said. I dropped my basket so I could take it, and my feet were stepping towards him. He opened his arms to me and I half walked, half stumbled into them. Then I was locked against that white t-shirt, my cheek warming against what it felt beneath. His skin, his muscle, his bone. *Mine.* His hand came up to hold me there.

'*Yes!*' cried the old man from behind, as if it were his arms I was falling into. Somebody, probably him, started to clap, and then everybody broke into applause and whooping and cheering.

'Don't make me regret this,' he whispered into my hair.

'I won't. I promise you, Zach. I promise.'

I looked up at him, and he was smiling. The people in the line behind us were smiling; even the deli girl was smiling. I felt like a sideshow, but it didn't matter. I was smiling too. All my pores were smiling.

55

'Iseult is crying again,' says Seaghán.

'Shhhh, boy!' she snaps. 'What have I told you about carrying your tales?'

'Iseult, whosoever you blame for your sulks, it is surely not Bichon,' scolds Maud. 'Please. Try to contain yourself.'

It is a blustery day in Le Havre but calm enough – regrettably to Iseult – for sailings to proceed. No, not regrettably. Such an emotion is simple-minded. If not today, she must leave tomorrow. A delayed sailing will not save her. Yet her feelings tell her that one more day, even one more hour, is something to hold. Every time she has the thought, tears rise again. Which means she wastes such time as *is* left to her in crying.

Oh, she is contemptible. Moura believes so, and she cannot blame her.

They step aboard. Moura first, her tall black back swinging across the ramp, her veiled head dipping under the low strut of the entrance to the ship. Iseult second, then Seaghán, Josephine and Willie in that order. The boy has been given charge of Coco the parrot, who keeps breaking into cackles of hysterical laughter. She and Moura hold a cage full of canary birds each, and she also has Minnaloushe on the other arm, sitting in a shopping basket upon a cushion of red velvet, disdaining to notice the commotion. One could learn much from Minnaloushe.

Down the slippery steps into the bowels of the ship. A carpet, some lights and trinkets attempt to give a feeling of luxury. They travel first class, of course. Moura's money has been decimated by the war, but it is one of her maxims to seek whatever possible comfort while travelling. She and Josephine will share one berth, while Iseult is in with Seaghán and Willie is a little further along the corridor.

Sailing, though not so dangerous as earlier in the war, is still far from safe, but a hundred U-boats lined up in the harbour taking aim would not stop Moura now. They go to England knowing she is unlikely to be allowed to travel onwards to Ireland, that to get there, she must break the law. But what is an English law to Moura? No more than a snap of the fingers. What is money? Friends? Home? Ties to country and culture? Snap, snap, snap, snap. She has liquidated her assets, her friends must come to her, her home is sold, Ireland is to be her country now.

And, thus, Iseult's too.

Maud pays the porter, and as soon as he has closed the door, throws herself upon her berth and sighs relief. This flamboyant breath almost blows Iseult out the door, up on to deck, across the gangplank and back by foot to Paris. Moura in this mood is intolerable, as showily exultant as a schoolboy who has won a sporting championship. She turns her back to her, fiddling with her sponge bag and arranging her cot.

Oh, no, here come the tears again, pouring silently down her face, in sheets. For two days she has done nothing but cry. This morning was the worst, closing up the small apartment, the trot-trot-trot of the cab horse clopping a sad and lonesome goodbye down the streets of Passy. How hard to disconnect from objects that had chosen her, to decide which to throw away, which to give away, which to keep. In the end, Moura had had to take control, and with her brisk energy she quickly whittled them down. Some dresses and other clothes. A box of only the most essential books – 'England and Ireland have wonderful libraries, *chérie*.' A few prized objects that symbolize childhood and France. Some letters and papers, school reports and the like. Dried leaves from Arrens, from that sad, sweet summer before the war. Tassie, her little rag doll.

All compressed into a small trunk and two small book boxes.

There they now sit, in the corner with Moura's and Seaghán's and Josephine's luggage, all they own reduced to a stack of cubes.

Last night she left the house and went for a walk along the dear familiar streets, but that too was unsatisfactory. The Paris to which she wished to bid *adieu* was already fled. The Tower of Babel could not have had more variety than Paris yesterday. Soldiers of all grades passed up and down. English Tommies and a great profusion of broad-hatted Americans but also Indians, Senegalese, Moroccans, Serbs and Portuguese. Chic officers on leave but still loving to sport their *pantalons rouges* and braided kepis. Slouching *poilus* in their baggy trousers and ill-fitting jackets. All looked as if they wished to shrug off their coats and roll up their sleeves – it was a warm evening – but they were too intent on being handsome soldiers.

She allowed no look on their part to penetrate her attention. Unlike Thora, she has no interest in wartime interludes, a touching and then a parting in thoughts of death. Like her cousin, it was once her aim to win the heart of every admirable young man she meets – it is what young, beautiful ladies are supposed to do – but she no longer wishes to play with hearts. Not because she has become a prude but rather because she has a growing feeling that if one is not in love, playing with love is not so much fun after all. It can even become a bore. A very great bore.

What she wants now is a love of her own. What she knows now is that she is almost certain not to have it.

Beneath her feet, the floor shudders. The ship engines striking up. There is still time. What would happen if she were to tell Moura that she does not want to go? If she were to take the trunk and book box and walk back across the plank and wave them off? She is twenty-three years old, nobody can stop her.

Except herself. It is not even a matter of having the courage to know that she would survive but the courage to know whether indeed she does not wish to leave. France now feels derelict, socially dispossessed – of good food, of culture, of fine talk, of the arts, of young men ... Most especially of young men. More than a million of them are dead. Whereas in Ireland there is (so far at any rate) no conscription. There young men roam freely yet. She takes out a handkerchief, blows her nose, tries to stop the ceaseless spring of tears. Is she being punished? At the harbour in Le Havre, before they embarked, she heard a clear voice saying to her 'Go back to God'. How far she feels from Him.

A diffident knock comes to the door. 'Willie, no doubt,' says Moura.

And indeed it is he, their faithful factotum, clutching his hat to his chest. 'I wondered whether anybody fancied a turn on deck?' he booms. 'To watch us pull out of harbour?'

'Iseult will accompany you, Willie,' Maud says.

Iseult shakes her head.

'Heavens, Iseult, do. It will do you good to get some air instead of moping about here. Seaghán, *mon cher*, come here and help me to feed the birds.'

Willie is not alone in his idea. Up on the top deck, a crowd has gathered, some strolling, some standing and waving to relatives who flutter handkerchiefs from the pier. They walk, Willie proud of all the people who turn to look at Iseult's tall, arresting figure. For her, the melancholia is wretched, but, once her tears are dry, it gives her an even more ethereal air, incomparably touching. Yet if he were to praise her beauty, she would act as though it is another he praises, or even that he is mocking her with praise of her mere opposite.

They walk, a small distance between them, comfortably silent. He has great feeling for the child, of course he has, her situation has all his pity as does her self-torture, but he has spent the recent days and nights in Paris recognizing that he is not, in fact, mad with love for her – merely concerned for her welfare. He has stood *in loco parentis* for so long that her rejection does not leave him too downcast. And her indolence, her erratic moods, her chain-smoking – even here, on this blustery deck, she does not forsake the inevitable cigarette – indicate that it is perhaps as well that they are not to be wed. He would, however, wish to do anything he could to see her free of unhappiness.

Maud has taken to repeating of late her conviction that Iseult is, in a sense, his child, a progeny of their connection of long ago. When carrying and bearing Iseult, she says, she was full of his ideas. This thought makes Willie squirm, and he cannot be quite sure that Maud did not say it with just such an intention. Shades of MacBride and Millevoye but such comparisons are invidious. He rejects them.

In any case, they no longer apply, now that he and Iseult are not to marry. He has agreed, instead, to become her guardian, to watch over her in the new life she faces in London and Dublin. He worries at the problems that accompany this promise. Above all things now, he needs tranquillity and order in his personal affairs. He is determined to marry by his astrological deadline in October and has another young woman in mind who will, he is all but certain, say yes. But can it make for tranquillity to bring into their marriage a beautiful young ward of the same age? Perhaps it would, after all, be more convenient if Iseult could find it in herself to agree.

'You know, my dear, you have a horoscope that makes me dread melancholia. Yet perhaps if you were to be free of Moura for a while –'

'Well, yes, but how am I to arrange it?'

'You know how you might.'

'Willie, I am ashamed of our marriage talk.'

'Why? Because of Moura?'

'Yes. Also –'

'Even though she gives so little heed to your situation?'

'She is too caught in her own passions.'

That Iseult is leaving the only home she has ever known must not be mentioned to Maud. Otherwise fury will come raining down and then, immediately after, tearful apologies and effusions. Maud despairs of what she calls Iseult's moods but is as changeable as the weather herself at the moment, careering in minutes from blazing political hate to despair to fervent love declarations.

Willie says, 'I made the mistake of sharing with her my belief that London would be a better place for you than Dublin.'

'What did she say?'

'She drew herself up into her most Roman and said: "Really, Willie? Is that what you believe?" Then unleashed upon me as cold a blast of fury as I have had from her in years.'

'You see? Even if I loved you wildly, Willie – and I tell you again, I do not – I could never marry you. It would distress her too deeply.'

'It is an impossible life for you, my dear.'

'Poor Moura.' She extinguishes her cigarette underfoot and turns to face the sea breeze. 'I cannot think of it any further. I am very sad and very tired.'

The brush of sea air upon her face stirs a small exhilaration in Iseult that seems to banish tears for the moment. She knows that loose strands of her hair are flickering across her face in a way that is pleasing to him, pleasing to any man who might be watching. With the thought comes scorn: how loathsome she is. All the man shortages in the world cannot make her love Willie, yet still she holds him close.

'My dear, do consider yet a while. I can show you a very different Ireland to Moura's world of activists and rebels, where you can make of yourself a poetess, surrounded by artists.'

'Babble of a different sort but babble still.'

'I too want quiet more than any other thing now. With me, quiet and habit create great affection.'

She lights another cigarette.

'I know that only in the country can you be free of this terrible mood for long. You would adore the countryside around

Thoor Ballylee, the Irish tower I have bought, and, when not there, we can be in England, so much closer to France than Dublin.'

'But love, Willie. What of love?'

He touches her hand, very briefly, where it rests on the railings. She notices that his hand is the oldest part of him, more wrinkled than the rest and patterned with a branch of veins that is very male and really not unpleasant. 'Love takes many forms, my dear, as you will realize when you are older.'

'Yet if I were to ask you: you wouldn't actually say you love me, Willie, would you?'

He cannot answer her.

Poor Willie. He so wanted a great love in his life and so wanted it to be Moura, long after it was evident that it should not be. Now he has convinced himself that to love her would fulfil that destiny, give meaning to his suffering.

When he finally speaks he surprises her by saying, 'You are more like your mother than you think.'

'Why? Because I refuse you?'

'When you talk of love, I see in you much that reminds me of Moura when she was a girl. Though she has forgotten her blood ever ran wild, I have not. You also were too wildly bred to mate with a man of fifty years.'

Really, sometimes he surprises her.

She pushes back strands of hair whipped by a gust of wind. 'When I went away by myself at Havre, Willie, such a rush of emotion came to me. I could almost hear the answer spoken: "Go back to Christ". Alas, is it true? Hermas and Cypris lead to knowledge but is peace only in Christ?'

With this question, she has moved herself again. She turns so her back is to him and the other people strolling the deck, and stands helpless behind the tears.

He says: 'My heart is too old, Iseult, to pay you the tribute of wild tears. That does not mean I do not love.'

'Willie, I am so ashamed. It is so selfish of me not wanting you to marry anyone else.'

'You have said nothing to me of not wanting –'

She looks down over the railings. The throb of the ship cuts the water in white slices.

'Does this mean –'

'It means I do not want to lose your *friendship*.'

'That will never happen. All your life you have been as a daughter to me. But perhaps your feelings are telling you some truths to which you need to listen. Feelings are always closer to the truth than thoughts.'

She opens her mouth to answer but he holds up his hand. 'Don't decide now what it means. In a few days I shall meet you in a teashop. You shall have had time to settle into London and see what you think of the place. And time to know better your own mind. You shall give me your answer then.'

'Come,' she says. 'Let us go down. Right now, the condition of sleep is the nearest to heaven I can picture.'

But in the bunk berth below her brother, sleeps evades her. When she does drift, it gives her no escape, just the shallowest drop out of this world into one still lined with the same thoughts and tears.

Poor Iseult. How I would like to go into that ship berth and press a cold compress on your stinging eyes and another on your heated forehead and hold your hand and soothe you with soft words. I would tell you something of your future, that your grief for France, for youth, for your dreams of independence, will soon ease its grip on you. That love, true love, lies not far ahead for you, across the black-night velvet sea.

56

I know what Iseult cannot know and also what she knows too well, the double-barrelled story she carries in her head. The dance of what is, the disruption of what might be.

On the third day of March 1983, I was once again at my desk and having a good day. The weather had improved, the cloud cover finally breaking into high colums of white fluff marching across a blue canvas. The thread connecting now to then, me to Iseult, my father to Zach, was twitching strong, and all I had to do was run after it, taking dictation. For the first time since my trip to Europe I was able to put writing first. No daughter, no job, no father to call me away. It was repaying that commitment. I had mornings when I woke, frozen by worries, unable to know which foot should go in front of the other, but I knew I could find my way to the desk and type my way into a day that worked.

I was in the middle of a sentence, pitying poor tearful Iseult in her bunk bed, when the telephone jangled beside me, making me jump. It was Mags Halloran, my lawyer, whirling in at speed. How was I doing? The date for the trial had come through, rather earlier than expected. She needed to see me. I felt like someone slapped out of sleep, but I managed to answer. I was doing fine, fine. Yes, I would come to Dublin. Tomorrow? All right, then, tomorrow.

I replaced the receiver in its cradle. The twitching thread of time disintegrated. I was Iseult Mulcahy again, back in my father's house, with the chair under me, the old mahogany of the desk smooth under my fingers, the tips of the trees outside the window, and, beyond them, the boughs and budding stalks of other branches, and through them shards of grey lake water.

The lake is visible from the house only in winter and then only in slivers. In another few weeks the leaves would be fully out, and the water and all around it would be hidden from view for another nine months.

Back in this strange limbo between my old life in Santa Paola and whatever lay ahead. Home to California or into an Irish jail. I needed to clutch hold of the two sides of my mind and draw them back over the fissure that opened whenever I considered this.

In my writing, I had reached the point where I was almost back where I started: at the events that spun me across the Atlantic Ocean. The pull of Pauline's letter telling me about my father's condition, the push of that terrible night when Star finally met Zach.

If I was to fight for my freedom, the time had come to tell Mags all I knew. To allow her to point up the other possibility. How could I do that to my own daughter? (Yet she had had no difficulty doing it to me?) How could I blame her, knowing what her life had been like? (Yet how could I let myself be jailed for life?) On and on the arguments went, slicing each other to ribbons. The writing that had seemed so powerful before Mags's call was diminished – a plaster on a gaping wound.

I see now that it was my double vision that disoriented me. I have come to know there is no what-might-be, there is only what-is. What a lot of suffering I would have saved myself if I had known that then.

Since Zach and I had last been together, he had got God. He didn't call it that, and he wasn't aligned with any particular religion or tradition, but that was what it was. After Brown's, I had brought him back to the café, enjoying the look on Marsha's face when she saw me swinging in with him, hand in hand. She sat him down in the corner table to share a pot of green tea and some get-to-know-you-time, then insisted I take the rest of the day off.

I brought him back to my house, his first time there, and, still holding his hand, showed him around while we relaxed into the knowing of what we were about to do. The west-facing entrance vestibule where I like to write. The open-plan kitchen and dining and sitting rooms at the back, opening out on to the yard. I didn't open the door to Star's room, black-painted walls covered in posters of Patti Smith and Blondie, Siouxsie Sioux and Lora Logic, Richard Hell and Tom Verlaine, the Stooges and Suicide, the Sex Pistols and the New York Dolls, all cut and pasted into enormous, explosive collages. And still, after not being inhabited for weeks, after being cleaned from floor to ceiling, somehow still smelling faintly of smoke and despair.

She was scraping through college as she had through school, managing to pass exams without doing much work. A trip to Mexico for the summer, working in a fruit factory with a friend, was supposed to distract, but she had come back browner, more enormous and more disgruntled than ever. Now she was back at college. I kept her door closed to Zach. 'Star's,' I said, and he nodded, respecting her privacy. I showed him the bathroom, which needed decoration: too frilled and flouncy for my taste now, and the spare room for guests and Marsha, who often stayed over if she'd had too much wine to drive home. All these delays that were a sort of commitment to our destination.

'This is great,' Zach said, almost wistfully. 'I can see your life since we parted, here, all laid out.'

'That sounds nice and boring.'

'Not at all. You're so rooted now, compared to before,' he said. 'Solid.'

'Solid? Charming. Makes me sound like a kitchen table.'

I put my arms around his neck and gave him the full-on kiss I'd been planning since Brown's. The holding back of our last time together would be no more. I had waited too long for this. I smelled the tang of him as our lips met, his own, unmistakable essence.

'I think it's time this table was laid,' I whispered in his ear, which made him laugh again.

Then he grew suddenly serious. 'Izzy,' he said, with a small frown, 'I have a lot to tell you about what happened to me.'

'We've a lot to tell each other, Zach. But we've all the time in the world to tell it. First . . .' I kissed him again.

'Izzy, Izzy,' he whispered into my hair, almost a cry, and again, after we'd slid each other's clothes away and tracked pathways along each other's skin with fingers and lips and were reaching to pull the nakedness of each other in close, he said it again, 'Izzy, Izzy,' only much louder this time, as if I were in danger.

Or maybe was *a* danger. I don't know.

I was determined that everything was going to be fine. With my ambiguities and reservations out of the way, happiness would be ours, that day and for ever, all the coming days.

'Stop,' he said.

I lifted my head. 'What is it?' Excitement was thrumming through me.

'Stop for a moment. Listen.'

'To what?'

'Just listen.'

I laid my forehead in the soft hollow beneath his shoulder, stopped the forward press of my desire for a moment and listened. I could hear the thumping of my pulse, birdsong outside the window, the ventilator in the bathroom, two kids shooting hoops next door, a car driving past and the hum of my own blood, pressing against my temples . . . And yes, the silence wrapped around each of the sounds.

'That's better,' he said, and he kissed me again, with cooler, gentler lips, a kiss that lasted on and on and on, until, again, I was lost to sound and to anything except touching and being touched. I drew him down, and we were together as we had never quite been together before, heartbeats knocking hard on each other's ribs. Two floating souls touching through heaving flesh.

Afterwards, after we had slept a while, we talked and he told me about the years we'd been apart. Some of it – his academic appointment and his publications – I knew. Now he told me what lay under all that achievement.

'After you left me, I didn't want to live. I blamed you for the way I felt. And at the school there was all this wrangling and competition, first for tenure, later for advancement. I found myself anxious all the time.'

'Anxious how?' I asked, from the pillow beside him.

'Just horribly, horribly anxious. Then one night I woke with a feeling of intense horror. Everything felt so utterly without meaning. I hated the world and what I hated most about it was me. I lay thinking what I'd often thought before: how could I bear this struggle any longer?'

'Oh, Zach.'

'I hope this isn't too heavy for you? I'm not like that any more. It feels now as if I'm talking about somebody else.'

'No, it's not too heavy.' I propped myself up on my elbow so he could see my face.

'I hated myself. I thought myself the most loathsome person in the world. Why had I said such and such to such a person? What did a, b or c mean by x or y or z? Thoughts whirling and churning until I thought I would drive myself out of my mind.'

He laughed and then kept on laughing, too long.

'What's so funny?'

'That's what I did,' he said. 'Which was precisely what saved me.'

'Sorry?'

'I didn't realize at the time that that was exactly where I needed to go.'

'You've lost me.'

'Out of my mind.'

'Zach, I –'

'Bear with me. A thought that kept flashing across my head as I lay there was: "I can't stand myself any longer." I had had

481

this thought before, but now, for some reason, I became aware of the illogicality of it. How could *I* not stand *myself*? Was I one person or two?'

He sat up on his elbow. 'As I tried to solve this puzzle, I felt – actually felt – my mind stop. I was awake, still wide awake in the dark room, but I wasn't thinking. A moment of peace. Then . . .' He paused, dropped his eyes, hesitating at the brink.

'Go on.'

'Izzy, I hope this isn't going to sound too crazy to you – as if my stopped mind was an aperture, what felt like a surge of white light came rushing in. My head felt ablaze with white.'

I kept my eyes open to him. To turn from what he was saying would be to turn from all the intentions I had brought into this bed. That much I knew.

'I could feel myself being sucked into it. I started to shake, all over,' he said. 'And then . . . then I heard a voice.'

'A voice?'

'A voice,' he said firmly. 'It seemed to come from my chest, but it also seemed to be outside of me.'

'What did it say?'

'It said: "Bow to what is."'

Again he looked at me. I didn't take my eyes away. I didn't laugh, or frown, or jeer, or turn away. I kept my face straight. Straight, straight, straight.

'So I let myself go. I fell, a long way, then I felt my heart growing warmer and then it was as if it were opening, like a flower blooming on fast-motion film.'

'Sounds like an acid trip.'

He ignored that. 'I felt peace and well-being washing over me. After that, I have no recollection. I must have fallen asleep, because the next thing I remember is waking, what felt like hours later, with light, early light coming in through my curtains. Light as I had never seen before.'

His face was alight just talking about it.

'I got up and walked around my bedroom, the bedroom I

482

had lived in for years but it was as if I had never seen it before. I walked round the room picking things up, simple things, a pen, a tube of toothpaste, a t-shirt, staring at them in wonder. They were so alive. *Alive* now seemed the most startling miracle.'

A third time he looked at me. 'Izzy?'

I needed to answer now. I needed to say something, find words that went beyond the obvious, half-frightened and half-cynical phrases that were leaping around my head. New Age mumbo-jumbo-spirit-psycho-nutter-freakery.

Zach had been so special to me; I had lost and mourned him, but life had brought him back to me and this was who he was, now. I needed to get beyond my own opinions, respect the heart of what he was saying.

As soon as I had that thought, a new word rose unbidden in my mind. I was able to reach across and brush his cheek with accepting fingers. 'Rebirth,' I said. 'You had a rebirth.'

'Yes. Oh, Izzy, you understand.' He reached for me and pulled me tight against him. 'You understand.'

57

Another evening, another air raid. As soon as the alarm siren goes up, Maud Gonne issues from her flat and walks towards Chesterfield Avenue at a measured pace, disdaining the hurry of the throngs. She is going for her Turkish bath and, like the French aristocrats who went unruffled to the guillotine, Maud believes the only becoming way to treat danger is to look down your nose at it.

At the baths, she undresses without haste and lays her form, tall and still trim for a woman of fifty, on a couch in the hottest of the steaming rooms, while more anxious types on the streets are merely sweating in their shoes. Usually, by the time she emerges from her bath the danger is past, but this evening events do not go to plan. She surfaces up the basement steps to the street, cool of cheek and hungry, to find the raid is only now unfurling, twin-engined Gothas and four-engine Giants swarming overhead in their close formations.

As she sets her face towards Chelsea, a number of explosions detonate close by, sending people scurrying in every direction. A special constable cries: 'Take cover, take cover!' and herds them towards the underground train station. Maud frowns, standing still to do it, the only person in the street not in fervent motion. The burly 'special' taps her on the shoulder, says aggressively, 'Take cover, can't you!' and pushes her towards the entrance. She endeavours to pull away, but the tide of humans in motion catches her in its flow and carries her down the slope.

'No,' she cries, preferring to be shot down by the anti-aircraft shrapnel than to go cowering into this burrow. With a pitched effort, she manages to squeeze her way back towards air.

'Oy!' shouts the constable after her. 'Get back here, you.'

It puts her in mind of the old days in Dublin. Dublin, Dublin, how she longs to be there. Here in London she has made friends among the socialists and suffragists, but in Ireland a new political party has formed, called Sinn Féin ('Ourselves Alone'), a young party full of idealists who insist that Ireland is entitled to be a free nation. The world's press is listening – America especially. Ireland's time is coming and she, and the children and Josephine, are stuck here in grim and grimy London, in a flat on the King's Road. The accommodation is too cramped. The weather is too cold. The food is too scarce. Seághan is too unruly, and Iseult, as ever, mopes. She mopes a little herself. Every few days, she visits the War Office, demanding her right of movement, but it seems they are not going to give in. She will have to take other measures.

Of them all, Josephine is the great surprise: she who was never outside France in her life is adapting best, simply by refusing to adapt. She wears her peasant costume, complete with clogs and a thick black hairnet. She buys her vegetables on a daily basis as she would in Paris and Normandy, asking at the greengrocer's for one parsnip or half a cabbage or a leaf of this or that. It is said the English hate the French, that they wished to be at war with them rather than the Germans, but the greengrocers and stallholders and shopkeepers are all charmed by Josephine's sturdy sense of self. They serve up what they've got to give, precisely to order, with a wink and a cheery 'There you go, love.'

But Josephine too will find Dublin more to her liking than England, Maud believes. One loves France for what she was but Ireland for what she is going to be.

Maud proceeds through the streets with no more trouble, and, when she gets home, finds Iseult is at the table by the window, eating a stew.

'Moura! You were never out in that. We thought you were at the baths.'

'No harm done. Where is Seaghán?'

'At Ezra's.' Ezra Pound has agreed to be Seaghán's tutor until he goes to Ireland. 'And Josephine is at her cousin's.'

'Oh, yes, I had forgotten. They may both have to stay put. This one looks like it may be down for the night.'

'Don't worry about Bichon; Ezra and Dorothy will look after him.'

'That food looks good.'

'Yours is in the pantry. You look unaccountably happy, Moura.'

'Happy? Do I? A small bit excited perhaps. Sometimes I think the only thing alive in London is the air raids. How I wish –'

Iseult interrupts. She is not able to bear Moura's longing for Ireland this evening, so begins to tell her instead that Sturge Moore, a friend of Willie's, has invited her to join a little society of a few who love poetry.

'That is kind,' says Moura, laying her plate of food on the table and taking the seat opposite. They feel so temporary in this flat that they have not claimed their own places at table.

'Yes, isn't it? I shall go tomorrow.'

'Is Ezra Pound part of the coterie?'

'I am unsure. Why?'

'I just wondered.'

Why had Moura asked that? And why had she not told her that, yes, Ezra should be there and that she is glad of it, for she would surely be too shy to attend without him.

'So how was it at the school today?' Moura asks, laying her food on the table. 'Will you like the work there, do you think?'

'Everything and everybody seems very nice. I hope they will be indulgent of my stupidity.'

'Would it not serve you better to hope to be capable?'

'I know it is but simple office work yet I fear I shall be unequal to the task. I still feel mentally very tired.'

Her mother returns to her food. She is irritated. Iseult does not blame her. She irritates herself with her constant thoughts

486

of failure or escape. To Colleville or to that place in the Pyrenees where she has told herself she will end her days in spinster-hood. Sometimes she wishes she were already there, but indeed she knows herself well enough to know that this is not quite true.

'What day do you start at the school?'

'The 20th.'

'Ah, the day of the wedding.'

'Willie and George? The date is set?'

'I believe so.'

'What a hurry.'

'Perhaps he is afraid she will change her mind.'

'Or he, his.'

They laugh together, guiltily, but poor Willie has made himself ridiculous with his prosaic marital arrangements.

Iseult feels dazed by thought today. Willie has organized this job for her at the School of Oriental Studies, which is a great kindness, and she is trying to be grateful, though for the first time in a long while she had been managing to read a lot and write a little. The pay is small but enough when added to her family income, and she will do her best to be happy there. She ought to succeed – both the Bengali and Sanskrit professors are charming, and Miss Iris Barry, with whom she is to work in her capacity as Assistant Librarian, has all the makings of a friend.

Miss Barry is proud of her reputation as a scandalous person. Her mother, she told Iseult, was the first woman in England to sue for divorce, citing her husband's frequent affairs and the gonorrhoea with which he infected her. She laughed her signa-ture, pealing laugh throughout the telling. Miss Barry – Iris – also writes. Ezra has read her draft novel and pronounced her nearer to Joyce (Ezra's highest praise) than any established female novelist. It has a chance, he says, of being literature.

Iseult does not admit how *she* should like to write something that would win such a judgement from him. Yesterday, he took her for tea at the ABC café, to dole out writing advice. She found him more thoughtful than when in company, less ebullient (though he did lean back so far in one of the chairs that he broke the leg and in such a way that she wondered whether it was deliberate), but, after the hubbub had settled, he gave her his full attention and a list of useful guidelines.

Poetry must be humble and simple. She must use the fervour of her life in her work, she must breathe into her verses, give her nature as it is, the evil with the good. Read Voltaire's *Dictionnaire Philosophique* in its entirety or something of that nature. Find a few things that no other living person has read, a few territories of print that she can have to herself – they are a great defence against fools, and the half-educated and dons of all sorts. She should get rid of poetic diction and all that is artificial or abstract. Being French should give her an advantage. Intellectual life demanded familiarity with French language and culture.

Then he surprised her. 'Write something for our next number,' he said.

'The *Little Review*?'

He nodded.

'"The Magazine Read by Those Who Write the Others"?' she said. 'Why should it take something from me?'

'Our next issue is French poetry: La Forgue, Corbière, Rimbaud . . .'

Her laugh is small and cynical.

'Why the hilarity?'

'I'm sorry, Ezra, but it is a little diverting to imagine the name of Iseult Gonne in the middle of that parade.'

'Maurice Gonne, don't you mean?'

She has decided to use a male pseudonym, as it gives her a better chance of being taken seriously. 'Well, yes, but none the less.'

'If you gave yourself over to me, you should soon think you were born in free verse.'

To deflect him, she said, 'I don't know how you find the time to do all the different activities. How do you do it? Or indeed, why?'

'I accepted the post at the *Review* because I wanted a place where Lewis and Joyce and myself might appear regularly. Much of the reviewing consists of saying the same thing over and over again. Joyce is a writer, GODDAM your eyes, Joyce is a writer, I tell you, Joyce . . . etc.'

'I have read *Ulysses*. It took me a long time to read because I could read but little of it at a time. He is too tragic to be bitter and not under any delusions but perhaps mad.'

He cast her his quizzical look. 'Goddam your eyes, woman, I tell you, Joyce is –'

'Don't be a bully.' She pressed a finger to her lips. 'I both admired it and disliked it. I can see the brilliance of the language, but it needed a real effort for me to get over the repugnance it inspired in me. His view of human nature is –'

'Repugnance?' Ezra threw himself backwards, clutching his chest as if she had shot him in the heart. The few people in the restaurant who were not already eyeing him – and the outlandish trousers he wore, which were almost the colour of a lime and tucked into his stockings – now turned their way.

It would disappoint him if she were to remark them or to care, so instead she smiled into his eyes and said coolly, 'Perhaps also I am exaggerating.'

'In a country in love with amateurs, I suppose it is well that one man should have a vision of perfection and that he should be disconsolate until he attains it.'

'Joyce?'

'Yours truly.'

'It sounds exhausting.'

'Ah, yes, it is. And you too must choose, my dear. To write or to marry.'

'That is what Willie says.'

'For once, the Eagle has it figured.'

489

'He has been so good to me, getting me this part-time job so that I shall have time to write.'

'So write.'

'In the past, whenever I got home from work, I was tired with a mind that ran everywhere, like a glass of spilled water.'

'That was war work, was it not? Or daily, consistent work. Three days a week card-indexing should not tax your mental energy much.'

'I do not seem to have as much mental energy as others.'

'Then you must marry. Only be careful. Follow the example of our friend Barry's ancestress – marry to govern a state. Don't marry three servants and a villa in Birmingham. It is no shortcut to leisure.'

And again he laughed his explosive laugh. His eyes seemed greener than they really were. They were actually a pale shade of grey.

Moura waves her hand before her face, making Iseult jump. 'Iseult, what on earth are you thinking of so intently? Did you hear what I just said?'

'Sorry, no.'

'Apparently Willie was boasting at his club of having found the perfect wife. Young, serviceable and able.'

'Poor Georgie.'

'A narrow escape for you, my dear.'

'Not so narrow, Moura.'

'I do wonder, if you had said yes to him, whether he would have described you thus.'

'Whatever words he would have used, it would not have been serviceable. Or able.'

'No, indeed.'

How is it possible that she should have this mother that is not one atom like her? 'And neither should I wish to be so described, Moura. I hope poor Georgie never finds out.'

'She will know soon enough, from his own attitude.'

'Ezra says she will be pleased to write and read for him, and to communicate with the living and the dead for him. Apparently, she is very psychic.'

'Perhaps she will see what is ahead for her and call it off.'

'Moura!'

'You know it is true. Once the poor girl realizes, then she must either run away or stay and become his slave. Either way it is better for her to make up her mind before the ceremony than afterwards.'

58

Zach's explanation of what happened to him that night was that his suffering was so intense that it forced his consciousness to stop identifying with the unhappy and fearful self he had become. As a result of which, unhappy and fearful Zach ('my false self') collapsed, and he was left with consciousness in its pure state, consciousness that doesn't identify with form and therefore does not suffer ('my true self').

Although he had shifts in intensity of feeling, he had remained in the same state of bliss since his metamorphosis. And metamorphosis it was. Out went the promising academic career: he no longer respected the emphasis on thinking and the mind. Thinking, doing, getting, achieving: all these seemed empty to him now. He just wanted to *be*.

'But how can you be without doing?'

'Of course you're right. We have to eat and dress and so on. What I mean is that once I awakened, I realized I needed to change the emphasis, the balance, in my life. Less doing, less thinking, more being.'

'Well, we'd all like a bit of that,' I said.

'I'm glad to hear you say it.'

'I said a *bit*.'

'Don't worry, Izzy. I'm not going to ask you to join me on my park bench.'

'Park bench?' My heart wobbled.

Yes, aside from some odd jobs, Zach had spent most of the past year on a park bench in Westside, LA.

'Like a . . . hobo?'

'Not too many hobos are in a state of deep bliss. And it was only during the day. I had an apartment.'

'I'm relieved to hear it.' My right foot was sticking out from under the quilt and feeling cold. I tucked it under, wrapped my leg around his. 'But how can you afford all this sitting around? Don't you have to work?'

'People ask me questions and some of them give me money for the answers. Or food. Or other stuff.'

'What sort of questions?'

'All sorts – Is there life after death? Why is love so difficult? How can I be free? Do I matter? Anything.'

'And you've got the answers to all that? Come off it, Zach. Are you fooling with me?'

'It isn't about the questions really. The questions are just entry points.'

'Hmmm. Are they religious, your answers to the questions?'

'Not in any conventional sense. My job, my purpose, now is to enable others to find their way out of the suffering created by too much thinking.'

'A guru?'

This made him sit forward off the pillows and turn to face me. 'No, positively, absolutely *not* a guru. A signpost maybe. A pointer.'

It frightened me, the awesome responsibility (the damn cheek) of answering such questions. 'Don't you ever worry in case you get it wrong?'

'It's not me, it just comes through me.'

That one would never stand up in a law court. And I didn't like this business of taking money from strangers, strangers who must be vulnerable and suggestible to be seeking answers from a man on a park bench.

'They need to give me something,' he said. 'I never ask. I really don't care whether they do or don't. I just accept what comes along.'

He sits up, takes my face in his hands. 'I understand why you're uncomfortable, Iz, but I operate from a different place now. I take my cues from the inner, not the outer world.'

493

He fixes me with his eyes until I feel I'm falling into them, down a tunnel, like Alice, where what he calls the outer world (what everybody else calls life) is floating around me, freed from gravity, light and loose as the snow-grey flecks in his eyes.

'Anyway,' he says, taking down his hands. 'It looks as if I'll be doing it differently back here. More formally. A group of philosophy students in Santa Paola have set me up in various venues and are charging a small entry fee so I can be paid.'

Apparently word had gone around among students that he was a modern mystic. 'You should come along on Thursday. That's the next one. See for yourself, Izzy, and put your anxieties to rest.'

The event was in Sportshall 2 on campus and had sold out, with a line at the door hoping for cancellations. It was a strange experience, seeing so many people avid to see Zach, not just students but men and women – mainly women – of all types and ages and colours. He had no props or special lighting, and made no concession to stage management: just him and his words and his calm, radiant presence. He spoke slowly and carefully, and had no problem connecting with the questions and finding answers that made sense. Nothing groundbreaking, just the concepts at the heart of all religions, stripped clean and put into clear, simple, modern words.

I was proud of him and, agnostic as I was, affected too. In that large hall, encased inside a silence so intense you could touch it, and a stillness so deep you could hear it, I sensed, rather than understood, what he was talking about. Peace was mine for those two hours, was there in the room for all who had come to hear what he had to say.

They loved him – yes, especially the women – but only I was allowed into the back room where he waited while they cleared the building.

We were back in love, but this time it was different. He was no longer the awestruck boy. He told me a little about other

494

women he had been with, only one of them special. A 'beautiful person' but demanding, with a 'sparky soul, a warrior spirit'.

'What about you?' he asked.

'Nobody.'

'Really?'

'Not a one.'

It wasn't a lie. There had been nobody serious, nobody worth mentioning.

He liked that. He was still the romantic who wanted what we had to be absolute, still uncomfortable with compromise. The shades and blurred edges of reality. My reality, anyway. But maybe he was right. Maybe life didn't have to be like that.

'We won't ever let each other go again,' he said, and that was just what I wanted to hear.

Now we had only one problem to face. Star.

'I think it's best if I meet her as soon as possible, Izzy, don't you?'

This time, I wasn't going to argue. Star was still making life hard for herself, still lovesick and heartsore, still relying on telephone calls. Mexico hadn't been what she hoped, and now she was just about coping with being back at college. Her hurt at being rejected was still coming between her and the rest of her life. And she still saw other people's love affairs as a personal insult.

However I played it, that her mother was in love while she was alone was going to feel wretched to Star, but Zach was right, it was never going to be easy. So the sooner the better. She would be back for Thanksgiving in three weeks. I would tell her then. This time, we shouldn't, couldn't, put it off.

59

On his wedding eve, the evening of Friday, 19 October, William Butler Yeats is struck with a feverish attack, followed by a great, indeed an overwhelming, exhaustion which – he writes to his friend Lady Gregory – may cause the ceremony to be post-poned. His friend responds by return, urging him to rally himself and requesting a telegram to inform her that the deed is done. Next day, Willie struggles to Harrow Road Register Office, supported by his best man, Ezra Pound, who is one of the witnesses, the other being Mrs Tucker, the bride's mother. Mrs Tucker is sister-in-law to Yeats's old lover, Olivia, herself mother to Dorothy Pound, the bride's best friend. With this marriage, the groom is stitching himself into a tight and intimate circle.

He has chosen Ashdown Forest for the honeymoon, but after the wedding he falls into a nervous collapse and is incapable of leaving London for two days. On the journey down, he com-plains all the way – of weakness, of neuralgia, of lack of energy and of headache. As soon as they arrive, he leaves his bride to the unpacking and locks himself away to write a poem that has been pounding his frontal lobes all these difficult days. A poem he vows his wife must never read, for it speaks of his love for another woman. A love that came to him unsought on the Norman upland of Colleville and that he feared would drive him insane from longing and despair and pity and fear.

The poem describes how he sought refuge from this true love in a smaller, safer relationship. 'I ran, I ran, from my love's side because my Heart went mad.'

Composition for Willie is usually a tortured process, but this lovelorn song of anguish empties from him on to the page.

With it comes a realization that the marriage he hoped would alleviate his mental turmoil has only aggravated it. He writes a long letter to Lady Gregory and an even longer, more troubled missive to Iseult, telling all – the poem, his love, his fear that he has made a terrible mistake and ruined the lives of three people.

Outside – as if in sympathy with his torment and that of his bride, who watches him gloomily writing, writing, writing, instead of consummating their marriage – the weather gathers to storm. A night of unusually severe gales ensues. The winds howl, the trees bend and twist, the rain lashes itself against the glass, while inside in the hotel room, husband and wife face each other across an abyss.

True to the form of a man who has always advanced his suit with one woman by bewailing his problems with another, he confesses. For Georgie, this is the worst moment of her young life. She had known there were others before her. Aware – who could not be? – of his long love for Maud Gonne, she had been prepared to face that spectre, but when he proposed to her, he had described himself as 'a Sinbad who after many misadventures had at last found port', and she had believed him.

When he went to Ireland after their engagement, he had written tender, ink-spattered letters that addressed her as 'My beloved' and spoke of how he dreamt of their future together, of finding her waiting for him at the end of his day's work, sitting by the fire or dealing with his household affairs. She had believed it all. For she loved him, had loved him for a very long time, despite the age difference that had made one of her cousins exclaim, upon hearing the news that she was to marry him: 'George . . . you can't. He must be dead.' For more than two years, she had yearned for this proposal, and finally it had come, only for her to find, after the wedding, that she was his second choice, held in reserve while he paid court to another. Another to whom he is still in thrall.

497

Sophisticated, intelligent, bohemian and proud, Georgie Hyde-Lees is not the type of woman to remain in a loveless match – married or not. What can she do but leave him?

My dear Willie

... I burnt your first letter; it made a very ghostly little flame in the chimney ... I felt your trouble as if it was mine, and it is just as well I did not write you at once, for it mends no ill, if someone says 'life is wicked', for someone else to answer: 'it is'.

I happened this afternoon to enter a little Protestant church quite bare but welcoming. I spoke to God there (for it was in the spirit of the place) as if he was a simple old friend, a kind of outlaw like ourselves yet with some influence on the authorities. 'Why should Willie of all people not be happy; why should I who have always loved him in all affection have had any share in causing him sorrow ...'

If only as one more kindness to me, try to be happy. It is too late and it is too early just now to look to yourself. An abruptly new condition is bound to have a little of the fearfulness of a birth, though it may be for the better. Though it may seem dreary to you, would it not be better to renounce for a time the life of emotion, and live a few maxims of the early Patricians.

But here I am speaking as if I knew when really all I know is that I share your sadness and will share your joy when you tell me: 'All is well.'

Give my love to Georgie; she has a sweet nature, and her kindness is no doubt the best wisdom.

Yours most helplessly
Maurice

Moura is on her way to Ireland at last, amid a flurry of back-blown kisses and promises.

'I shall send for you, darling, as soon as I am settled. You know that wherever I am, I must have you both with me.'

To fool the detectives, her new friend, Sylvia Pankhurst, has announced a meeting at which she is supposed to be speaking, and Maud has written to all her friends in Ireland, knowing the censor would open the letters, to say how broken-hearted she is to have to send Seaghán across alone, without her, to be put to school. Now, with the help of her suffragist friends, she has powdered her hair white and dressed herself in a dowdy grey coat with a worn grey muff and collar and a deeply unfashionable little blue hat that stands on her head like a post-box. This evening she and Bichon will take the mail-boat to Dublin as Mrs Grimes and son.

Iseult waves, as if she is the mother seeing off her child on an adventure. Moura expects her to follow shortly, but Iseult means instead to make a life of independence in London. Willie thinks she must and so does Ezra. She is, afer all, twenty-three years old now. And life with Moura has become impossible. Yet, as soon as they are gone, she feels flat. A little bereft. She goes to her bedroom to cry a little and is interrupted by her hall-door knocker banging.

She breaks into a smile when she finds her new friend, Iris Barry, on the step, complete with suitcase. Iris looks around the flat approvingly. 'How simply wonderful.' The suitcase is not set down before she is saying, 'Let's arrange a party.'

So they do, the first of many. The war and Maud's authoritarianism has delayed Iseult's adulthood, but now she plunges into a life that is freer and wilder and, above all, her own. Iris and Ezra introduce her to stem-necked aesthetes, cubist photographers and graphic artists. Iconoclasts and radicals and scorners of the bourgeoisie. Tyro-psychoanalysts and gramophone dancers and the occasional Dadaist en route to or from Paris or Zurich or New York. Such people swarm around Iris and Ezra like exotic bees.

At their parties, Iris stands tiny, slim and laughing in the midst of the excitement she likes to whip up, cigarette aloft, eyes seeking, black hair cropped, gold hoop earrings glistening.

499

Ezra runs from one person to another, always trying to get the 'lowdown', the inside story, the simple reason *why* . . .

Alcohol and other drugs – mescalin, 'magic' mushrooms, hashish – are passed around, and through it all they must avoid the baleful eye of Josephine, the faithful servant. Her presence, that knowledge that she will report all back to Maud, keeps in place some measure of decorum.

Adonis is not among these people, Iseult admits to herself, and neither is the God of wisdom. They have dogmas without faith and no hesitation. Their mental air moves but as if motioned by a ventilator. It is not the wind. Still, it is a new experience for her to consider an anti-aesthetic, anti-meaning, anti-moral view of life. She wants to know them for a time and try to understand. A movement must have something good in it, she feels, even if only in its intentions.

Iseult works hard at Sanskrit. The secret books of Buddhism and Hinduism – Pancha-Tantra, Bhagavad-Gita, Mahabharata – are endlessly revealing. She likes the way the Indian mind, rather than forcing story into one theme, conceives a story large enough to encompass all the themes. And she and Iris are much exercised by the concept of Nirvana and the theory that suffering is caused by attachment. The ideas are so much the opposite of all one has been taught and turn Western philosophy upon its head. 'I think, therefore I am' is inverted to 'I am, because I know myself to be more than my thoughts.'

But the extinction of desire: is it truly possible?

This is one of the questions that keep the two thinkers awake at night, talking into the darkness of their shared bedroom, with deliberation and detail, delighting in the other's ideas and how their hypotheses are stretched. Sometimes they diverge, and then the nasty side of Iris can emerge, tears and tempers doled out between the parties and confidences.

Ezra too draws closer. How amusing he is. No man has ever made Iseult laugh so. How attractive he is. Her sunny-head, she calls him, his face so radiant, his hair like the beams of the sun, lighting up all around him. How clever he is. She is only coming to an understanding of his ideas about the importance of the surface in literature, the work of language — what he calls melopeia, phanopeia and mythopeia. How kind he is. He devotes a quarter of his time to his own poetry. With the rest, he tries to advance the material and artistic fortunes of his friends — defending them when attacked, pushing their publications, lending them money, writing articles about them. How astute he is in relation to literary talent and how nurturing of his protégés — H. D., Tom Eliot, Joyce, Iris — of which she is now one (how is she to be worthy of that company?). How gentle he is, not at all the swashbuckling American she thought him first, but thrillingly gentle, as only a great man can be. How attentive he is. People call him egocentric, but he is always cutting the fruit and pouring the wine and passing the food and offering one books or papers or accompanying one to this or that event or introducing one to this or that person. How uniquely joyous and childish he is, with his outrageous behaviour and harrumphing great laugh.

How married he is.

'What about your writing?' is his constant refrain to her. And yes, she can report for the first time in a long time, writing *is* being done. Yesterday on the bus, her fancy was caught by a young woman holding a baby in her arms, so thoroughly detached from him and looking away, which seemed to Iseult to be the only decent attitude for a mother. She came home full of thoughts on the beauty of silence and could not wait to get to her notebook and add them to old thoughts on the same theme. What she wrote has stayed with her. She carries it around, like a baby itself, and, when she lays her head down at night, it comes alive again for her.

Yet she is unsure. Is it worth anything? The feelings that ignite her writing are so nebulous. When she reads back, she despises so much of what she has produced. Where she is indistinct, Ezra and Willie are unwavering, each burning with his own gem-like flame.

It seems that Willie's stars have brought him, against all odds, a good match. Some days after his wedding, George discovered she had a gift for automatic writing – putting herself in a trance in order to take dictation from the other world, the world that Willie thinks of as lying, tantalizingly, just beyond the veil. Now the newly-weds spend hours together each day in dialogue with spirits. From the wisdom this elicits, they are constructing a system of personality and history that will, according to Willie, provide the key he has so long been seeking to an ancient corpus of knowledge.

Iseult hopes he is not deluded, like Miss Eliot's Dr Casaubon. She finds it difficult to believe in An Explanation of Everything, preferring to reside within mystery – but that may be because she is too indolent for the effort. What George has to endure in pursuit of their revelations – daily sessions that can go on for hours – sounds exhausting, but she too is energized by the adventure and the affection it has ignited in her husband. Georgie really is very clever.

But she will not find him easy to hold. Moura was right. His is a nature that yearns only for what will not be his. In this he suffers – which is why she is not so cross as she ought to be at her sudden displacement in his affections.

Marriage has made Willie avuncular towards her. He has adopted the role of stern paterfamilias overseeing a child in danger of perdition and has written her a poem, 'To Young Beauty', in which she is flatteringly addressed as 'Dear fellow-artist', only to be admonished: 'Why so free/With every sort of company?' Ezra finds this self-appointed role most diverting; she finds it irritating to have a new father just when she's rid herself of parental domination. He induces as much guilt as if he truly were her father.

Moura's letters from Dublin, all the time asking Iseult to join her there, also make her feel remorseful. She had thought when Moura was far away, she should be free of daughterly self-reproach, but guilt is still her plague. Irrational, ever-present and, it seems, inescapable.

It is her father, of all people, who changes her feelings for Ezra from infatuation to . . . something else. Ezra calls to the flat one evening after Josephine has been dispatched to Moura in Dublin, bounding in in his usual oblivious way to give her his customary greeting – a loud smacking kiss in the middle of the forehead – before noticing that she is not herself.

'Feathermongers! Whatever is the matter?'

Embarrassingly, she finds herself unable to speak. She points him to the newspaper on the table. Her father, the man she refers to as the Wolf, is dead.

'My poor girl.' He leads her to a chair as the sobs begin to subside. 'You are alone? Barry –?'

'Is away . . . staying at Alan's.'

'But this is infamous, that you should be deserted. Hour of need and so on. Shame on Barry.'

'She does not know.' She takes the handkerchief he hands her. 'Thank you,' she says, dabbing her eyes. 'My eyes are sore with weeping. It is a great blow to me . . . I don't quite know why.'

'You and he were estranged, were you not?'

'When he lived, Ezra, I spoke and felt *so* unkindly towards him. But now . . . One never really knows just how much affection one has for someone until they are . . . lost.'

Ezra nods and pats her hand.

'Then one remembers with distress all one could have done for them and all that one failed to do and, worst of all, the hard things one has thought. And this feels so unjust and cruel.'

True understanding gleams among the grey-green speckles of his eyes.

'At least I have the poor satisfaction of telling myself that the last letter I received from him three weeks ago was very affectionate, and I answered almost immediately. We had really become friends again.'

She drops Ezra's hand and makes her way to the window, where she allows herself another squall of tears. She feels him watching her, but he does not try to console, as another man would. 'It is like this,' she says, as her breath settles. 'So long as one's father or mother is alive, one *has* to like them. So if they have failings such as might bring one closer to a friend, one does not forgive them. Then they die and the link that was compulsory – and a little shameful – dies also, because beyond this life, no such link exists. Now they are only little children yet unborn to whom much tenderness and pity can be given.'

'A perfect summary, my dear.'

'It is of little consolation.'

'And it shall be interesting to see if you can hold to this benevolent understanding when you next see your mother.'

Moura has settled in Dublin, in a house on St Stephen's Green once owned by Robert Emmet. She smiles. It stretches her tear-tightened face to do so. 'Poor Moura, I really should not be so critical of her. You should not allow it.'

'You know how vastly entertaining I find her – but she is not an easy person to have in proximity. And your father, I conjecture, was a similar kind. I don't think you should blame yourself for finding them difficult.'

'Thank you, Ezra. Truly. I am sorry for being so disintegrated.'

'Pishwaffle.' He crosses the room to stand beside her at the window and she hands him back his handkerchief. He is standing very close.

'May God have his soul,' she cries in a whisper. Here it comes again, a new wave of sorrow that insists on having her. 'Loup. Poor, poor Loup. In Christ's kingdom, the symbol of justice is not a weighing scales. The further a person has to

504

return, the more he is welcome. This is what I hope for him now.'

The tears take her.

'Come here to me, my poor dearymum. You will make yourself unwell.'

60

My dear Willie

*I am really at a loss to answer your letter. Ezra tried to kiss me?!!
My first impulse was to summon the good lady of Normandy so as
to get a little light, but then I thought it would mean tears and a
row and a reproachful letter to Moura which would not help
matters, so I decided not to say anything to her. The only thing I
could possibly imagine is that the poor old thing, fresh from her
village, must have been horrified at the way people call on us in the
evenings, and as Ezra comes rather often, must have drawn
fantastic conclusions.*

*What I cannot account for are the circumstantial details she
seems to have given; it would all be very laughable if it wasn't at
the same time rather distressing and humiliating . . .*

Iseult lies abed, beset by thoughts that fix her to the mattress, though she knows she should be up. About. Doing. Not
lying flat, unable even to be . . . anything. Josephine is gone,
to the shops in town, but Iseult no longer has to go to the
school because now she works instead for Ezra, three days a
week, an arrangement put in place by him and Willie and
George. The other days – of which today is one – are supposed
to be devoted to writing, but she knows that today she cannot
write.

Today is a bad day. A day for hiding alone in a corner. Today
le cafard is a giant, its shell-body swelling with black intent, its
angled legs ominously treading, treading, treading the room.
She cowers under her blanket, pretending to hope that it will
pass, but knowing (without quite admitting it) that she is

cornered, that she has been spotted, that it inches towards its target. Knowing that the best she can expect is that she won't be grasped too tightly or for too long. That it will tire of her and move off, dropping her back in her corner, exhausted and shaken, but relieved to be released. Not too long this time, not too long, pray God.

It is a relief, when she feels like this, to no longer have a flatmate. Willie kindly came up from Oxford, where he and George are now living, to rescue her from Iris, who, after they moved from Moura's flat, turned domineering and more than a little mean – omitting to pay her share of the rent or expenses too often for it to be accidental. In a tableau that made them laugh afterwards, Willie played the stern uncle sent by a concerned Moura to carry her off, while she played the submissive niece, who had to obey and allow herself to be installed in his rooms at Woburn Buildings.

It was the only way to deal with Iris, who even as it is, succeeds in making her feel guilty and in the wrong when they meet. It is Iseult's own fault of course; she cannot cope. She is . . . *Rat-a-tat*: the newspaper Willie has delivered daily clatters in through the letter box, cutting through her slothful thoughts. She pushes herself out of the bed and towards it, asking herself why, for what can knowing about the latest war offence, or the goings-on of Westminster, or the conduct of the English colonies, do to her today but further freeze the chill of her soul? Yet she finds herself picking the paper up from the floor and settling into the armchair with it and feeling the sordid words fail to stir the emotion they seek – her indignation or outrage or pride.

Then she gasps. An article under the heading SINN FÉIN GERMAN PLOT sucks her attention. It tells her that seventy-two Irish Republican sympathizers were arrested in Dublin the day before, and that, yes, Moura is among them, brought under military escort to the mail-boat under the Defence of the Realm Act, to be shipped to Holloway Prison in London.

According to *The Times* the Republicans are guilty of treason-
able conspiracy with the Germans, though it mentions little in
the way of evidence or how so many could be so implicated.
(She can already hear the Irish counter-cries of framing, of
this being a concoction to silence their anti-conscription
movement.)

The offenders, the paper says, are likely to be placed in solitary
confinement until further notice. Oh, Moura, no.

No doubt she would have had time to flee to the countryside
or back here to London had she wished, but had disdained to
do so. Now she will think herself happy, think she has found
her fitting place at the frontline of the struggle. Iseult remembers
the purity of the life of quiet Moura won for herself when
subdued by her divorce. This was the happiest time, for both
of them. Moura had sworn then never to return to the world
of hate. She did not see that the Dublin Rising, which stirred
so much emotion in her, was a test of that commitment to a
deeper, more subtle life.

A test she has failed. Nothing lies ahead for her but the
greatest suffering. The physical torture will be nothing to the
mental strain. Which means all around her must also suffer.
That makes Iseult think of Bichon. What is to be done for him,
alone now in Ireland? Fourteen is such a vulnerable age. Iseult
cannot cope with this alone.

She rises from the chair to send for Ezra and also to write to
Willie in Oxford. They will tell her what to do next.

By the time Ezra arrives next morning, Seaghán is also there,
having turned up on the doorstep ten minutes before. 'Well,
boy!' Ezra says. He proffers his hand, which Seaghán seems
reluctant to take. 'Lately arrived?'

'Out of the blue,' says Iseult. 'Dispatched back to us by
Moura on her arrest. Have you heard, Ezra?'

'Yes, from the Eagle. It seems nothing can be done, for now
at any rate.'

'No. Visits aren't allowed. I went up to the jail but was not even permitted to leave a note. I have applied for a permit and await the answer. Oh, dear, what a business.'

'I'm hungry,' Seaghán says.

'Are you?'

'Of course he is,' says Ezra. 'Boys are always hungry.' He flashes his eyes at her to put quite another meaning on the words.

'Josephine is gone to the market to queue for a carrot or half a cabbage, if we are lucky. She will look after you when she gets back.'

'But I'm hungry now.'

After his months in Ireland with Moura, Bichon has returned even more hyperactive and agitated and rabidly nationalist than before, full of drastic and foolhardy plans against the English.

'All right, all right,' Iseult says. 'I shall put on some toast for you. In the meantime, you'd better unpack.'

'I don't want to unpack.'

'Bichon, just do it, please.'

'Why?'

'*Please* just go to the bedroom I showed you. Take out your belongings and make a space for yourself. I need to speak to Ezra about some matters.'

'But . . .'

'In *private*. Thank you.'

He goes, scowling.

'Do you wish us to take him?' Ezra asks.

'You are kind and thank you, but we'll manage something. Better for him to be here. And nearer to Holloway.'

'So Madame is locked in perfidious Saxon chains?'

'Don't laugh, Ezra. It is most unfair. No formal charges have been brought against her, yet she is kept in a cell seven feet by thirteen. She is allowed no visitors, and no solicitor. She is too old for this.'

'Oh, stuff! If I know your mother, she will be enjoying it to the hilt of her foil.'

'That does not mean she will not wear herself out. And create the most perfect havoc for all around her.'

'But with dash and aplomb, *n'est-ce pas?*'

Perhaps but Iseult feels choked. Her freedom from Moura is over, already, before it fully began. She should have relished more her days of liberty while she had them.

'For myself,' says Ezra, 'I must admit I do not understand your mother's politics. She favours a socialist Republic in Ireland, but she was Boulangist in France, and they were royalists, were they not?'

'She is engaged by passion, not intellect.'

'How do you find the boy?'

She shakes her head, drops her voice. 'He has brought back a head packed with rubbish, having been brought to all the meetings and set in train for martyrdom. To read the English papers is to get a most misleading impression of Irish affairs. Bichon is a walking give-away of the real state of feelings over there.'

He moves in closer. 'So much for Miss Gonne's relatives. But what of the fair Miss Gonne herself?' He places a hand on her back, leans forward as if to kiss her. Which she has been permitting lately, perhaps a little too often.

'Ezra! For pity's sake!' She leaps from him as if his hand were fire, snapping round towards the door of the bedroom whence Bichon might, this very moment, be peeking out. 'Vile man! You must go now.'

He laughs, puckers his lip towards her.

'Please, Ezra, don't tease.'

'Then fix me a time when the boy is not about or the Normandy nun.'

Seaghán comes out and says he needs to go on a message.

'What kind of message?' Iseult asks.

He touches the side of his nose with one finger, an indication that it is Irish Republican business. And so it is he, and not Ezra, who is gone.

As the door bangs behind him, a silence descends. They stand at the window and he brings his hand up to touch her face. With typical Ezra awkwardness, he almost lands his finger in her eye, which has the merit of making them both laugh. Then his hands find her arms. She is wearing her blue taffeta with the tasselled shawl she likes to wrap around her when she is writing or reading. Two hands grip her, forearms first, then her upper arms.

When heart has been yearning, and flesh has been waiting, and thought has been burnished, as Iseult's have for weeks now, the smallest touch can be explosive. And so it is. She feels the heat of his hands through the thin material of her dress, she feels the backs of them, his knuckles, along the side of her breasts, and something new surges in her. She lets her head fall back, she lets his lips close on hers and his hands move from arms to waist. The tasselled shawl falls to the floor, and she lets it lie. She lets him place pressure on her shoulders while pulling her close and bending her knee with his own leg from behind. He intends to ease her down on to the carpet but actually causes them both to hit the floor with quite a bump, but now she doesn't laugh and neither does he, because they are both afraid to stop, both urging towards what is to come and there is distraction enough in the necessary unbuttoning and untying and unstrapping.

No, don't laugh or really look. Just kiss, kiss, kiss until released from the skin of clothes, ripe as a fruit. The surge of desire that brought her to here is ebbing now, and she is retreating with it, into her usual position of observation. Though she feels the press of his lips, the brush of his fingers, the prickle of his beard and moustache, it is all from the skin out.

She tries to search out his eyes, but they are trained upon her body or else, towards the end, raised to heaven, as if giving thanks.

And afterwards she cries again, hot tears against his naked shoulder. 'Your mother, I am hoping,' Ezra says, lighting two cigarettes and giving her one. 'And not our love tumbles?'

Which only adds puzzlement and makes her cry harder.

61

A dance. Star, Zach and I all at the same table at Marsha's AIDS Charity Ball. Was I crazy? I didn't know how else to do it.

Thanksgiving had come and gone and then Christmas, and I still hadn't broached it, but finally, on the first day of her spring break, I told her, with quavering voice and shaky hands, that I had met someone, someone important. She made it just as hard as I had expected. A shrug first (why should I care?), followed by a tantrum, supposedly about her bedroom (I don't care, I don't care), followed by a slam-out from the room (see if I care).

It was wrong of her and not to be indulged, Zach said, keeping up the pressure from the other side. Now that she knew, they must meet, and soon.

I considered having him round for dinner, but, every time I thought of it, it felt suffocating – the three of us, trapped in my small dining room for an entire evening. Way too intense. At the dance, we would be at a mixed table, some solos, some couples, some groups, so Star need not feel conspicuously single. He would ask her to dance with him, and they would be able to talk without my listening. He would be charming, and everybody else would love him, and Star would be unable to resist.

By the time that Friday came round, the breathing trick that Zach had taught me was letting me down. I left the café early, with provisions in my bag and a nest of nerves in my stomach. It's just a hurdle, I soothed myself, as I walked up Westcliff Road. Just a hurdle that needs to be jumped so that life can go on. Once Star got used to the idea, she would take Zach for granted, not see him as a comment on her inability to attract love. Wallpaper on the background of her life. That's where we had to get to, and this was the first step.

She was late home, of course. Zach was coming at eight to drive us to the hotel, and I had asked her to be back by six. By seven there was still no sign of her. I carried on, had my shower, dried my hair, put on my make-up, growing more and more anxious. My mother's jade-blue dress was laid out on the bed, waiting for me. I stepped into it, zipped it up. I'd had it adjusted so it fitted perfectly, and I loved everything about it. I loved the colour of it and how it flattered my skin and the jewelled detail across the bodice and down my back. I loved the way it bared my shoulders and supported my breasts, showing just the right amount of cleavage. I loved the way it cinched my waist, but not too tightly, then flared into fabulous folds all the way to the floor. I loved how it made me look and feel, and I knew Zach would love it too.

The door downstairs slammed.

'Star? Is that you?'

'No, it's the tooth fairy.'

I went out on to the landing, looked down over the banisters. One look at her face and I knew what I was in for. I weighed it up in my head. Which would be quicker – to go through the motions of sympathy and smooth her down or to be brisk and try to get her to speed along?

I plumped for sympathy. 'How was your day, darling?'

'Shit.'

'Oh, dear. Sorry to hear that.'

'I nearly punched this fool woman in the library. She's trying to say I owe $32 in book fines because her stupid system didn't record that I brought her stupid books back months ago. Then I had to wait fifty minutes – that would be, yes, five–zero minutes – to get over here.'

'That's awful, honey. There's some chicken salad there if you'd like a snack.'

'No, thanks. I had lunch with Suzy. What was I thinking of, agreeing to have lentil bake just because she's going on some stupid health kick? It's sitting in my stomach like a football ever since, I think it might come back up –'

'Star, you haven't forgotten the dance? Don't you think it's time you –?'

'Is that what you're wearing?'

'Yes, don't you like it?'

'It's lovely. Mine's rotten.'

'You liked it a couple of days ago. I love it. It's dead funky.'

'Funky? Jeez, Mom, where *do* you get the words?'

'Anyway,' I say lightly, 'too late to change it now. Will you pick up those shoes and things and bring them up to your room on your way?'

Mistake. Her face hardened. 'Don't you think you're being a bit pathetic, Mom? Do you really need to try so hard to impress this guy? If he . . . ahem . . . loves you, he's not going to care whether there's a pair of shoes on the floor, is he? As usual, you're making a mountain out of –'

'Okay, Star, okay. Don't pick up. I'll do it.'

'Oh, great, now the long-suffering Mom routine. God, Mom, what about me? I've told you I feel sick. That I've had the most horrible day. Don't you care about that at all? No, only precious Zach. *Zach*. What sort of a name is that, anyway?'

I did everything for you, Star, went the drip-feed in my head, the self-talk I always pretend not to hear. I did everything for you, but you can't do this one thing for me. You know this is important, you know exactly *how* important, but – no, not but, *so* – you can't let me have it.

I sighed. What was the use in looking for understanding that she wasn't able to give? Self-pity served no purpose, only made me feel worse. Wipe the ticker tape. Do Zach's trick again. Breathe in goodness and light, breathe out toxic thought.

She went up, and I came down and started fixing my hair,

piling it on top of my head. It took a long time to get it, and my make-up, right, and I was only just finished when the doorbell rang.

Ding dong.

My heart started to thud so hard it hurt.

'I'll get it,' I called.

Cooler air swept in as I opened the door. Zach looked gorgeous, spruced up in a crisp, white shirt, the hair he was growing back still a little damp from the shower. He held two orchids, one for each of us. A nice touch.

'Oh, wow,' he said, as he looked me up and down.

I did a little twirl so he could admire.

'Wow, wow, WOW.'

'Shhh,' I said, thinking of Star, but he pulled me in close, crushing the orchids between us to kiss me. A long, sumptuous kiss. I had never been with anyone – even the younger him – who made me feel the way I now felt. We were developing new, slow-going ways of being together that were connected to a deeper place, a channelling rather than a dissipating of desire. Sometime, sometime soon, I felt I might be able to –

Footsteps behind us on the stairs stopped my thoughts, and I pulled away from him, fast. I turned and started to say, 'Star, this is –' but, again, I was stopped.

Something was wrong. Zach's smile was contorting into the opposite of a smile. Star was looking at him as if somebody had struck her.

'Shando?' she said, her voice thick, as if she were clearing her throat.

'Maya?' he said, in exactly the same tone.

The two of them – so similar in their shock, mouths and eyes wide and aghast – turned to me, as if I held all the answers.

Then Star began to scream. 'Mom, Mom, Mom! What the hell, what the hell, what the hell is going on?'

Suffer as Your Mother Suffered

O you will take whatever's offered
And dream that all the world's a friend,
Suffer as your mother suffered,
Be as broken in the end.

W. B. Yeats,
'To a Child Dancing in the Wind'

Christmas Eve, 1982
Izzy

When his time came, he didn't go easy. He resisted, he clung, he struggled, to the extent that Star, back in the bedroom by then, became distressed by the sound of his breathing – the 'death rattle', I believe it is called – and the way his body twitched and shuddered in its resistance.

Once, as he slipped in or out of consciousness, he called for his mother – 'Mammy!' – in a way that made the word a prayer, an entreaty and an accusation. This hit Star worse than any scream or whine.

'You take a break for a while,' I said to her.

'Are you sure?'

'Step outside, get some fresh air. You don't need to be here all the time.'

'What if –?'

'Don't worry, I'll call you.'

I sat alone beside him. On the bedside locker beside him was his jug and tumbler of water, a box of tissues, a roll of mint sweets, the pill box, half full . . . His lips were dry, and I smoothed some petroleum jelly across them, as I did several times a day, so they would not crack or bleed. He was lying quiet now, except for the sound of his tortured breath, in and out. I didn't know whether he was awake or asleep. Sleep had become a thin, worn blanket for him, and it was hard to tell.

When the time came, I called Star as I had promised, and we both sat by the bed while I moved my breath to match his: in, out, in . . . Steady now, not jagged, but louder than was natural and rasping. And slow, so, so slow. I felt as if whole minutes were going by between breaths, waiting for him to let the air in or out, so I could do the same. In. Out. In. Out.

Until his stopped. The sound of this silence brought me back, out of the daze the slow repetitive breathing had induced. He made another, different sound, something like a dog makes when it's startled, a growl deep in the throat, fear and menace together: *Grr-uh-uh-uh.*

I took his hand and held it as a shudder shook him, from core to skin. The same sound again – *grr-uh-uh-uh* – and one more inhalation.

I waited for the exhale, waited and waited, and then I knew it was not coming. His fingers shrunk inside my own. I lay my forehead down to touch the white duvet cover that the day before I had cleaned and ironed and replaced. I inhaled the clean, fresh smell of fabric conditioner, knowing that when I lifted my head back up, he'd be gone. That there would be nothing of him left in his own face.

And so it was.

'Mom?' Star said, and that's when I remembered she too was there.

'He's dead,' I said.

'I know.'

'I'll go and call Pauline,' I said. 'She'll know what to do next.'

62

Iseult is eloping, if one can call it elopement when no mention has been made of marriage, or when the lady in question does not care if she ever sees a ceremony, in fact disdains the golden ring of marriage as a manacle. Call it what you will, her suitcase is packed, its handle an excitement in her hand, and she is on her way to a boarding house convenient to Euston Railway Station, where her beloved is to meet her, in the quaint phrase she used with him in making the arrangement, 'on the morrow'.

He had laughed at this, and she had explained how her English, learnt as much from books as conversation, is sometimes a little archaic.

'O let her choose a young man now and all for his wild sake,' Willie's fervent poem proclaimed in the wake of his hasty marriage, and that is what Iseult has done now, three years on.

Perhaps you picture Ezra's sunny-head, hair blown back, cat-eyes narrowed with daring, fleeing his wife at last? No, it has been more than a year since Iseult last saw Ezra, time spent in Ireland where, despite Moura's promises, she has not found much of the first rate. But then – is there much of that anywhere? The country has an entertaining variety and quite a decent percentage of intelligence, and, all in all, is a better zoo than London.

Except, no Ezra.

She left him at a bus stop in November 1918. The month the war ended and Moura was finally released. It was a painful parting, and he blustered through the days of arranging passports and boat tickets and suitcases to signify his displeasure. 'Bureaucratic imbecilities!' he had expostulated, all the way to the bus stop where they parted. Nobody expostulates like Ezra. 'God blasted ninnyred tape.'

She smiled a small apology at the gentleman in the bus queue behind them who had turned away, a little horrified – and who could blame him? Ezra in flight was more than a little alarming, but in reality he was no more to be feared than a strange bird of paradise. How she would miss him. She thought the world must stop for the sorrow she felt at their parting. It seemed unaccountable that the bicycles and perambulators of Kensington High Street passed, the omnibuses and shopping carts chugged on, oblivious.

'The entire Foreign Office should be brought on to a tug and set floating towards America. Noodleheads and nincompoops . . .'

This exasperation of his was one of their subtle exchanges, offered really as a balm to her, for it is she who is the more frustrated. It is she who, within five hours, must leave London for the night boat to Ireland, in service to an ailing and demanding Mama. It is she who will then live again within daily instructions on how to be and what to do, and within the knowledge that all one was and did gave disappointment.

Her consolation was that it would not be for ever. She sighed in his ear: 'I suppose, as you say, three months is really a cheap price for independence.'

In three months Moura and Seaghán should be well settled in Dublin among their revolutionaries, and Ezra would have sorted *his* visa altercations with the Foreign Office and then they would make their long anticipated bid for freedom. The Italian lakes was the latest choice.

She said, 'I shall miss you so much. I shall have no one to talk to. I can be six years old with you.'

He took her sleeve and pulled her down a side street, more of a lane really, with back doors into the shops and restaurants. There, only seconds from the shoppers and office workers, he kissed her to silence. She enjoyed his kisses. Kisses were her favourite part of their connection and especially here, where they could not be suddenly accelerated into that terrible need of his that leaves no room for hers, that is satiated only to begin again like the undulations of the sea. In the laneway, she gave herself over to what could begin and end only as a kiss, though to be sure he was pressing against her in a way that left no doubt that he should like it to be more. His beard tickled her chin. His teeth were too close to his lips as he kissed, but, when he pulled away from her, the air sliced in to divide them, cold as knife steel.

'Oh, my sunny-head,' she said. 'How I love you, how I shall miss you. I embrace you with all my heart.'

Which of course made him kiss her again.

If it were not for Moura . . . But poor Moura. It was not fair to think of her in that way. It was such a relief to have her out of that awful Holloway. She was so thin and unwell, like a great tree cut at the base of its trunk, magnificence retained but more than a little shrivelled.

This time she broke away in earnest. 'Ezra, if I should miss my bus and therefore my boat, Moura would never forgive me.'

And indeed, as they stepped back out into the lights and flurry of Kensington High Street, the Chelsea bus was trundling towards them. 'All aboard,' called the conductor, disconcertingly cheery.

'Goodbye,' Ezra said aloud, for the benefit of the bus queue, and he bent to kiss her cheek, with the kind of kiss any man friend would give. But while there, he whispered in her ear, 'Goodbye, sweet girl.'

The bus engine growled. 'I become shy to tell you that I love you,' she whispered. 'Because it is so true.'

'Return to me soon.'

'The end of February,' she promised. 'Be ready.'

'Come on, m'ladyship,' said the bus conductor. 'Hop aboard if you're hopping.'

She stepped up. Holding on to the rail, she turned to wave at him. 'Unless', she called out as the bus pulled away, 'I come back in a week.'

That was what she had thought then. Three months, if she could bear that long. Long enough to settle Moura, so weakened by her jail experiences, back in Dublin. Long enough for him to sort the post-war passport difficulties that prevented him from leaving the England that had become hateful to him. Just three months, then they would be together.

That is what she truly thought but I know what Iseult did not know or did not care to know. That on Armistice Night Ezra Pound walked among the hullabulloo of peace with another young woman, that at that time he was writing poetry about 'devirginated' young ladies – and had more than one on the go.

So it pains me now to read the letters she sent him in her early weeks in Ireland and must have pained her, to later think of them.

Every day I love you a little more than the day before in spite of the fact that I have forgotten how you laugh and my God how stupid it is that you are so far away.

I never really knew you and now I even forget what you look like. I only know you have something very fine about you . . . All the same I embrace you and I love you so much . . .

It becomes less and less easy as days pass to live without you, and yet there is some peace in being away from you, but I can't cope with that peace i.e. life is contradictious.

Tell me what you are doing and don't freeze people with business letters. I kiss you in your ear . . .

Ezra too was writing lamenting letters, not to Iseult but to his men friends, bemoaning the effect of armistice on his love life. To James Joyce, he complained about the 'competition' from returning troops. To William Carlos Williams, he looked back on London's delicious disproportion of females to males during the war years, 'making it', he wrote, 'THE land for the male with phallus erectus . . . THE cunt of the world.'

So no, it is not Ezra whom Iseult now goes to meet, suitcase in hand. Over the past thirteen months in Ireland, she has gradually put Ezra aside, except as an old friend. She has ushered his love out and another's in.

You can trace the restoration of her old defences in her letters.

First, ironic detachment: *I take up my beautiful pen; I wish I had words to write worthy of it and of your highness.* Then an emphasis on friendship: *I remain your friend till death in spite of my laziness.* Finally, forced nonchalance: *How's life, how are the love affairs?*

Iseult would disdain to cling.

Her new beloved has much in common with the old. A writer too, though only starting out and tentative. Socially awkward, cold in situations where Ezra would be bumptious. Equally full of scorn for the material and social world, more inclined to sulk. Her name for him is Grim.

One major difference from Ezra is that the new love is not older than her, but younger. Eight years younger. A troubled, sensitive, alienated, innocent youth, all stammers and blushes and blurted wisdom. A sweet boy, her blessed angel, her darling child.

He first piqued her interest when he blushed to hear Moura refer to her as her 'lovely niece' in her effusive way. At the words, he had winced, then grown pink of cheek, then withdrawn, like a snail into its shell, from the touch of Moura's hand on his. All of this made blood rise into Iseult's own cheeks, a new experience.

For weeks they had a lovely time together when he called to Moura's at-homes, playing draughts and chess, exchanging cigarettes and chocolates, she kissing him solemnly on both cheeks at the front door. Then she started visiting the mews room where he lived. There, under a high, horseshoe-shaped window, observing him living a life of which she approved, eating soda bread and tea, and ginger biscuits spread with Nestlé condensed milk, writing poems and being visited by a cat, she has come to admire his lassitude. He can sit for hours bent over the gas ring, seeing a glowing crown set with ultra-blue jewels.

He has only three valued possessions: a roll-top desk, which for him enshrines a little world in the middle of an alien universe; a volume of poems by Rupert Brooke, given to him by his favourite aunt, which started him on his life of writing; and a plaster-cast heron he had made as a boy at Rugby, a precious relic of his only good days at his sorry school.

He is tall, taller than she (perhaps not yet finished growing) and very handsome in a brooding way, though at this point in his life he still has acne and she suspects he does not wash daily.

He loves the civil unrest that has gripped Dublin, the bank robberies and assassinations and anything that diminishes authority. He draws parallels between the Irish Ascendancy and the Russian aristocracy. Both must go, the world has to change, to improve. (Dear heart! So young.) Complacency is what he distrusts most, especially among those held in high esteem in their own, closed circles. Like Ezra, he believes in the writer as lonely outsider.

Moura does not approve. 'Dear me, Iseult, why him? You know if you put a mind to it, you might have any young man you choose.'

'He amuses me, Moura. And he really is finer than he seems to those who don't take trouble to know him.'

'I have been making enquiries. His father was a madman, an alcoholic who hanged himself in an Australian asylum. And you know he is but seventeen?'

'Almost eighteen. He has feeling, Moura.'

'I don't doubt it. But as a marriage prospect, he –'

'Oh, marriage. Who said anything about marriage?'

*

Moura and Willie both live in Dublin now but they are not speaking to each other, having had a monstrous quarrel over the St Stephen's Green house. Moura rented her house to him while she was in Holloway, as George was pregnant and Willie wanted his child to be born in Ireland. When taking it, he had assured her that should she be released and allowed to return to Dublin, they would vacate immediately – which strangers would not.

Perhaps it would have been so, but when Moura arrived to the house from England, with Iseult and Seaghán and all the animals, George was ill. Extremely ill indeed with the dreaded Spanish influenza epidemic that was in the process of killing more people than the war. Willie could not risk having the Gonnes, and the chaos of rebels and police that would trail after them, in the house while George was pregnant and so unwell. So he refused Maud entrance to her own house.

The quarrel that followed was spectacular, and they were the talk of the town, with Dublin equally divided. Only Iseult and Russell refused to take sides, with the difference that Russell believed them both right while she believed them both wrong. For days she ran from one to the other, with Moura calling her a coward and Willie a martyr, while the truth was she was merely bored with them both.

She writes Ezra an amusing account of the 'definitive letters' they sent to each other, 'in the Noble Viking Style in Moura's case, in the Nobel Dying Bayard style in Willie's', and their meeting in St Stephen's Green, 'among the nurses and perambulators', where they proceeded to have it out:

'Moura: If only you would stop lying, Willie!

'Willie (indignant, with a gesture of arms): I have never lied, my father never told a lie, my grandfather never told a lie.

'Moura: You are lying now!'

In truth, Moura is like a woman possessed in Ireland. Sinn Féin, the party of Irish liberation, has set up an alternative government to Westminster, which meets weekly in the

Mansion House. And patriotic feeling is turning violent. Bands of Republican gunmen are attacking the British forces, who are responding with a strong hand.

Thankfully, the horrors of the European war have modified her more bloodthirsty tendencies and she works mainly now for the Sinn Féin press bureau. 'The people have voted for Sinn Féin,' she is fond of saying. 'Now we have to explain it to them.'

Intermittently, Moura turns her attention to Iseult's relationship. She goes to Francis's mews room to interview him as a prospective husband, telling him that Iseult has no father and no money, as if he is an heiress hunter. To which he, not unnaturally, objects. They do not understand each other. Iseult understands each of them too well.

Another evening she receives information that they are together at a friend's flat and takes it into her head that impropriety is under way. Their evening, in fact, had been perfectly chaste, for the boy was as frightened as a fawn, but Moura comes up the stairs shrieking accusations of dishonour.

If she only knew.

Not long ago she and Francis spent their first night together, up in the Dublin hills. They took a tram to the southern terminus and walked out through dingy streets. On the way, she slipped into a huckster's shop for a naggin of whiskey to prevent her fingers turning blue, and then walked on, out to where the city faltered and the fields took over, and from there onwards again, climbing far into the hills of south County Dublin, all the way out to where the soil speaks.

In a clearing of pine forest, they sat on a felled trunk and talked, passing the whiskey between them for warmth. The night was cold and the faraway lights of the city swarmed among the trees. Francis lambasted Roman Catholicism in his naive way, and she tried to educate him.

'I'm sorry, Grim, but you really shouldn't be so presumptuous. Catholicism is the theology in which so many great saints and mystics, and great writers and artists, find inspiration.'

He wanted to argue but he had no knowledge from which to speak, which incensed him.

'When I pray,' she said, more gently, 'it's the Blessed Virgin I see, not her face or figure but a calm, deep blue expanse, like the sky just before night falls.'

'Yes, but your understanding is not theirs. Theirs is the constriction of sham pieties.'

She screwed up her eyes to see him through her cigarette smoke, recalling the mission Willie set her to civilize Dublin Catholics.

'Have you read Jammes or Péguy or Claudel?'

'You know I have not. Why do you keep asking me what I have read?'

'I suggest you do. To become a writer, you must read. Read first as an artist,' she said, passing on some advice Ezra gave her. 'Later on you can stuff yourself up with as much erudition as you like, but for now read to see how writers achieve their effects.'

'I do not want to read. I want to write what arises from my own self, not to be influenced by others.'

She snorted her derision, then was sorry when she saw him flush. It was a little too easy to play with him. She said, 'I don't want to go back to Dublin.'

His eyes narrowed.

'What do you think, Grim?'

She saw she would have to take matters into her own hands. 'I saw a forester's cottage on the way up. I'm sure they would give us shelter.'

The door was answered by the son of the house; he bid them welcome and offered Francis a rug by the stone hearth. 'We have a bedroom, at the back, that would suit the lady,' he said.

'No,' Iseult said. 'I shall stay here too, in front of the fire.'

Francis, beside her, nodded but she felt terror leap in him.

'All right so. Y'can keep it burning all through, y'll need it, the night that's in it.'

After the boy left, they shared the end of the whiskey, then lay down, Francis placing his head on her thigh. Such was her awareness of the hard and heavy warmth of his head that she could imagine, she could see precisely, her long leg half swathed in nylon, naked at the top, and the layers above it: her white underskirt, the blue fabric of her dress pressed down by the weight of his skull. 'My suspender must be hurting your cheek, Grim? Do you want me to undo it?'

Not a word, just a sharp in-breath. His panic shuddered in the dark between them. She knew his precise thoughts: how was he to leap across the gulf from his body to hers? How was he to go through all the stripping and the shameful intimate postures of coupling with her, she whose hemline seems untouchable? And where precisely was the goal located anyway?

The depth of his agitation was horrifying to her. She didn't know how to help him without admitting to the scale of the problem. Oh, what a painful affliction sex is, what invalids it makes of us all. It was easiest to do nothing, so she moved her leg and switched to some small talk, and after a time she pecked his cheek to say goodnight. He lay beside her, rigid, intent on not touching until he slipped into sleep. Sweet blessed angel of a boy.

On the way back the next evening, it was windy, and, as they came into Dublin, along the canal, a gale blew up that sent the shop signs swinging wildly. The tree branches above the canal cracked and whined. Iseult let down her hair and offered it to the wind, which took it and whipped it into streaming skeins. She started to run, face raised to the stars and the small, torn clouds that were whipping across the darkening sky.

Her exultation troubled him. 'I do not like the wind,' he said. 'I never have.'

Holding his hand, she tried to draw him on but he wouldn't

be led. What a mite he was, jealous of everything. Even the wind.

She gave herself over to the element that had always stirred the depth of her soul. When she was spent, she returned to him, panting. 'Did you think I was running from you, Grim?' She took his arm. 'It won't be me who runs, you know. I am a willow, rooted on the river bank, and you are a black swan gliding past.'

Now she walks the streets of London, looking for a boarding house for them. The city is full of demobbed soldiers and visitors who have had to stay away during wartime. After the months in Ireland, she is much taken again by the black shine of the wide roadways and the smell of coal smoke and petrol and the red buses and the distant familiarity of the street names, each feeling like a different kind of excitement.

Yesterday Francis collected her suitcase from Moura's and met her with it afterwards, at the boat. Tomorrow he will follow her over to London. These arrangements were of her making, and he questioned them. If she was telling her mother that she was travelling alone, then why the secret sneaking away? If they have escaped without detection, then why travel separately? And for that, when is it intended that they return? Is London to be their home now?

Iseult declined to answer. Perhaps she does not know. Or perhaps she does not want these matters to be too settled between them. Not just yet.

63

After Zach and Star left that night, I was in shock. Clammy sweats, flying pulse, shot breathing, everything. For three days afterwards I couldn't go to work, or eat or sleep properly. I didn't know how to proceed.

My lover, my daughter, me, my daughter, my lover: that was the track that kept unfurling round my head. She was the 'beautiful person, troubled and demanding' he had told me about. He had even told me her name was Maya, but there were a hundred thousand Mayas in California and I never thought, how could I ever have thought, that Zach's Maya was my Star? He never mentioned her weight or a single physical detail about her. Her soul, yes (sparky), and her spirit (warrior) but not the colour of her hair, her age, her family history or any detail that might have intimated that his girl was my girl, except the name I never used for her.

As for him, Shando was his Buddhist name, taken when he joined the Buddhist centre in LA. Lots of people knew him as Shando, and he didn't mind what he was called. Name, life story, country, gender, colour: none of the badges of identity that are so important to people meant anything to him. ('Put them all away,' he had told me, more than once. 'They are not who you are.')

Star's Shando and my Zach were one and the same person. That's what my daughter and I had to grasp, that's what we were left with between us. My lover, my daughter, me, my daughter, my lover . . .

She coped in her usual fashion – by lashing out at me, storming and incoherent, as if I had set it all up just to hurt her, then slamming out of the room, saying she was going to Veno's.

Zach begged her not to go, to stay and talk it through, but no. After she left, he sat in the armchair, the orchids on the floor, his hands sunk between his knees, his head bowed.

'You do know this problem is not really between you and Star, but between you and the Source, don't you?'

'Please, Zach, not now.'

'Whenever you have a problem, however much it seems to be about others, it's always really between you and the Source.'

'Source, Source . . . If you mean God, Zach, why don't you say so?'

'The word God has become empty. People use and abuse it. "My God is the true God but yours . . ." People who have never come close to the realm of the sacred bandy the word "God" around. Or argue against it. When it's clear they don't know what it is they're claiming or denying.'

'Zach, *please*. This is not the time.'

He held up his hands, fingers spread wide. 'I know. I'm sorry. Of course it isn't. I thought you asked.'

He too was unmoored by what had happened and was turning to what he called the Source, knowing how this had saved him before. It was a good instinct. I could see it would save him again. But not me.

I spent the next two days out of work, reeling around the house. Star went back to LA, still not speaking. I persuaded Zach to follow her down, to make sure she was all right, and I spent hours envisaging his arrival on a scene similar to that which had greeted me when I got back from Europe. I felt I was a string of elastic being pulled between the two of them, stretching thinner and thinner, just waiting to snap.

Then, a letter arrived from Pauline Whelan, telling me my father was in need of help. He had been taken to hospital with a circulation problem but had discharged himself and refused to go back.

As you know, Pauline wrote, *he's over ninety now, and he's gone down a lot since Rose died. He doesn't feed himself properly and so has lost weight. We've organized meals on wheels, and I drop in to do his meds and as often as I can otherwise, but I know it's not often enough. He needs cover in the house or else to go to a nursing home — but of course he won't hear of either.*

By the time Zach got back, I was packed, ready to leave. 'Don't do this, Izzy. Don't make this any bigger than it already is.'

'I'm beginning to think you don't realize how big it is at all.'

'Of course I do. But we have to sit with it, the three of us, and see what it is saying to us. Not run away from it.'

'You can't be serious.'

'I know it's hard, but we must.'

'To what end?'

'I don't know what the end will be. All I know is that this has happened, and it must have happened for a reason.'

I thought: maybe there is no reason in this world of ours, Zach. For some of us, there is no Source. Just empty, random, cruel chance.

'We need to meet,' he insisted. 'We need to talk.'

'Even if I could face it, I'm quite sure Star —'

'She is willing.'

'Star?' I was unprepared for the spike of jealousy that spurted up in me when he said this, like mercury up a thermometer. '*Star* is willing to sit down, the three of us, and *talk*?'

'Yes, Iz.'

Could it be true? The thought of it, the thought of her allowing this in order to corner me, made me want to scream.

'We have to,' he says. 'Don't you see? The truth is the truth. What is, *is*. That's all we have to work with.'

'I can't, Zach,' I whispered. 'I just can't.'

He folded then, like a child's toy with the air let out. 'You're running away again, Izzy, shutting me out again.'

'I'm not, Zach, I swear. It's just that —'

'You promised you wouldn't do this again. You *promised*.'

64

Iseult finds them a furnished room with a small stove over a grocer's off Tottenham Court Road, at a cost of ten shillings a week. She leads him up the narrow, turning stairs to show him. As he steps in, his eyes take in the bed in the corner of the room. One bed. A single.

He recoils, unable to bear the expectations loaded on to this coming away together. How Thora would laugh at her dilemma. Ezra too.

'We'll take it,' Iseult says.

They eat a frugal meal in the electric gleam, then go out to take a promised omnibus trip around London. She shows him the school where she worked as a translator, the area around Euston near the rooms Willie lent her, the café where she rejected his proposal. They go to the cinema, and then finally there is nowhere to go except back to the room.

Once they return, she remembers that they haven't eaten and hears herself saying, in a hearty voice, 'I think fish and chips for supper! We shall need to fetch it from the shop down the road. Will you, darling?'

Darling. It is her first time using this endearment. His eyes widen around it. By now, he has her almost as jumpy as himself. Off he goes to do the errand, and, when he returns, she is in the wicked bed, her hair loose over the pillow.

'I can sleep on the floor,' he says.

'That's not necessary, darling.'

Not necessary ... not necessary. The words ring between them as they sit on the bed, eating the food straight from its vinegary newspaper wrapping. When they are finished, he blows out the candles, undresses quickly in the dark. She hears the rustle of his clothes coming off, the squeak of the floorboard as he approaches the bed. She feels the weight of him settling in on the mattress, the long-johns that cover his legs, the evidence of his desire beneath. She feels the fear that freezes his grip on the blanket, keeps him flat on his back, staring at the ceiling as if hypnotized.

So she begins to whisper to him, lightly and ironically, as she has before, about the attentions of other men – her cousin Toby, flirtations she enjoyed in Italy with Thora, Willie kissing her in Normandy and asking her to marry him. She even makes little of what happened with John MacBride, and the boy who attacked her in the hospital, and the debauchery she found there. She wants him to see she does not take sex seriously. She tries to say to him: dilute your intensity. Bring to this matter of sex, which is really so ridiculous, the cool disdain it deserves. It is not love.

When she mentions Ezra, his whole body judders, as if he has received an electric shock. 'But, Grim,' she says, 'I told you about Ezra long ago.'

'When?'

'Don't you remember, the night we walked to Killiney Hill?'

'I meant, when did it happen?'

'In 1918. When I lived at Willie's flat in Woburn Buildings.'

'Did you have the rapture with him?'

'Grim, stop. I *told* you.'

'Tell me again.'

'No, I did not.'

He sits up, groaning, his feelings too huge, too sweeping, to be contained by his body, spilling out of his mouth, bursting out of his skin. 'How you love your tower of idealism,' he erupts, his first ever criticism of her.

She knows what he means immediately, though it will be some months before he finds words to fully explain. To him, her amused superiority is a wall of judgement. A trap. Iseult Gonne judges sex (and, by implication, the rest of the world) as either evil or foolish, and yes, she may be right but what satisfaction is there in that – for her, or for him? Being morally right and getting no pleasure out of being so seems, to him, a most bitter thing.

All this she intimates, and it shakes her. Is he, in his youthful idealism, not right? He has all her pity, for his orphan upbringing (his mother has even less empathy than Moura), for his blind struggles and his prickling sensitivities that are even worse than hers – but he does not want her pity. From her, he seeks what she cannot give. Admiration. She has chosen him for quite the opposite reason, because he is young and unformed and delinquent and a little unsound.

He thinks Willie and Ezra his rivals and flails against them, like a toddler kicking Papa for taking Mama away, but the real adversary is his disdain for himself. If only she *was* his mother, instead of what she is – his poor, unsatisfactory love.

Now he fires at her a thousand useless questions about Ezra, all the answers adding to the case he is building, so he will have an excuse to do what he must do. If not Ezra, he would have found another spur to make him leap from the bed and put his clothes back on.

'Where are you going?' she asks, but his only answer is the stomp of his boots from the room.

65

When I arrived at Doolough, my father answered the door with food in his mouth, chewing, and when he saw it was me, he turned, leaving the door swinging open, and shuffled back down the hall on thin old man's legs.

In the kitchen the television was loud, too loud. A boiled potato was split open on a plate with two fried eggs on top, oozing yellow yolk. He sat back down to his food and began to eat again as if I wasn't standing there watching. He ate slowly, food falling off the fork, his old mouth making loud suckings and swallowings. The veins on the back of his hands were swollen, tributaries of blue.

He was a shrunken version of the man Star and I had left five years before. He had two cavernous O's for eye sockets, and two sharp cheekbones jutting through below, all padding gone.

I sat opposite him. 'Did you get my letter, telling you I was coming?'

His hair was unwashed, and the smell in the room whispered incontinence. Yellow egg leaked down the front of his shirt, mixing with older stains, making me long for one of those plastic bibs that Star used to wear. His long life had made a child of him again.

'Are you going to speak to me?'

Another shaky mouthful, half of it missing its mark.

'If you don't answer I'll have to leave.'

On the table were several vials of pills in different colours. The room was in disarray, dishes everywhere, dust widespread, dirt trails all over the linoleum.

'They always were pure nosy, those Whelans.'

'You mean Pauline? She's only concerned for you.'

He pushed his plate away, half finished. 'I'll never get out of this dump again.'

'It's as nice here as anywhere. Nicer than lots of places.' True, but it must have sounded hollow coming from one who had escaped.

'It would sicken you when it's all you see from one end of a year to another. I'd like to have got out again, just once more before I died.'

'I could take you for a drive. We could go anywhere you wanted to go. The West?'

'Yerra, don't talk soft, girl.'

I picked up the dishes, for something to do, while he headed off on a list of complaints. Nothing but funerals in this damn place. Maggie Moran yesterday and don't give him any palaver about the afterlife because he doesn't believe in it and neither do the rest of them, which can be heard clear in the way they talk about the dead.

Funerals, or else the young sergeant going about in the squad car like he was in one of them Grand Prix. Or children calling to the door selling flags, letting on they were for the school or the GAA but he knew better and he wasn't going to be funding their sweets. When he had exhausted himself complaining, he sat contemplating its hangover, one knobbled thumb spinning around the other.

Then: 'I tell you one thing you *can* do for me, if you want to make yourself useful. You can get a basin of hot water on the go. My corns are a scourge this past week.'

He shuffled across to the fire, the only homely thing in the room, and took off his boots. A smell of feet leaked out to mingle with the tang of cooking oil and fried eggs. I boiled the kettle, mixed it with cold water in the basin, put in a dash of Dettol.

'You'll get a towel in the back kitchen and the blades are in the bathroom press.'

The towel was threadbare and grey. The razor blades were double-edged, each in a separate wrapper.

I brought them through. 'Here we go,' I said with false cheer. Instead of taking them from me, he raised one of his gnarled feet. 'Will you give them a scrape for me? I find it hard to reach down that far these days.'

The foot dripped blotchy red into the bowl. His eyes, though rheumy, were as sharp as the blades in my hand. He knew exactly what he was doing. And I thought I did too, as I knelt and took his foot between my hands.

In those days after I returned, I could feel my sanity quivering as I spent days and nights chasing round the endless loop: my lover, my daughter, me, my daughter, my lover . . . My whole life seemed to have collapsed into this one line of thought.

I did my duty by my father, no more. I didn't have any more in me to give. And I did it for me, not him.

With Pauline's help, I changed the parlour into a bedroom and moved him downstairs. At night I slept upstairs with my door and his open, so I would hear him call up if he needed anything. I slept only fitfully, on the surface, skating across crazed dreams, sleeps that left me exhausted when it was time to get up in the morning. In the afternoons I'd find myself napping in the fireside chair, falling into an unconsciousness somewhere between asleep and awake.

Pauline was my only connection with normality. Whenever she arrived, I was shocked to see her red-cheeked smile, so open and ordinary and *nice*, breaking the trance within which I lived in this house. As I led her into my father each time, and afterwards as I drank a cup of tea with her, I would feel a piece of myself coming back into myself. My neck and shoulders and forehead would relax, and I would waken a little into the real time of the outside world.

The other hours, the alone hours when I wasn't cooking or cleaning or caring for him, I spent in my bedroom. Not writing, no spirit for writing. Just staring, unseeing, out the window, pursuing my thoughts round and round, until I felt I was going to spin loose and be flung off the planet.

A few weeks into my time there, Pauline said she was going to have to fit my father for a urinary bag. Next time she came, she asked me to stay to help irrigate his catheter.

'Will it hurt?' he asked us, in a little-boy voice I'd never heard him use before.

'Not too much, I'd say, compared to what you're used to.'

'What I'm used to is not too good.'

'No, I wouldn't think so.'

He seemed to find her matter-of-factness comforting. She put her hand on his, wrapped her fingers round his twigs of bone. 'You know it's important that you're not in pain, don't you, Mr Mulcahy? You know that's what the morphine is for?'

His head dropped, a great lollipop cracking at the neck. Silence. Then something fell on their conjoined hands. A tear. *Plop.*

I was his daughter but I was the intruder. A voyeur.

'You shouldn't suffer any more than you have to,' Pauline said in the same gentle tones.

He nodded. 'I'm sorry now. I'm usually better than this.'

'You're surely allowed an old cry.'

That annoyed him, and he threw off her hand. 'It's not a girl you have.'

She only laughed, as if to say being male won't save you from tears, not in a sickbed. Not even Pauline could turn my father into a good patient, but she never minded his crabbiness.

'Should I help him wash?' I asked her afterwards, when we were back in the kitchen, having our tea.

'That shouldn't be necessary. There's a rubber mat fixed to the side of the bath, and I've taught him ways to sit on the edge and slide in, in stages. He should be safe enough. So no, not yet. Let's wait and see.'

'Wait for what?'

'A stink,' she smiled.

I wrinkled my nose.

'I know. But let's not meet trouble halfway. For now he's able to do for himself in that department and needs to be encouraged. It's something to give a shape to his day.'

My own days – and nights – were formless too and broken. I don't know why, but ordinary, everyday things always seem to be harder for me than for everyone else. When Star was small, I remember watching other mothers, the careless, expert way they would swing their baby on to a hip or wipe a cut knee. Effortlessly, naturally. Pauline was like that with my father, but everything I did felt as if an invisible force was all the time pulling me back or tripping me up.

The fatigue didn't help. Being beside my father day after day, the effort of not remembering the last time we lived alone here together, was taking its toll. After weeks of fractured sleep, night and day had melded. I was never fully awake, never fully asleep, and my bones were sore with tiredness. Pauline advised me to exercise, to tire myself out physically. 'One good night's sleep would get you back on track,' she said, and I knew she was right. I would find myself yearning for the Wicklow Hills, as if I were still 6,000 miles away from them, but not doing anything about it. I felt myself trapped in that house, held in place, even though Pauline said she would come and sit with him any time.

One afternoon, I was napping by the fire when I heard – or dreamt that I heard? – the creak of the kitchen door. I opened my eyes. Or dreamt I did. I saw two jean-clad legs. Long. Familiar. I followed them up the torso, all the way to the top, to his beautiful, beloved head.

Zach.

I reclosed and reopened my eyes.

Still there.

'You didn't hear the doorbell,' he said.

I reached my hand up. I felt his arm, flesh and bone, and I felt my own fear rising. He came in close to me, put both arms around me, kissed my cheek. A waft of his smell.

'You're real,' I said. 'Dreams don't smell.'

'What?'

'I thought I hallucinated you.'

He laughed. His laugh. 'You might at least say "dreamt", Izzy? Or "envisioned". Something that doesn't make me sound like a nightmare.'

He pulled me in close, on to the white cotton of his t-shirt, on to his broad man's chest.

'Zach, we can't. I can't . . . Star . . .'

'Shhhhh. We'll talk later. We'll sort something. Just hold me for a minute.'

'But . . .'

'Izzy,' he said, stern this time. 'Rest. Stop thinking. You look awful.'

'Thank you.'

'We're not doing it your way any more, Izzy.'

'We're not?'

'No.'

'Thank God.'

I let him hold me, and for a moment I held him hard back, but it was no good. Distress and bewilderment reared up again. My daughter, my lover, me . . .

I pulled away.

'Look, Izzy,' Zach said, sitting back on his heels, beginning a speech he had obviously prepared. 'You need help. I knew it all the way across the ocean; I know it now that I have you in front of me. Let me help you.'

'But –'

'Later, afterwards, when you're stronger, I will do whatever you say. But for now, just let me.'

'You mean stay here?'

'Yes.'

'Daddy would never allow that.'

'Allow it? My dear Izzy, how confused you are. The question is, will *you* allow it? The question, my dear Izzy, is: what can you allow yourself to have?'

I thought of what it would be like, having him around here, helping, a shield against my father. How tempting it felt.

'I can't ask him.'

'Leave it to me.'

He jumped up.

'But, Zach –'

He was gone. Within five minutes, he was back, giving me a thumbs-up.

'That's it? Already?'

'Sure,' he said, shrugging, deliberately nonchalant. 'Is there tea in that pot?'

'No. I'll make some. But first tell me what happened.'

'Nothing startling. I asked him if I could stay and he said yes.'

'Just like that. Come off it.'

'Izzy, think about it. What else could he say?'

'Anything. He could have said anything. Tell me some of the details.'

'Why?'

'Jesus, Zach. Tell me.'

'So you can obsess over them. I really don't –'

'Jesus God, Zach –'

'Whoa, no need to swear. I told him who I was and what I wanted – what *we* wanted – and he said, "This is still my house." And I said, "We know that, sir. That's why I'm asking your permission to move in." He said, "What if I don't give it?" I said, "Izzy and I would understand that to be completely your right, sir, and we would move out." "Move out? Move out where?" he asked, and I said, "I'm not sure, sir. Izzy and I would have to discuss that, but we'd make sure you were well looked after, you can rest assured about that."'

'Oooh,' I said, laughter gurgling up from somewhere. 'You're good.'

'You know, Izzy, it is really very simple.' He took my hand. 'He has no power, hon. Not unless you hand over yours.'

The clock ticked, too loudly.

'Think about it, if you decided to leave, what would he have?'

'I won't do that, Zach.'

I hoped he wouldn't ask why. It was an act I couldn't begin to understand, my coming back here. Not being able to cope with the California situation was only part of it. Something primitive between me and my father was in it too.

'I'm not asking you to. I love that you're compelled to care for him even though . . . y'know. But we could easily move to Avoca, or into another house near by, and you could do it from there. Or get him a nurse and just visit.'

How lovely it sounded. Especially that 'we'. I used it: 'We've no money, Zach.'

'We'll find the money if you think it's the right thing to do.'

I shook my head regretfully. 'No. He really does need live-in help at this point.'

'Okay. But if we stay here, you must drop him as a burden, in your head and heart.'

'I can't seem to do that.' No matter how I tried, no matter how near or far from him I was.

'You can. You don't do it by trying.'

'Then how?'

'I'm going to show you. We'll start tomorrow. For today, just remember: whatever he was in the past, now he's just a sad old man.'

'Hmmm. I'd wait till you know him a bit better before you jump to that.' I looked at my watch. 'It's time I gave the sad old man his meds.'

I strode in, playing brave, but it was all right. He was reading the paper, unwilling to confront. As I went about the small chores of dealing out the pills and the water, of plumping the pillows and straightening the covers, of clearing away the assorted debris of the morning – newspaper, lunch bowl and teacup, biscuit wrappers – I hardly looked at him. I was afraid of what he'd bring up, but also I needed time to think. To sort myself. A man like Zach wasn't going to want to be around a snivelling wreck for long.

My brain was blistering with small knotty questions that were so much easier to think about than the big one: Star. Star. What about Star?

When I went back out, I stood over his fireside chair and said: 'I know we're not going to be able to go on like this, Zach, as if you're a teacher and I'm your pupil. I want you to know I will be strong again.'

He held his two hands up to me and drew me down until we had reversed our positions of earlier, and now I was the one sitting on the floor. He pulled me in, between his knees, and I sat, looking up at him.

'You just don't get it, Izzy, do you?'

'I can't have sex with you.'

He shrugged.

'Not at the moment, anyway,' I said, chickening.

'That's okay.'

'Really?'

'Of course. I understand why.'

'But remember what you said?'

He laughed. How could he *laugh*? 'No. I don't,' he said. 'Tell me.'

'You said a relationship without sex was a relationship in trouble.'

'Poor, Izzy. You're getting everything wrong, fretting, fretting . . . Here's what's going to happen. We are going to get you better. I am going to live here and help you get strong again. Then I know – I just know and you, for now, are going to have to trust – that everything else will work out.'

'But how?'

'I don't know how myself, but it will. It already is.'

I found I couldn't raise Star between us again, but he must surely see that to love me was to not love her and for me to love her was to not love him.

It was he who spoke her name. 'You're thinking of Star, aren't you?'

'Have you seen her?'

'Yes.'

'Oh, God. Is she still angry?'

'Furious,' he said, eyes lighting up, as if Star's fury were something wonderful.

Tears, my constant companions, sprang up. 'She loves you so much, Zach.'

'And I love her, Iz.'

That spike again. He let this statement sit there, between us, out and open. Neither of us had the slightest clue about what to do with it. After a while he said, 'She's actually coping with all this rather well.'

'Not like me.'

'It's harder for you.'

'Is it? What about you, Zach? You seem so calm.'

'I'm reeling too, of course I am. But I'm trusting the Source. This is in our lives for a reason. I trust everything will come out right, if we let it.' He tightened his hold on my hands. 'That's what you've got to learn to do, Izzy. Trust.'

I looked up into his eyes. Electric-grey, beautiful, overflowing with love.

'Trust,' he said again, a whisper this time.

My skin quivered, grew porous, opened. In that moment, I chose him.

66

'Thank you for coming, my old friend. Oh, it is such a tragedy. I don't like to speak of it or think of it, and I certainly wouldn't do so to anyone else. The boy is an imbecile, his own relations regard him so. My own fear is that he has second-degree syphilis. His father was an alcoholic lunatic who committed suicide in Australia. You know he is only twenty years old and they're already married two years? But mentally he is short even of that age and utterly unsuited to be a father. What is certain is that he is selfish, he takes no thought for her in any way.

'He has no education, and neither the power nor the will to work. He has £350 a year, but it is his intention to spend this only on himself. He expects Iseult to take and pay for the flat. She has about £100 a year from me, and I fear will have to dress, feed and lodge herself on this. With her disregard for worldly matters, he and his mother have manoeuvred her into that position, and she would not allow me to interfere.

'And, by the way, might I say that she certainly took your advice to pay no notice to what I advised. Yes, you may well look sheepish, my friend. She told me one night in an argument. But I forgive you because you have come to us now with such alacrity, and I suppose you did not understand, although, really, Willie, you should know that I should not be so concerned for her without cause.

'When I tried to take steps to protect her, back at the beginning, they bolted to London, his mother seeing them off and providing money for the escapade. For over a fortnight I was left without an address – his mother had it but pretended not. Of course they *had* to marry then. She had made it impossible to do anything else, announcing to various people in Dublin that they had been together to London.

'How dismal the ceremony was, just me and Helena on Iseult's side and his mother and an aunt on his. His aunt was a loud woman who smoked a pipe and wore trousers and she laughed the whole way through. Her tone of jollity and her expensive present – the most magnificent pearl necklace I have ever seen – were utterly inappropriate. I had no heart for it, and Iseult wanted only to be gone . . .

'Now, this.

'Willie, I am at my wits' end. She will not hear anything said against him but it is impossible, absolutely impossible, that she should go on living with him. I am sure she will not be frank with you, so it is left to me to tell you the worst. It is so awful, Willie. Like history repeating itself . . . I cannot believe that this unspeakable sordidness has arisen in my life again. The curse of the Gonne women has done its worst this time.

'Take a seat, my friend, and let me order some tea. Oh, but it is good to have you to talk to . . .'

He knocks on Iseult's bedroom door, and her voice, so much gentler than Maud's, calls out: 'Come in.'

The room is in half-darkness, curtains closed. He can dimly see the bed, opposite the window.

'Willie, oh Willie. Moura said you might come. I didn't expect to see you so soon.'

'How are you, my dear?'

'I am f . . . No, I can be honest with you. I feel like I am living within a heavy black mist. I cannot see, and it weighs down my every move, my every thought.'

'I am so sorry.'

'As am I, that you find me like this. I'm afraid the effort to remain firm and not let my nerves get the better of me has reduced me to even more practical incapacity than usual.'

She pulls herself upward on her pillows, a great effort. Her skin is grey; her hair, tied in a loose knot at the base of her neck, is wan.

'Sit down, Willie.'

He takes the chair by her bedside, pats the hand that lies, like a dead bird, upon the counterpane. 'I have spoken to Moura. You understand why she is so concerned for you?'

'You know Moura and her overdeveloped sense of the dramatic.'

'She insists that the boy's conduct makes it impossible for you to go on living with him.'

'She is always telling me to leave him.' She sinks back into her pillows. 'And he is always wanting me to leave here and go away with him.'

'You must not agree to this, Iseult. He wants to take you from your friends, those who care for you, the better to have power over you.'

'Perhaps. But he seeks this power only because he feels so powerless. He is young and does not know as much as he thinks he should. It frustrates him. If I give in to him on something, we are often happy for days.'

Willie sighs. 'Is it true what Moura tells me? Perhaps she exaggerates?'

'Perhaps. They do not get along.'

'She fears he is mad, perhaps through syphilis.'

She shakes her head. 'No, he is not mad, though he sometimes acts as if he were. Usually when provoked.'

'But it is true that he has locked away food, keeping you hungry?'

'Yes.'

'Deprived you of money?'

'Yes.'

'Kept you from sleep to cause you distress?'

She nods.

'Knocked you down?'

'He has done me no injury.'

No injury. Such passivity is almost beyond understanding. Suspecting she might deny, Willie had armed himself by investigating Maud's claims with neighbours in the area. The elderly woman who lives next door spoke of how Stuart drove Iseult out of doors in her dressing gown and then heaped her clothes in the middle of the floor and burnt them. A young man found her one evening weak and hungry, and had to get her food. Another spoke of his keeping her without sleep by night, making scenes, once banging so hard on a door she had locked that he broke the panel. They spoke of his lying in bed, all day every day, compelling the pregnant Iseult to fetch wood for the fire down an uneven swampy mountain path a mile and a half away.

This is what she preferred to the protection and care he would have provided for her? What a fearsome, inexplicable thing is sexual selection. It was her destiny to be the hare who must run wild, but who will draw upon herself the tooth of the hound. A shade of the terror that had gripped him in 1917 passes over him now, sitting by her bed, and gratitude floods him once again for his marriage.

Destiny delivered unto him, as promised, the perfect wife who has made his life serene and full of order, instead of the certain chaos that would have been his with Iseult. George's seership, like Maud Gonne's in earlier years, provides a scaffolding for his philosophy and poetry, and the work they do together will eventually culminate in an explanation of the social state – made not with a young man's yearning but with a mature man's weighing of earthly life, and of all that is beyond life, in fine balance.

The only salvation for the world is to regain its feeling for revelation. This has been his own salvation. One of the first things George's hand wrote was that he would neither regret nor repine, and he thinks certainly that he never will again.

'No injury?' he queries. 'To knock a pregnant woman to the

floor? To starve her of food? Is it true he set fire to your clothes to keep you in the cottage?'

'Willie, it is what is in my own mind that injures me.'

'Thus Griselda speaks.'

'I goaded him, Willie.'

Yes, yes, she had. Willie or Moura would say that did not justify what had happened, which is true, but the truth is also that she knew just what she did as she snatched up Francis's precious plaster cast, his most precious heron, and held it aloft. She knew she was trying him beyond his endurance. He had warned her – 'If you break that cast, Iseult, I tell you: we are no longer married' – but she raised her hand over her head and flung it as far as fury could carry it. And exulted, and then trembled, as it hit the wall and smashed.

It was no surprise when he grabbed her and roughed her to the floor, his face a contortion of rage.

Her mouth opened around the words 'No, Francis, no', but something in her disdained to cry out, and she watched, with detached fascination as he took her arm and pushed her out into the yard, taking the paraffin can back in with him. He locked the door, and grabbed her dresses from the wardrobe and brought them into the kitchen, where he threw them in a pile on the floor and splashed paraffin all over them. The tang of it reached her nostrils through the window as she watched, petrified. He struck the match, its flare a declaration, then he dropped it with a flourish. The top garment was made of a stiff tapestry and it only smouldered, but then – *phum!* – the flame caught the line of the liquid and leapt along it. A sky-blue dress burst to flame, then a shawl with tassels.

Once he knew it was going to take, he opened the door, went outside and, without looking at her, ran up into the glen, clambering among the boulders with the box of matches and the paraffin, setting fire to the gorse bushes as he had done before. To see him thus, others – and not just her mother – would think him mad. Just as they would if they saw him rush from the bed in pitch black, as he often did, throwing himself on the bracken used as bedding for cattle. Yet she understands how the large, coarse ferns or the dry crackle of flames and the cloud of smoke drifting down the glen are offerings to the great, sensual spirit, revealing to him some secret.

'I think he turns you mad as himself,' Willie says.

'If he *is* mad, he but needs me more. Surely you, of all people, can see? What good was I doing with my life anyway? I may as well spend it this way.'

Afterwards, having dowsed the flames inside with water, she had gone out to him and found him lost behind a billow of smoke. She took his hand, gently walked him back to the house and sat on his lap in the kitchen while he apologized, crying the way men do, in jagged breaths, fighting his own tears. They had held each other for a long time, trembling, hushed by their frailty. Then, unable to stay at the ruined cottage, they had set out for the station that would take them to her mother's. A ten-mile walk, but they hardly noticed it.

She hadn't known what to do with him, with what they had become, so she had turned to Moura and her healing energy. Which was possibly a mistake.

'You have more than yourself to consider now, Iseult,' Willie says.

He means the baby.

'If you permitted a repetition of what happened at Barravore, the child might die.'

He is right, she does know that. Perhaps that is really why she has brought herself here to Maura. Able to demand for the baby what she cannot ask for herself. She pulls herself up higher on her pillows. 'Tell me what I should do.'

'Send him a message, saying that you will see him only once, here in the nursing home. He is to avoid raising subjects that give you emotional pain. And if he wishes to return to live with you, he must give guarantees of good behaviour and he must settle an income on you and his child.'

'These are Moura's instructions.'

'Moura is right in this, my dear.'

The tears come then, slow sliding down her cheeks. 'He *is* selfish, Willie, but his selfishness is not of a low nature. I wish you to know this.'

'You worry me the way you speak of him.'

'He has an adoration for you that amounts almost to a religion. You have often told me that I am your spiritual child; perhaps he is that even more than I. He has, like many young people, imitated your manner and your style, drawing on things that are well known about you, or from your books. But when I see in him a reflection of things in you that only I know, then I am amazed.'

'It may be better to have someone else deal with him if you are not strong enough.'

'No, no, I shall do it.'

'You must impress upon him that there must be no more . . . scenes . . . or you will leave him for ever.'

'I shall be firm, I promise.'

'Good, good. I can offer some news that should give you cheer. I have looked up your dates. When you married, Venus and Saturn were in conjunction and when you decided to go to the nursing home, Venus and Neptune were in conjunction. In combination I believe this should mean that the worst is over.'

67

Zach banished the gnarled thinking, the shallow sleeps, the hours of staring, unseeing, out the kitchen window, by taking hold of my time. What I needed, he said, was less thought and more practice.

'Practice', as he used it, was a Buddhist word, with a special meaning. Our days were to begin with meditation. In the morning, after giving Daddy a cup of tea, but before making his breakfast or organizing his meds, I was to sit down on a cushion on the floor, legs crossed, and for thirty minutes focus my full attention on to my breathing. When thoughts arose in my mind – as they would – I was to label them 'thinking', then bring my attention back to my breath. Especially my out-breath.

It sounded easy, but it wasn't for me. The first day I jumped up after two minutes, overwhelmed. Gently, insistently, Zach led me back. 'You can't do it wrong, so long as you're sitting there, making the attempt,' he said. 'See the thought. Don't judge it. Just let it be. Then return to the breath.'

I sat back down, quieted again, but, as soon as I stilled, hurricanes of thinking rushed in, firing me with feeling. Rebellion, restlessness, craving, agitation. I wanted to sob at my mother's large-knuckled hands and the pity they always stirred in me. I remembered how my dentist once burst an abscess on my tooth before the painkillers had kicked in. I remembered how I felt when Mossie Mangan, a boy from Doolough with a too-long chin, dumped me when it should have been the other way around. The plug of dread begotten by my father that always sat in the pit of me rose up, until I could feel every layer of it. I imagined escaping him, going back home to Santa Paola or onwards, somewhere else, somewhere beyond him. What would such a place look like? It would have a flat, open plain, with the mountains far in the distance, a ranch, a paddock, horses in a corral . . .

Everything I had ever heard or seen or felt or even imagined seemed to be still in my mind, and I didn't want any of it. I had to hold it at bay. Otherwise it would drive me over. I would go insane. I would cut off my ear or choke my father or step into Doolough Lake, my pockets weighted with stones. Better to leave well alone. Better to keep it all damped down.

Yet, after sitting with it, I felt better. Calmer and cleaner in my head, as if my brain had had a shower. And taller, somehow, inside and straighter.

Next came what Zach called free-writing. Writing down, fast and by hand, three pages of those thoughts of mine. Whatever arose in my head. Opinion, idea, commentary, stories. Nonsense, bitterness, pettiness, jokes. Annoyance, fury, fun, hope. All to be placed upon the page, as mixed up as it wanted to be.

'Think of meditation as one leg and free writing as the other. You need them both to get moving.'

Like the meditation, I wasn't to judge what emerged during the writing. The meaning of the words was secondary to the act of writing them.

But I had Real Writing, my book, to be getting on with. Wasn't structured work like that more valuable than these pages of mish-mash? And why did I have to use a pen when my typewriter was so much faster?

'Oh, fast,' said Zach, as if speed was a vice.

'But you said to write as fast as possible.'

'A fast pen is quite fast enough. This isn't a race. You're after depth, not distance.' He pointed to the pages. 'Look how much more of *you* is there than on a typewritten page.'

'Hmmm.'

'Your handwriting is as unique as your fingerprint. An expression of *you*. That's what we're after.'

'Hmmm,' I said again, even more sceptical. I was not at all sure that I liked the sound of that.

'The deep down you, Iz. The one you can count on. Just do the practice, then the rest will look after itself. I promise you.'

'Hmmm.'

'Trust me: the more you resist this, the more you need it. Come on, here's the pen. Another three pages today, fast as you can, starting now. Go!'

And he was right. As the days passed, I became aware of the different dimensions and different voices inside me. Thoughts and feelings still tore through me, but, as I separated from them, they lost some of their power. Over time, a remarkably short time, my feelings shrank. I had become big enough to contain them.

I would never gain control of my mind or my heart, that's what Zach taught me. You can't command the ocean or strap up the wind, but you can observe and get to know them. What he gave me was a structured way to do this, a way to flex and strengthen my inner self, so I could rely on it. So I could feel free and safe, whatever the outer circumstances.

Three pages complete, it was time for breakfast. Daddy's first: some porridge or mashed banana or soft eggs. Going into his room was still an ordeal, but with Zach out in the kitchen, within calling distance, it was an ordeal I could face. Once he was looked after, we took time over our own meal, and then it was down to three good hours working on the book.

Break at twelve thirty. Prepare the soup or home-made blanc-mange or whatever slippery concoction was my father's for that day and bring it in to him, while Zach prepared ours. And, after lunch, a walk: Daily Practice No. 3.

'When Pauline is here,' he said, 'I will sometimes go with you. But it is important that you often go alone.'

Right again. The step-by-stepness of those solitary hikes in the Wicklow Hills somehow synchronized with the pages of free-writing stacking up on my desk, and the witnessed breaths of my morning meditations. Beat by beat, regular practice gave a new rhythm to my days. I found myself beginning to smile again, to laugh, to listen to music. I started cooking us some of my favourite recipes from the café. I bought a camera and started taking photos of Doolough, of the mountains and the lake.

My father was no longer the only focus of my day. At night Zach and I sat by the fire, telling each other stories that compared Ireland and California or reading or dancing to a music show on Radio Éireann that played songs of the sixties.

With three simple tools – meditation, walking and writing – Zach nursed me back. The way he taught me was the way he followed himself. On the outside, we looked like two simple people living simple days, but, inside, we were warriors, fighting a true fight.

Zach loved Ireland. He loved the Wicklow Hills, the mystery that hung about the mountain peaks and the lakes. He began to speak of finding a space where he could offer workshops and even retreats. Which gave rise to an idea in me. One evening, as we sat by the window looking out at the trees, I said to him, 'Have you thought any more about a premises for your workshops?'

'I have committed myself to the idea now,' he said. 'If it is meant to happen, it will come.'

'Do you see it being in the city or the country?'

'The country, definitely.'

'What about here?'

'You mean Doolough?'

'I mean this house.'

The location was perfect: isolated and on the doorstep of some of the finest scenery in Ireland but close enough to a main road to take a car to Dublin in less than an hour. The house would need refurbishment but . . .

'Daddy won't last for ever. You could do it here when . . . after . . . he's gone.'

'Are you serious, Izzy?'

'I think so. Yes, yes, I am.' The idea excited me. To see this house used for such a purpose. It would reverse the rot.

'Does this mean that you want to help? Do you see it as something we could do, together?'

That I could not give him. I was with him now because I'd needed him so badly, but, as my strength returned, I could feel our time together running out. Even Zach was not able to overcome the problem of Star.

'It was just a thought,' I said. 'That man in there is a tough old boot. He could see us all out yet.'

Then, as if I'd conjured her up by thinking about her again, the call I had been dreading and craving arrived. I answered its ring, and there, at the end of the line, was her voice. 'Hi, Mom, it's me.'

It gave me a moment's vertigo. I moved to the wall to steady myself. 'Star. Darling, how are you?'

She answered in a new voice, crisp and clipped, repeating prepared sentences. She was well. She was taking time out. She was thinking of coming to Ireland. Two weeks from now.

'Star, that's wonderful. Absolutely wonderful.'

'Just one thing. Is *he* there?'

'No.'

'No, not right now? Or no, not at all?'

'Not at all.'

Okay, then. She would come. She should be with me by Christmas Eve. She went on, talking about flights and arrival times, but I was only half listening. So tangled in thought I didn't notice she'd stopped talking.

'Mom?'

Not knowing what to say, I asked, 'Are you in the hall or the kitchen?' Hearing her voice made me lonely for California, for warm nights and beach days. It had been eight months since I left, and I missed Marsha and the café, and the click of palm trees and the dart of lizards and most of all the evenings, watching a hazy sun sink into the sea. Evenings here crawled up from the mountains, ever earlier each day.

'I'm in the hall,' she said. 'Are you listening to me?'

'Of course I am. I just wanted to imagine you there.'

'For Chrissakes, Mom. Don't put me off coming before I even leave.'

'No, sorry, of course not. Are you –'

'Look I have to go. We'll talk when I get there, okay? Bye.'

68

The room is dark and full of sound, great gusts of breath broken by cries. They are upstairs in No. 73 St Stephen's Green, Maud Gonne's house. Dr Solomons is in attendance, but he has gone home for dinner, so in the room are Mrs Ogilvy, the midwife, Miss Owens, the nurse, and Maud herself. Iseult is breathing and crying, crying and breathing, into a crescendo, and her suffering racks Maud with a complexity of feelings too tangled to understand.

The darkened room seems somewhere ancient, like a cave. For some reason, she keeps thinking of Tommy and the time when she was a child and heard that babies came out of a woman's body and she took the question to ask him and he said, 'Yes,' with a laugh and a twinkle and then, 'I know what you mean. Who can believe that it is so?' Which somehow made it all right again.

Iseult is oblivious to all but her pain. People should hear more of these sounds, the panting and the crying, Maud thinks. It would help them to live. Maud finds herself instinctively panting with her daughter, attuned to her pain and to what lies beyond the pain.

She feels her stretch wider than skin can stretch, feels her top breath become a gasp and her top cry a scream, feels her tear and feels, through the scream of the tear, the other smaller cry that is there.

Sees new breath, soft and speedy and fragile.

'A girl, Iseult,' she cries. 'A beautiful little girl.'

Mrs Ogilvy takes her and wipes her eyes, and nose and mouth and ears, and then Iseult, of course, is reaching for her.

It is fortunate that she had the foresight to choose a female name as well, just in case. Maud sees her whisper it into the little baby's ear. Dolores. Dolores of the Sorrows. Does she think of her man, so unfaithful and so unreliable, so much worse even than her father? Does she wonder whether a boy might have settled him better?

'Dearest,' Maud whispers, and Iseult looks up at her with brilliant eyes, eyes too big in the face that has become too thin, but they are glowing tonight, and her skin is luminous. Her soul is reignited by the child, gleaming as it has not in months. No, in *years*.

'Moura,' she whispers. 'Oh, look at her.'

Maud sits on the bed beside them both, cups the new skull in her hand. It fits perfectly. A throb of life pulses into her palm. The pad of her fingertip is the same size as the tiny, curly conch of an ear. She bends and touches the cheek with her lips. It is cool, which surprises her. It smells of Iseult's insides, of blood and secrets.

'Well done, my darling. She is beautiful and so are you. Well done. Now you must rest.'

This is a strange and new kind of love, Iseult thinks. Dolores smells of lilac and honey. She has square patches on her skin, under her hair. The dip between her skull bones breathes. She is out in the world now, within her own separate skin, but somehow they still overlap. When Dolores is hungry, Iseult feels it in her own stomach. When she is tired, Iseult yawns. When she sleeps, Iseult feels not quite awake. After she has been fed, and lies sated with little mouth open. Iseult too feels full.

It is so hot in their flat, up on the third floor, under the roof, but Francis refuses to let them go to Moura's. Everyone is talking about the heat, the hottest summer since 1881. Young people divest themselves of clothing and old people mutter at the sky. It is as if nature herself is celebrating, Moura says, for the British government and the Irish Republican Army have reached a truce. The raids and the shootings, the flare of explosions lighting up the night sky, have ceased, though the nights are still disturbed as the young men – all soldiers now the danger is over – go careering around in motor vehicles.

Iseult writes to Willie for an astrological chart for the baby and tells him all is well. She does not mention that Francis is in a monstrous sulk since being brought to heel. Halfway through her pregnancy, he took himself off to London to sell the pearls his aunt had given as a wedding present and, while there, struck up an affair with a ballerina. He refused to attend his daughter's christening, instead writing a poem about being elsewhere, an awful piece of self-justifying tosh that had him conversing with the sky and the grass, half thinking he was among those who will have most sway over Dolores when she grows.

'That's really quite dreadful, darling,' Iseult had said, when given it to read. 'I preferred the ones you wrote for your dancer.'

Yes, she knew of his affair, knew it was his way of coping with the heat and the baby and the soldiers on all sides and the lack of money and the disapproval of her mother . . . And the growing fear and pressure and demands of practical matters. She fears too. Just keeping the baby fed and clean is overwhelming. As for Moura's strictures about bottles and nappy changes and hygiene . . . No doubt they are excessive. Children survive African jungles and Amazonian rainforests, do they not, and Dolores is content, whether fed or changed or not. She is such a good baby, so rarely crying.

A nice surprise arrives when Lily, Francis's mother, offers them rooms at her seaside bungalow in County Meath. It will be cooler there, everybody says so, although when they arrive, Lily's dog, Butternut, lies panting on the veranda, pinned down by heat. Francis finds himself a new mistress, a motorbicycle, which he installs in the spare bedroom – it must be kept hidden in the house because he does not have a permit. He moves into the room with it, leaving Iseult and Dolores alone while he sits on the saddle for hours, the chrome controls and brake levers under his fingers, the shiny expanse of tank between his legs, his eyes full of images of other places.

Away, away, that is all he thinks about. She hears him through the wooden walls, muttering or humming to himself of imagined roads and destinations. Always, always, these delusions of elsewhere.

Whatever Francis doesn't react against violently, he comes under the spell of. There's nothing in between for him, no detachment, no balance, no perspective. He suffers, and he finds that an adventure too, but that's because he doesn't know the worst suffering — when everything seems dead, and oneself dead, and adventure and romance and joy mere empty words.

But he will come round, in time. As has she. One cannot argue with a baby. Dearest Dolores. She is a symbol of all the intangibles, surrounded with a shimmer of mystery. Certain things that she does mean something that it is impossible to explain.

Iseult squashes out another cigarette on the underside of the bedside table and leaves it stuck there with the rest. Rows of stubs are lined up under that table, like the multiplying grave-stones being laid for dead soldiers all over Europe. No, don't think about that. Take Dolores out of the cot instead to admire again her forehead (incredibly white), her eyebrows (faint, as if sketched in pencil). Her little eyes are open and she seems to smile, though Nurse says this is impossible, that it is just wind. Can she be right? It seems so like a smile.

She really is most adorably pretty and seems to be far more advanced in mind than babies months older. Iseult lays her down in the bed beside her so she can watch her sleep, admires the way her hands have folded under her chin, as if she were praying. After all the longing, here it is. True love come round at last.

69

But Dolores dies.

70

And so we have come round to the beginning. To where there is nothing left to do but tell. No, says my mothering instinct. Keep silent. Make something up. Protect. Go on protecting. But I did not write all these words to sully them at the end with a lie. I have to tell my truth, if only to the page.

Or maybe to the police?

My trial begins in three weeks, Mags says. If I am going to speak, it must be now.

I think Mags knows.

I have started to imagine the trial. Star has been called back for it, of course, as has Zach. I have started to imagine them, arriving together each morning to the courtroom, leaving together each afternoon, and sitting side by side all day. While I am brought to and from a hotel room to the defendant's stand, alone. They are both wandering around Ireland. Is it possible that they are together? Last time I saw him, he said, 'Don't worry about Maya, Izzy. She'll be okay. Her warrior spirit will win through.'

Maya.

Warrior spirit.

He knew a different person.*

The day she telephoned to say she was coming over, I told him he'd have to go.

He didn't want to. He said there was nothing to fear, that we would never get beyond this thing – this admittedly terrible

---

* The truest words my mother ever wrote. And I ask you to consider whether a man like Shando would ever have loved the surly, spoilt, self-obsessed lump that my mother depicts in these pages.

thing, terrible for him too – if we didn't go through it. He didn't know why it had happened, but it had. We had to be open to what the Source was trying to tell us. Each of us.

Enough time now had passed for the three of us to be able to sit down together and understand what it all meant. He had telephoned and told her so.

'Zach, you didn't.'

'Why not?'

I couldn't tell him I'd lied to her about his being here. He wouldn't understand. He wanted me to be better, stronger, than I was.

'No,' I said, jumping out of my seat, pacing the room. 'I can't, I can't.'

The only way I could cope was to have only one of them in front of me at a time.

So this time, I chose Star.

I didn't blame her for being angry. I deserved whatever she was going to deal out to me when she arrived. The accident of being loved by the man who had rejected her was bad enough, but it was what I did afterwards that was unforgivable. Taking Zach into my father's house, being with him once I knew what he had been to her.

That I did it only because I was in terrible need would hold no water with Star.

And so it turned out. She arrived with her anger, her blistering anger that wanted to set fire to all the fields and dump poison into all the rivers and hurt everybody in the whole wide world (especially me). Only such an anger could have led her into what she did. She had little time for my father, but that degree of hatred, I know, was something she reserved only for me. She did it to punish me and perhaps to see me off to prison so she and Zach could be together.

Or so I had long believed.

Unless . . .

Unless. Such a small word, so often used, so rarely noticed. Not a word to announce itself, yet, as soon as it came to my attention, I wondered why I hadn't paid it due consideration before. It had grown in me, over the months in my father's house, through all the writing, so that now it seemed a lever, lifting possibilities many times its size.

It kept buzzing around my brain, like a fat bee banging against my skull. Unless, unless . . .

So this is something else that I have started to imagine. It is our visit back here in 1976, and I have gone to Dublin to the book launch. Daddy and Star leave the house at about four o'clock to go blackberry picking, promising Rose they'll be back for tea. He brings Star to the brambles on the upper field, then down towards the lake. They hardly speak. He is twisted inside thoughts of his own, and Star is miserable, guilty about not having gone to Dublin, wondering why her grandfather has brought her out if he is going to be so silent.

They pass through the high field, black and brown cows munching grass, one raising its head to look at them. The pigeons are loud in the trees as they approach the woodland that thickens round the lake in summer. My father steps into the drowsy mass of green, and my daughter follows. The trees smell of fresh breezes, and the breeze smells of the earth. It swooshes through the branches, making a sound like the sea.

Her hair gets caught in a branch, and she has to stop to pick out the pine needles. He chivvies her, his nerves at him. 'Come on.'

The trunks of the trees draw closer together, the light dims. He stops against a fallen bough near the lake.

'I don't like it here, Granddad.'

'Don't you, now?'

A rattle in his voice makes her look into his face and see something. She feels what is coming her way before she knows that such a thing can be.

She moves to turn.

He catches her by the wrist.

She shouts: 'No!'

He says, 'Now, now. Don't be like that.'

He pulls her down. Down into a secret that is the dull light of the lake, and the pigeons cooing, and the wavy wind in the trees, and the ground going from under her feet, and the berries spilling out of the can, and the twigs digging into her back . . .

'No!' she tries again, and he claps his hand over the sound.

Then it is the weight of him urging down on her. His knee thrusting hers apart. His mouth by her ear, breath wet, breath hot. The splaying of her open. The burning of him in her. The green scum on the edge of the lake lap, lap, lapping. The ferns curling away beside me.

And nothing ever again as it was.

This is what I need to know. Did this happen? Was this part of the mix of her motives? If it was, how can I have her further punished? If it is all pure fancy, if the real reason was revenge on me and Zach, how can I not?

And what of Zach? If he knew what she did, would that be the end of her and him? Was that – come on, out with it, tell the worst – what a part of me, a deep-down, low-buried, loathsome part of me wanted?

The answer to both questions was the same.

Yes, it would.

Yes, it was.

Unless . . .

71

It is the nurse who admits Dolores who first says the word –
and that is the consequential moment, the moment when hope
drains away.

On the way in, Iseult catches sight of herself and her mother
in the mirror at the end of the ward and is surprised, as always,
to see her physical resemblance to this woman whom she thinks
of as her very opposite.

Who is so intent on forcing the word from the nurse. 'We
would rather know,' she said, as Iseult shrank.

'I'm afraid it's not good news, madam.'

It was the heat that did it. Iseult is sure the baby was all right
until the heat came down, but the heat had made it so hard to
do anything. Ordinary air was so stifling that the thought of
smoke from a good cigarette felt like a clarity in the nostrils,
but then too many cigarettes made her feel ill from nicotine
poisoning, and she wasn't able to do all she should. Not that it
would have made any difference, Moura says.

A hot forehead under her own hot hand: that is how it begins.
Hotter than the weather outside, hotter than seems normal (but
how is one to know?). Iseult puts her on the bed beside her, as
she likes to do. Wrapped tightly in her blanket, like a little
mummy, she sleeps or watches as her mother deals out hands
of Patience on the counterpane. Ace, king, queen, jack . . . Iseult
knows she should get up and clean the room and help Lily
prepare some food for lunch or dinner but really, the heat
makes one too indolent to do anything.

She makes a vow to renounce smoking entirely for nine days,
and the playing of cards and the foolish, time-wasting letter

games too. For nine days she will accomplish as closely as can be all duties, big or small, inward or external, and have an outward serene manner. But first, just one more hand, one more cigarette . . .

As evening comes on, Dolores vomits, not just a baby sick-up but a violent projectile throwing. Her forehead scorches. She is flushed of face and pale, both at once. Iseult takes her outside to the garden. The sky too is pale and torn, with light, high clouds and night sliding in over the sea. She feels the old pull of the waves, the cry of gulls heading out from land, like a kind of dream. Dolores's hair is plastered flat and moist across her skull. Iseult opens her little robe at the throat, shivers as she holds the hot skin close.

She goes to the spare bedroom. 'I think the baby is unwell, Francis.'

He looks up from shining the chrome on his motorbicycle, silent. On the table are sheets of paper covered in writing. A new poem.

'She is not feeding now, or sleeping.'

He looks at her as if to say, What is it to do with me? She could be angry, but she knows he too is overwhelmed.

Later she returns, this time in darkness, to pull him out of sleep. 'Francis, please, help me. I think she is weakening.'

His eyes glitter in the reflection of the candlelight.

'What?' he says.

'Oh, my God, if only Moura were here. I don't know what to do.' She puts the candle into his hand. 'Take pity on us, Francis. Please, fetch me your mother.'

Lily is little more use than her son. She does not know, she cannot tell, she is not sure, she wouldn't care to advise . . . Iseult cannot lie in bed. She takes her sleep in snatches, rocking in a chair in the kitchen, with the baby in her arms, waking every few minutes to check that she still breathes. She cannot shake off the feeling that it is too late, that she has done too little. Not just now but all along, since the baby was born.

571

The morning dawns early, bright and sunny again, a light too sharp to be Irish. A pitiless light. Lily calls up to a neighbour to organize a hired pony-and-trap to collect them for the train. As the train pulls into Dublin, she sees the tall black figure that is Moura and almost weeps for relief. Moura will know, Moura will tell her whether she is right or whether she overreacts, Moura will offer advice in clean, strong lines.

She hands the baby over to those gentle, expert hands. Having touched the little forehead, her mother looks up at her and says, '*Oh, chérie*,' in tender tones that are like the toll of a bell.

'Oh, Moura.'

'Come now, we need to be brave. And to pray. Dolores needs our prayers.'

Iseult leans back into the strength of her mother's organizing presence, as a taxi is hailed and bid to hurry to Harcourt Street Children's Hospital. The surface of the road is as cracked and dry as old paint. In the city, away from the sea edge, the heat has a different quality, orange instead of yellow. Dirty and dry and shaded with gloom. The leaves on the trees they pass are shrivelled, some already turning colour, months early. Everybody walks too slowly through the streets, as if in mourning. A gust of warm wind sweeps her face, bearing a choking eddy of dust, making the cab-horse cough and further coating its blinkers white. Iseult pulls her shawl across Dolores's nostrils and mouth and tries, as Moura said, to pray.

The moment of admission is the worst. Not the jollity of the nurses, who remind her of her own nursing days, whose grim cheer speaks to the dread knot in her stomach. Not the first sight of the infant ward, row after row of white cots. Not the feel of Dolores's five fingers closing over one of hers, as she fights, a skinny gladiator baring toothless gums, and clinging to the only things she ever owned, her life.

Not the later moment when, as Iseult stoops over the cot, the baby grabs the crucifix that dangles from her neck, grabs it so tightly that she detachs it from its chain. Iseult wants it to be a sign that what is happening is explicable in religious terms but her faith is not so primitive or robust. As she says to Francis when he finally arrives, after the death but before the funeral, the baby in her last agony would have grasped any object. Moments later, in any case, she lets it fall.

Worse even than the final slipping away, which is so ordinary, like a basin of water being emptied. Or the funeral, with Francis standing dry-eyed through her silent weeping and her mother's not so silent but equally copious tears. Or the graveyard and its small oblong hole in the yellowish clay, or the priest's inadequate piety, or her husband choosing for the headstone a small, upended coffin in grey stone, or the visit to the grave a few weeks later, to place this ugly headstone and plant a rose tree.

On that day, she determined that she would never visit that cemetery again – and she never did.

None of these compares to that moment of diminishment, standing beside her mother, hearing the word delivered. It seems as if all her life before and after culminates in this moment.

'Do tell us, nurse. It is ridiculous to be mute on the matter. We insist on knowing.'

'It looks like it's . . . I'm sorry to have to tell you that it's meningitis.'

On hearing the word pronounced, a vision rises in Iseult: she and Moura, faces white and haggard above long, black clothes, circling a hole in the ground, a damp pit wherein lie all hopes and all deceptions.

Moura drops to her knees. 'Tell us that it is not that. Not that.'

These dramatics are unbearable to Iseult. 'Get up, Moura,' she hisses, and something in her voice makes her mother obey.

'I am sorry, my darling. I –'

'Please, Moura. I beg you. For once, do not speak.'

Iseult sees what this will do to her marriage. She knows that she and Francis are like moths who have loved each other on the flowers of a roadside. Tarnished by dust, but side by side. She knows this is a wind that will whirl them away from each other in clouds of dust.

Poor, poor Dolores, to be born to such inadequate parents, who failed to keep her alive.

Thora comes to Ireland for the funeral, and afterwards, when it is over and everybody has been seen away, they sit together in Moura's house and Iseult speaks a little of Dolores, of how she grasped the crucifix, of her burial in the yellow-coloured mud, of the coffin made of a special material so light that Iseult could have carried her alone. 'I don't think she suffered much, not after the first convulsion. She was mostly in a kind of coma. Sometimes she would regain consciousness and gaze at me with the most pathetic eyes.'

She starts to cry again, and, at her request, they move to discussing other matters, and Thora manfully keeps up a long string of chatter about inconveniences and enjoyments, the particular qualities of the Irish and English and the inadequacies of husbands.

On the way out, as she pulls on her gloves, she asks outright what she must ask. 'How is it, darling? How are you?'

'Broken.'

'Can you cope?'

'I don't know.'

'The cockroach?'

'Worse. Different. This is inside and out. It has got into the birdsong.'

'Are you in actual pain?'

'I cannot speak of it any more, Thora. I . . .' She closes her eyes, puts her fingers to her temples. 'I'm sorry. Each time I say it, it is as if I am making it happen again.'

'My darling, have you any hope?'

'No. No hope.'

'But you have courage.'

'Perhaps.'

'And nobility. Yes, you have, always. Courage and nobility.' Thora places a hand upon her cousin's shoulder. 'Always, Sir Maurice.' She takes Iseult's hand then and places it upon her own shoulder.

Iseult contrives a smile, though she no longer believes in their ritual. How vain, how childish, to think one can surmount one's destiny. Life surges, only to pull away, leaving one as lonely as a stranded sea creature betrayed by the tide.

'It was good to see you,' she says.

'Dear Maurice. I'll come again soon.'

It is Iseult's cue to take away her hand, to let her cousin go, but she finds herself still holding on to the shelf of bone. Gripping it hard. And now she is bending her head and pressing her forehead down into the crook of Thora's neck. 'Oh, please do,' she hears herself saying, as her forehead grinds into her cousin's shoulder. 'Please do, please do, please do . . .'

72

We began each morning of the trial with a man banging a long stick on the ground and shouting, 'All rise!' Called a tipstaff, after his long wooden crown-topped stick, this person has been a feature of Dublin's Criminal Court since it opened three hundred years ago. Once he had alerted us, the judge followed in, overweight and bewigged, in dark-rimmed, Buddy Holly glasses, with an irritating way of tenderly placing his well-upholstered posterior upon the well-upholstered bench. Settled, he would take a brisk look at me over his glasses, then nod at counsel, and we were off on another day of question-and-answer games.

Around me mouths opened and closed, opened and closed, around the same questions over and again. The pump. The pills. Pauline. Zach. Star. Me. My father. Yet, much to Mags's surprise, the trial seemed to be going our way. She was taking the line that too much of the Department of Public Prosecution's evidence was circumstantial and doing a great job of persuading the court that I was not the only person who might have done the deed.

As things looked better and better for me, I felt less and less present. All this courtroom chatter seemed unreal. Irrelevant. What seemed important was Zach and Star, sitting beside each other each day. Zach's grey eyes looked at me and seemed to ask me every question under the sun. Star's blue eyes looked at me and were as blank as a doll's. I saw those four eyes all day in court, and when I was ushered back to my cell, I saw them still. I saw them while I was awake and while I slept.

By day when I controlled the dreams, I saw my daughter and me in a world where none of this had happened, living a life where we went to the mall to shop, where we enjoyed pizza and ice-cream sodas together, where she introduced me to some nice boy I'd never met before and I was happy for her. An ordinary, normal mother and daughter. What we hadn't been for oh so long.

How long?

I had no answers. I had no words. I didn't even know what to wish for.

What lay ahead for me, if Mags got me off? My heart whispering for Zach, the only man I'd ever really wanted. A proper man, strong enough to be gentle, and the only man I couldn't have. But my blood whispering for Star.

And none of us able to be together.

I couldn't think about guilty or not guilty because there was no freedom for me, for any of us, either way. The choice between a physical or emotional prison was no choice at all.

Lover? Daughter? My mind's eye played with one and then the other, until some mouth would open around some new set of words that would drag me back into that horrible courtroom, back to unreal questions for which there were also no answers.

Days droned past. The cyst of confusion and trepidation inside me turned solid.

Then came an exchange between Zach and Star, a small moment that told me what to do. While the prosecutor, Manny Bradshaw, was cross-examining Dr Keane, Star leant sideways to whisper something in Zach's ear. He shook his head at whatever she asked, then reached across and patted her hand, a small protective pat. She turned from him to hide her expression, so he didn't see the look that crossed her face, but I, sitting opposite in the defendant's dock, viewed it full frontal. Adoration. Pure and total adoration. No other word for it.

She flicked her eyes in my direction and saw that I had seen. That chased away the blankness of the stare she had been dealing me for days, and, as she looked at me properly for the first time since all this had happened, as I stared into those blue eyes so like my own, I felt as if I were falling into water. They had everything in them now, those eyes. Pity and pity's opposite, her complete scorn.

And she was right. Whichever way I looked at what Star had done, a finger pointed back at me. The night before, I'd dreamt she was a baby and I was feeding her a bottle, but when I looked closely it had no milk in it, only dust and crumbled, dried-up leaves.

I wanted to go back, that was what I wanted.

My daydreams took me there. Back to the days before she knew either of us had a father, back to when I was her all in all and she was my twinkling twinkling little star, and further back, to when we were even safer, to before I was born myself, when she was already buried fast inside me, a tiny egg, a whispered promise.

A line from Iseult Gonne's writing came to mind – 'Judge yourself by the fruit; judge others by the blossom' – and Star's eyes now seemed to beg a question. What would you give to go back? they asked. What would you give?

It came to me then, all in a rush: the only answer.

In front of me was a pencil. I picked it up and wrote on a piece of paper that I passed to Mags. Her eyes boggled as she read the words and – predictably – she shook her head furiously at me. I nodded, insistent. Calm now. Serene. Untouchable.

I took a big breath, letting the knowing settle in me. Around us, the court began to grow restless. I closed my eyes. I could hear their growing unease, the coughs and the shuffling of papers and the shifting of feet, but I knew what was coming and I took the time I needed to take.

I pushed my chair back, went to stand to make the announcement, but Mags pulled at my arm, forced me back down.

She stood herself. 'M'Lord,' she said, before I had a chance to speak, 'I wish to request a recess. I need to speak to my client.'

He wasn't impressed, but he granted it.

In the inner chamber, Mags slammed the door theatrically behind us. 'If you're not careful, he is going to throw the book at you for wasting the court's time. I refuse to do what you wrote down in there.' She couldn't even bring herself to say it.

'It's what you wanted me to do.'

'Yes, back at the beginning. Not now. For Christ's sake, Izzy, if you do that, you'll get the absolute worst of both worlds. He'll give you life.'

'So be it.'

'You can't! I won't let you. It's going well in there, there's a good chance of getting you off. Why would you do this?'

'I'm sorry, Mags, I know it's inconvenient for you but –'

'Incon – bloody – venient! It's a bit more than that.'

'I know it's hard for you. I wish I'd known earlier, but I didn't. I'm sorry, but if you don't tell him, I will.'

Something in my voice communicated itself. She sat down. Her shoulders slumped. She looked so unlike herself I almost laughed. I could have, easily, but I didn't want to confuse her any further.

'Have you any idea what prison is like? You'll be an old woman when you come out.'

'So be it,' I said again.

'I don't get it,' said poor Mags. 'I just don't get it. Tell me why.'

How could I explain that stepping into prison was going to liberate us? That this was the only way for us all to salvage . . . something.

I didn't even try.

'I should never, never have taken this case,' she said, slamming her pencil down on the desk. 'I knew you were trouble, from the first day. Christ! I am *never* going to forgive you for this.'

We went back out.

Mags approached the bench. 'M'Lord, my client wishes to change her plea to guilty.'

Pandemonium erupted. Reporters woke up out of their snoozes and followed their colleagues rushing for the exit. Star's hands flew to her mouth, one over the other. Zach found my eyes and held them and sent me a small smile, knowing somehow, without yet knowing the details, that I was doing right.

Many Changing Things

But O, sick children of the world,
Of all the many changing things
In dreary dancing past us whirled,
To the cracked tune that Chronos sings,
Words alone are certain good.

W. B. Yeats,
'The Song of the Happy Shepherd'

Izzy
1984

When I started this book, I intended to write the whole of Iseult's Gonne's life. I have stacks of notes about things that happened to her after the time we've got to – she lived for another thirty-three years after that – and some events that are outwardly very interesting (falling in love with a Nazi spy, for one). But I can't seem to get beyond Dolores's death. For me, that was the incident that defined Iseult, the day beyond which there was nothing more to be said.

We all have one – a day on which our whole life pivots. The day in that courtroom was mine.

I wish I could explain this to Star but we can't talk about any of it, yet. During her visits we discuss the doings of other inmates, or the latest challenge of the centre, or the lousy weather or . . . anything, really, except the complicated, tender territory between us.

This prison isn't Doolough's lock-up room, my father's house or the kitchen I felt tied to when Star was small. This is the real Victorian deal, complete with clanging steel doors, hard beds and chamber pots. In here they laugh like crows and cry like owls and hardly know the difference – yet I'm managing to make a good life here.

I have turned to writing travel books. In *prison?* Yes, it is a little unusual. I rely on memory and research in reference books sourced for me by the prison librarian. My *Guide to Glendalough* has been translated into ten languages.

Could I live so well in here without my writing? I think not, but it's a two-way thing. My writing would not live so well were I not here. On the outside, it took me fourteen years to bring order to this tome. Eighteen months in here has already produced two books.

Books of a different order – but still . . .

I don't write about Iseult any more because I have done what I wanted to do for her – prised her from the poet's fingers, breathed her own life back into her.

And because I've learnt what she had to teach me. The difference between defeat (how she handled her health, her writing, her husband) and acceptance (how she handled my father, Moura, John MacBride). The need to relinquish the search for meaning.

Iseult has taught me that meaning and happiness are incompatible. Meaning must have past and future to fix upon, but happiness is always here and now.

What first attracted me to Iseult Gonne was her effect on me and my father, how being in her presence seemed to turn us into different people. Later, when I understood her life, I kept in mind always the old lady I had met with him. She was sad, yes, but she had peace in her too, sitting in her garden. The glory of her later years lay in that garden; I sensed it even then. It offered her something akin to the transcendence she experienced when she was a young woman dancing in the wind and touched my father and me as her dance had affected the poet.

Iseult Gonne lost her child and her writing, she endured poverty and depression, she suffered loneliness and heart disease, but she was still open to those moments.

So the loose ends no longer bother me. If this manuscript is to be put out some day, it will need to be tidied up, but for now it wants only one reader.

But how am I going to get her to sit down and read it?

In here, where the outer days are harsh, beset with rules and ugliness, we prisoners are supposed to be sitting out our time, waiting for the release date when life will strike up for us again.

Not me. For me now, the outer is the lesser half of life. I'm dancing to an inner rhythm, set by my writing and the practices Zach taught me.

They are what keep me safe and well and, yes, happy, in here. Each day I write, I read, I walk in the exercise yard, and I call a halt to my thunderous thoughts by meditating. If I let these stabilizing practices slip, I get resistance, fear and struggle again. If I stay with them, I get trust, surrender and acceptance. Even joy, sometimes.

This prison is 'decrepit, inadequate, overcrowded, unsanitary and inhumane', according to the most recent penal reform report, and full of broken angers, but in this unlikely place I find my writing flows, as Iseult once said charity flowed from Maud – like a live fountain springing from the soil.

In here, in prison, I am free and safe at last.

It's what I hope for Star: that she will drop the questions that have no answers and allow herself to be free and happy too. That she will let Zach show her how.

Sometimes, not too often, really not often at all, I allow myself a small imagining. Not a why-oh-why, or a what-if; something closer to a dream.

I am out of prison and back in Doolough, and Star has read this book. It is dusk in summer, and we are walking towards the lake. The fading light has greyed the water that we can glimpse through the trees. The wildflowers are out, wood avens, honeysuckle, greater bladderwort and, on the lake's eastern shore, a cluster of white water lilies.

I tell her to keep her eyes alert for young hedgehogs or badgers or foxes that might be coming out to feed. We go down to the water, admiring the stillness that makes it look half solid, like mercury. We circle round it, pushing through the spot where the pathway knots with nettles and strings of the weed we call 'Sticky Nelly'. I pick fuchsia and show her how to suck the flower for honey.

I deal no reproaches, I let no shadow fall.

We stay out until the bats start to appear, and then we leave the lake and turn back the way we came. I pick another flower, an orchid for her hair, and we walk, with me just a shade ahead of her, through the slow-gathering darkness, back to the house where my father no longer lives.

Afterword(s)
Star
2008

Imagine. That's what people always say, whenever they hear our story. Imagine: the mother, the daughter, the same man! Just imagine!

So do. Imagine us, my mom and me, last Christmas morning (her final Christmas, though we didn't know it then), driving through Wicklow to Mass. In the years after she came out of prison, especially once the twins were born, Mom liked to go to church with me for Christmas. Not that she ever, as she would put it, 'got God' but for the tradition of it. We avoided the gossipers of Doolough by taking Mass at St Kevin's Church in Laragh, and she loved the outing with the kids.

Our kids, mine and Shan's. (Always Shando, never Zach, to me.)

Her grandkids.

Two little miracle babies, born through the wonders of science, and now – how can it be already? – six years old.

So imagine us in the high seats of my Land Rover, driving our way to that village just east of Glendalough, where Iseult Gonne lived and died and my father grew up. The jeep ignored the potholes in the rutted roads, and we glided through a frosty, blue-white winter morning, through scenery my mother described in her *Guide to Glendalough*. Mountains dropping sheer on each side of us and a mesh of rivers emptying into the two long lakes at the valley's heart that gave the place its name – *Glean Dá* (two) *Lough*. Lakes long and deep enough to take the rivers' gush and hold it still.

We drove within that stillness, the twins growing drowsy in

the back. At Laragh I turned left up the hill to St Kevin's Church, crunching the gears to a halt outside the church doors. Even after twenty-six years in Ireland, I still haven't got used to driving a stick shift.

I walked round to the passenger side, to help my mother down. Her illness and its treatment had made her frail, more frail than a 65-year-old woman should be, but she still had beauty. The tan that faded during her prison years was revived by travel afterwards in Italy and Greece, so that now she looked like a white settler, leathery skin against long ashy hair that she twisted into a knot at the crown of her head.

Dean was already unstrapping himself and hopping out, poised to run. (Are all children always in such a rush? My two can never just *wait*.)

'The hand!' he shouted, leaping to the ground.

Aimée fumbled with her seat belt. Life is more of a struggle for her than for her brother, has been from the start, when oxygen deprivation during their birth left her with a small drag in her foot. But she's a fighter. Tumbling out, she took up her brother's call. 'The hand! The hand!' They meant the water feature in the church grounds, the bronze arm and hand of Saint Kevin.

According to legend, this man, the patron saint of Glendalough, was praying in his tiny cell one day, with an arm stretched out the window, when a blackbird came and landed in his upturned palm and laid its eggs.

'No hand yet,' I said. 'Mass first.'

'Noooooooo,' says Aimée.

'Sorry, sweetheart. We haven't time now.'

'That's not fair,' said Dean, mutinous as always. Aimée started to cry but not convincingly.

'Now come on, you two. We'll go down to the hand straight after Mass. But first we want to see Baby Jesus in his crib, don't we?'

'Stupid Baby Jesus,' said Dean, running towards the church

before I had time to chew him out. He always did that, made himself feel better with a little burst of rebellion. Aimée giggled and ran after him, and my mother and I, pretending not to smile, brought up the rear.

When Mass was over, we followed them back down the slope as they ran towards the hand. I walked at my mother's pace, feeling too large as I always did beside her though I am thin now, or reasonably so (148 pounds, if you must know – and I won't be referring to it again). I got my father's looks, not hers, and was never beautiful, but now I know myself to be what Shando calls present.

Myself.

A robust tweed beside a silken gauze.

The kids had begun to climb the sculpture, in what was becoming a Christmas tradition.

'He's so right,' my mother said, as she sat down on the nearby bench, her legs to one side, like a lady riding side-saddle.

'Who?'

'Seamus Heaney.'

Another of her poets. 'Huh?'

'In saying the whole thing is imagined.'

'What are you talking about, Mom?'

'Don't you remember? We read it last year.' She was pointing to the plaque and I went across and read it again. Lines from a poem, 'Saint Kevin and the Blackbird', which ask us to imagine being so at one with nature that you'd hold out your arm, like a branch, because a bird had laid eggs in your hand, and keep it there for all the weeks it took the eggs to hatch and the baby birds to fledge. To imagine the feel of the warm eggs in your hand, the beat of the bird's breast, the scratch of its claws. To imagine what it would be like to have trained your whole body to 'become a prayer, entirely'.

'It's good,' I said, sitting back down.

'You should learn it by heart. Poems have to become the marrow in your bones.'

All my life, she'd said things like this and ignored how I ignored them. I saw Aimée was climbing too high, dangling from Saint Kevin's arm. 'Aimée!' I shouted. 'Get down. Now!'

She did, and I relaxed.

My mother said, 'You know my book about Iseult Gonne?' She hadn't mentioned it in a long time.

'Sure.'

'I need you to finish it for me.'

'I thought it was finished.'

'It has lots of loose ends, bits that need tidying up. And I'd like you to add an afterword, to say how everybody ended up.'

I didn't know then that she and I and our lurid story were part of it, but I was reluctant anyway. Disinclined to please her but for better reasons too. 'Mom, I can't. I wouldn't know how.'

'I need you to. I have no energy for it. And without that polishing off, it doesn't work.'

'I'm sure it's fine.'

She sighed and reached up to remove the grip that held her hair in place It tumbled down, the same colour as the cloud-filtered light above us, and she pulled it across one shoulder, so it fell over the place where her breast used to be. She stroked it down, trying to keep her composure.

'Star. Please. It needs you.'

A thinness had taken over the skin around her eyes. Another person wouldn't have been able to tell, but I knew I was making her tired.

If only I had agreed, taken it from her, there and then. Nothing would have pleased her more.

I knew it. And so, I didn't do it.

That's what I live with, now.

The day she went to prison, my mother was not allowed to see us, so she explained what she wanted in two long letters, seven pages each, to Shando and me. I can summarize each in two sentences.

Dear Zach,

I want you to work with Star, to take my father's house and turn it into your centre, to work on it together, to be together. That is my wish.

Dear Star,

He will need your help to make this work, so be there for him. Be together, that is my wish.

And it was our wish too. Fragile as we both were after all that had happened, it was a way forward. So we entirely remodelled my grandfather's house, with Mom encouraging us at each prison visit to use as much of his money as we needed. 'What better use could it be put to?'

Downstairs we knocked down walls to make a large catering kitchen, where Janet and Bríd, two local cooks, prepare wholefood. We added a sun lounge on the south-west façade and a dining area at the opposite end and extended the front rooms into a yoga studio and classroom. The Better World Centre, we call it, in tribute to Mom and Marsha's café, and we carried over some – big and neat – ideas from there. Marsha too came over, when she could, more often after she retired and Mom came out of jail.

At first we had a struggle to keep going. We were ahead of our time in Ireland, and it was a challenge to build a clientele and to win trust among the locals in Doolough. Mom's trial was only part of it. All sorts of crazy rumours flew. We were part of 'a cult', we were witches, we were offering orgies and pagan practices. Pauline Whelan, who worked part time for us in the office, would deliver the latest nonsense to us, shaking her head. I would have given up many times, but Shando never wavered.

'You can't control what people think,' he used to say. 'If we stay true to the vision, everything will work out.'

He was right. By the mid 1990s, we were thriving.

Life was hard on my mother – even I can admit that. The final blow was breast cancer, diagnosed the year after she got out of jail. She battled it, as they say (stupid metaphor), and went on to tour the world and write more books. Six years later it surfaced again, and this time it had spread. She took treatment for a while, but it failed and she gave it up. As she weakened, we had no choice, after all she had given us, but to invite her to live with us at the centre.

And she had no choice but to accept.

Her illness added guilt to my internal swirl of resentments. I even resented her cancer for allowing her into my life again. Irrational, or what? As if she had arranged to have tumours gnaw at her just to get at me.

Shando worked with me to dismantle these rages, which were really most unfair to her and destructive to me.

I did see that, even when I was simmering in them.

The night before Christmas, I had woken around 3 a.m. to a noise that made me sit up out of sleep, discarding whatever dream I had been dreaming. This movement changed the rhythm of Shando's breathing beside me, and I froze still. And heard it again. A cough? A call? With care, I slid from the warmth of the covers, chill December air pouring across my naked skin. Naked in bed is a privilege I have allowed myself since losing weight.

At the door I put on my robe and slipped out to listen down the corridor. All quiet. No guests that week. With my mother ill, we had decided to forgo the usual Christmas retreat and make it family only. I paused by one of the corridor windows, made a circle in the condensation-covered glass to look out. Nothing to see, except winter darkness, blanketing us in.

Often on deep winter nights like these, Santa Paola comes to mind. The click of palms and the rustle of eucalyptus. The hot wind that smells of laurel and burnt offerings. The warmed-up, blue-black skies.

I sighed, flip-flopped down the corridor in my slippers, stopped outside her door and put my ear to it.

Yes, movement.

I stuck in my head. The room was dark.

'Who's that?'

'It's only me,' I said. 'I heard a noise. Are you okay?'

'Fine, fine. I just went down for a drink of water.'

'Do you need anything else?'

'I'm *fine*, Star.'

'I was only asking.'

'I know, I know. Thanks but really no need. Go back to sleep.'

You'll see that we'd swapped roles by then, which neither of us was quite able to cope with, though most of the time we managed.

As I made my way back to bed, I did the work Shando taught me to do, took my focus off my coiling emotions and put it on to my breathing. Breathe in . . . and fill the belly with air. Breathe out . . . and all the badness with it. And again . . . in. And . . . out. There. Everything was fine. No cross words, not really, and tomorrow was Christmas Day.

I slipped back into the warmth of our bed. 'Daddy could sleep for Ireland,' Dean used to say, an expression he picked up from the schoolyard that made us all laugh, especially Shando. I arranged myself around the curve of his spine. His heat transferred itself to me, and I kissed the knobbly bone at the base of his neck. If I slid my foot along his shin, he would be likely to waken. Our legs would straighten out and he would turn and we would feel the length and centre of each other.

I'm sorry but I needed to write that. I know it must be hard for you to read, that it must stir in you some shade of the feelings we have all learnt to live with. Disbelief, distaste, perhaps even disgust. I don't blame you. It took us a long time to allow ourselves to be together in that way and our strange history will always be there between us. A ditch we continually navigate and into which we sometimes stumble.

We cope by accepting things as they are, by not wishing they were otherwise. In the interest of that, Shando says there's no need for me to be writing any of this about us, together, in bed. But I must. It's not that I want to make you uncomfortable, but I have to claim him back. For all that you have read, it's important that you understand that he is *my* husband.

Mine.

And that there's a whole story you haven't been told.

So let me tell you, just once, how I loved slipping back under the covers beside him. He was sound asleep and I decided not to disturb him, just to lay my hand quietly across his chest and enjoy a different pleasure, the feel of my naked front all along his naked back.

So unlike those nights I endured after I found out that my mother – who had had so many men – had also taken mine. Nights that used to slowly pulse past – *beat – beat – beat* – each second a throb of jealous rage.

He was my first love, and he will be my last – I know that. Even if I wanted, I wouldn't have time enough to learn again how to be so free, how to take and give with our mix of abandon and familiarity. Whereas she and he had only months together. Not even a year, if you put both times together.

His love for me is very different to what he felt for her, I knew that even before I read her book. For a long time, the longest time (sometimes even yet?), I thought mine second best. Shan always wanted to talk about it, but, if my imaginings came close, I lobbed them away with some other thought.

The best I could do.

It's foolish, I know. He and I have shared so many years, the effort of building the centre, of getting (and staying) pregnant, of having and raising our kids, that it's a two-way thing now, how we hold each other up.

Where, I would have liked to ask my mother while she was alive, is the poet that has done justice to *that* kind of love? The intimacy that takes years to build? The lovemaking that has within it all the other times you've been together?

Not, of course, something I could ever ask her.

This, then, was my life before I read my mother's book. In the room next door my two children safe in sleep, soon to waken with yelps about Santa Claus.

In my bed, my husband's heartbeat under my hand.

In the rooms around and below us, our home and work, our life's purpose (Shando's words, not mine, but true, I guess).

Down the corridor, trying to get some sleep, my mother.

And at my core, despite all, my own heart still pumping jealousy and fear.

They made her serve more than sixteen years. One hundred and ninety-five months of avoiding the drugs and sex and dramas that got the other inmates through the days. She told us very little, during her time or afterwards, about the dirty secrets that seeped out from under the cell doors – the punctures and jabs of drug abuse; the sex connections that were a kind of hate; the aggression and belligerence and occasional violence; the screw who forced himself on the most hopeless of the hopeless cases; the self-harmers who broke plastic cutlery to cut themselves . . .

Instead, she recorded her thoughts in hard-backed note-books, often filling pages with the details of these days that, from the outside, looked so identical to all the other days around them.

At first, her aloofness annoyed the others. 'Her Ladyshit', they called her. 'Her Ladyshit thinks her shit don't smell.' Which made me smile, I have to admit. Before long, she was the old hand, the lifer watching the small-timers come and go, and, as her acceptance of where she found herself settled in her, the others came to acknowledge it.

She categorized her cellmates into two types: the ones who cried for their children and the ones who cried for their men (which, back then, had me wondering: which type was she?). The particular details of neglect or abuse that led these women to their addictions or shoplifting became her subject. She wrote books that told these true-life stories and, with the help of the prison's librarian, who came to be a friend, she had them published to success and acclaim.

But still, it was *prison*. 'How did you stand it for so long?' I asked her, after she came out.

'Whenever it got tough, and self-pity started up, I would ask myself: "Can I bear this moment here and now?" The answer was always yes. Thoughts of the past or of the future might be agonizing, but the moment I was in was always liveable.'

Happy in prison. Her Ladyshit, serene in the face of hostility. That's who my mother became.

When, after sixteen years, they let her out early for good behaviour, she was forbidden from travelling to the States, and that, Shando said, was the hardest of all for her. She longed to see California again, to drive a top-down Chevy through Big Sur, to go for a walk at sunset by the Pacific, to admire the soar of a red-breasted eagle, to lie under a moon burnt red by the Santa Ana. It wasn't to be, and that too she accepted, travelling instead in the opposite direction, to Spain and Italy and the Greek islands, and writing travel books as she went.

Not a bad life.

When she died, a good contingent of prison staff turned up to the funeral and all said they'd never had an inmate like her.

Some people are born special – like Maud Gonne, six foot tall, rich, gifted, marked – but my mother started ordinary. It was how she lived her life that transformed her.

*

So: the loose ends. What came after for Iseult and her entourage?

Ireland's fight for freedom ended in a Treaty with the British that was too much of a compromise for die-hard nationalists and led to a bitter and squalid Civil War. My grandfather was happy enough to compromise, as it meant jobs and security, but the Gonnes, *naturellement*, plumped for the idealistic – and doomed – anti-Treaty side.

Iseult Gonne was arrested in a round-up and, during a riot in one of the women's prisons, once again encountered my grandfather, where he was a Free State policeman. There, despite the charged atmosphere, he and she managed to have a conversation, in which she shrugged off the event that he had been squirming over for eight years.

'They were strange times for all of us,' she said, smiling that smile that, apparently, no man could resist.

'You're a lady,' he replied. And he protected her from the beatings and abuse inflicted on some of the other women by Free State soldiers and police.

I would have liked to read my grandfather's version of this event, but his diaries and letters are nowhere to be found. It seems my mother must have destroyed them, a deed that interests me and begs a question. Why, when she had 170 of his letters and six diaries, did she never once give him – or indeed me? – the privilege she afforded to Shando and Maud and Iseult and W. B. and even John MacBride: our own words upon the page, without her interpretation?

The rest of the 1920s saw the Stuarts moving to Laragh, opening a poultry farm (!) and having a baby boy called Ian. Francis escaped regularly to London to live the life of a bright young thing – or as bright as a boy-about-town can be when he's broke. Maud founded 'The Mothers', a protest organization, and spent every Sunday of her life marching down O'Connell Street in Dublin, calling attention to the latest Free State scandal.

In the 1930s the Stuarts' marital estrangement grew; a daughter, Kay, was born. W. B. decided to have a 'Steinach' operation for sexual rejuvenation, the Viagra of its day – thereby making himself, once again, a figure of Dublin fun. He and Maud made up their quarrel, and he kept his friendship with Iseult, visiting the Stuarts whenever he went to Ireland and taking every opportunity to puff Francis's writing. They all fell for Fascism and for the promise Germany offered to ennoble and purify the world.

In the flush of his sexual rebirth, the 69-year-old W. B. took up with a 27-year-old actor and poet, beautiful of course, called Margot Ruddock, whose other defining characteristics were her instability and her longing for greatness. She left her husband and child to follow him to Majorca, seeking reassurance about her poetry and her life's worth, saying: 'I told Yeats if I could not make a poem that would live, I must die.'

The poet critiqued her work with supreme self-interest – at first, with extravagant praise and later, when he had moved on to another woman, with extravagant brutality ('You take the easiest course – leave out the rhymes or choose the most hackneyed rhymes because – damn you – you are lazy'), and Ruddock went temporarily insane, dancing in the rain down by the seashore. Mom wrote reams about this woman, who was later committed to a lunatic asylum, where she lived out the rest of her life. She was troubled, as was W. B. himself, by the harshness of his criticism, by the image of her dancing, by the echoes of Iseult. Might Iseult's writing have flourished if she'd had a better teacher? The question haunted Mom. For her, the unborn writing was a loss to rival that of baby Dolores.

The decade ended with the outbreak of the Second World War and W. B. dying in the South of France, with faithful, put-upon George in attendance. During this war, Ireland remained neutral and Francis Stuart surpassed himself by emigrating *into* Nazi Germany in 1940. Back home, Iseult welcomed a Nazi spy in from the cold.

Like Maud and her husband and her exes (Ezra Pound was

jailed for anti-Semitic broadcasts), Iseult Gonne believed in an aristocracy of thought. Her only known comment on the outcome of the war was: 'There seems to be no "becoming" in anything. What disenchanted days we live in.' Mom might have been able to explain all that away, but for me it takes dreamy utopianism a tad too far.

In the 1950s Iseult's chief pleasure was in visiting her mother, now an old lady in her eighties who liked to hold court from bed. Iseult would sit in a rocking chair, and the room would fill with blue cigarette smoke as they reminisced over memories, recalling people they never saw any more. She has left letters that give a good indication of her life and thinking at this time. One to her husband is especially eloquent – it speaks of how tired she was of crying and of not sleeping and of not being able to think well of him but granting him 'all the phantoms of the spheres, and as many Russian dancers as two arms can hold (indeed, this is not quite true)'.

Always, with Iseult Gonne, the equivocation.

She died a year after her mother, as she had predicted to my grandfather that she would, with her son holding her hand as she peacefully slipped away. Her daughter, asleep in the bed beside her, is said to have slept through the event. They spelt her name wrong (Isuelt) on her coffin and disregarded her wish to be cremated, and she was hardly into the ground when her husband married the German woman he had long wanted to bring to Laragh to live in a *ménage à trois*.

At least Iseult's self-abasement had stopped short of allowing that.

Stuart lived on for another forty years, writing a string of flawed and solipsistic novels that lashed out at his wife and the world. He made a personal mythology out of egotism and alienation, and the Irish writing establishment – red-faced at having underestimated the genius of that other mad egotist, James Joyce – thought they'd better hedge their bets and offer him the title of *Saoi*, the nation's highest literary honour. At this,

his much flaunted outsider status was cast to the winds and he hopped happily upon the insider's throne.

He spent the rest of his life exploring in words the various ways in which he was damaged and damaging, but he never found a facility with language, and his ego always came between him and artistic truth.

So there you have it: Mom's two hundred pages summarized in a thousand words. You can read between the lines of the novels and poems and biographies if you want more.

Enough. The end. Chop chop.

There is not much in the life of Iseult Gonne to make anyone jealous but I do envy her those smoky, talk-filled days in her mother's bedroom. I never spent a minute more in my mother's company than I had to, so I never got to where I could have said to her, 'Why did you do it, Mom?'

Which is why the end of this book came as an awful shock to me. To Shando too. We're reeling from it still.

She didn't do it. That's what her book makes clear. Not only that but she thought it was *me*. A thought that could make me as mad as hell – if I hadn't jumped to the same conclusion, in reverse.

Now I know, I wonder how I ever could have thought her guilty.

I didn't think, that's the truth. Blinded by anger, I believed the surface story: she was under arrest, so she must have done it.

I never wondered, *I* never imagined; I'm not the type.

Or, maybe, deep down, so low I didn't quite know it was there, I thought she had help. From the great helper himself. *Shando*, for pity's sake. I thought she was capable of anything and I thought any man, even the *goodest* man in the world, would do anything for her.

What does it say of me that I could so misjudge the man I

married? What does it say of me that I could think that of him – even for a flash, even deeper-than-deep down – and still take him as a husband?

Maybe, as he says, I am being too hard on myself. After all, he thought she was guilty too.

But she wasn't. She didn't do it. And so now I am left having to reimagine her.

Shando and I used to visit the prison separately, one of us taking out the old Hiace van we had then to make the drive to Dublin and come back and report to the one left minding the business. She made a great effort for those visits, I know that now from reading her notebooks. I suppose I always knew it, that it couldn't have been easy to be so pleased to see us, so open to being entertained and amused, as my mother always was for visiting hours.

One day we had big news for her, news we had to go together to deliver. I was so nervous that Shando had to stop the van twice on the way to let me be sick and, approaching the meshed door of the visitor room, I balked. 'You tell her,' I said. 'I'll wait out here.'

'Don't be silly.'

'It's not fair to her to have to deal with us both at once for this.'

He was having none of it. He made me go in and took my hand in his to tell her the news. She was better than good about it. The smallest flicker, just for a fraction of a moment, then she turned her eyes to hold us both and said, in her mawkish way, 'A new life! How wonderful!' As if she was any other prospective grandmother.

Exactly how Shando had said she would respond (and in case you're wondering, yes, it *is* irritating to be married to Mr-Right-All-The-Time, especially when he's so indulgent of your irritation). Still holding my hand, he reached across and took one of hers. I blushed blood-red, but they were smiling. We sat there, a small chain of hands, with the two of them looking so serene, while my circuits sparked into overdrive.

It was only afterwards that I realized I should have reached over and taken her other hand, to close the circle. I was so young then, not yet able to grasp what Shando instinctively understood: the depths of my mother's need for reparation. Prison was her penance; she opened herself to it, utterly.

My feelings, as always, were more conflicted. The thought of her locked away from us – from *him* – consoled me one minute but plunged me into guilt the next. That day, the hand-holding day, resurrected all. I began to torture myself again with imaginings about what she and Shando said during those visits while I was not there. I would boil myself up to a pitch where I *had* to say something – usually something stupid. He would respond with his trademark calm and then I would pick a row about his coldness. I would storm and he would be condescending and, in the middle of it all, I lost the baby.

It was to be another nine years and two IVF attempts before I was pregnant again.

And what about the straggliest, loosest thread of all: what precisely happened in this house in the years before my mother ran away to America?

Her book gives us the scene in the bathroom with Miss September, but nothing after that. She touches against John MacBride's sexual assault on Iseult, but doesn't draw any parallels. She tells us what she told that demented psychologist, but was it the truth? She pictures my grandfather attacking Iseult Gonne in the hospital, but why? She shows us the rebirthing weekend but doesn't answer the salient question.

Always she is skipping around and away from the topic. And then, at the end, it is *me* she puts beneath him.

That never happened. Yes, he brought me fishing but there were no blackberries and I was dead to the cows and the pigeons and the trees my mother describes, dead to everything except the mental showdown I was having with her in my head. As I followed my grandfather down through the field and into the wood, I was sharpening the sting in my answers to all she'd flung at me that morning, the ripostes I'd deal her when she got back from Dublin.

At the lake, my grandfather began demonstrating what to do with a fishing rod, flinging it forward and back with instructions I half heard. Then he shoved the rod into my hand. 'Now you do it.'

'Me? But I don't know how.'

'Amn't I after just showing you how? Go on.'

I stood with the line in my hand, helpless, until he said, 'Do it,' in such a bossy voice that my well-primed anger spilled out. 'No.'

'No, is it?' Sinews strained in his neck, like twigs. 'I'll give you "No".'

I thrust my jaw up at him, furious at him, at my mother, at the whole world. 'No, no, no, no,' I shouted, like a toddler in a tantrum.

'You little fool. That mother of yours has you as bad as herself.'

I threw down the line, turned to walk off.

'Get back here,' he called after me, but I could hear the snarl of fear in his bluster. I stomped on.

'You fat lump, get back here . . .'

His power was already slipping by then, and once Rose was dead he had no one left to bully. Until Mom showed up one day, willing.

But then she brought in Shando. That would have driven him wild.

Doing what he did to himself was my grandfather's final flex of power. We should have seen that, Mom and I, but we were so caught up in each other, we lost sight of him. Of his elemental need to win over.

Sometimes I play Mom's trick and picture him collecting his

stash of pills, hiding them where she couldn't find them, salivating over them like a miser over gold when she wasn't around. I imagine him opening the tissue paper or handkerchief in which he kept them, I see him putting them between his wasted lips, his tainted teeth . . .

With what poisonous thoughts?

With what mixed motives?

Unanswerable questions. My life is full of them.

So picture us then, my mother and me, on our last Christmas together in Laragh: two women in a winter churchyard, one a little overweight and reaching middle age, the other still lovely but on the edge of old.

'It's your story too,' she said to me, and I, unable to give her what she wanted, called out instead to the children, 'First to the car gets to open the Christmas crackers!' Bribery, as usual, worked better than nagging, and they jumped down, Saint Kevin's hand forgotten for another year.

I can't turn back time. I can't change the facts, so I ask you to imagine us just as we were. The children, their new, young bodies running. Four short legs (one dragging, just a little) pumping up the hill to the car that will take them home, to presents and to Daddy and to Christmas dinner. My mother and I behind them, a gap between us as we walked.

I was thinking: what was the point in this drive to create? Whether it succeeded (Willie Yeats) or failed (Iseult Gonne) or hovered somewhere in between (Izzy Mulcahy), it didn't seem to make any of them happy. With all his goals achieved, but still unable to give pure, simple love, W.B. wrote his saddest line of all: ' "*What then?*" *sang Plato's ghost.* "*What then?*" '

And that was before his poet's tower was turned into a greasy till, selling Aran jumpers and tin whistles.

Even if my mother's book was read, I reasoned as I walked beside her, it would vanish, sooner or later, along with everything else. There were so many books – far too many – and only a fraction survive and then not for long. A few centuries if a writer was really gifted and really lucky, a tiny beat of time on planet earth.

So I turned her down.

If I could go back now to last Christmas, I'd take her by the arm and drive her home and bring her for a walk by Doolough Lake.

I'd look at all the Irish country things she showed me and see them through her eyes.

I'd accept her orchid for my hair and ask her all the questions I should have asked, and give her all my answers. I'd read the manuscript she wanted me to read, so that while she lived, we'd both learn what we needed to know.

Yes, that's what I would do.

Imagine if I had.

'She felt a need for reparation,' Shando says, as I try to work it through with him, why my mother volunteered to be punished for a crime she didn't commit. 'She was taking herself out of the situation, letting us get on with it.'

'Her way of making up?'

He nods at me, eyes soft and grey as clouds.

'For you, you mean?'

'For everything – us, your childhood, your father . . .'

'But what a way to do it.'

'That was the way that presented itself.'

'But . . . It . . .'

'Yes?'

'It . . . She . . . I . . .'

He is holding still, deathly still, like I am some shy animal he's just surprised in a wood. My insides quiver. My husband opens his arms to me and, as I step into them, I'm talking not to him but to my mother. I'm calling her name. 'Mommy,' I'm saying. 'Mom. Mommy. Mom.'

*

Too late. The saddest two words in the English language. But is it really too late for my mother and me? I've realized that your relationship with somebody doesn't stop just because they're dead. It goes on changing, especially when there's a big book full of their words to have and hold.

And if she were still alive, we might still be scraping against each other. That too is true.

Sometimes I even think it's all just as it should be. Shan says so, and I do have times when I know what he means.

My favourite thing to do now is to go walking by Doolough Lake, imagining all the things I would have said to my mother if I'd read her book in time – and saying them anyway. I speak them out loud and listen to her whisper, through the water and the mountains, back to me.

It's her book, not mine, so I leave you with her word. Imagine. Just imagine. Because – as she said to me on that last Christmas morning, before I knew enough to understand – it's all imagined anyway.

Acknowledgements

This novel treats Iseult Gonne and other people who actually lived as fictional characters, but I have tried to render as accurately as possible the outer and inner details of their lives, where known. I depended for information on a great number of sources, including the following:

For the letters between Maud Gonne and W. B. Yeats, *Always Your Friend: The Gonne–Yeats Letters 1893–1938*; for those from Maud to the literary patron John Quinn, *Too Long a Sacrifice: The Letters of Maud Gonne and John Quinn*; for those from Iseult Gonne to Yeats and Ezra Pound, *A Girl Who Knew All Dante Once: Letters to W. B. Yeats and Ezra Pound from Iseult Gonne*. Material in Chapter 5 is a modification of the account of meeting Lucien Millevoye given by Maud Gonne in her autobiography, *A Servant of the Queen*.

For permission to draw heavily from these texts, I am indebted to Iseult Gonne's granddaughter Christina Bridgwater and her niece Anna MacBride White. My warmest thanks to them both.

The exchanges between Maud Gonne and John MacBride around the breakdown of their marriage are based on selected letters and statements held in the Manuscripts Department of the National Library of Ireland. Those of John MacBride to his friend Victor Collins are taken from a document written by John MacBride for his lawyer (NLI MS 1937, 29814–29820). Thanks also to A. P. Watt for permission to quote so extensively from the poems of W. B. Yeats.

Francis Stuart's novels, especially *Black List Section H*, provided much insight into Iseult's marriage.

My interpretation of the pivotal events of December 1898 in the Gonne–Yeats relationship owes much to the analysis by Deirdre

Toomey in *Yeats Annual No. 9: Yeats and Women*. The simple act of imagining those days from Maud Gonne's perspective, rather than from Yeats's, yielded a new interpretation, not just of those events but of the entire liaison and the poems arising from it.

Other biographical work provided much of the background and foreground of this book. Particularly useful to me were: Roy Foster's two-volume work, *W. B. Yeats: A Life. The Apprentice Mage* and *The Arch-poet*; Terence Brown's *W. B. Yeats: A Critical Biography*; Ann Saddlemeyer's *Becoming George: The Life of Mrs W. B. Yeats*; *A Serious Character: The Life of Ezra Pound* by Humphrey Carpenter; *Francis Stuart: A Life* by Geoffrey Elborn; and Nancy Cardozo's *Lucky Eyes and a High Heart: The Life of Maud Gonne*.

To these scholars, who are trained to hold wanderings and wonderings in check, I offer a small apology for any imaginative excesses, together with my thanks and admiration.

All these books and documents, as well as Yeats's *Memoirs* and poems, and other poetry and prose by Ezra Pound, Francis Stuart, Maud and Iseult Gonne, have been ransacked and plundered for details of scene, action and character. I have worked on the basis that what is ultimately expressed in a poem or piece of finished prose is often ruminated over, or discussed, first.

Many thanks also to my editors at Penguin: Patricia Deevy for her patience as this book found its form; Donna Poppy for her meticulous attention to detail.

No writer manages to produce without a support system. So deepest thanks to Ita O'Driscoll, of Font Literary Agency, for so deftly combining the roles of reader, representative and friend. To 'the kids', Ornagh and Ross (yes, I know, kids no longer), for their constant encouragement – and for the loan of their names for my pseudonym. And, of course, to Philip, for understanding it all.

Orna Ross
Dublin, 2008